AMBER ARGYLE

SUMMER QUEEN

FAIRY QUEENS 4

First Edition: April 2015
Library of Congress Cataloging-in-Publication Data
LCCN: 2015905629

Argyle, Amber
Summer Queen (Fairy Queens Series) – 1st ed
ISBN-10: 0985739479 | ISBN-13: 978-0-9857394-7-8

TO RISE FROM
THE ASHES,
FIRST YOU MUST
BURN.

To Ellen Smith,
for always believing

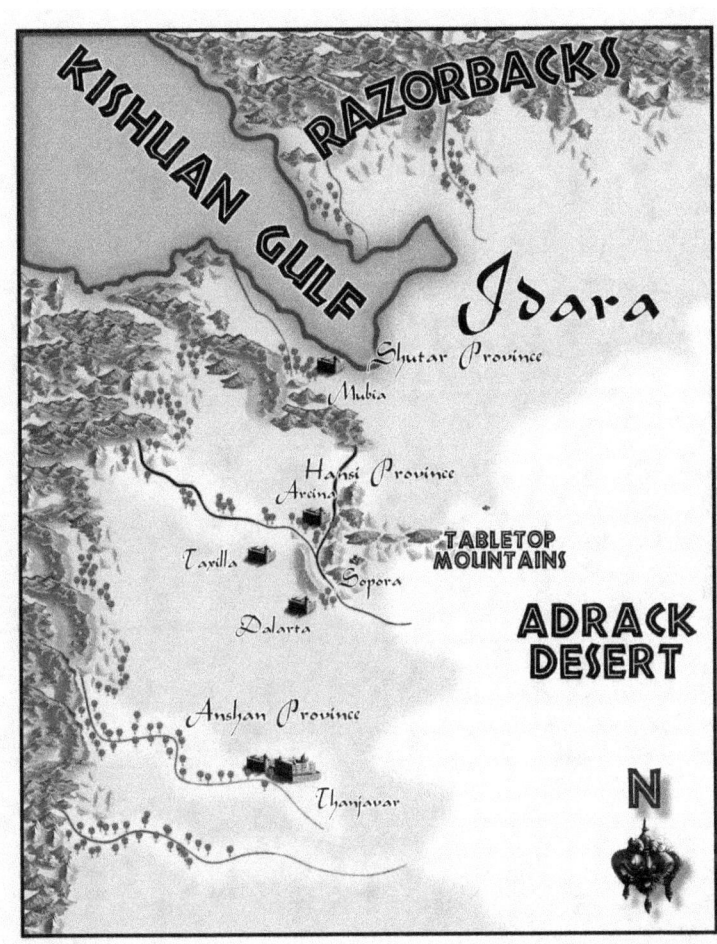

CHAPTER ONE

Holding her breath, Nelay sucked in her ribs as tight as she could. Still the hooks on the back of her bodice refused to meet.

"Arms up," Jezzel commanded. "Maybe that will help."

Nelay stretched her arms above her head as Jezzel strained behind her. "Got it!" she said. With the first hook down, the others fell into place.

Nelay wanted to sag in relief, but the blasted bodice was too tight. She would have been far more at ease in her simpler, modest acolyte robes, but meeting with the high priestess required full ceremonial attire. And afterward, Nelay had a king to seduce. She sighed. "It wasn't this snug at the fire dance."

Jezzel collapsed on her bed in their tiny acolytes' room, fanning her face with her hands. "Yes, well, tell your bosoms that," she teased.

Nelay sat down to pull on her adorable little boots with tips that curled up like a new vine.

"I wouldn't do that. One of those things is likely to pop out." Jezzel snorted at her own joke.

Nelay looked down at her full breasts, which threatened a rebellion against the plunging neckline. She shot Jezzel a withering look, and the other girl's snort turned into a burst of laughter. Nelay couldn't help but chuckle in return. Perhaps she should be more nervous. But then, the priestesses had trained her to win the game of fire since she'd arrived at the temple seven years ago. All she had to do was align the players perfectly. And if anyone excelled at winning games, it was Nelay Arel Mandana ShaBejan.

She stood, and the silk slid like water across her hips. Her fingers traced the cinnamon-colored tattoos that fanned across her temples before winding along the shaved scalp just above her ears and ending at the nape of her neck. They displayed her rank as the most powerful acolyte in the temple. "How do I look, Jez?"

Jezzel's gaze traveled critically over Nelay's bodice, her bare midriff, the voluminous trousers, tight only around her waist and ankles, so they flared like bells. "Good enough to distract a king," Jezzel finally said.

Nelay wiggled her eyebrows. "That's the goal."

She left their room and stepped into the priestesses' private courtyard, squinting against the bright sun. To her right were the sand-filled training grounds. To her left, the stables. Directly before her was the temple. And beyond that, the Summer Palace.

As she walked, the desert wind blasted her, leaving her mouth tasting of baked earth. Just after midday, the wind always turned, bringing with it the hot, dry air off the desert—the ovat—during which everyone retreated into the cool stone structures to nap. At night, the winds reversed, bringing cool air down from the mountains—the tavo, opposite of the ovat in every way.

The flagstones radiated heat through the soles of Nelay's boots. Many trees decorated the courtyard, but their shade pooled in useless little puddles directly beneath them. Even the twin bathing fountains looked wilted under the heat.

She cast a regretful glance at the assortment of weapons stored under an overhang along one wall. In the sand courtyard during the pre-dawn cool, the acolytes learned the fine arts of killing. Nelay's fingers itched to take one of the shamshirs down.

To feel the perfection of the motions, the elegance of the forms. But she now headed for a different kind of battle—one waged with wits instead of weapons.

This time of day, the massive temple doors remained closed against the merciless heat. With the doors' size and weight, it took four well-muscled guards to push them open. Nelay usually slowed to admire those muscles. But this time she was too relieved to step into the cool shadows of the bethel, the worship room for the hundreds of priestesses residing at the temple.

An echoing thud sounded as the guards shut the doors behind her, plunging her into near darkness. She drew in a breath of the smoky, sweet myrrh incense—this was, after all, a temple dedicated to the Goddess of Fire.

As Nelay's eyes began to adjust, she could make out row upon row of gold-plated, twisted columns holding the high, arched ceiling of mosaic gold tiles in the patterns of the stars and the sun. A ring of oil with five burning wicks surrounded each column. Besides showing off the priestesses' vast wealth, the gold reflected the candlelight and illuminated the entire room, shining across the surface of the circular pool of water before the altar. The flickering light made the reds of Nelay's bodice and pants richer, darker, and the gold trim almost crimson.

She crossed the vast room, sidestepping the kneeling cushions, and made her way to one of the cleansing rooms at the perimeter of the temple's center section. The servants already waited for her. The perfectly square room featured an altar along the far wall, with a pool of water in front of it. Clay bowls filled with incense floated in the still water.

A cube of crumbling incense also burned inside the hollow glass statue of the dancing Goddess of Fire, the smoke filling the glass in mesmerizing, curling tendrils before escaping from slits in the Goddess's fanning wings. Tonight, the younger acolytes would take the idol apart and polish the pieces until they shone, then put everything back together.

Nelay's entrance stirred the smoke, which made her throat itch with the need to cough. She ignored that itch, just as she ignored the desire to take a full breath against her restrictive bodice. As she knelt on the cushion before the altar, the servants converged on her.

One applied rich-smelling soap to her scalp, while another sharpened a razor on a strip of leather. A third servant wrapped a towel around her neck and pulled back her thick mane of hair to expose the shaved portion of her scalp. The servant with the razor positioned it carefully on Nelay's temple and pulled it back in sure, even strokes, cutting the thin bristling of hair just above her ears, lest it obscure the tattoos. Another servant lined Nelay's dark eyes with even darker kohl. Two more applied a stain to her skin, using cool brushes to draw intricate designs on her hands and arms.

By the time they anointed her hair with holy myrrh oil, Nelay's knees felt numb and she had a cramp in her foot. The servants draped a delicate gold headdress across her head; the blood-red ruby felt cool against her brow. They added more of her ceremonial jewels—a skirt of tinkling gold coins connected by delicate chains, a heavy gold necklace that dangled into the cleft between her breasts, and a ring attached by a more delicate chain to a bangle at her wrist. Last, they inserted her nose ring, which was connected by a third chain to her heavy ear cuffs. Having finished bedecking her in finery, the servants bowed from the room and shut the door behind them.

Nelay slipped her hand into her pocket and took hold of her small glass idol, the side of her thumb fitting perfectly between the woman's folded wings. She didn't have to see it to know a lifetime of touch had rubbed off the shine, leaving a matte finish.

"Goddess of Fire, I pray you forgive me." Suddenly, Nelay's bodice wasn't the only thing that was too tight. She closed her eyes and forced herself to take a breath of air that seemed thick and heavy, nearly impossible to draw into her lungs.

"I have given you my best. I have studied and trained harder than any acolyte. I have kept the rules—I've even left the guards alone, though I've been sorely tempted by more than a few." Her mouth twitched in an almost smile that quickly faded.

"And still, I would not go, but I must save my family." Nelay imagined the Clansmen attacking her family's home, killing her parents and brother. She shook her head to dispel the images. "I have no right to ask anything of you, but I will, for them."

She took a pen and a fibrous square of paper that had been soaked in myrrh oil. After dipping her pen in the ink, she wrote, "Grant me all my cunning and all my arts that I might succeed." Choosing the shape of a duck, as they were considered lucky, she meticulously folded the prayer. Her fingers flew—she'd done this hundreds of times in her early years as an acolyte.

She touched the tip of the duck's head into a burning brazier of embers. Then she blew until the paper caught, glowing in a stripe of orange immediately followed by black, like a tiger's stripes. Balancing the duck on her fingertips, Nelay dipped her wrist into the water. The paper started to float, sending out gentle ripples.

She took a deep breath. "Grant me this and when I return, I will serve you all the days of my life." Without waiting to watch the flame go out, for the ashes to drift lazily through the water, she bowed and rose, smooth as smoke in a windless room.

With her jewels tinkling and water dripping from her fingertips, Nelay crossed the echoing halls at the temple's center, where all the priestesses' chambers were located. She had not been to the high priestess's apartments since she arrived here at the age of nine, but she knew where to go. As she approached the woman's central chambers, two guards snapped to attention and pushed open the doors.

Nelay swept into the room and knelt on the silk cushion before the raised dais, which was surrounded by a star-shaped pool of water. Floating on the surface were clay lanterns with wicks made of twisted prayers—the kind of prayers only the richest Idarans could afford.

For the most powerful woman in Idara, High Priestess Suka looked perfectly ordinary—middle-aged and a little on the plump side. Nevertheless, her gaze was as sharp as the razor that had shaved Nelay's head. Suka also had a love for incense that sent even pipe smokers coughing. Keeping her watering eyes properly averted, Nelay bowed.

Suka shifted, the chain that connected her rings tinkling gently. "Acolyte Nelay, do you know why I have called you here?"

Now that she had been addressed, Nelay could speak with impunity. "No, High Priestess."

Suka raised her hand, palm out. "I'm sure you have heard that the Hansi Province is under attack."

Nelay's palms began to sweat. *This is a game,* she told herself. *I will position the players perfectly. And I will win.* "Yes, High Priestess."

"Need I remind you that we are your family now? I am your mother, and your fellow priestesses and acolytes are your sisters."

"Yes, High Priestess. You are my family." It goaded Nelay to say it, but there was nothing to gain and much to lose by defying Suka.

"The Goddess is a jealous one, daughter. Be careful that you put nothing and no one before her."

Nelay bowed her head in a show of deference, but also to hide the anger simmering just below the surface.

Suka leaned back in her throne. "You were always my favorite—I'm sure you know this?"

It was the reason Nelay and Jezzel had gotten away with so much as children, a fact both of them had taken advantage of many times. "As you say, High Priestess."

Carefully, Suka picked up a cup of tea and sipped. "Since you came to us, you have received only the highest marks." Of course she had. As the top-ranking acolyte of her class, Nelay would have the freedom to choose her future—no rotting away for years in some small village or being sent on a long expedition. "And the Goddess's fairies are most pleased with you," Suka went on.

Nelay had heard this ever since she arrived at the temple, yet she still wasn't sure what it meant. As a child, she'd been one of a handful of priestesses blessed with the Sight—the ability to see fairies, with their delicate wings and inhuman faces.

But her Sight had slowly faded in her. One day the fairies were blurred, the next they were hazy, then gone altogether. Nelay couldn't say she was sorry—she hated the fairies even more than she hated snakes, and snake fairies more than both combined.

"I no longer have the Sight, High Priestess." Nelay loathed to admit as much, but a show of humility would make Suka feel superior—another nudge in the right direction.

Suka waved her hands, her rings flashing. "It is of little consequence. What is important now is that all of Idara is in danger. You do realize this?"

Nelay was surprised the high priestess was willing to admit as much. "I do." Fire was many things. It brought warmth and comfort and light. But it could also be greedy.

The rise of Idara had begun with old king Kutik and continued after his death with his son, Zatal. Over the span of nearly a century, Idara had devoured kingdom after kingdom, whose kings became vassals to King Zatal.

If fire is stretched too thin, it risks going out altogether. Almost twenty years ago, King Zatal had committed the majority of his armies to subjugate the stubborn Clanlands. But a freak blizzard wiped out nearly their entire army. The loss left Idara reeling and weak, setting off a series of rebellions among the vassal kings. Over the space of two decades, Idara's armies had been routed from one kingdom to another. Just a few months ago the conquered kingdoms, led by the Clanlands, had banded together to snuff out Idara altogether.

"After our duty to the Goddess, our loyalty lies with Idara," the high priestess declared, her gaze brooding. "We must do all things to protect those who watch over us and our way of life, for the Clansmen worship the Goddess of Winter."

Through all Suka's sermons, one thing had always been abundantly clear—her hatred of the Winter Goddess. She cleared her throat and took another drink of tea—apparently the ridiculous amounts of incense bothered her too. "Dark times come, dark times which only the Goddess of Fire can illuminate. All of us will be required to make sacrifices."

Nelay tried to calm her racing heart. So far, everything was going exactly as planned. Suka clearly felt in control and relaxed. "What do you wish of me, High Priestess?"

Suka rose to her feet, motioning for Nelay to follow her. A servant who'd been kneeling in a dark corner shot forward and rapped on the doors. The guards pulled them open, their muscles heaving beneath their oiled skin.

As they moved through the doorways and halls toward the public bethel, the high priestess said quietly, "Sacrifices—all of us will have to make many if we are to survive. You most of all."

It was so blatantly clear what the High Priestess was getting at. Did she really think she was being secretive? "And what sacrifice would you ask me to make?"

"I know you wish to be high priestess. That you've been working towards it."

Nelay's breath caught in her throat.

Suka's brows came up. "You think I didn't notice? Don't forget, I won my own game of fire once. But I'm afraid you have a different destiny, daughter. One of far greater importance. You take the first step toward that destiny today."

"Why me?" Nelay said as they approached the bethel and the guards moved to open the doors.

"Because there is no one else." Before Nelay could ask what she meant, Suka took a deep breath and stepped into the bethel.

CHAPTER TWO

Nelay walked into the public worship room, which was always hotter than the rest of the temple, since the pivot doors between the columns were always open to the public. But the room held no commoners. Instead, soldiers in loose trousers and leather breastplates stood before every entrance, their shamshirs crossed in front of their chests. Nelay recognized them immediately. The Immortals were the king's personal army, so named because when one soldier died, he or she was immediately replaced. In that way, the Immortals always numbered ten thousand—no more, no less. They were the most elite soldiers in the world. And if the Immortals were here, so was the king.

It didn't take Nelay long to find him, with his head covered in tattoos marking him as the King of Kings. Zatal knelt before the altar of the Goddess, which rested in the center of a calm pool. He lit his own prayers on paper, which an acolyte must have folded for him. The phoenix shape matched the gold mantle on his chest.

The king had only arrived at the Winter Palace last week, after fleeing the Summer Palace in Idara's strongest city of Mubia, which had fallen in a matter of days. He'd brought his mistress and their two children to the safety of the holy city of Thanjavar and the comforts of the Winter Palace.

The clans had made themselves comfortable in their stolen city. Nelay's spies said their enemy would march on Arcina any day, and that Zatal planned on marching back out to meet them soon. Nelay had seen the king as she performed her fire dance, but that was from a distance. Now she took the opportunity to study him as he rose to his feet and approached.

He sported all the latest fashions of Idara—a close-cropped mustache and a perfectly curled and oiled beard. He was in his mid-forties, with a hint of gray touching his temples. He wore fine linen robes and trousers with a wide, pleated fabric belt under a golden phoenix buckle. The toes of his calf-high brown boots curved toward the ceiling.

Before her stood the man who just a few short years ago had ruled most of the known world. He'd conquered kingdoms, tribes, and empires simply by recruiting power-hungry natives and turning them traitor. While they created internal strife, he positioned his armies and attacked without mercy. Then he left the traitors in charge, making it clear the only thing standing between them and their angry people were his armies. His brilliant and ruthless tactics had worked. At least for a time.

As Nelay looked at him now, she felt nothing but disdain. He had overreached. His tactical errors had cost hundreds of thousands of Idaran lives and placed their once-great nation on the precipice of collapse. Had placed her parents in peril.

Nelay and the high priestess bowed. "Zatal, King of Kings," Suka said by way of introduction, though Nelay was fairly certain the title no longer applied, since all the vassal kings had rebelled against Zatal and routed his armies.

Probably wasn't prudent to bring that up.

The king bowed back, his expression reluctant. "This is the acolyte?"

"Yes," Suka replied.

He grunted. "She is . . . not what I expected."

Nelay bristled.

"Tread carefully, King of Kings." Suka's voice was filled with scorn. "A viper is dangerous the moment it hatches."

Suppressing a shudder at the mention of snakes, Nelay glanced between the two. It was clear they were speaking about something besides the Clansmen, but what danger could be worse than the armies on their doorstep?

"Do you insult me, King Zatal?" Nelay asked flatly.

He looked her over, his gaze lingering on her breasts, but with surprise rather than lust. "No, I do not."

Zatal turned to Suka. "I will speak to her alone."

"Of course." The high priestess bowed. Just before she turned to leave, her gaze swept over the image of the Goddess of Fire, and Nelay thought she saw hate flash across Suka's eyes. With an inward gasp, Nelay stared after her retreating form.

The king gestured for Nelay to walk with him. They crossed between the enormous columns—these made of marble instead of gold, which was too easy to steal. He paused when they were out of earshot, but she kept going, swaying her hips seductively. She was counting on the king following her. They needed to be out of Suka's line of sight for Nelay's plan to work, and she wasn't yet ready to abandon her plans to seduce him. To calm herself, she slipped her hand in her pocket and rubbed her thumb on the back of her idol.

"What has the high priestess told you?" the king asked from close behind her.

Nelay let out a tiny breath of relief. Objective one accomplished. "I know only that some great sacrifice is required of me to serve Idara and the Goddess."

"Is that what Suka said?" Zatal was clearly amused.

Steeling herself against her disdain, Nelay cast him an ironic smile. "And this sacrifice has something to do with you."

The king grunted. Though a priestess could take a lover, they never married. Tying herself to one man and losing her rank as a priestess was certainly a sacrifice. And now he knew she had guessed the reason for this meeting. Nelay congratulated herself on a successful play toward cleverness.

"I am not an eloquent man, Priestess. I am a soldier, so you must forgive my straightforward manner. I'm told I can be a bit . . . harsh."

They had reached the edge of the columns, well beyond where Suka might see them. The guards stood like deaf and dumb statues. Before Nelay were the wide stone steps surrounding the entire temple. So far, she was playing the field perfectly. "It is well, King Zatal, for I am also a soldier, trained from my youth to fight for the Goddess."

Again, he openly appraised her. She was muscular yet soft—opposing traits the men of Idara seemed to find most attractive. Her eyes and mouth were large, as was her nose, and her chin a bit too small, but overall, she was considered evocative if not beautiful.

"What do you wish of me, my king?"

His gaze strayed to the hand in her pocket. "High Priestess Suka met with me not long after I arrived. Apparently, the Goddess wishes us to wed."

Nelay withdrew her hand and swept her gaze over him, lingering on his numerous scars. His features were too strong to make him handsome, and he was old enough to be her father. But Zatal's most repulsive trait was his failure—even with the strongest army the world had ever known, and the best strategists and engineers, he'd lost their capital city in a matter of days.

She itched to ask him if the rumors were true—if the Clansmen wielded a terrible new weapon. But that would make him defensive and wary, and she needed him distracted and open. "Priestesses never marry," she reminded him.

The king's face remained impassive. "Unfortunately, your high priestess was right—marrying me would be a sacrifice, for I have made little secret that I already love a woman who has borne me children. But she is of low status and forbidden to be queen."

Of course Nelay knew that. "So you propose a marriage in name only?"

He slowly shook his head. "No. Though she has borne me two children, I have no heirs. Provide me with three, and you shall be free to do as you wish."

Nelay made a show of turning away from him. Where he couldn't see, she closed her eyes. She had watched her mother bury so many children. Her brother, Panar, had mocked her, saying he would be a man of standing, while she would be nothing more than a mother and wife. She'd sworn then to never be either.

If she failed to beat Suka in a game of fire before her wedding to the king, Nelay would be forced to bind herself to this failure of a man—in exchange for her family's safety.

"Are you really asking me?"

King Zatal hesitated. "I would prefer your compliance."

At least he was honest. Under different circumstances, perhaps they would have gotten along.

Nelay turned to face him and canted her head to the side, exposing her neck at the best angle. "I will marry you on one condition." The king's head came up. "My family lives in the Hansi Province, northeast of Sopora. I want them secured within the city. And I want access to them."

Holding her breath, she waited for his answer. She hadn't seen her parents or brother since she'd arrived at the temple. For the first year, she had cried every night for missing them. She even missed the fights with her brother.

"Despite your many charms—" Zatal's eyes swept over her mockingly "—it's not as if you have a choice."

Hot humiliation and then anger flushed her skin and settled sharply in her belly.

"Nevertheless, I would gladly honor your request," the king went on. "But I am afraid it is too late. Arcina is already under attack. I just received a report this morning."

Nelay's heart dropped in her chest. Arcina was the capital of the Hansi province. If her family hadn't already found safety within the city's walls, they may well be beyond the king's reach.

Suddenly lightheaded, she realized she'd been holding her breath. She gasped, not bothering to hide her fear. Panar would be eighteen now, almost two years her senior. Their parents would be old and gray. If her family had made it to the city, would she even recognize them?

"Then will you send the Immortals to retrieve them?" she asked the king.

He smoothed his curling beard. "I will not sacrifice my men for a fool's errand. If your family is alive, the Clansmen will have taken them as slaves they call tiams. And they always refuse any offers of ransom."

The news struck Nelay like a dagger. She'd failed them—failed her family.

"I will, of course, send emissaries to see if your family can be found among the refugees." King Zatal's voice was softer now. His gaze strayed to her breasts again. "I know what it looks like when a woman is trying to seduce me. Not that I blame you. I would do that and more to save my family."

Nelay clenched her teeth. She'd been a fool for thinking she could manipulate the most cunning man alive.

The king's eyes flashed with amusement. "You know, I believe you and I will get along just fine." He knew he had won, and he was gloating. When she didn't respond, he turned to look out over the temple's gardens. "They say there are two kinds of people—those who build and those who break. But I have learned that sometimes we must break before we can build." He faced her again. "I will break you. It will be painful, and I'm sorry for that. But you can build yourself up stronger than you were before."

Her main objective—to have the king go after her family—had failed. Now Nelay would carry out her backup plan. "Very well. Only let me say goodbye to my fellow acolytes."

He bowed to her. "I will give you a few moments."

"You will wait for me here?"

This time he hesitated before nodding to the closest Immortal to let her pass. "Of course." Just as Nelay started off, King Zatal reached out and grasped her shoulder. "To be a true leader, one must not simply be strong. One must also be selfless." His eyes shone with admiration. "You will make a fine queen."

Selflessness was not a trait Nelay had bothered to cultivate. With a smile she hoped looked sincere, she strode down the steps to the side yard without looking back.

A feeling nagged at her that she was making a mistake. After all, Suka had said Nelay's sacrifice was necessary to save Idara. Nelay pushed the thought aside and crossed the guarded gate into the acolyte sector. Then she broke into a run, her jewelry bumping and jingling against her body. She passed no one; it was still too hot out. Out of breath, she burst into her tiny room and slammed the door behind her.

Jezzel shot to her feet. "Well?"

Nelay met her friend's gaze. "I just outmaneuvered the most cunning man in the world."

CHAPTER THREE

"So he's going to marry you?" Jezzel asked.

A muscle flinched near Nelay's brow. "Not exactly."

Jezzel scrutinized her friend from head to toe. "So how exactly did you outmaneuver him?"

Nelay shot Jezzel a flat look and slipped off her shoes. "When I enacted our contingency plan—I tricked him into letting me go without Suka noticing."

Jezzel obviously wasn't impressed. "I just can't believe he didn't ask you to marry him."

"He did," Nelay huffed, then slipped off her trousers. "Now help me out of the bodice."

"Say please," Jezzel grumbled.

Nelay took a breath and checked her temper. "Please."

Jezzel unfastened the bodice, which was much easier to take off than put on. "I don't understand. If you failed to seduce him, why did he still ask you to marry him?"

Nelay tossed her jewelry onto the bed. "Suka went on and on about sacrificing and the marriage saving Idara—as if marrying an acolyte would gain the king favor with the Goddess or something. You know how dramatic the woman is."

Nelay pulled her glass idol out of the pocket of her discarded trousers. It was a gift from her father—the only thing she had from home. A few months after she had arrived in Thanjavar, she'd gone to the glassmakers and had them fasten it to a simple leather cord, which she now slipped over her head.

She tugged on the sand-colored robes of the desert tribes and said, "Get my baldrics, will you?" Moments later Jezzel dropped two of them across Nelay's shoulders.

"They're going to know you helped me," Nelay warned. She felt guilty, but they'd taken enough punishments for each other to be beyond keeping score anymore.

"I'll claim you told me Suka granted you permission to search for your family."

Out of habit, Nelay checked her shamshir and knives. Perhaps the priestesses of fire had taught her too well how to plot, how to fight.

By the time Jezzel finished, Nelay had donned the headscarf and tied the veil over her face, with only her eyes showing. In the plain brown robes, she looked like a woman of the tribes, all of whom had a reputation for tetchiness and shamshir skills.

"Nelay?" Jezzel voice had lost its teasing tone. "Be careful."

She crossed the distance and embraced her friend. "I'll be back in a couple of months."

Jezzel grunted. "You know that even if the high priestess believes me innocent, she'll have me running barefoot over hot sand for months."

Nelay pulled back to arm's length to look at her. "I'll pay you back when I'm high priestess."

Jezzel rolled her eyes. "I'll be the commanding priestess of the Goddess Army long before you're ever high priestess."

Nelay tipped her chin toward the door. "Any fairies out there that will report me to Suka?" Nelay hated to ask, hated that she depended on someone else for anything. But her lost sight left her blind to the dangers the fairies presented.

Jezzel peeked out the door. "There's a spider fairy in the palm tree to your left. She's looking right at the door."

Nelay grimaced. "If Suka dares make a deal with the treacherous creatures, she'll find me long before I can escape the city!"

Jezzel held out her palm in a calming gesture. "I'll take care of it. You slip out and keep your face covered. If you can get to the desert and then behind the Clansmen's lines, you'll be out of Zatal's reach. When I give the signal, hurry. Suka will turn the whole city apart looking for you."

Nelay squeezed her friend's arms. "Thanks, Jez."

"Just don't get yourself killed," Jezzel called as she rushed out.

Nelay waited, the sweat running down the sides of her face. *I don't have time for . . .* the thought was interrupted by the hoot of an owl, which wasn't an owl at all. She slipped back into the ovat, which whipped at her robes. A huge, dead spider lay at the base of the tree, flat on its back, its legs curved around an arrow shaft. But it wasn't really a spider at all. It was a fairy, visible only to those with the Sight.

From experience Nelay knew the fairy would steal the body of another spider within moments. She had to be out of the courtyard before then. She exchanged a goodbye nod with Jezzel.

There were no guards posted on this side of the priestess courtyard, and the ones on the other side said nothing—after all, their job was to restrict ingress, not egress. Nelay climbed the stairs that wrapped around the public bethel, then slipped into the wedge between the door and the wall. King Zatal still stood with his hands behind his back. Grateful for the shadows of the temple, she cocked one foot casually against the temple walls and waited.

It didn't take long. "King Zatal?" Nelay recognized Suka's voice. "Nelay?" Then her tone changed, becoming almost threatening. "Where is she?"

"She went to say goodbye—" Zatal began.

"Pasha, Meho, check her room," Suka shouted. Two acolytes burst into view, running past Nelay. "You two, check the stables."

Imagining the high priestess ordering around the king's Immortals, Nelay smiled beneath her veil. She had planned this moment for days, preparing to flee at a moment's notice. Suka was sending all her acolytes in the wrong direction.

"You think she'd run?" the king asked, his voice becoming more distant

Suka growled. "I told you not to let her out of your sight." Nelay peeked around the column and caught a glimpse of their quickly retreating figures. The Immortals followed them.

"She seemed amicable . . ." the king began.

"She is trained by the priestesses of fire. She can appear however she wants whenever she wants."

They didn't know it yet, but it was too late. Nelay had won the game when she'd convinced the king to let her go back to her rooms alone. She moved casually forward. Immortals were stationed between the temple and the populace. The Immortal closest to the temple wall was watching the chaos unfold at the temple and didn't notice when she slipped past him.

Immediately Nelay joined the crowd waiting for access to the temple. Since everyone wore a veil during the ovat, she blended in perfectly. A few dozen steps more and she'd be beyond the palace's high walls. People took one look at her plain Tribeswoman garb and quietly stepped out of the way.

Nelay was crossing the palace gates when Pasha and Meho showed up to look for her. Their gazes slid over her disguise, but then one of the girls whipped back. It was Meho, burn it! She had the Sight, and if the high priestess had managed to strike a bargain with the fairies, there was nowhere Nelay could hide.

A Tribeswoman wouldn't keep her head down, so Nelay didn't either. Meho gave a sudden shout and, judging by the crowd's reaction, started coming after her. Nelay didn't run. Running would confirm who she was. Instead, she crossed the street and stepped into an incense shop.

She gave a nod to the owner, who handed her an unlit torch and slipped out, a bundle of incense in his hand. The lock snicked behind him. Just a shopkeeper showing his complete devotion by going to the temple to worship during the ovat—no doubt with some of her bribe money jingling in his pocket.

By the time Meho pounded on the door, Nelay stood in a crowded back room. Before her sat huge, heavy-looking crates that were actually empty and made of light wood, the bottoms nailed to a trapdoor. She removed a loose board and pulled the handle underneath to reveal a pitch black hole. Under parts of the city ran tunnels that at one time had been connected to the now-abandoned luminash mine on the southern side of the palace.

Nelay dropped into the tunnel and settled the trapdoor back in place. She opened one of her pouches and scattered luminash powder all over the torch before scraping her flint across the striker. The luminash instantly caught fire. Multicolored light danced with the shadows on the rough stone walls. The luminash burned bright and long. It was the priestesses' own compound, the secret ingredients so carefully guarded only three women in the entire kingdom knew them all.

Holding up the torch, Nelay glanced around. Behind her was the portion of the tunnel that some long-dead king had ordered collapsed in an effort to secure the palace grounds. Before her, the tunnel stretched on into blackness.

She heard the front door shatter open and ran, slipping through the empty tunnels, nothing more than a spark in the shadows. She counted trapdoors as she ran. At the fifteenth, she settled her torch in the bracket, climbed the ladder, and pushed. As she came up in a stable, a donkey started and brayed. Nelay cringed at the loud noise. Despite the heat, a smoky fire burned in a brazier, just as she had requested. Fairies hated smoke.

Nelay hesitated before leaving the barn. Hopefully she'd lost her pursuers as well as the fairies by taking the tunnel, and with her face covered, there was little chance they would recognize her. But she must be cautious. She looked about, making sure no one was around, and wished she could tell if there were any fairies.

She brushed off her robes, stepped through one of the more respectable inns in Thanjavar, and emerged into the upper market. This time of day it was nearly deserted. She had traveled east and a little north. The palace was now behind her and to the right. Near the palace were buildings of stately marble and granite, but here they were constructed of mud brick and plaster.

One hand on a knife, Nelay moved at a good pace, her gaze sliding to the right and left as the gaze of a Tribeswoman would do. The few people she passed wore robes, bell-shaped trousers, and headscarves in bold colors with decorative prints and embroidery. One obviously rich woman wore a fitted bodice that bared her midriff, with swaths of vibrant fabric wrapped around her. Instead of robes, sometimes men wore bell-shaped trousers with a vest. Many men had curling beards or long, curving mustaches. Everyone wore a headscarf to keep the hair clean and to protect against sun, wind, and sand. When the wind was especially bad, the veil was pinned over the face.

Taking numerous twists and turns, Nelay moved steadily into the part of town that serviced criminals and whores. Here the buildings were derelict and the air stank of leather tanneries, which used feces and urine to treat the hides.

Nelay slipped down alleys, went through a bar and out the back entrance, and twisted down two more blocks to make sure she hadn't been followed. She climbed up a wall, using a windowsill and beams as steppingstones, before hopping onto a roof.

She crouched, staring at a man of the desert tribes. Though she'd contracted with him to smuggle her out of the city, she'd never met him. They had communicated only through her spies, so now she scrutinized the man who held her life in his hands. He wore the robes and headscarf similar to that of an Idaran, but in muted colors that blended in with the deserts. With his veil tied up, only a thin slit of his eyes showed.

The skin around those eyes crinkled in amusement when he saw Nelay. "So, this is the woman willing to pay a king's ransom to slip behind enemy lines."

"I don't owe you an explanation, Rycus." She didn't want him to say anything that would give away her identity to any listening fairies.

He tugged his veil down under his chin, revealing a surprisingly young face, only a couple years older than her. His nose was a little on the big side, and his forehead reminded her of a shovel. But he had liquid eyes the color of sand at midnight and a nice smile, with brilliant white teeth against his dusky skin. This was the most renowned smuggler in two kingdoms?

"No," he replied, "but we'll be sharing close quarters for two months, so we might as well be friends."

Nelay had enough experience with criminals to know they had their uses, but they were also incredibly unpredictable, and therefore dangerous. "I don't need friends," she said.

"Everyone needs friends."

"If I'd known you were going to be this talkative, I would have picked someone else."

Rycus grunted. "No you wouldn't have. You wouldn't have settled for less than the best."

Nelay tossed him the bag of coins she'd received in exchange for two of her ceremonial rings. When the high priestess found out, she'd be furious, but Nelay would deal with that later. "We must hurry—the Immortals are nothing to be trifled with."

Rycus pushed the bag into the folds of his robes without counting the money. He would receive the other half when he returned her and her family safely to Thanjavar. "You don't have to come with us, you know," he said.

Nelay snorted. He might have a reputation as a fair man, but it didn't mean he wouldn't cross her—say, if the king offered more money. "I already told you. It's not a place marked on a map."

"I could figure it out," Rycus replied.

"No offense, but I don't trust you."

He shrugged. "And afterward, you're sure you wish to return? Whatever has you running away will still be here then."

"That is not your problem." She might be Suka's favorite, but even the high priestess couldn't overlook what she'd done. Nelay's only hope was to stand in the public bethel and announce herself the next high priestess. Then she had to beat Suka in the game of fire, the winner of which would become the next high priestess. King Zatal wouldn't dare touch Nelay then.

And if she failed . . . she shuddered. She'd have the wrath of a king and a high priestess to face.

"What are you running from?" Rycus questioned.

"Am I paying you to ask questions?" Nelay shot back.

Another man climbed onto the roof. What remained of his hair was a dull gray, and he wore an eye patch. The skin visible above his veil was scarred and wrinkled. He gave her a steely look with his remaining eye. "No, but you are paying us to keep you alive. It would help if you weren't so goat-stubborn."

She rose to her feet, her gaze hard. "Being stubborn is exactly what's kept me alive."

"Easy, Scand," Rycus said.

The man tossed something to Rycus before resting his hand on his sword. "There are Immortals everywhere. They're looking for a runaway priestess." Scand studied Nelay suspiciously. "Somehow she managed to escape the temple."

Rycus swung his gaze back to her. "However did she manage that?"

She wasn't about to tell them about the tunnels; she'd spent a small fortune finding them and paying to use them. She and Scand glared at each other. Clearly he was making it a contest, one Nelay was only too happy to win.

Rycus glanced between them, one brow cocked in amusement. "Nelay, this is Scand. He's like a cactus. If you can get past his thorns, he's soft and squishy on the inside."

Scand grunted and climbed back down the way he came. Nelay had to suppress a grin of satisfaction. She turned her gaze back to Rycus, trying to figure him out. He seemed almost playful, but criminals didn't do anything without a reason. Perhaps he wanted her to lower her guard, get her to trust him. Well, she wouldn't fall for it.

He uncorked the top of a jar the old man had given him and approached her. "Hold still."

She tensed up but allowed him to wipe something cool around her eyes. It tightened and began to itch as it dried. She reached up to scratch it, but he batted away her hand. "Leave it be."

"What is it?"

Rycus grinned. "Something to make you especially pretty."

"What's that supposed to mean?" She gently touched her face and felt heavy wrinkles. He'd made her look old. Her mouth dropped open. "It better come off."

"Vain, are we?" He chuckled, then motioned for her to follow him to the edge of the roof. A caravan of desert camels was filing out below, Scand leading the way. Rycus swung down from a beam and landed easily in the next camel's saddle. It wasn't a move Nelay had practiced, but then sometimes simple was best. She hung from the beam until a camel came into position beneath her, then stood on the saddle before easing down. Not nearly as showy as Rycus's move, but with the same result.

Surrounding her were Tribesmen and women—probably two dozen of them—all dressed similarly to her and mounted on camels that reeked of urine and the unique odor of camel. Nelay swayed from side to side with the rhythm of her camel. The whole troop kept moving, holding a hand to their shamshirs, for Tribesmen didn't trust cities or Idarans on principle.

Soon they approached the city gates. The king's Immortals stopped the caravan but didn't dare touch the Tribesmen's women, who were about as forgiving as the Adrack Desert. Nelay heard the cry of an eagle above them and wondered if Suka had struck a deal with the fairies and they had found her.

A female Immortal, the tattoos on her bald head revealing her lower ranking, paused to scrutinized Nelay, who stared right back, daring her to try anything even as her heart pounded in her chest.

CHAPTER FOUR

The Immortal slowly backed up. "She's not here." As they filed out, Nelay let out the breath she'd been holding.

When they were well out of the city, she looked back at Thanjavar, wondering how much trouble Jezzel was in, and if they had found the tunnel Nelay used to escape. But mostly she simply felt sad. Thanjavar was her home. She reached up, holding her glass idol in her hand.

Rycus rode up beside her, his veil tied up again so only the wrinkles around his eyes showed. He glanced at her hand before tossing her a damp rag.

Immediately she set out to wipe the stuff from her face. It peeled away in long strips that left the skin around her eyes feeling raw.

"Now I think you will learn the true meaning of fire. For in the desert, there are no cool stone buildings to hide from the heat."

Nelay scrubbed her face till it stung. "We should rest until the ovat is over."

He spread his arms as if he enjoyed the blistering heat. "The Adrack Desert is the ovat, high priestess." He said the last bit in a mocking tone.

Her head jerked up. She figured he'd guessed who she was, but how could he possibly know her plans to become the high

27

priestess? But he only chuckled at her and moved his camel to the front of the caravan.

Nelay reworked the players. She considered heading out on her own right then and there, but Zatal must have guessed where she was going. Soon the Immortals would search for her all through Idara. The only way to reach her family safely was through the desert. The only way through the desert was with a Tribesman as her guide. She determined to watch Rycus even more closely. But for now, there was nothing else to do but adjust her headscarf to shield her eyes from the relentless sun.

Nelay wasn't ignorant of the dangers awaiting in the Adrack Desert. She'd grown up along the border in a one-room mud-brick home surrounded by dying fields. Her memories of that time were distant and disjointed. The smell of fresh-cut wood as her father's calloused fingers had brought wood to life, curled shavings littering the ground around him. The feel of her mother's soft body, the lull of her voice as she'd held Nelay. The bleat of the sheep as she and her brother and father had driven them to water holes—the silly little names she'd given them. Her brother's hatred, the feel of his hands so tight around her throat. The sight of her mother's dead babies.

But what Nelay remembered more than anything was the hunger that had carved her gut into a hollow, much like her father's knife had carved the wood. She might lose everything she'd gained over the years since then, but none of it was worth having if the price was turning her back on her family.

That night, they made camp under a brilliant, star-strewn sky. Nelay shivered in her robes as she helped raise the massive tent. Her inner thighs felt like they'd been pummeled by a wooden mallet. Once the tent was up, the Tribesmen strewed the ground with camel-hair rugs. A fire was lit and the strongest black orray she'd ever tasted was passed around as if it wasn't time for everyone to go to sleep.

After only a polite sip, she curled up in the sheepskins Scand had tossed her way. Keeping her veil up even now, afraid a passing fairy might recognize her face, Nelay turned her back to the tent and gripped her shamshir. She watched the men and women laugh together in the way of those who have known and trusted each other for years.

This was the first time she'd been away from the temple since she was nine, the first time she'd truly been on her own. Already she missed the routines and the friends she'd made—especially Jezzel. She was the only one who understood Nelay.

The priestesses taught that life was simply a game of fire. The world was the playing field, and everyone and everything a player. Living was just a series of moves and countermoves. Only the best of players learned how to manipulate other players to change the game. Together, Nelay and Jezzel could manipulate dozens of them.

Nelay rubbed her thumb along her pendant and then felt something tickling her. She shifted to see a spider the size of a large shoe on her arm, staring under her veil. She jerked her arm to throw off the spider while simultaneously drawing her knife. She stabbed down and impaled the creature right though the center. It wriggled, legs thrashing and pinchers rearing back to hit her. Nelay twisted the knife. She squinted at the intruder, trying to get her Sight to work, but saw nothing other than a spider, which she felt certain this was not.

She took a lunging step toward the fire and flung the enormous spider into the flames. Its coarse hairs caught fire and it darted out of the blaze, its body burning. Nelay promptly kicked it in again. On its back, it writhed and twisted before eventually growing still. Breathing hard, Nelay realized everyone had gone silent and was staring at her.

"Well," said a man named Delir. "I for one feel we are very safe from spiders."

Everyone laughed, some more nervously than others. Nelay, cheeks burning, returned to her blankets and adjusted her veil. She could only hope the spider fairy hadn't seen her face. Hearing a hiss from the fire, she knew the spider was cooked through, because at one time she'd eaten insects for survival. Some weren't too bad. Crickets, for instance, tasted like nutty shrimp when roasted. And that particular species of spider was actually pretty good.

That made her think of home. She wasn't sure how she felt about the people who'd never bothered to make the two-week journey to come see her, always stating that her father couldn't leave the sheep and her mother couldn't go without her father. Never mind that Nelay had sent them enough money to buy their way into society.

When Idara had been invaded, she'd written a letter, begging them to come to Thanjavar. The longer she went without an answer, the angrier she'd became. If sheep and land were more important than their daughter, more important than living, so be it.

Then the nightmares started. Nelay had one almost every night now, the guilt of living in safety and security weighing on her. She couldn't stay in Thanjavar—not if she wanted to live with herself. And though she was a fool to risk a bright future for the ghosts of the past, she could live with being a fool.

She shook herself and turned to see Rycus watching her with a searching expression. Then someone spoke to him and he glanced away, laughing. Nelay tightened her grip on her sword and forced her eyes to stay open.

The next day, she kept her veil tucked down tight and a wary eye out for anything that might be a fairy. She saw nothing but didn't let herself relax. Just before midday, they climbed a rise and Nelay saw the tops of the palace and temple through the heat wavering off the sand.

A pang of homesickness tore through her. For all her training and experience, she'd never truly been alone. Now she was surrounded by people she couldn't trust, didn't dare even speak to for fear she'd drop her guard.

"You owe me too much money to fall behind and die of thirst," a voice said loudly. "Keep up."

Nelay looked up and saw Rycus. The rest of the caravan had moved on, and he had come back for her.

"We need to move fast," she said evenly. "I have a feeling they know where I am."

"I'm not the one falling behind," he pointed out. She shot him a glare. He held up a hand in a sign of peace. "Even if they did, we go where no man can follow."

She met his gaze. "Unfortunately for us, they aren't using men."

He studied her with a frightening shrewdness. "What are you running from?"

That wasn't the first time he'd asked her that. She turned her camel and kicked it into a trot, but Rycus kept up easily enough. "What has this to do with the king?" he asked.

Nelay refused to look at him. "I'm not running from anyone. I'm going to rescue my family."

They caught up to the others and fell into step behind them. "You're lying," Rycus said. "If the priestesses were after you, they'd have sent the Goddess Army. The Immortals are the king's men."

She ignored him. He was a variable she couldn't control, and she didn't know him well enough to use him. Yet. Silently she would watch, and she would learn.

That night, she took her share of simple travel fare—dates and dried meat and nuts. The nightly bread had been burned. "You need to post a watch," she said as she passed Rycus.

He didn't bother to look at her. "I post a watch every night."

After a thorough inspection for fairies masquerading as spiders, Nelay took her usual place against the tent wall and studied the people around her, cataloging their intelligence, skills, proclivities, alliances, and so forth. There were two distinct groups—the caravan of men and women, and Rycus and five other men. Except Scand, those in Rycus's group were around the same age and looked so much alike they had to be related. But they hadn't been bickering like brothers. Cousins perhaps.

It didn't take long for Nelay to draw conclusions about all of them. Cinab was the youngest, the hair on his face still downy and patchy. The others teased him mercilessly, but with his fairly good nature it didn't seem to bother him. He also had a tendency to burn dinner, as evident by the blackened bread. Delir was quiet and watchful. He was by far the biggest of the men. He didn't speak often, but when he did, it was usually something profoundly funny or simply profound. Ashar was a bit of a loner whose sharp eyes matched his intelligence. Often Rycus had him scouting out ahead, or left him in charge when he and Scand were busy. Bahar almost never spoke. His haunted look made Nelay think he had lost someone, a tragedy that followed his every waking moment. And Scand, well, if he did have a soft, squishy inside, Nelay hadn't seen it yet.

The next morning, Rycus plopped down beside her. She stiffened, wondering what he wanted, but he only began to eat, taking small bites and long sips of water. Nelay did the same as the silence stretched out between them.

Finally, Rycus brushed his hands off on his trousers. "Really, high priestess," he said without looking at her. "If we were going to kill you, it would be simple enough to poison your food. You've hardly slept the last two nights. Accept that you're at our mercy—after all, we outnumber you two dozen to one. Sleep. Eat. Relax. Otherwise you'll be in no shape to deal with anything when we arrive in Idara."

If she was only worried about Rycus and his men, and the others in the caravan, it would make things so much easier. She glanced over to see him examining her.

"Or is it something else altogether?"

Nelay looked away, refusing to answer.

"Well then, I assure you, my men are more than capable of defending you."

When she still didn't answer, he got up and stalked away. He ignored her after that, but she continued to watch him more than the others. It didn't escape her notice that he'd doubled the guard.

For eight days, they traveled in the Adrack, farther away from the life Nelay had known and the people she had grown to love. She kept to herself, feeling like the outsider she was. Of course she was relieved when no Immortals came barreling through the desert or sneaked up on them in the early hours of the morning.

On the ninth night, they arrived at a cistern carved into a small outcropping of rock. It would be impossible to find unless a person knew where to look. Rycus said the caravan would rest here for a day. The cistern was reached by a narrow fissure large enough for one camel to enter at a time.

About ten camels could be watered at once, a relief since each could practically drink its weight in water, and Nelay was sick of hauling it up from wells. The whole camp drew water for bathing, and the men and women took turns. It wasn't as efficient as the bathing fountains of Idara, but with a clean body and clothes, Nelay wasn't complaining.

When everyone finally finished bathing, she settled down and ate some almonds, dates, raisins, figs, and dried meat. She finished off with a swig from a wineskin, as the Tribesmen believed this good for the health. Then she watched them talk and laugh. Missing Jezzel and her home at the palace, Nelay felt miserable and empty.

"What's that necklace you wear?"

She started, as no one had really spoken to her in days, and glanced up to see Rycus watching her sympathetically. She hadn't even realized she was holding the idol in her hand. She tucked it beneath her robes. "It's the Goddess. My father gave it to me."

Rycus tipped his head to the side. "All your jewels and all your finery, and you wear a bit of glass on a leather cord."

Nelay studied him, trying to decide if he was being rude or not. Before she'd made up her mind, he walked away. She gazed at the sunset again, but the sky was now mostly charcoal and navy, so she turned to watch the fire where the others had gathered to share a wineskin.

Cinab suddenly dropped beside her, scratching at his patchy beard. "Tell me about your priestesses."

She considered ignoring him, but she couldn't stand another second of silence. "The Tribesmen have priestesses."

"Yes, but our priestesses marry and have children. No one pays them to fold their prayers. And they don't shave the sides of their scalps."

Turning to look at him, Nelay noticed the way he leaned toward her as if truly interested. She sighed, giving up on her vigilance. Rycus was right. If he wanted to cross her, he would have done it days ago. And by now, the Immortals should have caught up with them. "What do you want to know?" she asked Cinab.

"What's this game of fire you all play?" He crossed his legs in front of him, his eyes practically sparking with curiosity. "I've heard of it, but it doesn't really make sense to me."

"Well, it's a game of strategy."

He waved his hand. "I know, but how does it work? Can we play?"

Nelay shook her head in dismay. "No, it's too complex."

"Please?" he said, pouting a little.

She sighed. "No. But we play it every year at the temple at the fire festival. Close your eyes."

He obeyed.

"There are five players per team—a scholar, a spy, an artist, a warrior, and a thief. The scholars are given a topic to study, and the artists, a medium. The thief, an object to steal without getting caught. The warrior is to win a tournament. And the spy must stop a crime that has been set in motion. We are always judged by the high priestess."

Nelay found herself looking in the direction of Thanjavar. "The last time I played was at the fire festival. The game had begun days before." Her favorite role in the game of fire was warrior. No frenetic studying of the chosen topic, none of the plotting necessary for the role of thief, and not nearly as much vigilance as was required for the spy. The latter of which was, unfortunately, the task she'd been assigned. Suka had chosen someone from the temple to "assassinate" herself. Nelay's job was to identify the person before he or she could perform the deed.

For weeks, she had been listening and watching, trying to figure out who had been assigned to "kill" the high priestess, all with no luck. So she'd done the obvious thing and spied on the other spies. Since they were all as clueless as she was, it hadn't helped. While the rest of her teammates engaged in battles of wits, fighting skills, and fire dances, Nelay sat in a tree, examining the crowd in growing frustration.

Suka oversaw the proceedings, cheering as the final winner of the fire dances climbed onto the back of one of the horses, its withers draped with roses, and parading around the courtyard. No one tried to slip past Suka's guards. No one acted suspiciously or bothered the high priestess's food and drink. Midnight neared as the last battle, between Pasha and Jezzel, took place. The other winners waited atop their horses prior to the parade through the city streets.

From Nelay's team, Meho had won the scholar contest. Jezzel was about to finish the warrior contest. That put them in the lead, so it wasn't vital that Nelay figure out who would "kill" Suka.

Then the impossible happened. Jezzel, the most skilled warrior in the entire temple, lost. She stood outside of the line drawn in the sand, her face tight with barely controlled fury. Pasha screamed in excitement, her teammates hugging her and cheering. With two winners, they were in the lead. If Nelay didn't figure this out, they would lose. And she hated losing—more so now that her team had won the contest for the three years in a row.

She scanned the crowd, as she'd been doing all night, but saw no acolyte or priestess who seemed to pose any threat to Suka. As Pasha made her way to the waiting horse, Jezzel, her head down, stormed toward the temple, probably to head to their room so she could rage in private. Thick and pulsing with excitement, the crowd jostled her out of her way.

Nelay wracked her brain, trying to determine what was out of place. Suddenly she knew. She swung down from the tree and shoved people aside as she raced to the temple steps. The crowd fell quiet when she grabbed Jezzel by the arms.

"It's you! You lost the fight on purpose so you could get close to the high priestess!"

Jezzel's scowl melted into a grin and she pulled her robes aside to reveal a wooden dagger in her grip. She tossed it in the air and caught it again.

Suka clapped Nelay on the back. "Well done, Acolyte Nelay!"

"That's not fair," Pasha cried from atop her horse. "They're best friends and on the same team. Obviously Jezzel told her."

Nelay shot Pasha a glare that should have melted the flesh from her bones. "I beat Jezzel. She did not let me win."

"I chose Jezzel for this task because I knew she was the only person who had a chance at fooling Nelay," the high priestess declared. "But since you doubt the honor of your classmates, we shall have a rematch. Pasha, you and Jezzel in the circle."

Pasha hesitated. Even if she believed she'd won fairly, the chances of her beating Jezzel again were miniscule.

Suka motioned with her hand. "Now."

At that point, Cinab eagerly interrupted Nelay's storytelling. "She won didn't she?"

Nelay laughed. "In two moves, Jezzel had Pasha pinned. The two of us rode through the streets, to the cheers of the crowd and the smell of roses."

"Oh, what a woman! If I ever met her . . ." He let his voice trail off, a gleam in his eyes.

Nelay looked him over. Probably fourteen years old, he was all arms and legs. But in a couple years, he'd be handsome. So you never knew.

Cinab leaned back, gazing at the stars. "You miss them, don't you?"

Nelay scooped up some pieces of gravel and tossed them into the darkness. "They are my family," she said softly.

"You could at least try to make friends here," Cinab responded just as quietly.

Nelay said nothing and was glad when he didn't push it, instead delving into a story about Rycus, Scand, and a shipment of feathers during a sandstorm.

CHAPTER FIVE

O n the tenth day, Cinab woke Nelay when the stars were still bright against the blue-black sky. She blinked blearily. After she'd finally fallen asleep, her dreams had been riddled with fairies with sharp teeth attacking her parents while they worked in the fields.

Once everyone had loaded up the pack camels, the women and some of the men took them and headed deeper into the desert. Nelay was left with Rycus, Scand, and his four cousins—all of them paid for with her gold. "Where are they going?" she asked.

"They were just our cover and strong-arms in case we were attacked," Rycus answered. "But this far into the desert, we should be safe. We'll be going the rest of the way with my armsmen.

Nelay didn't like being the only woman. She could handle Rycus, but the rest of his men . . . even she couldn't defeat six Tribesmen. But she didn't think it would come to that. Tribesmen prided themselves on their honor. Besides Rycus and Scand, none of them had even looked at her disrespectfully, and all did as Rycus directed.

"What's our route?" she asked him.

"We move parallel to Idara, keeping a safe distance into the desert. Our next rest is at another cistern. After that, you'll have to lead us to your home, since it's not marked on a map." He turned to climb on his own camel.

"How many more days?"

His camel lumbered to his feet. "About twelve if the weather holds."

"And if not?" Nelay asked.

Rycus grinned down at her. "Then you will owe me more gold."

She shot him a glare, unhappy that circumventing Idara was costing them nearly a week. But there was no other way to sneak so far behind enemy lines.

They traveled until the midday heat made her head feel light and heavy all at once. Every time she took a sip of water, it seemed as if the heat wrung it from her body within seconds. Rycus was right. Living within the cool stone walls of the temple and feeling the cool morning breeze off the Razorback Mountains had not prepared her for this.

Finally he called a halt, and they set up the tent with only the canopy and one wall for shade. Nelay dropped down onto some sheepskins, utterly exhausted and cranky. Rycus set a reed basket inside and went back for another.

"I thought the Adrack Desert was the ovat," she said in the same mocking tone he had used with her the first day.

He squinted up at the sun before carrying another basket inside. "The Adrack Desert doesn't have the ovat. Only the cities south of Arcina do. But even Tribesmen rest during the hottest part of the day."

"Then why didn't we stop the first day?" she asked with a grimace.

He gave her a lopsided grin as he settled down far too close to her. "Because we were in a hurry. And you . . . well, let's just say I was trying to take down your" —he paused as if searching for words— "confidence a few notches."

"She needs to be taken down more than a few," Scand growled from where he was pulling the saddle off his camel's back.

Nelay glared at the tent canopy. "I've earned it, old man."

"Doesn't make you better and doesn't make you right," Scand said.

"But I am better and right." It was true. She was smarter, faster, stronger, and more determined than anyone she had ever met.

As Scand moved past her, he shook his head. "Life has a way of teaching you the lessons you least want to learn."

She wanted to argue, but what was the point? He was just a jaded old man.

They ate flatbread, mangoes, and a little dried meat before curling under the shade to rest while the camels huddled together.

Nelay finally felt safe enough to truly relax. Just as her eyes grew heavy, Rycus sat down in front of her and said, "I have question for you, high priestess." He was wiry and tall, intelligence sparking behind his midnight-sand eyes. "Do you know why Tribesmen are stronger than Idarans?"

She tugged her robes in and out to stir a breeze around her sweaty breasts. "I always assumed the strong smell was because they never bathed."

He chuckled. "Because to everyone but the Tribesmen, the Adrack Desert is a deathtrap."

"You can keep your desert, smuggler. We don't want it."

He took a drink of cold orray. "Zatal's grandfather tried to take it."

"Yes, and I believe the Tribesmen fed him to a lion."

Rycus tipped his cup at her. "Jackals. Lions are much too noble for such carrion."

"Are you insulting me and my kingdom, smuggler?" She rested her hands on her hilts, ready to show this smuggler his place if need be.

"Sadly, no. Though I would love to dance blades with you, high priestess, I merely wish you to understand that Tribesmen have no alliances, because we don't need them. We alone can survive the realm of the Goddess of Fire."

She raised an eyebrow. "Which is why the chieftain's daughter was so eager to marry Zatal's father—because the desert is such a lovely place in the summer?"

Rycus chuckled. "When a man is unruly, we give him a stern wife to keep a firm hand on him."

Nelay huffed in frustration. "So you really believe the Tribesmen had the King of Kings in their grasp and just let him go?"

"Yes," Rycus answered.

She shook her head. "That's not how it happened. King Kutik ventured into the desert and found it a worthless wasteland. On the way back, they had a skirmish with some Tribesmen. King Sansit was killed from behind, his body dragged off as a trophy.

"After the cowards slunk off, King Kutik went in search of his father's body. A sandstorm arose, and when it was over, his army had become hopelessly lost. Marif emerged from the desert. Having seen the trickery of the Tribesmen, she was determined to right the wrongs of her people. She showed King Kutik the way home. By then he had fallen in love with her. They married shortly thereafter."

Rycus laughed out loud. "Is that what your priestesses told you?"

"The story is the same through all the histories," Nelay said with a scowl.

"And who wrote the histories?"

She threw her hands up in exasperation. "And you know better, do you?"

He leaned toward her, his gaze intense, almost intimate. "I'm a smuggler by trade. The story will cost you."

"Rycus, with you, any price is too steep." Just like the blasted fairies.

He leaned a little nearer, close enough to kiss her. "One of us needs to wash the dishes."

Nelay's face turned hot.

"So, you are right and you are better. But are you also lazy?" His voice held a challenge. "And besides, you're not paying us enough to pamper you like your temple servants."

If he thought to peg her as some weak city dweller, he'd be wrong. She set her jaw and pushed herself to her feet, took the pile of dishes, and set them in the sand to scrub out. She felt his gaze on her back. "Well? Let's hear your story." She emphasized the last word. Rycus stayed silent so she looked at him over her shoulder. "I'm not going to drag it out of you. Talk, smuggler."

He gave her a lazy grin. "King Sansit had conquered every kingdom within thousands of miles, but for the Clanlands and the desert tribes, which fact he felt was an embarrassment. After all, the Adrack shares all of Idara's eastern border. So the king hired a traitor, as he always does, loaded up his Immortals, cavalry, and infantry, and ventured into the desert. But the king forgot that a man is only as strong as his greatest weakness."

The only response was Scand's thunderous snores, but Nelay noticed the others were awake, listening. "And what was his greatest weakness?" she finally asked.

Rycus glanced up at her as if he'd forgotten she was there. "He was completely dependent on the traitor, who turned out not to be a traitor to her people at all. The woman led the king seven days into the desert and abandoned him."

Nelay's eyes widened. Cinab gave up lying down and moved closer to hear better.

"Two days later, their water ran out. A day after that, the men started hallucinating. A woman appeared on the horizon. She came alone and unmolested into camp, for it was said the sentries believed her a mirage. By then old king Sansit had died, but his son Kutik still lived. The woman promised to lead them to water on two conditions. First, that King Kutik marry her and make her his queen. Second, that he swear never to venture into the desert with his armies again."

Rycus leaned back on his elbows. "And that is how Marif, a chieftain's daughter, became the strongest queen to ever live, and Zatal's mother."

Nelay had finished with the bowls. She piled them neatly in their crate, then smoothly drew her swords and turned to face Rycus. "Are you threatening me?"

Delir, Bahar, and Ashar scrambled to their feet, while Cinab gaped at her. Scand continued snoring, oblivious.

Rycus eyed her steadily. "Why would you think an old story a threat?"

"Don't be asinine."

He gestured for his men to stand down. They sat reluctantly, their bodies still tense.

"Not a threat, High Priestess. A lesson. In your temple, there are only games. A loss for you simply means you don't get to ride rose-draped horses through the city streets. Here, a loss means you die or you wish you had."

Furious, she tightened her grip on her swords. Obviously he had eavesdropped on her conversation with Cinab—had probably sent the boy to speak with her in the first place. "You think I don't know that?" she said.

Rycus set his jaw. "No. You don't."

She leveled her sword at him. "I grew up just inside the Idaran border. I remember the hunger. I remember what it felt like to watch my father dying. He lived, but my siblings weren't so lucky. The dreams of my mother's keening still wakes me at night. So don't tell me I don't know what loss is."

Rycus studied her with an expression of surprise. She shoved her swords back into their scabbards. "You don't get to teach me any more lessons. You don't get to look down at me as some weak, pampered Idaran. Another word in disparagement, and I will crush you. Is that clear, smuggler?"

He inclined his head. "It is, high priestess." This time there was no mockery in his tone.

Nelay lifted her chin and strode to the other side of Cinab. He was the only one who hadn't jumped to defend against her, even if he had been ordered to be her friend. She lay down, glaring at the tent. Cinab watched her for a moment before sheepishly lying down. Fuming inside, Nelay closed her eyes and pretended to be asleep.

She heard the boy shift so he was facing Rycus. "Since King Kutik couldn't conquer the desert, he turned to the Clanlands?" Cinab asked.

"The Clanlands don't even have a standing army—it's all militia," Rycus replied. "Zatal took their continued resilience as a personal insult to his military prowess."

Cinab's voice dropped to a whisper. "They say the Winter Goddess herself protects the Clanlands. That her lover is one of their men."

It wasn't the first time Nelay had heard as much.

"Don't believe their nonsense," Scand snorted, rolling onto his side. "And keep quiet! Some of us are trying to sleep."

"If only you kept your own advice," Delir shot back, and the others snickered.

After a moment, Cinab persisted. "But do you believe it?"

It was Delir who answered. "Personally, I think it's their very, very large battle axes."

"You've fought them?" Cinab asked in awe.

Nelay had yet to even see a Clansman. She turned her head quietly and opened one eye as Delir's enormous hands waved in the air. "They are pale, their skin white like a maggot's," he said. "Unless they're upset—angry or sick. Then it turns red or even whiter—really, you've never seen such disgustingly colorful people. And their hair comes in the color of copper." He paused, then said quietly, "But the strangest thing . . . the strangest thing of all is that their skin is cold to the touch. And when they speak, cold vapors flow from their mouths."

Cinab's eyes looked like they would pop out of his head.

"He's teasing you," Nelay said. "They have pale features, but other than that, they're just like us." Or at least that's what the priestesses had taught her when she'd learned Clannish. With a glare aimed at all of them, she held her shamshir to her chest and settled down. This time she didn't fight sleep.

CHAPTER SIX

N elay commanded her camel to kneel. It did so jerkily, going first to its knees, then dropping to its hindquarters, then sitting back to let its front legs relax. She stepped toward it to mount but stopped to watch a lizard scurry off. Another fairy sent to find her? As horrible as having the Sight had been—as scary as the fairies were—at least back then she could see her enemies. Now she was blind to them, and that was worse.

She had just started to climb on the camel when a hand landed on her shoulder. Nelay knew immediately who it was. She grabbed his hand, wrenching his knuckles down and his wrist up, and shoved him back. "You don't get to touch me." She glared at him, actually hoping he would rush her and she could work out this tension instead of trying to stuff it all inside.

Rycus shook out his hand, looking at her with his brows raised and mischief in his eyes. "If you're this angry over a disagreement about histories, I'd hate to see what happens when you lose at gambling."

She leaned forward, a challenge in her eyes. "I don't gamble and I don't lose."

He shrugged. "Probably for the best. I'd beat you easily."

Angry he hadn't taken the bait, Nelay got on the camel and kicked it to make it rise. As they moved out, Nelay turned back to see Rycus watching her. She'd thought she'd made her point and he would leave her alone, but he rode up behind her. "You know you can't actually outrun me, since we're traveling together. Also, my camel is faster than yours—you have to pay more for the fast ones."

She ignored his teasing—ignored him entirely—though she still itched to hit him. But he wasn't done yet. "Have you heard the story about how the stars came to the sky?"

Nelay cast her eyes to the heavens, silently asking for help from whichever goddess would listen. "You told enough stories last night."

"Ah, but that wasn't even close to my best one." He cracked his knuckles as if preparing for a fight instead of a storytelling. "A wise old priestess tired of the world being lost to the dark of night. So she created a new kind of luminash, one that never stopped burning."

Despite herself, Nelay's interest was piqued. Luminash that never ceased to burn? The possibilities of such a substance were endless.

"The priestess formed an expedition and climbed the highest mountain in all the world," Rycus explained. "From there, she tossed the burning luminash into the night sky."

"Only someone with a death wish would do that," Nelay interrupted.

He shot her a pointed look and went on. "It caught her on fire, as she'd known it would, killing everyone in her party. As she lay dying, she watched the luminash scatter across the sky, settling in place to form the stars."

Nelay kicked her camel into a trot, determined to outdistance Rycus. But he simply hustled his camel after her.

"Then something happened that she did not anticipate. Some of the luminash fell back. As her soul departed her body, it passed through the burning particles."

Despite herself, Nelay tipped her head to the side to listen.

"Her soul became so bound to the luminash it burned like cold fire. Even more than the burning substance around her, her soul lit up the night sky. And so she decided to remain, offering light to all those in darkness. Over time, her name was lost to the ages. And so the world called her moon."

Nelay didn't know what to say. Suddenly Rycus urged his camel to the front of the group, leaving her in her oppressive silence.

That night at camp, Nelay was staring at the inside of the tent, cold and lonely. Rycus's voice again rose, loud enough for her to hear even though he was again on the opposite side. Every night and every morning it was the same—more tales of love and loss, betrayal and hope. Each one contained an undercurrent of sacrifice, of giving of oneself to make others' lives better.

Despite Nelay's distrust of Rycus, her determination to keep him at a distance, she could not make him angry. And she tried. For twelve days she tried. Eventually, it became almost a game between them. She would toss out a dig, and he would end up telling a story, which she would listen to in rapt attention while pretending not to.

On the twelfth day the wind blew dirt into her eyes and ears and mouth. She was hot and bored. Though resisting the urge to engage with Rycus on principle, she found herself riding closer and closer until she was beside him. "Is there a reason for the slow pace, smuggler?"

He looked her over. "No. I just enjoy annoying you."

She made a show of rolling her eyes. "I paid you a lot of money. The least you could do is keep it interesting."

A slow smile spread across his face. "Are you asking for one of my stories?"

"Of course not!" she huffed, yet she couldn't bring herself to ride away, either. Smirking, Rycus let the silence stretch. Finally, Nelay let out an exaggerated sigh. "Well, anything would be better than listening to the wind howl."

He grinned at her, and something softened in her. She liked it when he grinned. Liked the way his eyes lit up when he teased her. Liked how he always looked after everyone, telling jokes and tales to keep their spirits up.

"How about the very first Tribesmen to cross the Adrack Desert?"

She pretended to hate the idea. He pretended to believe her. Somehow, it had become a thing between them.

"Hazree crossed the Adrack Desert," Rycus began, "before even the founding of Idara."

"Proof that the Tribesmen descended from imbeciles," Nelay said.

"All it proves," Delir called from behind them, "is that even imbeciles know to choose the Adrack over Idara!"

Rycus snickered and Nelay shot them both a glare, but there was laughter just beneath the surface. And this time, she wasn't sure she kept it entirely hidden.

"I'm not telling any stories unless you promise to stop interrupting, high priestess," Rycus said, his arms crossed over his chest.

"Well, if—" she began.

"Not another word!" he growled teasingly.

Nelay bit her lip in a show of silence.

His gaze snagged on her mouth before he quickly looked away. Something seemed to catch inside her—catch and refuse to tug free no matter how hard she pulled at it.

He cleared his throat. "Hazree crossed the Adrack before even the founding of Idara. He went in search of the elice flower to heal his dying wife, but instead found a canyon with high walls. He explored these canyons and discovered several underground lakes of brilliant blue water. He thought it would be easy to divert some of the water to irrigate the canyons' rich soil. Inside one of these caves he found the flower he'd been searching for. He returned home with all haste and healed his wife. Then he took his family and his family's families deep into the desert to this hidden canyon. And that was how the Tribesmen were born."

Nelay noticed the camels perking up and picking up their pace. Blinking her sand-scratched eyes, she shot a questioning look to Rycus, whose eyes crinkled the dirt on his face as he smiled. "The cistern is ahead. We will rest for a day. You may bathe, else we will not be able to bear your company any longer."

She leaned over to smack the back of his head, and he had the decency not to avoid the blow. They didn't carry enough water to waste on bathing, and for the first time in her life she wished for smoky incense to cover the stench of sweaty bodies and camel hair.

Kicking their camels into a gallop, Ashar and Delir rode on ahead to circle the cistern for signs of an ambush. Nelay didn't see the entrance until they were nearly upon it—an outcropping of rock, a black void beneath it. Her camel must have smelled the water for she broke into a gallop. But the entrance wasn't tall enough to accommodate Nelay riding the camel. She pulled back hard on the reins, hard enough to pull the peg out of the camel's nose. But even with blood leaking from its nostrils, the animal forged on.

CHAPTER SEVEN

"Nelay!" Rycus called. "Slide off her back!"

Nelay saw the top of the cavern looming toward her. She pushed herself up and over the saddle, slid off the animal's backside, and landed hard on her bottom.

Rycus dropped off his camel to kneel beside her. Despite his concerned gaze, Nelay could tell he was trying very hard not to laugh. She glared at him, her headscarf twisted so she could only see him with one eye. He reached out and righted it before bursting into laughter. He sat and cocked one arm around his knee, his sides shaking. The others were laughing too, even Scand. Nelay felt a smile spreading across her face. Then she too was laughing.

Rycus helped her up, and for once she didn't shy away from his touch. She moved toward the cistern and her wayward camel, but Rycus held out his hand. "Not yet, high priestess. A cistern is a dangerous place."

She examined the shadows. "Are there snakes?" The reptiles loved to hide in dark holes from the heat of day. The scar on Nelay's ankle seemed to twinge as she thought of the time she and her father had been bitten. "I hate snakes."

Rycus scanned the horizon. "Snakes aren't what I'm worried about."

The itch from a mixture of sand and several days' worth of salt from her sweat seemed to worsen by the second as she forced herself to wait until the other men returned to confirm they were alone. Only then did Rycus nod for her to step inside the cistern.

Inside, it was immediately cooler, the air damp against her skin. But that wasn't what took her breath away. The first cistern had been little more than a cave. This had grand columns interspersed throughout, the water blue-green. Her camel stood in it up to her knees.

Rycus waded out, took hold of the reins, and pulled the reluctant animal out of the water. Standing at the edge, Scand heaved on a pulley, which released a torrent of water into a shallow trough carved into the ground. He called for the others to let their camels in. The beasts drank from the trough almost as fast as the water filled it.

Nelay felt a tug on her arm and turned to find Rycus behind her. "This is my favorite part," he said. He led her around a column, part of a pair that flanked the entrance. Behind it was another trough, this one much deeper. He lifted a pulley, filling it with cool water. "It's for bathing. That way the drinking water stays clean."

Nelay didn't wait for an invitation. She stepped into the cool water with a groan of pleasure. It was deep, reaching halfway up her thighs. With cupped hands, she splashed it on her face. Even that wasn't enough, so she submerged, clothes and all.

Rycus crossed his arms, laughing at her. "Don't drink anything yet, high priestess. We must boil it first."

She was too happy floating on the still surface to acknowledge him.

"How's your backside?" he asked.

"It throbs."

He chuckled. "All right. We'll make camp while you play."

A while later, she sat up when Rycus splashed her. She grinned at him, too happy to affect an imperious air. But at the sight of him wearing only a dhoti, she felt herself go still—her insides catching again. He was hard and wiry everywhere she was soft. And though she was still fully dressed, her clothes were plastered to her body.

He held up a cake of soap. "For you, I bring myrrh-scented soap. But you better hurry. The rest of us want a turn." He tossed it to her and disappeared again. She wasted no time stripping out of her robes and setting her necklace carefully on the edge.

She scrubbed herself twice for good measure, her hands running across the soft bristling of hair that had grown on her scalp in the weeks since they'd left Thanjavar. She turned her arms over, studying the ink stains that were mere echoes of what they had been. Once she was clean, she scrubbed her desert robes and wrung the water from them, wishing she'd thought to grab her training clothes to change into. She wrapped the damp robe around her body like a towel and moved onto the sandy stone, then winced as she realized her feet were no longer clean.

Stepping outside, she found all the men wearing only their dhotis, their dark skin glistening with sweat under the relentless sun. When they saw her, they hustled past her into the cistern. Rycus slowed down, his gaze lingering on her bare shoulders and legs, before he hurried to catch up to the others. There was splashing and laughter.

Nelay moved to her camel packs and withdrew a dry set of robes. After dressing, she settled down in the shade of the tent the men had set up and began combing her long hair. She'd just worked out all the snarls when the men emerged. Smiling, they nodded at her and returned to their banter.

Their lack of interest in her as a woman was baffling. When she danced the fire dance for the men of Idara, their covetous gazes had followed her with more than a little fear, for priestesses were well trained in the art of death, and fairly impervious to the law of the land. Not to say that the high priestess wouldn't make an acolyte wish she were dead, but that was different from a prison or a death sentence.

Nelay was something to be revered, feared, and desired—usually in that order. And yet these men didn't seem to see her as anything but a friend. Warmth blossomed in her chest. For the first time since leaving Jezzel, Nelay no longer felt alone. She took a deep breath in, smiling with happiness.

When she opened her eyes, she found Rycus unabashedly watching her and the catch in her lower belly felt more like a tug. Perhaps, she thought, the men's distance has more to do with the way he has begun to look at me.

Dressed in clean robes, Rycus plopped down beside her. "I have to admit, clean is a better look for you than filthy."

She repressed a grin as she started weaving her hair into a braid. "Personally, I like you dirty. It hides your unsightly face."

He laughed and then sobered. "My favorite is your ceremonial attire."

Her head jerked up. She lost hold of a section of her hair and her braid came loose. "You were at the temple?" Had he known all along who she was? And how much did he know about what she was doing? Heat touched her cheeks. Her attire had been positively scandalous. And for some reason, his opinion of her mattered.

Rycus only flashed a conspiratorial grin. "Saw you slip out of the public bethel after speaking with the king. Masterfully done." She glared at him, and he held up his hands. "We had to make sure you weren't followed."

Methodically, she sectioned her hair and began braiding it again. "What do you know?"

He took his time answering. "You might think me just a smuggler, but I have my ethics. I don't help murderers, I don't transport opium, I don't . . ." He hesitated as if searching for words. "Help bad people. And I had to make sure you weren't one of them."

Nelay finished braiding her hair and tied off the end. "How much do you know?" she asked again.

"All of it."

She studied him askance. "You risked angering the king by taking this job. Why?"

Rycus cocked a lopsided grin. "I like angering kings. A little defiance keeps them humble."

They were silent for a while, and then she shook her head. "You've been watching me a long time, smuggler."

His easy expression slid away, replaced with something like regret. "I shouldn't be." Before Nelay could ask what he meant, he pushed himself up and dangled her necklace in front of her. "You forgot this."

Horrified at her own carelessness, she grabbed it and slipped it over her head. "Thank you."

"I'm getting some food," Rycus said. "Bahar's cooking." Nelay's mouth watered at the thought. "I'll bring you some."

She watched him go. She didn't bother putting on her head-scarf—the breeze felt too good on her damp scalp.

After they ate, the men passed around a bottle, laughing and joking with each other. When it was Nelay's turn, Rycus held the bottle out to her. "A desert crossing must be marked—fire with fire."

She took a drink and choked, her tongue trying to escape her mouth. She passed the bottle to Delir as the heat spread all the way to her toes.

He took a drink and snorted at the look on her face. And then choked. "It burns!" Tears streamed down his face and he blew his nose until Nelay though he might invert his face.

"You're supposed to drink it, not snuff it!" Cinab was laughing so hard he could barely speak.

Nelay laughed until her ribs hurt. When they finally settled down, they passed around the orray and pipes and began to speak quietly among themselves.

In less than a week, she would arrive at her family's home. Every day she wondered what she would find there. Images of the house, ransacked and burning, flared in her mind.

Unable to sit still, she crept outside the tent. The wind howled off the desert, the tavo in full force. It drove her into the cistern. She sat at the edge of the water, watching the faint light shining on the still surface.

Worry for her family stole the warmth from the alcohol. Nelay started shivering in earnest but hesitated to go inside the tent. She was still sitting there when Rycus found her and draped a scratchy wool blanket around her shoulders. "Are you all right?" he asked softly.

"Of course."

He rubbed the back of his head. "It's just . . . it's freezing out here."

She sighed. "If this is really the Goddess of Fire's realm, why do you suppose it's always so cold at night?"

He hesitated before sitting next to her. He gazed out over the water, his face obscured by shadows. "Have you ever held ice?"

His face was turned toward hers, but she couldn't make out his expression. "Yes," she admitted. For some of their jubilations to the Goddess of Fire, the temple had ice packed in sawdust and carted all the way from the Razorback Mountains.

"And did you notice its touch leaves you with the same sensation as fire? It burns. Fire and ice have much in common. They are opposite ends, like men and women. We fight, we love. But we are always better together than apart."

"The Balance." Something the priestesses taught, about all things having an opposite. Light and dark. Mercy and vengeance.

Women and men. Nelay took a deep breath of the sharp night air. "So tell me, are all Tribesmen descended from imbeciles?"

Rycus chuckled. "You could ask nicely."

She pretended to consider it, then said, "No. No I couldn't."

He shook his head. "I have seven brothers and one sister. About two hundred cousins—my armsmen." He jerked his thumb toward the tent. "They are some of those cousins. Scand is actually our great-uncle."

Nelay raised her brows higher with every word. "Well, that explains the crotchetiness—it must be a family trait."

Rycus snorted. "There's" —he tapped his fingers as if counting— "twenty aunts and uncles. And each of them has . . ." More tapping.

Nelay held up her hand. "Really, two hundred cousins covers it." Though secretly she was jealous.

He leaned closer to her. "Your voice has that tone, like you've eaten something sour."

She hesitated, debating whether or not to tell him, but it wasn't like he could use the information against her. "I was just thinking how wonderful it must be to have all those people looking out for one another."

"When they aren't fighting."

And then he leaned toward Nelay, his fingers grazing her cheek where her tattoo began. He traced the curling pattern to the soft bristling of hair that had grown in, and ended at the base of her neck. The catch in her belly went to a hard tug and she found herself leaning toward his touch.

"Why are you so sad?" Rycus asked softly.

His hand spread out, cupping the back of her head. His gaze went to her lips and a thrill of anticipation leapt through her. "You have to stop," he said, "or I'll be forced to kiss you to make you happy."

He was giving her a chance to back away. There was nothing to gain from kissing him. And perhaps that's why the idea was so appealing. There were no spies here—no one to report back to the temple. No political alliances to secure. No egos to stroke. She could do what she wanted. And Nelay found she very much wanted him to kiss her. She wet her lips. "I'm not sad," she lied breathlessly.

"Then prove it. Smile."

She tried. She really did, but her mouth simply would not cooperate. He leaned toward her. She felt his breath on her mouth and her eyes slipped closed.

"You know better!" a voice said loudly. Rycus and Nelay quickly moved apart. Scand stood at the entrance, his face cast in shadows. "There's a rule with chasing women—don't start something you can't finish. That girl will get you killed."

Rycus pushed himself to his feet. "Who's in charge here, Scand?"

"If you're in charge, then act like it!"

Nelay felt Rycus's gaze on her, but she refused to look at him. Her face burned with embarrassment. What had happened—almost happened—was a mistake, a result of loneliness and worry. Nothing more.

"Are you coming?" he finally asked.

"In a little while," she responded, her voice tight.

He seemed to hesitate.

"Rycus," Scand said sharply.

He stormed toward Scand. "You will remember your place, old man."

"I know my place. Now don't forget yours!"

Their voices faded along with their footsteps, leaving Nelay with only the lapping of the water. She had never seen Scand's authority supersede Rycus's. But that was exactly what had just happened—over something as trivial as almost kissing her.

She dropped her head in her hands. She couldn't let something like that happen again—she was out here to save her family, not get distracted by some criminal. I don't even like Rycus, she reminded herself. So why was the tug in her belly nearly painful at the thought of their almost kiss?

CHAPTER EIGHT

Nelay dreamed about fairies again, only this time she couldn't see them. She ran, trying to get away as their sharp claws and teeth sank into her flesh. They tore at her hair and clothes, scratching at her eyes. And then she wasn't running away, but toward something. Her parents screamed, begging for help. Nelay finally emerged from the base of a gully choked with brush to see her parents being attacked by monsters who resembled men but had skin so translucent Nelay could see the blood and muscles beneath. But perhaps worst of all were the fairies, controlling the men with strings like marionettes.

With a start she woke to a hand on her shoulder. Rycus looked down at her in the gray light, his expression hooded. "It's time to get moving." She rolled out of her warm blankets, buckled on her weapons, and stepped out of the tent. The landscape had grown hillier the closer they came to Idara, and she made her way around a little rise to relieve her water in private.

As she reached for her trousers, a hand clamped down on her mouth. From behind, arms wrapped around her, pulling her back into an unyielding embrace. She tried to bite, but he was pushing so hard her jaw touched her neck. Two more men came forward in dark robes, headscarves obscuring all but their eyes. They bore ropes tied in loops.

Nelay screamed, but the sound was so muffled she doubted Rycus and the others would hear. She kicked and twisted, throwing her head back and writhing to make it difficult to hold her. When that didn't work, she peed on the man holding her. He hissed in annoyance but didn't release her.

They shoved her wrists and ankles in the loops and pulled them tight. They stripped off her weapons, leaving them where they fell. Other men jumped up from where they'd been hiding, urging their camels to stand as well. When her captors picked her up, Nelay kicked out with both heels, connecting with the man holding her feet. Then she twisted, bucking out of their arms. She fell to the ground. The man she'd peed on knelt on her neck, while the other two pulled her heels against her wet backside and tied them to her neck so that if she straightened her legs, she'd choke herself.

They hoisted her in front of a man on a camel. The other men jumped on their own camels. Nelay managed to look back and see that Rycus still wasn't coming. Idiot smuggler, couldn't he hear the scuffle? She couldn't make noise, but it was noise she needed. So she did the only thing she could think of—she bit the camel. She got a mouthful of camel fur, but it had the desired result, the camel jerked and when the men tried to hold it still, it nuzzed in dismay.

Poor thing, but they had to hear that. Nelay looked back, waiting for them to round the bend. Her captors were already turning their camels and kicking them to full speed. She kept watching, silently willing Rycus to realize something was wrong.

Cinab appeared a moment later. He took a few running steps as if to come after her before he seemed to change his mind and headed back to the others, shouting at the top of his lungs. Within seconds, Nelay saw Rycus on his camel and hoped it was as fast as he claimed. The others weren't far behind him.

The man holding her gave the order for two of his men to drop back and hold them off. Her captors pulled out their bows and started swinging around.

Burn it, this was going to hurt. Nelay bucked, ripping herself out of the man's grip. The way she was tied, it was impossible to land on her feet. The rope dug into her windpipe, making her face hot and bloated. She hit the ground hard, trying to roll, but she crashed through a bush, landed on a rock, and rolled over a cactus.

She couldn't get up and run away. All she could do was keep rolling until Rycus and the others slid in around her. He dropped from his camel and cut the rope around her ankles and the gag from her mouth. He hauled her to her feet and threw her belly first over his camel.

"I'm not running!" she gasped. "Give me my weapons."

"I don't have them," Rycus said as he lighted up behind her. He turned his camel and headed back, while his men took out bows and began firing at the enemy.

"Why didn't you bring my weapons?" Nelay cried.

"If I'd have known you were going to get yourself captured, I would have planned better!"

They arrived back at the hill. Rycus cut her arms free and she pushed herself off the camel, wobbling as she hit the ground. She scooped up her baldrics and dropped them over her shoulder. Then she turned to assess the situation. Six men were fighting five Tribesmen. Three more men were headed their way.

Rycus whipped out his bow and strung it in a second. Nelay already had her sling out and filled with a stone. She whirled around and let loose before Rycus had freed his first arrow. Her first stone hit a camel, and the animal cried out and dodged to the right. The rider couldn't seem to get it under control again.

Nelay and Rycus both took aim at the final two men. He missed. She would have gloated, but she missed too. And then there wasn't time for more shots. She drew her swords and forced her bruised body into a defensive stance.

The men charged in swinging, the high ground giving Nelay and Rycus an instant advantage. One man cut viciously at Rycus. The other kept trying to get inside Nelay's guard, as if to take her down. Rycus was holding his own, but the third man, the one with the out-of-control camel, had jumped off and headed for them.

Nelay twisted her wrists and feinted to the right, but upper-cut from the left. She cut into the man, leaving him gasping. Guilt immediately tore through her. But there wasn't time to dwell on it. The second man was on her—actually, judging by the shape, not a man at all but a woman. Nelay faded back, drawing the woman forward, then leapt, deflecting her opponent's parry and sliding past her guard. The woman was dead before she fell.

Nelay turned to help Rycus, but his man was already down. Her searching gaze found the rest of Rycus's men, already running back towards them.

Nelay stared at the dead woman at her feet. Something about her felt almost familiar.

"Well?" Rycus said to his men.

"Killed two of them, injured three. The rest ran off," Scand answered.

"Thieves?" Rycus asked.

Nelay bent down beside the woman, removing her head-scarf to reveal intricate tattoos across her scalp. Her breath caught in her throat. "She's a priestess."

It was the first time Nelay had killed someone—and they were her own people. "They wouldn't have hurt me. And I killed them."

Scand knelt beside another. "An Immortal."

Nelay turned abruptly and ran but only made it to the other side of her tent. There, she fell hard to her hands and knees, gasping for breath that would not come.

She felt someone behind her. "You knew they were coming—that they would find us."

Rycus's voice was soft, lacking any of the recrimination she had expected. She shook her head. "No. But I knew it was possible."

He knelt beside her. "How?"

She closed her eyes. "That wasn't a spider—it was a fairy."

His head came up. "It led them here?"

Nelay nodded. "The woman—she must have had the Sight. She led the Immortals here."

He let out a long breath. "Nelay, you didn't know who they were. And even if you did, you have a right to defend yourself."

The right to kill. Was there even such a thing? Ending a life that spread like the gossamer strand of a spider web, one strand touching thousands of others. And Nelay had cut two of them down.

"Here, hold still. This is going to hurt." Rycus yanked on the cactus spines sticking out of random places on her body. She winced, pretending the tears were from the pain instead of the heartache.

"You hurt anywhere else?" he asked when he had finished.

She shook her head. "Just bruises."

He was silent a moment. "There are some things you never get over. After they happen, everything changes. But you can choose to change for the better."

She turned her tear-streaked face toward him. "How?"

"By helping those who need it."

"Is that what you do, Rycus?"

"You're not the first person I've helped escape Zatal. And you won't be the last."

He rested a hand on her sore shoulder, but she welcomed the pain as a distraction from the turmoil inside her. "You take what you've done this day," he said, "and imagine yourself locking it up tight in a box. Then you bury it deep in the sand and you leave it there."

The others were already taking down the tent and loading the camels. After Nelay had washed herself and her clothing again, she joined the others and they rode out as the sun rose in the east.

That evening, they ate supper in subdued silence. Nelay finished her food first, gathered up the sheepskins and blankets, and headed out of the tent.

Rycus jumped to his feet. "Where are you going?"

"To keep watch. I assume you are going to keep one tonight?"

He nodded, seeming reluctant.

"Good. I'll wake someone in two hours." She stepped into the cold night, the wind of the tavo tugging tears from her eyes, and chose the highest possible vantage point. She settled the sheepskin on the ground and wrapped up in a wool blanket.

Not long after, Rycus came to sit beside her. After their almost-kiss the night before, she wondered what he wanted. "What will happen to them—the Immortals we chased off?" she asked.

"Well, without someone to lead them to water, and with injuries, they won't be able to come after us again. If they're smart, they'll head toward Idara and hope they find water or people before it's too late."

Nelay mulled that over, her heart heavy in her chest.

Rycus pointed to a bright star. "That is the tip of the Goddess Staff. If ever you are lost in the Great Desert, you can follow it to find my tribe's permanent home."

She looked at the star, memorizing it. "I would die of thirst before I ever arrived there." Her brow furrowed. "I thought the Tribesmen lived in tents and moved with their flocks."

"We do. But the story I told you earlier was true. We have cities, built into the mountains above the canyon's floodplain. There are also lakes deep within the caves. We channel those lakes to water our fields."

She looked into his eyes. "The priestesses never told me that."

He reached over and traced the faded ink lines on her hand. "They don't know, and I'll ask you not to tell them. It is not knowledge we like outsiders to have."

"Then why are you telling me?"

Instead of answering, he reached into his robes and pulled out a cylinder. He lengthened out the spherical compartments and handed it to her.

She pushed it open and closed a few times to see how it worked. "A telescope. I've seen these before." The Immortal commanders had them. She lay back on his stomach and peered at the stars, noting they were not all white as she'd once assumed, but red, gold, and even blue.

She swung the telescope across the starry sky, finding the Goddess Staff again and wondering what a city built into canyon walls looked like.

Rycus showed her more constellations—the Winter Star, the Hag, Wings of Fire, and Sky Mountain. Nelay knew many of them, most by the same or a similar name. But she learned new ones as well. After a while, she handed the telescope back to him. "You should probably go. I'm not doing a very good job of keeping watch."

He was silent for a moment, then said, "Tomorrow, I'll take first watch. I could show you some more then."

She looked away, searching the darkness for any sign of something amiss. "You might get yourself killed," she remarked with a touch of mockery, echoing what Scand had said the night before.

"I already took care of Scand." Rycus pushed himself up and went back to the tent.

Later, she woke Cinab so he could take his turn. He rubbed sleep from his eyes and shuffled outside. Nelay climbed into his warm blankets and fell straight asleep and into her recurring dream of the fairies tearing at her as she searched for her parents, only to find them murdered by Clansmen with puppet strings.

Before dawn the next day, the travelers were on the camels, riding away from the cistern. Nelay learned it was possible, although not recommended, to sleep in the saddle.

When they stopped for the evening, she dropped down, wincing as she rubbed the crick in her neck. Rycus took the watch after dinner and rubbed at the knots in her neck while quizzing her on the constellations, playfully mocking her when she got them wrong.

"Let me ask you something," he said.

Nelay blinked her eyes open and looked at him.

"Is there really a luminash mine under the palace?"

She rested her chin back on her folded hands. "Not under the palace—no one would build a palace on top of a mine. It's below the southern gardens."

"Why mine anywhere near the palace?"

She smiled as she remembered Jezzel catching her hair on fire with a torch the first time they'd explored the mines. High Priestess Suka had caught them sneaking back in to the temple. She'd taken one look at Jezzel's singed hair and made them both run on the hot sand for a full day. Jezzel had been more upset about her hair taking over a year to grow back in. And that had been nothing compared to the time they'd brought an elephant to the temple.

"The mine was there first," Nelay said finally. "It was the most prolific one in all of Idara. The priestesses of old built their temple there. After the mine was tapped out, the Winter Palace was built beside the temple."

"Could you sneak into the palace through the mine?"

"No. The Immortals were very thorough about destroying any tunnels out of the mine." *Which is unfortunate,* she added silently.

"You sound awfully certain of that."

"Well, Jezzel and I searched them. We were caught." Once.

Rycus fell silent and she glanced up at him. "Aren't you going to ask the question everyone wants to know?"

"The ingredients of luminash?"

She nodded.

He shrugged. "It's the priestesses' most guarded secret. I doubt you know. I doubt more than a handful of priestesses know."

He was right. All Nelay knew was that different types of luminash took different ingredients. Relieved he wasn't trying to wrangle more secrets out of her, she fell asleep with the sound of his voice naming the stars, the feel of his fingers still thrumming through her body.

Midday next, the flat ground gradually rose up, turning to flat table mountains. Telescope against her eye, Nelay studied the landscape. She'd traversed these lands hundreds of times as a child. A vague sense of familiarity washed over her, but she couldn't be sure she was seeing home until the twisted, ancient juniper tree come into view. She pointed it out to Rycus. "My home is about three leagues from here."

"Our camels are no match against the speed of the Clansmen's horses. Our best chance now is to slip in and out unnoticed."

Nelay reached into her packs and removed her scale armor. While the men turned their backs, she stripped down to her underthings and buckled on her breastplate, leather scale skirt, bracers, and greaves and made sure they were all invisible beneath her robes. She checked her baldrics and throwing knives and then braided her hair back, showing off the tattoos barely visible through the hair now touching the tops of her ears.

Rycus looked her up and down as if he had never seen her before. He wore his own armor, though none of it was as fine or as complete as hers. "From now on, you must lead the way, High Priestess."

They left Cinab to guard the camels and started out, Nelay in the lead.

CHAPTER NINE

The landscape continued to change. The flat plains of the desert became interspersed with table mountains, so named because of their steep sides and flat, barren tops. Between these mountains were dry riverbeds choking with brush, some as high as Nelay's waist, others as tall as two men. As she pushed through it, many of the brittle branches broke, giving off the medicinal scent she remembered well.

Suddenly she recognized the terrain from her nightmare. With every step she took, fear reared up inside her. She found herself looking for the fairies she could no longer see. Every bird became a fairy with black, depthless eyes. Every insect, a fairy with stingers. And every snake . . . every snake became Siseth, the fairy Nelay had made her horrible bargain with.

Hunching over, she braced her arms on her knees and pinched her eyes shut in an effort to banish the fear and the memories.

"Nelay?" Rycus said. When she didn't answer, he turned to the others. "Get her some water."

She barely heard him. She was remembering the promise she'd made the fairy all those years ago—that someday she would perform a service, any service the fairy required. Nelay also thought of what the fairy had revealed to her—that as a child, her mother had made a similar bargain. Only Mandana had bargained for an elice petal to save Nelay's life.

The magic in that petal had changed Nelay's body. She'd never been sick, not even so much as a stomachache, but it had also changed the course of her life. An overwhelming sense of doom nearly choked her. Whatever the fairies had done to her, they weren't finished yet.

Bahar pushed the water into her hands and crouched in front of her. She looked into his eyes and something passed between them. She knew he could see the pain her past had brought up. She knew he had similar pain. He didn't say anything. He didn't have to.

He rose and held out his hand to her. "We're with you."

Taking a deep breath to steel her courage, Nelay started out again. At the sound of bleating, she veered off course, slipping through the taller brush. She found a flock not far away, next to a spring.

Their wool was shaggy, much too long for this time of year, and full of briars. There were only a dozen or so animals, but she recognized the marking in their ears. These were her family's sheep, though surely only a fraction of the original flock. There was no shepherd, only the huge white dogs that protected the sheep. All three of those dogs stared at her, but none moved to attack, for she was no threat to their charges. One of the dogs was limping. Another was missing its right ear, brown blood matting its fur. All were scarred and starving.

Nelay's heart sank. Without the shepherd to tend the flock and dogs, the lions and hyenas would pick them apart in a matter of days. Her father would never let the flock come to this. During her childhood, she and her brother had gone with him for weeks at a time, traveling with the flock as they grazed for food over the arid ground.

She closed her eyes as memories reared up to strike her from the pit where she'd buried them. Of the day her father had almost died. The day her infant brother hadn't been so lucky. Nelay could still hear her mother's keening—a high-pitched wail that haunted her sleepless nights. Mostly, Nelay blamed herself. Whatever blame was left she laid on the fairies.

Rycus came to stand beside her. Some of her turmoil must have shown on her face, for he rested a reassuring hand on her shoulder and his voice dropped to a whisper. "You do not have to do this, Nelay. You could come back with me to our cities. We have need of priestesses for our own temples. And women who can fight."

"Perhaps my family has already fled." But a voice inside her whispered that her father would have never abandoned the flock. He would have taken them with him. She imagined herself violently crushing that voice beneath her heel.

She steeled herself and continued on toward her home, crossing the lands that had been in her family for generations. Abandoned luminash mines riddled the mountains, for though the ingredients for it were abundant in the province, none had ever been found on her father's land. Her life would have been entirely different if it had.

Nelay wove through fields of grain, their heads heavy and drooping, and the grove. She finally slipped through the last of the trees and saw her home, with its broken tile roof and pitted mud-brick walls. It was so much smaller and shabbier than she remembered. Why hadn't they used any of the money she'd sent them to fix it up? When she closed her eyes, more memories attacked her from where they should have stayed dead and buried.

Nelay was eight. It was a year before the priestesses would come for her. Two years into the drought that had lasted for five. She remembered the hollow, carved feeling of her stomach. Her father and brother had gone in search of a lost lamb, leaving her alone. One of the dogs had suddenly stiffened, his hackles rising. He'd let out a low growl that had sent her spinning for her spear.

Her heart beat like a fist against her ribs, the carvings her father had etched into the spear leaving patterns across her palms. The sheep milled, turning useless circles around each other. She needed to keep them from bolting. Keep them together. She tried to whistle for help, but her mouth was so dry barely any sound came out.

She worked her pasty tongue against her lips and tried again. A weak whistle left her lips just as one of the dogs lunged. A sleek, golden form exploded from the brush not ten steps from her. Snarling, the dogs took off after it. Nelay shouted for the dogs, her tone brooking no argument, but they were beyond hearing. The predator was running, and they gave chase.

She did not follow them, did not leave her charges, for she knew the first lion had been a decoy to lure the dogs away. She didn't have to wait long. Blurred forms exploded from the brush. The sheep scattered like a burst water skin, running and bleating in terror. Screaming, Nelay stabbed at the closest lion, but the beast did not divert, did not even slow as the spear punctured its flesh.

They streaked past her, so close she could feel the wind stirred up by their passing. She jabbed her spear after them, screaming, tears of fear and frustration blurring her vision. The lions stayed away from her, for she had a spear. The sheep had nothing—nothing but her. She pulled out her sling and lobbed stone after stone at the lions. When they finally retreated, each had its teeth locked around the throat of a sheep, some of them still kicking uselessly.

Nelay had watched the lions take her only friends and her family's livelihood with them, knowing she couldn't go after them, that she had to gather what was left of the flock. Her father and brother had found her that way, with tears streaming down her face, her spear in hand. They'd started running when they'd heard her screams, but they had been too late. They had never seen the dogs again. Nor could they afford to purchase new ones.

Nelay started at a sudden touch to her arm. She hadn't realized she'd been crossing the yard, that the stench of death wasn't in her memories, but before her. All around her.

Rycus held her gently, his gaze full of pity. "Nelay, don't go in there."

She swung her gaze back to her house. The yard was deserted. There were no clucking chickens. No barking dogs. No slinking cats. But there were prints that didn't belong—jackals. My family fled to Sopora and from there to Dalarta, she told herself. They were safe and well. She just had to find them and bring them back to Thanjavar.

A breeze pushed past her, playing with the unruly strands of hair that had escaped her braid. The door shifted a little, revealing that it was partially open. And Nelay knew. She knew without stepping inside, because her mother had been fastidious to a fault, sweeping their dirt floor a dozen times a day. Even if they had fled in too much of a hurry to take the flock, she would have latched the door.

Nelay jerked free and darted forward.

"No, Nelay! Don't!"

But it was already too late. She'd already pushed open the door. And her world stopped.

There were two bodies, their flesh picked to the bone by scavengers. The smaller one would have been her mother. She lay in the far corner, a cooking knife beside her.

Her father was by the door, his carved cane beside him. Nelay remembered him carving that cane, long curls of wood littering his feet, the smell of sap. Both her parents wore the remnants of their nightclothes as if they'd been startled from sleep.

King Zatal had been right. It was too late. Too late and too little.

Rycus was behind her, his hands on her upper arms. He tried to pull her away. To spare her or to comfort her, she didn't know. She dropped to her knees, her clenched fists holding her glass idol. Her eyes shut tight as the tears burned her throat.

She wasn't sure how long she sat crumpled like that. How long the sobs ravaged her. But when she finally finished, she felt empty, dead but for the fact that she still breathed.

Holding her sleeve to her mouth, she moved past the threshold and pried off the loose bit of mud brick under her parents' bed. She retrieved the thin ring her father had bought her mother for their wedding. It was far more than a shepherd could afford, and the only piece of jewelry her mother had ever owned. Then she took her father's shamshirs. They were her grandfather's, who'd used them in the war against the Tribesmen decades ago. A thick band of silver circled the hilt—a gift from the old Noble Keef—and the runes for her grandfather's name stamped in the pommel.

Nelay sprinkled the last of her luminash on her parents' remains. The funeral luminash was better—it burned hot and fast—but she didn't have any. The ceremonial kind would have to do. She took her flint and knife and coaxed an ember to life in some kindling, then lit the roof beams on fire. She went outside to look for the burial herbs, but Bahar had already gathered them.

He passed them to her without a word, tears filling his eyes. "It won't break you if you don't let it."

"I am already broken," she said without looking at him.

"No, you're not. Only battered."

She took the herbs and tossed them onto the flames. Her voice broke as she sang the song to set her parents' spirits free. Her feet felt too heavy for the dance. She took her father's cane when Scand held it out to her. She stared at it a long time. It wasn't as long as the flaming poles they used in the dance. Her family could have never afforded the priestesses' rites—especially one so powerful as Nelay.

But her parents deserved the best. She spun the cane above her head and slammed the end down in a clap. She pounded her foot in rhythm with her song. She commanded the flames to char the bones to ash. Commanded those ashes to spin with the wind, spinning through the world. Become part of all things—part of her. She breathed in the smoky air, taking her mother and father deep into her lungs. And she spun the spear about her. Speaking of the battle of life—it was all jabs and spins.

As her dance ebbed, her voice softened. Into wind. Into ash.

When she was done, she turned to find the Tribesmen watching her in awe and sorrow. Her gaze caught on the tears streaming down Rycus's cheeks. Nelay turned back to the fire. She considered keeping her father's cane. But he would need it with him. She tossed it into the flames.

With her hands empty of her family and her mouth empty of words, she walked away. She turned back only once, when the roof collapsed with a roar of flames. She watched as they licked away the evidence of her past. The bowls and utensils her father had carved from scratch. The blankets and clothes her mother had woven from their wool.

Rycus was still beside her. "We need to keep moving. The smoke might draw the Clansmen."

"I had to." Her parents deserved to have their ashes dance with the wind.

"I know," was his only response.

"My brother's body wasn't with them." Nelay took a deep breath, forcing her mind to take the players she had and form a plan. "There are dozens of mines, some sealed up after a cave-in or the minerals ran out, and only a local would know where to look." She crouched down on the packed dirt, using her knife to draw in the silt. "There are seven he might have gone to. There are six of us. If we each check one, we can meet up tomorrow and slip back into the desert."

Rycus shook his head. "It's safer if we stay together."

"Is it? If we all go together, it will take us three days to check them. And any Clansmen we meet will surely outnumber us. You said it yourself—our biggest advantages are stealth and speed, not numbers."

He and the others exchanged glances.

"The Clansmen were bound to leave soldiers to keep the area secure, Rycus." Scand said. "We need to be gone before that smoke draws them here."

"We'll be quick," Ashar agreed.

The muscles tightened along Rycus's jaw. "We don't know who we're looking for."

Nelay closed her eyes. "His name is Panar. He looks a lot like me." Or at least he had. "If you find anyone in the caves, just ask for him."

Rycus stared at the map as if not really seeing it. Finally, he lifted his gaze to hers. "All right. But we stay hidden. We don't try to fight them."

She gave a jerky nod.

He gave terse orders, directing each man to a specific mine. Then Rycus stood and kicked dirt over the map. "We meet back at the juniper tree by nightfall tomorrow." His gaze locked on Nelay's. "Don't be late."

He stepped into her, gathering her into his arms and pressing his lips hard against her forehead. "And don't do anything foolish." Then he turned and jogged away.

With the impression of his lips against her skin, she closed her eyes, trying to force the grief into the pit where she shoved all her bad memories, trying to force her legs to stir. And then she smelled the smoke, saw bits of ash drifting around her, and the heaviness lessened. Her parents were with her. Because of the ceremony she'd given them, now they always would be. That thought gave Nelay the courage to work her way toward the most well-hidden mine, the one she'd have gone to if she had needed a place to hide.

She moved until it grew so dark she tripped on every other step. The tavo blasted her, leaving her shivering with the cold. Finally, she gave in to the exhaustion and climbed a tree for safety from lions, snakes, and Clansmen, to wait for morning. She did not sleep, for whenever she closed her eyes, she saw her parents' bones. She did not eat, for her stomach rebelled at the mere thought of food. Instead, she took small sips of water and huddled in the single blanket she'd brought.

Sometime in the night, she caught sight of eyes flashing in the moonlight and leaned forward. A pride of lions passed beneath her, nearly silent and invisible. A lioness peered up at her, and Nelay longed for her spear—a much more effective weapon against lions than a sword. But then the beast looked away again and moved on. Nelay didn't even relax when she heard one of the males roaring some distance off. She'd seen lions use tricks to placate their prey, and she wasn't going to fall for it.

When the world had turned from black to charcoal, she slipped from the tree and continued on, swords in hand and grateful for the movement to warm her chilled body. Sometime later, she crossed a thready stream that steadily grew in size, though never so large that she couldn't jump across it.

At midday she came upon a small spring emerging from the mouth of a mine hidden by a copse of trees and bushes. Clear and cold, the spring was bottomless, layers of rounded rock slowly receding into the belly of the earth. Nelay crouched and studied the entrance, searching for any sign of life. Then the breeze changed, bringing a hint of smoke. Someone was in there. Either her fellow Idarans or a small company of Clansmen. Larger groups wouldn't maintain such perfect silence.

To enter the mine, Nelay would have to step into the open. The thought sent a wave of sick fear through her. She edged around the bushes for a better look, but froze at the feel of a spear at her back. She'd been so focused on the mine, she hadn't paid enough attention to her surroundings.

"What's a Tribesman doing here?" He spoke in Idaran, with the inflection of her province.

Some of the tension leaked out of Nelay as she slowly pivoted round to face a boy, no more than fourteen, his legs as thin as a bird's.

"I'm not a Tribesman," she whispered as she pulled down the veil that had covered her face. "I'm just dressed as one." She slowly pulled back her headscarf, revealing the tattoos on her temples. The rest were obscured by her hair.

His spear immediately fell to the side. "A priestess? Out here?" he said just as softly. She could see his mind working, trying to figure out who she was, and then his eyes widened. "Nelay ShaBejan? The shepherd's daughter?"

She barely managed a nod.

His eyes dropped. "You know?" He could only mean the death of her parents.

The lump in her throat threatened to choke her, but Nelay said, "Yes. Have you seen my brother? Is he here?"

"Panar," the boy said more to himself than to her. "No. Not in a long time. He left for the city shortly after you did."

She perked up. "City? What city? Sopora?

He lifted a thin shoulder. "I don't know."

She felt the first bloom of hope. If Panar had gone to Sopora, he would be evacuated with the rest. But why hadn't their mother told her in their letters?

Nelay took a breath. "What's your name? How many are in the mine?"

"Benvi, and there are fourteen of us."

"Benvi? Named after your father?" He nodded. She knew this family, dimly recognized this youth from when he was a young boy. She had almost been betrothed to Haddi, Benvi's brother. But that was many years ago.

"Listen," Nelay began. "You must all come with me. I have six Tribesmen waiting for us at the border. They'll take us deep into the desert and bring us safely to Idara."

Benvi stared at her hand on his arm, a blush lighting up his cheeks. "We can't leave our homes. We still have dead to burn. The army will drive the Clansmen out. We just have to wait for it to happen."

Nelay withdrew her hand. "Mubia fell in a matter of days. The king himself brought his family all the way to Thanjavar for safety. And when Arcina falls, the Immortals and the army will retreat to Dalarta."

His shoulders slumped. "The king will let us fall to the Clansmen, just like that?"

Nelay tugged down her headscarf and secured her veil. "The king's fire burns too low to char his enemies now. Let's go."

She started to step out of the brush, but froze at the sound of a scuffle. One of the bushes just to the side of the mine thrashed as if coming alive. She slowly lowered herself, her heart a knot of fear in her chest.

Benvi shot her a look and peered past her. "We have a sentry there." He half stood, but she locked a hand on his arm and jerked him down.

"It might be a lion," he said, almost sounding hopeful.

"If it was a lion, he would have cried out. Someone silenced him." Nelay didn't miss the irony. Lions were once their biggest fear. What she wouldn't give for that to be true again. "Follow me."

She eased toward the disturbance, careful not to shake the bushes. There was a soft thud, and a limp hand plopped into sight. Benvi made an almost soundless whimper, his hands opening and closing around his spear.

And then Nelay saw them—a dozen or so unnaturally pale men emerging from the trees at the side of the mountain. They wore tunics to their thighs, with breeches beneath. And around their waists were intricate belts, each unique and colorful. They bore axes, shields, bows, and even some spears.

They were Clansmen.

CHAPTER TEN

B envi drew a sharp breath. And somehow, his panic calmed Nelay—it was as if she knew both of them couldn't crack. She looked pointedly at his spear, reminding him to stay focused. He lifted it and his gaze hardened.

Her training kicking in, Nelay assessed her surroundings. In the space of a dozen heartbeats she chose her players and planned moves and countermoves. The sun was at her left, perfect for blinding her opponents if she came up behind them. "If something happens to me, head three leagues past my family's home. You know the old juniper tree?" Benvi nodded. "You won't see the Tribesmen, but they'll see you. If they attack, don't fight back or they'll kill you all.

"Call for Rycus. Tell him the deal has changed. He is to take you and the others. Acolyte Jezzel of the Temple of Fire will pay my debt to him." Nelay would pay Jezzel back as soon as she could sell more of Nelay's ceremonial jewels and gold.

Nelay slipped around the spring, not waiting to see if Benvi followed, and came up just behind the Clansmen as they positioned themselves to enter the mine. She assessed the players out of habit. They were all taller than her. She would cut at their legs. They wielded axes—extremely powerful, but slow, especially on the recovery. She would have to be fast, striking first. Her sword was longer, so she would keep her distance. The terrain was uneven, and she could easily be pinned by the bushes, which meant she would have to drive forward.

Nelay shook her arms to loosen her muscles, slipped one of her throwing knives into her hand, and gave Benvi a slight nod. Stepping into view, she threw her knives in quick succession. One hit hilt first, making a Clansman stumble forward. The second struck true, dropping another man.

She shot forward just behind her knives. Her shamshir spun, cutting the tendons behind the knees of the first Clansman as he turned to face her. She twisted her wrists, rotating her swords back. Before she could completely recover, a third Clansmen hacked at her from the side. Benvi struck him down before jabbing the butt of his spear into the belly of the Clansman coming at him from the rear. One thing about lions, they taught you how to use a spear.

Having lost the element of surprise, Nelay screamed to alert the Idarans in the mine to the attack. Her assault wouldn't work unless they helped her. A minute later, Idarans, mostly women and children, spilled into the light, spears in hands. The Clansmen were now pinned between them.

Nelay sliced at another Clansmen. He deflected her sword with his shield and arced his axe toward her unprotected right side. She couldn't bring her other sword across her body fast enough to block, so she reversed her momentum, barely managing to catch his axe haft with the dull side of her shamshir. She slid her blade behind the axe-head and jerked the man forward.

As he stumbled toward her, Nelay kicked his feet out from under him. Her sword slipped past his shield, stabbing into his chest as she stepped to meet the next foe. He aimed a colossal swing at her. She dropped to a crouch, cutting his legs. He landed hard, and her blade shot into his guts, effectively killing her third man. Before she could recover, another man tackled her, pinning her body with his. His strange blue eyes locked on hers, his hair the color of dried grass and his beard the color of fire. In a contest of strength, she would lose.

So she kneed him in the groin. His face paled before going a magnificent shade of red, the veins in his neck standing out. She locked her neck and head-butted him. Blood spurted from his nostrils. She shoved him off and stumbled to her feet, her ears ringing.

Blinking back his blood, she raised her sword to block a downward stroke from another Clansman and slashed, unseeing, at his legs. She felt her shamshir cut through muscle before shuddering through bone. Good enough to drop him, though he still held his shield. A flash of regret shot through her—he was an old man. Before her blade could finish him, someone shouted, "Nelay!"

She whirled to find Benvi and the others backing away. Somehow she'd become separated from them. There were less than ten of them now, Benvi the closest thing they had to a man. Suddenly she realized they were going to run for it, and she was still in the midst of the Clansmen.

Nelay charged after her fellow Idarans, but a Clansman darted in front of her. She warded off his blow and kicked him in the gut. He stumbled back. Benvi jabbed with his spear, trying to clear a path for her. The man shifted to deal with them both.

From the corner of her eye, Nelay saw the man with the broken nose chopping down at her. She brought up her sword, and the axe blade stopped a finger's width from her nose. Her opponent jerked his weapon back, the hooked edge ripping her sword from her grasp and nearly taking her arm with it.

The old man lunged toward her and pushed her arm up her back. With her free hand, she twisted a knife free of its sheath and jabbed toward his side. Before she could make contact, he caught her hand in a viselike grip. The knife was pried from her fingertips. She stomped on the old man's foot, and his grip relaxed enough for her to free one arm. She drove her elbow upward, into his gut. He fell back and she scrambled free.

Not sure where her knife had gone, she snatched up her shamshir and darted toward the others. But she drew up short. The way was blocked by Clansmen. Six of them stood between her and Benvi—the other Idarans had taken off. The old man rose to his feet, blood streaming from his mouth and lower leg, his gray hair stuck to his face with sweat.

They all backed up, assessing each other. Nelay reassessed the players, trying to make them fit in a way that ended in her freedom. But she had lost her knives. Perhaps if Benvi took half and she took the other half . . .

But no. She could fight two men with her shamshir and win—it wouldn't be easy, but it was possible. But three? One would always be in her blind spot—impossible to defend.

Nelay had seen the women and children. They wouldn't survive without Benvi, and he was the only one who knew where to go. Though good with his spear, he wasn't good enough to fight three Clansmen.

All the moves and countermoves she could possibly make all ended the same. "Go," she said to the youth. "I'll give you as much time as I can."

"Nelay . . ."

She met his eyes. "You can die here with me or live to keep them safe."

He let out a long breath and backed slowly away. Three of the men moved to go after him, but one of the Clansmen barked, "Let him go," in Clannish, which she understood perfectly. All priestesses were taught the languages of Idara's conquered lands.

"Surrender. You tiam. You live," the one with the broken nose said in nasally, halting Idaran. She looked at him, surprised he spoke her language.

She did not want to die, but it had always been a possibility. And she'd rather be dead than a slave. She made a great show of spinning her shamshirs before melting into a low fighting stance. The old man with the leg wound charged her first. She sliced his other leg so he'd have a matching set. He dropped with a howl of pain.

She twisted her blades, trying to force the others back. She slashed at the man before her, but something solid connected with the back of her head. The sky spun in a dizzying circle before her legs went soft and she crumpled in a heap. The old man limped toward her. Her mind screamed at her to get up, but her body wasn't working properly, her heels scraping uselessly across the ground.

The old man stood above her. The hatred in his eyes felt like a physical thing, something alive and sharp and consuming. Nelay managed to raise her arms, though they felt doughy and soft. An animal sound escaped her mouth. She hated her body for betraying her. Hated that she'd lost her dignity.

She couldn't stop him from killing her, so she determined to meet her death in stillness and calm instead of as a writhing, moaning mess. Glaring at him, she went still, her arms falling to her sides. The old man raised his axe. But the man with the broken nose took hold of his shoulder. "Dobber, no." His eyes were locked on hers, so blue she was sure she was falling upward, toward the sky. And he was falling with her.

Dobber tried to jerk away, but the man with the broken nose held him fast, speaking so rapidly in Clannish she couldn't follow.

"Leave off, Harrow," Dobber told the man.

Another man, this one with an even more intricate belt, knelt beside her and pulled her headscarf back. He touched her tattoos. "What does this mean?" he directed his question to Harrow.

Harrow knelt on the other side of her. They unwound her headscarf and fingered the tattoos on her temple, lifting her hair to peer at her scalp. She wanted to push them away, but it was like riding a camel with no reins. She had no control over her body. A moan of fear escaped her lips as Harrow traced the tattoos to the nape of her neck.

"She is one of their holy women," he said.

"She's killed four of our own. She doesn't deserve to live," Dobber spat.

The third man, obviously the leader, ignored him. "Their holy women fight?"

"Idarans worship the Summer Queen," Harrow responded. "And if winter is a cold death that steals your life away unnoticed, summer snatches it away in a blaze of battle."

To call the Goddess the Summer Queen was ridiculous. Nelay would have told them so, had her voice worked properly.

"Clan Chief—" Dobber began.

"Shut it, Dobber," the commander said without breaking gazes with Harrow. "Have we ever taken one of their priestesses?"

Harrow shook his head. "Not to my knowledge."

The commander grunted. "Treat her and get her on a horse. There might be more of those blasted Idarans around."

As he rose to his feet, a voice said, "We caught one of them."

Nelay shifted her eyes toward the voice. A girl who couldn't have been more than thirteen was shoved to the ground. She landed on her knees and cowered, a grimace of fear on her face.

For a split second, Nelay met her gaze, and so many things passed between them. Knowledge that they were in the hands of the enemy. Understanding that though they didn't know each other, they were all either of them had. And a promise they would help each other survive.

"Any others?" Dobber asked as he looked darkly at the girl.

The man who'd found her shook his head. "Three dead."

"Bring her," the clan chief said. "We need something to show for all our dead."

Harrow clamped manacles around Nelay's wrists and hauled her up. She didn't struggle as he carried her toward a horse. The world was going soft, the edges blurring. She felt as though she were being sucked backward, sucked inside herself.

And then she remembered no more.

CHAPTER ELEVEN

Nelay woke with manacles around her wrists, five links between each cuff. Her hands were cold and numb. Everything appeared warped, twisted like the heat wavering from the courtyard paving stones. It was night, the shadows stacked upon each other, gray upon darker gray.

Her head throbbed as if it had been trampled by a hundred camels. Someone was curled around her body for warmth. She had just enough time to make out a young girl before she rolled away and vomited bile into the dirt. When the dry heaves stopped, Nelay had the distinct impression her eyes were crossing and she couldn't stop them. "Where's Rycus?"

"Easy," said a girl's voice. Nelay jerked instinctively at the feel of hands on her. "It's just me. It's Kalla."

The girl, Nelay remembered. Chains clanking, she rested her palms on her forehead and tried to recall what had happened. Rycus and the others—they had separated. She'd fought the Clansmen and they'd taken her captive.

By the Goddess, she might never see Rycus or Jezzel again.

Nelay inched her hands toward the throbbing at the back of her head, hissing through her teeth when her fingers found the edge of a swollen knot crusted with old blood. She blinked a dozen times before her eyes would focus.

Beside her knelt the young Idaran girl . . . Kalla? Her hands were chained together as well. "What happened?" Nelay's voice sounded like it had been broken and clumsily put back together.

"Benvi and the others got away. We were the only two captured."

Nelay's hands traveled to her neck. She didn't feel the cord of her necklace. Her frantic fingers searched, but her pendant was gone. A profound sense of loss and anger tore through her. Taking a deep breath to calm herself, she carefully looked around, assessing the players of the game. She and Kalla were backed against the steep side of a tabletop mountain, the nearby fire throwing light that danced with the shadows. A guard glared at her from across the thick bushes on the other side of the camp.

Nelay counted seven men sleeping around the fire and had to stifle a fierce grin of satisfaction. There had been twelve to start with.

"They couldn't make out what your tattoos meant." Kalla pointed to the sleeping man with a nose so swollen it deformed his face. "Harrow asked me. I explained that they told your story. He said their belts do the same."

Nelay grunted, upset that Harrow had been right. She tried to plan her moves and countermoves, but the players moved around her like a desert wind, touching her before spinning away, and she couldn't hold onto any of them. She rested the side of her head on the ground. "I can't think straight."

"Just rest," Kalla said. "I'll keep you safe."

Nelay looked the girl over—she was skin and bones held together with determination. "We make quite the pair, don't we," Nelay murmured before slipping back into unconsciousness.

When she came around next, there were still more shadows than light and her head throbbed in time to her heartbeat. But her thoughts were clearer. This time, she was able to take stock of the players of the game. She went through different scenarios, but there was no way to make them all fit. She either needed more players or she needed to manipulate the field in her favor. So that's what she would set about to do.

It wasn't long before the camp came alive. Two men helped Dobber go into the bushes, likely to relieve himself. When he came back he walked past her, wrinkling his nose in disgust. "She stinks!"

Despite herself, Nelay blushed as she realized Dobber was right. She reeked of urine, which meant she'd lost control of her bladder at some point.

Kalla started out of sleep and sat up abruptly. Wide eyed, she took in the situation.

"Arcina is only a few days away," Harrow said. "After that, they're someone else's problem."

Sitting up beside the girl, Nelay noted that her headscarf was missing. She felt exposed without it to shield her from the fairies' unseen gaze.

A mocking laugh, and then Dobber spoke to the Clansmen who were busy saddling their horses. "Everyone knows your family has a soft spot for Raiders." His cruel gaze landed on Harrow. "Don't they, traitor's son?"

Who are the Raiders? Nelay wondered.

Harrow's head shot up. "Says the man who was too drunk to defend his family when the Raiders slaughtered them."

Raiders, that's what they called Idarans, she realized.

With a roar, Dobber lunged to his feet and started toward Harrow. Harrow sprang up, his fists clenched at his sides, something close to relief in his gaze.

"Shut it, both of you!"

Too fast, Nelay turned to see who spoke. Pain flared in her head and momentarily stole her vision. She slumped against the cliff and slid down to her haunches, shale falling all around her. She was useless, and she hated herself for it. She blinked a few times and spotted the clan chief, tugging his trousers on straight and buckling the beautiful belt around his waist.

He shot Dobber and Harrow looks of disgust. "None of the clans would have any of us. That's why we work together. Either of you lift a hand against the other, I'll brand you as outcasts and you'll have no refuge with any Clansmen. Understand?"

Harrow sighed. "Yes, Clan Chief."

With a wince, Dobber half fell back onto his blanket, fresh blood staining his bandages. "Aye, Clan Chief."

Nelay huffed. It was clear Dobber and Harrow were on a collision course. One of them was going to kill the other—the clan chief was only delaying that. She tucked the information away, sure she could turn the rivalry to her advantage.

Kalla squatted beside her. "What was that all about? Can you understand them?"

Nelay studied the girl again. She was all sharp angles, pointy knees, elbows like broken sticks, and a narrow face. Her expression wasn't afraid as much as defiant. Not much of a player, probably more of a liability than an asset, but Nelay had been dealt worse.

"Yes, but we can't let them know I can," she said without moving her lips. It was one of the only advantages they had. "They decided we get to live. Again. They're taking us to Arcina."

"To make us tiams?"

Nelay studied the ragtag band. Their belts looked new, which went against her understanding of clan customs. The belts were given to a child upon reaching adulthood. They identified the wearer's clan and roles.

She'd never paid enough attention to the meaning of the shapes to understand what these meant, but she guessed a new clan had been created in the midst of Idara, and these men would inhabit it. "And there's more. I think . . . I think they're criminals. Like they were outcasts from the Clanlands, and they formed their own clan here." The thought brought a flare of anger to her chest.

Kalla took a deep breath and let it out slowly. "Me, I'm just a child to them. But you? You killed or injured most of them. And even hurt, you're dangerous. Why are they letting you live?"

"I'm something they don't understand. I think they're hoping that by bringing me in, they'll gain favor."

"Favor? How?"

Nelay's smile was brittle. "I'm not sure, but I intend to use the knowledge to my advantage."

Kalla gaped at her, clearly frightened, but Nelay simply added another detail to the players.

Harrow made his way toward them with a bowl of water in his hands. Careful not to slosh it, he handed it to Kalla, who immediately offered it to Nelay.

Nelay shot her a look of gratitude and drank the muddy water. Grit coated her tongue and stuck to her throat. She paused when half of it was left, but Harrow shook his head. "Finish. Lots," he said in halting Idaran.

When he left, Kalla spoke softly. "Harrow tried to explain, but he's hard to understand. Tiams are to pay back the damage Idara has done by rebuilding our cities—which the Clansmen destroyed. But I haven't done anything."

The cities wouldn't need rebuilding if the Clansmen hadn't attacked them, Nelay thought bitterly. "Doesn't matter. All that matters is that we get away." She cleared grit from her throat. "How long was I unconscious?"

Kalla's gaze seemed drawn to the distant mountains. "Just since yesterday."

"Have they ever left you unguarded—even just to let you pass water?"

Kalla blushed. "No. We're always in the center of camp and chained."

"Have they hurt you?"

Kalla's gaze found Dobber. "Not yet."

Harrow came back with the second bowl of water. He shook his head in disgust as he handed it to Kalla. "I don't know how you stand this." He'd switched back to speaking Clannish, his voice wistful. "Where I come from, in Tyron, the water is sweet, and your throat aches as you drink it for the cold."

There is such water in Idara, just not if you dig it from dried-up streambeds, Nelay grumbled in her head.

Harrow handed them both bowls filled with a gruel that Nelay didn't recognize. It was so thick she had to chew it, and it tasted vaguely of meat, as if they hadn't cleaned out the pot well enough from one meal to the next.

Harrow watched them eat. "You don't understand what it's like to see the meadows covered in green wheat that grows so tall you can get lost in it. You don't know what it is to see winter snow, so bright your eyes almost refuse to stay open." Nelay could have sworn he looked lost. "You don't know what it's like to miss something you hated so much."

Nelay was shocked at his words. How many times had she felt that way about her childhood? She hadn't been happy; there had been too much hunger and heartache for that. But still, she missed so many things—the bleating of the sheep, the voices of her parents, gazing at the stars every night until she fell asleep.

Nelay stared into Harrow's eyes, refusing to show any signs of comprehension. What she wanted to say was, "Haven't you seen the scarlet and gold sunrises? The verdant fields to the west, which my people learned how to flood from the rivers that came down from the mountains? The cactus blooms and delicate flowers after the rains? The beauty of our cities, cool stone fashioned by the best artisans in the world? The fountains for the children to play in? The colors in our weaving?"

Nelay finally looked away. She should be meeting Rycus and the others at the tree today. What would they do when they found Benvi and the others instead? She'd thought she was going to die, so she'd told Benvi to instruct the Tribesmen to take them to safety and collect their payment for Jezzel. Nelay's only hope was if Rycus ignored that order and came looking for her. Not likely. Despite his many good qualities, he was still a smuggler.

Maybe it wasn't such a bad thing that she'd lost her headscarf. If the fairies reported where she was, perhaps Zatal would send a rescue party. She let out a long breath. She'd killed the last Immortals he'd sent after her. If he found her at all, he'd likely do the same to her.

Fire and burning, her head hurt. "We're on our own," she said to Kalla.

"Harrow, get them up and on the horses," the clan chief said. All the men were already mounted and waiting for them.

Kalla helped Nelay to her feet, holding onto her to keep her steady.

When they reached the horse, Nelay was relieved it wasn't as high as the camel. She managed to take hold of the horn, but every time she tried to get her foot in the stirrup, she missed.

Kalla patiently guided her foot. So now Nelay had a hold of the horn and a foot in the stirrup, but her arms had turned all watery and she couldn't pull herself up. Kalla tried to help, but the girl couldn't lift her.

A hand planted itself on Nelay's rump and pushed. She settled in the saddle and glanced down to see Harrow with a look that almost dared her to complain.

He held onto her hips. "You stop?"

She thought he was asking if she was going to fall off. There were no reins—the man in front of her had a lead rope wrapped around his saddle horn—so she grabbed onto the pommel and concentrated on staying still. "Yes."

"She's going to slow us down and you know it," Dobber ground out. "She's weak. She'll probably die anyway. Let's just put her out of her misery."

Nelay shot him a glare that would have burned a more as-tute man into a pile of contrite ashes. Why did he hate her so much?

Harrow turned to face him, his eyes flashing. "Just leave them alone."

Dobber leaned over and spat on the ground. "You'd like that, wouldn't you, traitor's son. That way you can have them all to yourself."

Nelay glanced between the two men. Dobber had called Harrow an Idaran lover, a traitor's son. Could his father have been one of the natives King Zatal had recruited? But why would the Clansmen hate him for that? At most, he was only a few years older than her—a child at the time of the clan wars.

The clan chief rolled his eyes. "Dobber, take the rear. Har-row, the front. Move out!"

"Oh, come on," Dobber ground out.

The man dismounted, marched over to Dobber, and hauled him from the horse, then pushed him into the ground and held him there. "Who's the clan chief?"

"You are," Dobber ground out.

The chief shoved him hard and stepped away. "Get on the horse."

Dobber staggered to his feet and looked at the others for help. But no one would meet his gaze. He grumbled something as he hobbled, unaided, to his horse and mounted.

The horses started forward with a lurch, and Nelay had to shut her eyes against the sudden nausea that rose within her. From the horse behind her, Kalla said softly, "You're not going to die, are you?"

"No, Kalla," Nelay answered. "I'm not going to die."

CHAPTER TWELVE

That day in the saddle was one of the longest of Nelay's life. The Clansmen didn't seem to understand the concept of midday rest, and they foolishly pushed on through the ovat. Then, just when they should have been moving out again, they stopped. Nelay had given up any sense of dignity and draped herself across the front of the saddle in exhaustion.

A man slapped her leg, motioning for her to get down. She roused herself and looked down at the ground, wondering how she was going to get there.

When she didn't move, he slapped her leg harder.

"I'll take her," Harrow said. "I'm supposed to be in charge of them anyway." Mindless of her stink, he helped her down from the horse and supported her while she walked, then set her on the cool earth by the cliff.

Hovering like a mother bird, Kalla placed a hand on Nelay's forehead and said in a hysterical voice, "She needs water!"

Harrow stared at the girl's lips, obviously struggling to understand the upset Idaran.

"Water!" she cried.

"I'm just weak, that's all," Nelay insisted.

Kalla didn't seem to hear her. "Please don't die, please don't die," she chanted as Harrow handed them his water skin. Apparently, the girl rambled when she was nervous.

"I'm not going to die." It was true, but at this point, Nelay just wanted her to shut up.

"You might!" Kalla seemed upset that Nelay had contra-dicted her.

She reached out and held the young girl's hand. "I've never been sick. Never had a wound fester. I hear better than normal people. It's why the priestesses chose me. And . . ." She trailed off as she sensed movement and realized Harrow was listening behind Kalla. Nelay shifted to see him looking at her slack jawed. She clamped her mouth shut. Exhaustion had loosened her tongue.

The Clan Chief squatted down beside them. "Have you found anything else out?"

Harrow rubbed his scalp above his ears while staring at her tattoos. "A priestess like her must be very powerful. So why was she in the middle of the skirmish and not well protected behind Thanjavar's walls?"

"Let's just hope someone is willing to pay to find out." The man slapped Harrow's back, stood, and walked away.

Repressing a shudder, Nelay wondered why Harrow was so kind. Why did his own people seem to abhor him for something his father had done? And most importantly, how could Nelay use that to her advantage?

After Kalla helped her slowly drink the water, Nelay slept for a few hours. She woke later and drank more and ate a bit of food. As evening fell, Harrow arrived and gently tried to help her to her feet. When she protested, he demonstrated scrubbing his skin. Her heart expanded with hope. If she could get him to take off the manacles, she could be free. With Kalla holding onto one arm, Nelay shuffled through the main camp. Taking only a few steps made her gasp for air. Maybe she could be free if Kalla managed to tie her onto a horse first.

For the first time, she had the wherewithal to look around. The Razorbacks loomed in the distance, their white caps seeming to stretch into clouds. The group was about a day's journey from Arcina. They'd left the Table Mountains and brush of her home for the fertile fields and trees brought about by the clever irrigation techniques of the Arcinians.

Nelay's jaw tightened as she realized the Clansmen and their allies held everything from Arcina all the way to Mubia and the ocean. Half of Idara. What was left of her once-great nation was encircled by mountains, desert, and enemies.

Harrow herded them into scraggily trees Nelay didn't know the name for. Eventually, she heard the rushing river. She slid down the embankment, holding onto Kalla for support. Putting on her most hopeful look, Nelay held out the manacles for Harrow to release her. He shook his head, pointing to his broken nose.

She dropped her hands in a show of frustration. "Then how do you expect me to wash?" she grumbled in Idaran, for she couldn't let them know she understood Clannish—it was one of the only advantages she and Kalla had.

He tossed her a strange-smelling cake of soap the color of faded leather. She remembered Rycus giving her myrrh-scented soap, and a pang shot through her. Keeping her frustration in check, she searched the water and its banks for any sign of crocodiles or alligators. With the water moving fairly quickly, she decided it was probably safe.

Carefully, she stepped into the river, fully clothed, with Kalla still at her side. Nelay started with the worst parts, washing her clothes and then scrubbing herself with the soapy cloth. Harrow's gaze darted to them, then quickly away as if he was trying to give them privacy.

"Be kind to Harrow," Nelay whispered to Kalla.

The girl glanced up. "Why?"

"Because right now he's our best chance of escape."

He rose to his feet and looked directly at Nelay. "Guards." He pointed to the trees and tapped his axe. She assumed he was trying to say the guards would kill them without hesitation if they tried to escape.

Wanting to allay his suspicions, she gave him a small smile. "You speak Idaran."

"Understand." He nodded. "Speak." He gave a small laugh as he shook his head. He studied her as Kalla washed her hair, then pointed to Nelay's tattoos, a questioning look on his face.

She considered not telling him as she started on Kalla's hair. But perhaps he would relax if she acted friendly. She pointed to the patterns nearly obscured by her growing hair. "Our tattoos show our rank."

Harrow touched his ornamental belt in understanding. "Trained?" He pantomimed sword fighting. "Soldier."

"No, I'm not a soldier," Nelay said.

He copied some of the words awkwardly and nodded, then said in Clannish, "How do I make you understand that if you try to escape, the chief will let Dobber kill you?" His voice caught. "And I won't be able to stop it."

"Why would you help us?" Nelay asked without thinking, but he didn't seem to notice she'd responded to his Clannish statement.

He looked down at the ground in shame. "Father, mother."

She thought she understood. She ducked down and rinsed the soap from her top half, then worked on her bottom half. She'd heard of this custom in other cultures—a parent's shame transferring to a child. "It seems to me, all of these men—" she gestured back toward the camp "—are from shamed families."

Harrow scoffed. "Father." He swallowed several times. "Traitor." He pointed to himself. "Bastard."

"Priestesses aren't allowed to marry," Nelay said, lowering her voice. "We may take lovers, but if we have a child, we must give it up. It's the same with the women soldiers. Sometimes the father raises them. Sometimes they are given away—and always such children are viewed as blessings."

He stared at her in open disbelief. "But . . ." He switched to Clannish. "They are a dishonor."

"It's wrong marking a baby as something less because of the actions of his father." Nelay studied this man who was an outcast for something his father had done. "Your father was in league with Zatal?"

At the hatred that flashed in Harrow's eyes, she knew she'd guessed right. They appraised each other. He was so pale he was almost translucent, unreal. But for the first time she saw past that. Perhaps . . . perhaps these Clansmen were not so very different from Idarans.

Such thoughts made her head hurt.

She sloshed out of the river. "We are cold."

He gestured for them to walk ahead of him. Back at camp, Nelay and Kalla crouched shivering by the fire as their clothes dried. Harrow didn't ask them more questions—didn't acknowledge them at all, in fact. It was as if he wanted to hide his kindness toward them from the others, which made sense if his father had been in league with Idara.

Finally, when she was dry enough to sleep, Nelay curled up in thick furs beside Kalla. She awoke sometime later, shivering, feeling like something had brushed against her face. She sat up to find an owl staring at her with its enormous eyes. It looked over her shoulder, toward the camp, before spreading its wings and flapping away. A fairy? Nelay glanced around. She was used to starting her day now, in the gray hours before dawn. The Clansmen didn't even stir yet—the fools didn't know how to survive in the desert.

Her head still throbbed as she rolled over to find Kalla's warmth, but the girl was gone. Nelay's hands shot out, feeling the wool blankets. They were cold. She hadn't just gone to relieve herself. "Kalla!" she cried as she pushed herself to her feet. The sudden movement left her dizzy. Stumbling, she turned in a circle. "Kalla!"

Harrow was at her side in an instant. "Did she run?"

Nelay searched the sleeping men as they staggered to their feet. "Dobber is gone!" She suddenly noticed the owl, watching her from a tree. As soon as she saw it, it spread its wings and glided away. She shot after it. Harrow's hand reached after her, but she slipped free and entered the dark trees. She heard him cursing and calling out the others as he came after her.

The manacles prevented Nelay from pushing the branches out of the way. All she could do was hold her raised hands before her head as she pushed through the brush, which whipped and scratched her mercilessly. Though she was aware of the injuries, there was no pain.

She emerged from the trees and realized she could no longer see the owl. She whirled, searching. "Come back! Show me where she is!" The owl didn't appear. "Kalla!"

The other men had spread out, hunting for her. Nelay closed her eyes and took a few meditative breathes, restoring her balance as the priestesses had taught her. Then she methodically lined up all the players, trying to figure out what a man like Dobber would do with a girl. He would take Kalla somewhere secluded. Somewhere that would muffle the sounds.

"The river." She shot toward where they had bathed earlier. As soon as she'd cleared the embankment, she saw them. Kalla was thrashing and crying. Dobber shoved something toward her chest. The girl screamed.

Nelay barreled into him, knocking him away from Kalla. Straddling him, she balled up both her fists and brought them down on him, making sure the chains and cuffs hit first. He sagged beneath her and she stretched the chain tight, shoving it against his throat.

Someone grabbed her, throwing her off him. Unable to use her hands to catch herself, she slammed hard into the ground. She staggered back to her feet. Most of the Clansmen had gathered, some of them watching her with their axes drawn. But others were staring at something behind her.

Kalla, Nelay thought. In her rage she'd forgotten her. Her gaze followed theirs and found the girl lying on her back, her body oddly still. Nelay crawled to her and gasped at the blood soaking Kalla's chest. The girl twitched and raised a bloodied hand toward the sky. "My family . . . at last."

Tears filled Nelay's eyes. "What did he do?"

Kalla choked, blood running from her mouth. "Couldn't . . . understand." She wheezed.

Nelay reached out and took Kalla's hand. She heard the scraping of a boot and turned to find Harrow facing Dobber. "You murdered a child," Harrow said.

Dobber looked at the other men as if seeking their help. "She was escaping. I caught her, but she fought me. I had to defend myself."

Harrow grunted in disbelief. "A little girl, her hands in chains, was too much for you? And you couldn't bother to call for the sentinels? For any of us?"

"I—" Dobber began, but then seemed to change his mind. "She's just a whore Raider. She has no right to live while my daughters are all dead."

Harrow's fist slammed into Dobber's temple. And then Dobber was under him and the Clansmen had to pull Harrow off.

Nelay turned away, focusing her attention on the dying girl in her arms. The priestesses spoke of the elice flower. A single petal from the bloom was strong enough to save a life. Every year, Idarans went in search of it. But none ever found it—except for Nelay's mother.

She looked up to see the owl from before watching them. "Please," she whispered. "Just one of the petals from the elice flower. Please."

The owl simply spread its wings and flew away.

Kalla's was not an easy death. Nelay stroked the girl's head as she coughed and gagged and choked on her own blood before finally drowning, bloody foam coating her lips.

When she was finally still, Nelay cried for her. Cried for the life she should have led, the children she should have borne, the death she should have had as an old woman, surrounded by her children and their children. Not like this. Not as a girl murdered for having the audacity to survive. Nelay cried for failing to protect her. Cried with rage at the fairy's indifference.

She finally finished weeping after the sun had slipped above the horizon and washed its light over her. Harrow stood beside her. Still holding Kalla's body, Nelay noticed for the first time the grave the men had dug in the soft sand of the riverbank. She knew when the river was swollen with water from the rainy season, Kalla's bones would be washed away. "She should be burned, given back to the Goddess of Fire. I will administer her last rites."

Crouching down, Harrow reached out to lay a hand on Nelay's shoulder, but she shrugged him off. And suddenly, the last player of the game slipped into place. She knew what she had to do. "A man who stands by while an evil is committed is just as guilty as the villain."

Guilt burned in Nelay's chest as Harrow closed his eyes in silent agony. He was a good man. He had done everything he could to protect her, and she knew burying Kalla wasn't his decision. Nelay was using him. But it was the only way she could turn the game to her favor.

She rose to her feet, her chains clinking. Harrow picked up Kalla's body and deposited her gently into the grave. The other Clansmen pushed dirt onto her body. Nelay did her best, tossing the leaves that were meant to be burned with the dead and singing the last rites. But Kalla would never rise with the wind and become part of the world, part of those she loved. That knowledge was as painful as her cruel death had been.

When they were done, Nelay looked down at the earthen mound. "Such a filthy death, rotting in the ground. Our ashes are meant to join the sky. To dance with the wind."

"I'm sorry," Harrow said again. She didn't answer him as they led her to a horse and left that horrible place.

Only once did Nelay's eyes stray from straight ahead of her, and that was to see Dobber, barely sitting in his saddle. His face was swollen nearly beyond recognition, and across his throat were bruises in the shape of chain links. A bolt of grim satisfaction shot through her. Even five horses in front of him, she could hear him wheezing through his damaged throat. She could still feel his body beneath her.

She swore he would die for what he'd done.

CHAPTER THIRTEEN

That night, Nelay forced herself to eat the Clansmen's horrible food. She would need her strength to kill Dobber and escape.

Harrow sat down beside her, her pack in his hands. He set it aside and wrapped his arms around his knees, staring at something in his grasp. Finally, he held it out for her. Curled in his palm was her necklace, the glass idol hanging off the side. She snatched it from him and put it over her head, her thumb settling into its customary place between the wings. "You had it? All this time?"

Instead of answering, he made a great show of going through the compartments. Her Idaran acolyte clothing, the packed food. Even her baldric, empty of all weapons. The coins were long gone. "Well, there are no weapons here, so I suppose you can have it back."

He held it out for her. With a dull hope, she took the pack. She tucked them in her robes and opened the compartments of her baldric. Inside one of them, she could see the keys to her cuffs. Her head jerked up, her gaze locking on his.

He sat beside her. "I know you can understand me," he whispered in Clannish. She gaped at him. How long had he known? It had to have been at the river. She must have given herself away.

He handed her the necklace and called out to one of the men. "Are Shev and Tor on duty tonight?" He pointed off in the trees.

The man nodded. "You're not up until tomorrow."

"Remember that," Harrow whispered to her. He was silent for a beat. "The elice flower. It changes you. Makes you more, and maybe less."

She ducked her head to hide the shock playing out on her face. How could he know this . . . unless he too had been changed by the flower? She was desperate to know what he'd lost in the bargain, but she dared not reveal her secret.

He sighed. "Just be careful. The fairies, they're not like us. They're dangerous."

She looked back at the knife in the baldric. "Why are you helping me?" she said in his native tongue.

"Because what happened to Kalla was wrong." Harrow stretched and stood, brushing his hands on his trousers. He looked pointedly at her and walked away. She stared after him. He was like her. The only other person she'd ever met, and she couldn't even talk to him about it.

Nelay's plan had worked—she'd manipulated one of the players into helping her. Even as relief washed through her, her guilt rose. If the Clansmen found out, Harrow would pay a terrible price. But the only way to spare him was to remain a captive. Not an option.

Carefully, she reached into her pack to her. She tucked the keys in her robes and opened the compartments of her baldric. Inside one of them, she could see the gleam of one of her throwing knives.

Shocked, she glanced up to find Harrow watching her. He looked pointedly at Dobber and then lay down, pulling his furs over his ears. Knowing she wasn't schooling her features, Nelay buried her head in her arms. She'd sworn to kill Dobber, and it wasn't like she hadn't killed before. But always in battle, defending herself. This would be different. This would be murder.

And while a part of her trusted Harrow, he was still a Clansman. Was he using her to kill Dobber in order to avoid the consequences himself? But then the image of Kalla coughing blood flooded Nelay's mind. She could still feel the girl fighting to draw every breath.

And suddenly Nelay remembered the satisfied look on Dobber's face as he'd forced the knife into her chest. This wasn't the first Idaran he'd murdered. And it wouldn't be the last if Nelay didn't stop him. She eased the compartment's flap closed as casually as she could and lay down to feign sleep.

Shivering without Kalla to keep her warm, Nelay waited until halfway between watches, when all the men's breathing was deep and heavy. Then she silently withdrew the key and unlocked the manacles, which came free of her raw wrists.

She drew the knife from her pack and held the blade flat against her arm to conceal it. Keeping her hands together as if they were still bound, she moved toward the trees as if to relieve her bladder. She paused beside the sleeping Dobber. In one quick motion, she pressed her hand to his mouth and thrust her knife in his heart, making sure not to miss as he had with Kalla. Then she twisted the blade to make his death faster.

His eyes widened and locked on hers before they rolled back. Nelay looked around to make sure no one had heard anything. There was only silence. She turned Dobber over onto his stomach, so the blood would seep into the ground instead of pooling for all to see, and pulled the blanket over his head. Then she moved silently into the trees.

She nearly jumped out of her skin when she found Harrow waiting for her in the shadows. Was he here to kill her? He'd obviously seen her slay Dobber. But he didn't sound the alarm, only motioned for her to follow him. She did so hesitantly. When they were out of earshot of the camp, he handed her two shamshirs and quickly stepped back, as if afraid she might use them on him. They were her father's shamshirs, and she took them gratefully, relieved to have them in her grip.

"Two sentries." He pointed. "Stay directly between them and you should be able to pass through without being seen. Make as much distance as you can. I'll try to see they don't come after you."

"What if they suspect you?"

Harrow wouldn't look at her. "My father should have protected my mother, should have loved her. Instead he used her in the worst way. Of all the men in her clan, no one protected her, no one stood up for her. Except another worthless Tiam." His gaze locked on Nelay's. "I won't be a man who stands by and does nothing."

"You are not the monster I thought you'd be," she replied.

"Nor are you. Goodbye, Nelay. I hope we don't meet again." He took a step toward the camp, but paused. "And beware the fairies—their interference always upsets the Balance."

"What did they take from you?" she asked softly.

"Think of the upheaval one fairy can cause by meddling with the Balance. Now imagine if all of them did."

She shuddered. "The whole world could be destroyed."

Harrow gave her a gentle push in the opposite direction. "Some laws are not meant to be broken." He turned and within moments was gone.

Easing from one shadow to the next, Nelay headed to the place he had shown her. Once she knew she was clear of the sentinels, she broke into a run.

She might be in her homeland, but she was well behind enemy lines.

Nelay felt weak from her injuries, from running all night and slipping through occupied territory for half the day. So when she caught sight of an orchard a little off course, she headed for it. It would provide food and shelter from the ovat, which would begin to howl any moment. She slipped inside the cool shadows, the smell of rotting fruit making her a little nauseated. She stopped frequently to listen and watch.

At a flash of movement in her peripheral vision, her gaze darted around the orchard in careful sweeps. But there were only lazy wasps buzzing drunkenly around the pears. Nelay reached up, picked a pear, and crouched at the base of the tree. She bit deep. Hot, sticky pear juice dribbled down her chin and soaked the front of her robes, which clung to her chest. She tossed the core away and rose to quickly pick several more pears, then cradled them in the folds of her robes.

Dobber's dying face flashed in her mind. Closing her eyes, she shoved the memory deep inside the pit where she banished everything she wanted to forget. No sooner had she done so than she saw Harrow's face. She hoped he wasn't suffering for helping her. She hoped the Clansmen didn't blame him. And then those memories too were shoved deep in the pit.

As her fingers wrapped around another pear, a sharp sting radiated from one of her fingers. Shaking off the wasp, she sucked in her breath with a hiss.

"Thief! Get out of my orchards!" a gruff voice cried in the rolling language of the Clanlands.

Nelay's anger flared hot. These were not this man's orchards. He'd stolen them from her people. A stone's throw away, he dropped from a tree, his short apron bulging with his plunder. He was pale and ugly as larvae under a rock.

Holding the pears in her robes, Nelay emerged from her half-hidden position and smoothly drew her shamshir from her scabbard. He stopped short. She considered killing him. It wouldn't be hard—the priestesses of fire had taught her well.

"She's an Idaran!" he cried.

Another man dropped from the same tree. A third came running up behind her. Her gaze darted between the three of them, her mind automatically assessing moves and counter-moves. Fighting would take time, allowing more Clansmen to arrive. Their main army was too close for Nelay to risk it. Abandoning her position, she sheathed her swords, hugged the food to her chest, and ran.

She risked a glance back to see the three of them giving chase. She increased her speed, desperation adding lengths to her stride. She was still weak from her injuries, and the strength she might have garnered from her feast of pears hadn't had time to seep into her muscles. Even though the men were older and a little fat, they were catching up.

Unwilling to let go of the food, even for a moment, she sent her practiced mind searching for something to use to her advantage—anything that might give her a chance to escape. At the sound of rushing water, she veered to the right. The orchard gave way to trees choked with brambles. Perfect. Nelay threw herself into the thorns, vaguely aware of the pain they inflicted on her flesh and clothing, and grateful for the protection provided by the leather armor she still wore under her clothes.

She winced and stumbled as a jagged stick pierced her leg. With a cry, she stumbled back, her robes ripping to reveal the tender flesh beneath. For a moment, she stood there, held upright by thorns imbedded in her arms. Juice from mashed pears soaked through her tunic and mixed with her blood. *Burn it, now the fruit will be bruised!*

Over the sound of her rasping breath, she listened. Half-muttered cursing and snapped branches confirmed it. They still followed her. Were they so desperate for more slaves that half of her country wouldn't suffice?

Surging to her feet, she forced her way through the last of the brambles, ignoring the pain. As soon as she was clear, she dove into the murky brown water, praying to the Goddess that the crocodiles and snakes would look the other way, just this once. She struggled in the water, her armor weighing her down and her robes making it hard to move. She kicked for the opposite shore, letting the current take her further downstream.

When Nelay couldn't hold her breath a moment more, she broke the surface and took another gasping breath. Then she dove again. She didn't stop until she felt the embankment beneath her fingers and the mud oozed into her torn flesh. Coughing and wheezing, she clawed up the bank and rose to her knees to look behind her.

One of the men from the orchard shouted curses at her, shaking his fist in the air. She patted her robes, desperately searching. She only found one—muddy, bruised, and misshapen, but still a pear. She smiled weakly with relief and tucked it back in her robes.

Movement caught her gaze. Farther downstream, about an arrow's flight away, was a bridge. That bridge was lined with about a dozen cavalrymen dressed in the multiple colors of Clanlands.

Of course it was. Nelay froze, hoping they hadn't seen her, but then the three from the orchard pointed her out. She should have killed them when she'd had the chance.

Half limping, half running, she pushed past another barrier of brambles and emerged from under their shadows to enter another orchard. She found herself rushing through the remnants of a battle between the Clanlands and Idara. Blood, brown with age, smeared across broken weeds like paint from a madman's brush. Smashed, worthless pieces of battle gear lay scattered haphazardly. Revulsion and fear mixed with a dim hope in Nelay's heart. Just days ago, the clans had clashed with her people. The king's armies had been here! They could still be close!

Her hope was short lived. Bent low over their horses, the Clansmen were devouring the distance to her like a wildfire driven by the ovat. She examined the players of the game. She limped badly now, her lips and fingers tingling from overexertion. They were going to catch her, and she'd best be ready for them when they did.

Halting was one of the hardest things Nelay had ever done. But she turned to face them and drew her swords. Keeping one of the trees at her back, she practiced her breathing and felt her fear melt away. She'd been trained in the art of killing since she was a child.

One of the priestesses' abiding principles was to use men's underestimation of a woman to her advantage. So Nelay didn't lift her weapons, for that would reveal that she knew how to use them.

The soldiers encircled her, sizing her up. They sported neatly trimmed beards and ice-blue tunics that bore the image of the Clansman axe. "It's a woman," one of them said in surprise.

"An escaped tiam," another sneered.

"No," came the answer of another. "She's dressed like one of the Desert Tribes. They train all their women to fight. It explains the sword."

"Let's bring her in," said the first.

They didn't know she could understand Clannish. Or perhaps they didn't care. She waited as three of them dismounted and came at her.

Just out of range, they paused and one of them spoke in terrible Idaran. "Come. Won't hurt."

In answer, she spat at him. They exchanged glances and charged her from three sides. She lunged, hitting one of them in the throat—stupid of him not to bring his shield. Then she dove, slashing at another's arms with her shamshir. One charged her. She stabbed, hitting his vitals.

She was beyond remorse. These men were thieves, murderers, and slavers. One of their own had killed Kalla just yesterday. Better them than her.

Before the last man had even crumpled, Nelay took both sword hilts in one hand and leapt into his still-warm saddle. Jerking the reins around, she slammed her heels into the horse's sides. Grunts and cries of outrage from the nine remaining Clansmen pierced the air behind her.

They were on her in seconds, but the trees prevented them from coming in close. Sheathing her swords, she urged the horse forward. All the men were large, while she was a small woman without any baggage. And she'd grown up less than three-day's journey from here, so she knew the countryside.

She started pulling away, leaving the orchard to strike out onto hard, unirrigated ground, watching the terrain before the horse carefully lest he step in a viper's hole and break his leg.

Nelay spotted the owl again, flying toward her. She whipped her head around as it went past. "Not helpful!" she cried. As she looked at the soldiers chasing her, one of them pulled out a recurve bow. Fear slammed into her.

She pressed herself flat against the horse, her elbows pinned to her sides to protect her vitals. If she could just manage to get out of range, she would be safe. As the first round of arrows whizzed past her, she locked her gaze ahead and refused to consider that she had no way to defend herself. Her fear was so overwhelming that the appearance of a group of horsemen drew her up in the saddle. She recognized their robes and headscarves, the veils drawn across their faces so only their dark eyes showed. They were desert Tribesmen. In Idara.

"Rycus?" He'd come for her! Her relief was almost tangible, so mixed up with a wash of joy that she nearly smiled. Judging by how rumpled they looked, they'd obviously been searching for days. Where had they found horses?

The thoughts were halted by a flash of light so intense she thought she'd been struck by lightning. And then the pain hit, so all-consuming that it drowned out all her senses. One of the Clansmen's arrows had found its mark in her left side, at the base of her ribs. Nelay clutched the horse's mane to keep from tumbling from the saddle. With each of the horse's strides, the arrow shifted inside her. But she'd managed to stay in the saddle. She might still make it.

Her horse suddenly jerked, rearing up and tossing its head as it screamed in pain. Before she could react, the animal violently shook its head. And then they were falling. Nelay hit the ground and pain blinded her again.

When she finally came to herself, her left leg was pinned under the thrashing horse. Nelay wished the darkness would take her, give her relief for even a moment. She was vaguely aware of the sounds of battle. She blinked to focus, watching as six desert Tribesmen killed nine Clansmen. Delir ran toward her and pinned the horse's head, then drove a dagger into the animal's neck.

The horse's thrashes settled to twitching. Rycus bent over Nelay. She looked into midnight-sand eyes set against dusky skin. "You came for me," she said in disbelief and more than a little wonder.

He didn't acknowledge her statement; he was too busy studying the arrow. "It hasn't passed all the way through. You can't ride with it inside you. I have to take it out."

"I know," she said through gritted teeth.

One hand rested beside the wound, the other took hold of the arrow. Even that small shifting sent a shock of pain through her.

"Brace yourself," he said as he jerked.

Her bones caught fire. She screamed and passed out.

She came to as gentle hands lifted her. She couldn't have been out long, because the horse was still twitching. Nelay was aware of a bandage tight around her ribs, of blood soaking her robes. Her wound seemed to pulse fire all the way into her shoulder and down her leg, but it felt so much better to have the arrow out.

Scand and Ashar passed her up to Rycus, turning her so she straddled him. They expertly tied her arms and legs around his body. The movements brought on another blaze of pain so bad she had to bite her bottom lip to keep from screaming.

Rycus gripped her tight, pressing hard on her wound, and turned the horse. He leaned forward, his mouth beside her ear. "There are Clansmen everywhere. You mustn't scream."

She closed her eyes and promised herself that no matter what, she would remain silent. He whirled the horse around and kicked it to a full gallop.

She wished the blackness would come for her. Wished it would take away the pain. But she stayed aware, her whole life revolving around her vow not to scream.

CHAPTER FOURTEEN

A t first, Nelay had gripped Rycus, holding onto him to keep from being jarred as much. But the horse's movement kept reopening her wound and her blood poured out, taking her strength with it. Now she was slumped against Rycus, her eyes closed and her head resting on his shoulder. He called for Scand to ride up beside him. "She's not going to make it much farther. We have to find a place for her to rest."

"The two Clansmen she wounded have escaped." Nelay heard the displeasure in Scand's voice. "They will report to their army. They will be looking for us."

"I hope they find us. I'll make them pay for what they've done to her," Rycus said, his voice full of heat.

"But what of the people we left at the cistern?" Nelay thought it was Cinab who said it, and she wondered why he wasn't tending the camels.

She perked up a little to ask, "Benvi and the others? You didn't take them to safety yet?"

Nelay felt an inaudible growl of frustration in Rycus's throat. "We've been too busy looking for you. Keep getting distracted by all these Idarans we need to take back to the cistern. There have to be over thirty of them now."

She smiled a little. "Rycus, one would almost think you cared."

"Believe me, I'm adding them to your debt. You owe me a gold coin for each, especially after all the food they keep eating."

Nelay would definitely be much poorer after this. She'd probably have to clip all the coins off her skirt. Such a shame—she loved that skirt. She lifted her heavy head and tried to catch her bearings, trying to force the players of the game into alignment. "There are mines all around," she said. "Find one."

"Surely the Clansmen know of these mines as well," Scand grumbled.

She tried to lift her head to look at him, but it dropped down again—she simply couldn't hold it up. "You have a better idea?"

"Spread out," Rycus said. "Search for a mine."

"Find the owl. It will lead you to safety," Nelay muttered. The world was beginning to spin, so she closed her eyes to block it out.

"We have been. I figured it was like the spider, which would mean it isn't an owl at all, would it not?" Rycus's voice was tight with wariness.

"Exactly like that." Hot as it was, Nelay was shivering with cold. "Just leave me and come back after you take the others to Thanjavar."

"That would only cost you more coins," he murmured, rubbing her freezing arms.

"Fire and burning." As if from a distance, she noticed her words were slurring. "I'm going to have to sell more of my jewelry. High Priestess Suka is going to be so angry at me. Not that she'll dare say anything after I'm high priestess." Nelay sniffed. "We'll see how well she likes running barefoot in the hot sand." She imagined challenging the high priestess to a game of fire. Suka couldn't turn down a challenge like that, not if she expected to keep control of the temple.

"Is that how you're financing this?" Rycus asked. When Nelay didn't answer, he pressed his lips to her temple. "I'm not leaving you alone. Tell me what I need to do to help you."

She was vaguely aware of the horses' hooves clacking against the rocks as they maneuvered a rise. "Ask the fairy for an elice flower. It will heal me."

He let out a long breath. "No one has ever located one."

"My mother asked a fairy for one. It saved my life as a baby." A sudden image of the fairy burst into her mind. Black mouth. Fangs. Slitted tongue.

"I found something!" Ashar called. "This way!"

Rycus turned the horse to the right and asked Nelay, "How would I ask a fairy? I can't see them." But she was too tired to answer. He nudged her. "I need you to stay awake."

She groaned, annoyed he wouldn't let her be. "Lost my Sight."

"I didn't know that was something you could lose."

"It's not . . . it's not supposed to be."

She tried to remember how it had happened, tried to explain. "It went blurry . . . then faded. Then it was . . . gone. The balance . . . was punishing me. Shouldn't have used my Sight." She drifted off again.

Rycus nudged her. "What are they like? The fairies, I mean."

Nelay shuddered and pain flashed through her. "Terrible. Wonderful." Then another image of a fish fairy struck her, gliding through the water, swimming with wings. Its body flashed with silver scales. "Bulging eyes . . . bald!" she gasped in horror.

"What?" Rycus said next to her face.

More images of fairies popped into her head. A beautiful butterfly fairy, its wings violet and white. But as it turned toward her, its eyes were faceted black orbs sticking out of its face. Nelay recoiled.

"It's all right," Rycus told her quietly.

She saw another one. This one wasn't so terrible. With cobalt and pink wings, and eyes a solid black. She had rainbow feathers for hair. Her clawed feet curled under her when she flew, her wings a blur. "Hummingbird."

"What?" Rycus asked.

Even with her eyes closed, Nelay began to sense movement. Shadows within shadows on the back of her eyelids. She stared at them until shapes began to appear. There were snakes, thousands of them. Black, with slithering tongues and dripping fangs. They moved slowly, hazily, but they kept growing bigger and bigger.

"Do you see them?" she whispered so they wouldn't hear. "The snakes?"

She felt Rycus's head shift. "There are no snakes, Nelay."

The snake's backs expanded, stretching like shadows. They had wings! The creatures dived, striking her, their fangs piercing her flesh. Thousands and thousands of times. "They're biting me! Rycus! Help me!"

He pinned her arms. "Nelay, your eyes are closed!"

Why wasn't he helping her?

"Scand!" Rycus called, panic in his voice.

Finally, Nelay felt unconsciousness coming for her. "The snakes will get you, too."

The next thing she remembered, Rycus pressed his mouth next to her ear. "Remember," he whispered, "don't scream."

She searched for the snakes, but they must have been hiding, waiting to strike again the moment she let her guard down.

Rycus passed her down to Delir. The pain jolted her eyes open, but she wasn't even tempted to scream. She was simply too tired and in too much pain. As she settled in Delir's arms, she noticed Rycus's stallion was soaked in blood from its withers to its knees. Her blood. She hadn't known there was that much in her body.

Delir carried her inside a mine and set her down on a wool blanket. Scand knelt next to her, ordering, "Start a fire."

Delir shifted on his knees to do as instructed. Cinab set down an armful of wood, his gaze locked on Nelay's, worry weighing down his young face

Rycus knelt beside her, carefully rolling her onto her back while she bit her knuckle. Scand cut through her robe. She held the remaining fabric to her breasts.

"Rycus," she whispered through chattering teeth. He leaned closer. "If you were trying to get my clothes off, there is an easier way." She was shivering so hard her teeth chattered.

Rycus didn't laugh. He didn't even take his eyes of whatever Scand was doing. "I'll remember that."

Nelay smelled smoke. She felt so dizzy, her heart beating frantically in her chest.

"Quiet now," Rycus said softly. She was about to ask what he meant when pain speared through her, barbed hooks shooting outward. She bolted up. Rycus caught her in his arms as she screamed, sobbing and clawing at his chest.

Scand tossed a red-hot knife toward the fire, and Nelay realized he'd cauterized her wound. As Rycus held her, the old man poured something sharp-smelling down her back and scrubbed at her raw flesh. She screamed again.

"All right. It's clean as I can get it and the bleeding is starting to slow," Scand said. "Lay her down on her side."

Rycus eased her onto a wool blanket and covered her. "Nelay?"

In too much pain to respond, she watched Scand rummaging around. He stuffed a few chunks of what looked like fibrous resin and dried leaves into a pipe, which he lit with the end of a burning stick. He puffed a few times to get it going before handing it to her. "Breathe deep and hold it. It will cut off the pain."

She knew what this was—opium mixed with tobacco. She breathed in the sweet smoke eagerly, hungry for relief. After a few puffs, she felt the pain easing back to something almost bearable. "Why didn't you give it to me before?" she asked angrily.

"We didn't have time—you were losing too much blood. Keep breathing it in, girl." Scand poured some leaves into a mortar with shaking hands, then added a scoop of what looked like yellow spices but smelled like eggs. While Rycus went to work mixing it, Scand crawled around to her other side.

"How bad is it?" she asked.

"You shouldn't be conscious with as much blood as you've lost." Scand's face was ashen and sweaty. Rycus shot him a dirty look, which he expertly ignored. "If the arrow hit your spleen, you might live. If it hit your intestines, you'll die."

"I won't die," she said flatly.

"That's the opium talking," Scand replied, then took a swig from a bottle of pungent-smelling spirits. She realized that was what he'd washed her with before.

They gave her a few sips of water, until her stomach felt queasy and she refused anymore. She glanced carefully around. "Where are the others?"

"Keeping watch," Rycus reported. "What happened? We met the group you saved. They said you and another girl were captured."

"She was killed. I escaped," Nelay ground out, refusing to think of Kalla. Rycus searched her gaze but didn't press her.

She looked at Scan. "Are you finished?" Her thoughts were getting hazy again.

Scand took the mortar from Rycus and examined it. He packed the contents between two pieces of linen and pressed it to Nelay's back, wrapping it while she gritted her teeth. "It'll need stitches, but not today. The wound is too swollen and it needs to drain."

"Thank you for not giving up on me, Rycus," she whispered.

He bent closer. "Rest. We will take the watch." After a few more determined puffs of opium smoke, she rested her hand on her pendant and remembered no more.

When she woke again, it was pitch black except for the dancing light of the low fire. The pain had gone from a deep ache to burning again. The night air was chilly, as it always was in the desert. She shifted and saw Rycus, one arm cocked over a knee as he stared into the fire. "It hurts," she said hoarsely.

He took the pipe and lit it, then puffed until it was burning. Nelay took her first pull and held it in her lungs for as long as possible before letting out. Almost immediately, her body relaxed. Still, she had to think of something to take her mind off the pain. "What are we going to do now?"

Rycus shifted to help her drink from a water skin. "The border along the desert is crawling with Clansmen. The only way to safety is to keep ahead of them, heading straight to Sopora and on to Thanjavar."

"What about all the Idarans you left at the cistern?"

"We'll have to go back for them after we get to safety. They have enough supplies to hold them out until we do."

Nelay started to feel fuzzy again. "Do you think we'll find my brother in Sopora?"

"I don't know. Why didn't your family tell you?"

Why hadn't her parents told her Panar had left them? Why hadn't he written her himself? She was ashamed they hadn't cared enough to let her know. "He's the only family I have left. I need to find him."

"Nelay, you're not going to be in any condition to search for your brother. Pay me and I'll find him."

"I'm in no condition to challenge Suka as high priestess, either. If I go back now, I'll either be married off to the king or killed on sight."

"Would it be so bad to be a queen?"

She stared at the mine walls without actually seeing them. "In the state Idara is in, it might just be fatal." He didn't say anything. "Even if we beat the Clansmen, I would be a queen in name only. The king has all the power. Better to be high priestess and decide my own fate."

"Is that what you want? Power?" Rycus asked as he pressed the water skin into her hand. "Drink as much as you can hold. You lost a lot of blood."

She did as she was told. After all, she had to get her strength back to prove him wrong. She shifted to look at him, immediately regretting the slight movement as her back twinged painfully. She combated it with a deep inhalation of smoke. "No—I want the freedom that comes with power." Her eyes closed. "I watched my mother bury many of her children. I never wanted that for myself. Never wanted a life of servitude as a wife and mother." Nelay was silent for a time. "All I want is to be a priestess." She sighed, deciding not to fight the sleep dragging her down. "I'll be ready to fight in a week."

Rycus gave a doubtful grunt.

When she awoke again, a brilliant shaft of golden light streamed from the entrance. It stabbed into the mine, hurting her eyes. Immediately, she searched for the opium pipe. Scand already had it ready and pressed it into her hand. She frantically puffed, willing the sharp burning to ease. When it finally did, she looked around. Rycus was asleep on the other side of the fire. "It's midmorning," she said. "Why haven't we left yet?"

"We leave now and you'll bleed to death." Scand lifted the bandages to check her back. "I don't know how the swelling has gone down so much, or why you don't have a fever."

"I told you," she mumbled. "I'm very hard to kill." An effect of consuming the elice petal.

With a huff, he poured something thick and dark into a cup. He held it to her lips. She sipped. It tasted like cooked meat but had the texture of thick gravy. "What is it?"

"Cooked blood to replace what you lost."

Nelay's lip curled in distaste, but she reminded herself she'd eaten worse and sipped until her stomach threatened to rebel. "What kind?"

"Sheep. There's a lot of them running loose around here." Scand changed her bandages and slipped outside.

Desperately needing to relieve her bladder, she looked around. She didn't want to wake Rycus, and everyone else seemed to be gone, so she rolled to one side and tried to stand. A stab of pain shot through her back and she gasped.

He was awake in an instant. "What are you doing?"

"I have to relieve myself."

"Oh." His brow furrowed. "That's harder for women."

"Yes," she chuckled, then winced at the movement.

"Have you smoked some opium? That should help."

At her incredulous look, he shrugged. "Help with the pain. Not necessarily the awkwardness."

After five puffs, she felt well enough to let him help her to her feet. He led her outside and helped her squat behind a bush. Then, thankfully, he moved a few steps away.

When she was finished, he supported her as she walked back to the blankets. "You should never have come here," he said, handing her a water skin.

Nelay was tempted to be angry, but the concern on Rycus's face was real. "What would you have done if you were in my place?"

He hesitated and tapped the water skin. She drank a few swallows. "Had I the money, I would have hired men to find my family for me," he said.

"And those men would have given up the moment they found my parents' bodies. I knew where to look, knew which mines people might hide in. And I found Benvi, who knew something of my brother's whereabouts."

Rycus was silent for a time. "You are very brave and very stubborn and a more than a little foolish."

She thought about that for a moment. "Yes."

He laughed outright.

"Don't worry. I'm going to be fine."

She was already falling asleep, but she thought she heard him say, "I hope so."

The next time she woke, it was dark out. She could smell food cooking. "Oh, lamb stew."

Rycus smiled at her. For a Tribesman, he smiled a lot. Or maybe all Tribesmen smiled a lot, just never around Idarans. "I thought that might wake you up."

She ate far more than her share. When she was finished, she couldn't seem to get warm, no matter how much she tugged at the furs. Finally, Rycus came to sit beside her. He lifted the blankets and shifted very carefully until he lay next to her. He gently wrapped his arms around her. She automatically stiffened, unsure what to do with a man this close and this . . . warm.

He sighed. "I'm not going to take advantage of you—unless you want me to."

She sort of did, but she wasn't going to admit that. "Do you do this in the desert with your men?"

"Sometimes." His answer surprised her. But it was working—already she felt warmer. She also had a very good view of his chest hairs. Not too many, but enough that he was definitely a man.

"So . . . do you want me to take advantage of you?" he asked.

She looked into his eyes, which gleamed with mischief. "Do you want to keep your man parts?"

Rycus chuckled and stared at the cave ceiling for a time. "So, snakes?"

She repressed a shudder, still feeling the ghost of their bites, over and over. "I hate them."

He breathed in deeply. "I hate being in small spaces. The only reason I can tolerate this cave is because I can still see the sky."

Nelay studied the slice of sky, mentally naming a couple of constellations.

He ran his fingertips along the side of her face. "When I saw you in that orchard, it was like finding something I thought I'd lost forever. And then that arrow hit you, and your blood was all over me." He kissed her forehead, and something in her softened. "Rest, Nelay. I'll take care of you."

CHAPTER FIFTEEN

Someone touched her face. "Nelay." She opened her eyes, only to be greeted with pain. Rycus crouched before her with the smoking pipe. He handed it to her. Behind him, the other smugglers were leading horses out of the mine. "Clansmen are headed this way. I fear it is too soon, but we must go."

She tried to wet her lips with her tongue. "Water."

He helped her drink from a water skin that tasted of goat—not especially appetizing but she'd had worse. She drank carefully, knowing the journey might cause her stomach to rebel. Rycus handed her a cup of cold lamb stew.

"The scouts say it's clear, but we will have to move fast." Worry filled his eyes. He leaned in and whispered, "These men deserve my loyalty. I can't risk their life for yours, no matter how much it pains me."

"You don't have to apologize." Eager to banish the fear in his eyes, Nelay started to push herself up, but he moved in before she could and scooped her into his arms. She winced. He must have noticed, for she could feel him watching her. With exceeding gentleness he handed her up to Delir, then passed her the pipe. "We have to ride hard. I'm sorry."

With that he mounted his own horse and they took off. A wave of nausea and pain swept over Nelay. She puffed on the pipe until the haze distanced her from the pain, but she was not oblivious to the trickle of blood running down her back. Or the fact that she had to lean over to vomit lamb stew into the blurring countryside.

Throughout the day, they carefully passed her from one smuggler to the next so as not to tire the horses or themselves. Rycus watched her with a tense expression. But she knew how hard she was to kill. When they finally arrived at Sopora near dusk, Nelay glanced around in a haze. The village seemed just as she remembered from her childhood visits to the dry season markets, when their family had sold their sheep's wool and purchased the supplies they needed to survive the coming year.

Rycus pulled her from the horse and carried her into an inn with a tile floor and mud-brick walls. He entered the first room he found and laid her on a soft bed. A very young, very pregnant woman came in and leaned over her. She pinched the skin on Nelay's hand, clucking her tongue when it didn't immediately spring back. "She's desert sick. She needs water."

"She throws up anything I give her," Scand reported.

Scowling, the woman turned on her heel and started out of the room. "I have something to help with that."

"My father bought me my glass idol at the market here." Nelay touched it through her clothes, her eyes aching with unshed tears.

"Rest, Nelay," Rycus said gently.

As if his words worked some kind of spell, her eyes grew heavy. She closed them, not sleeping so much as resting.

She heard someone pull out a chair and sit heavily on it. "We can't leave those Idarans at the cistern forever," Scand said. "They'll be out of food any day now."

Rycus sat next to Nelay on the bed, the wool mattress slumping under his weight. "Give the men a day's real rest and then you all go back and lead them to safety."

"The fire's too hot, Rycus. You're going to burn your sausages." Scand's voice was surprisingly kind.

"I'm staying," Rycus grunted.

Scand drew in a long breath and left, his soft-soled boots scuffing across the floor.

When the woman returned a short while later, Rycus helped Nelay sit up and sip a sweet, spicy tea that eased the rolling in her stomach. His face relaxed as she drank cup after cup. She ate more lamb stew, which was much better than even Delir's cooking, before finally lying down again. Rycus fetched Scand, who inspected her wound.

"The swelling's gone down enough to stitch it." He sounded surprised. He gave her more opium and started rooting around in his bag—a bag Nelay was coming to hate.

Moving to kneel before her, Rycus pushed her hair out of her face before turning to address the pregnant woman. "What's your name?"

"Maran," she said softly.

Feeling much more alert, Nelay remembered why she'd left the safety of the temple in the first place. "Do you know a man named Panar Favar Denar ShaBejan?" she asked, almost afraid to hear the answer.

There was a pause before the woman said, "No, I do not think so."

"Is there someone else who might know him?" Nelay pressed.

"We're the only inn in the village. If I don't know him, no one does."

Nelay didn't have the energy to argue.

"How many have fled Sopora?" Rycus queried, and Nelay couldn't help but wonder why a desert smuggler cared about Idara.

"Most of the women and children have already left for Dalarta," Maran responded.

Rycus's gaze lingered on her swollen belly. "Why have you not gone with them?"

"My husband insists that Arcina will not fall. He doesn't like leaving the inn unattended."

Rycus leaned back on his haunches. "Arcina will fall. If it hasn't already."

"The Immortals are the finest army the world has ever seen," Maran said in a mousy voice, as if repeating something she'd heard but didn't quite believe.

"Not anymore," Rycus muttered.

The woman stepped away and Nelay heard her push open the shutter. "If what you say is true, how long until the Clansmen arrive here?"

Rycus watched Maran, pity in his gaze. "There were patrols a day's ride north of here. Sopora doesn't have defenses to speak of. If the Clansmen attack, it will be a massacre."

Maran closed the shutter and headed to the door. "Then I best warn my husband."

Scand pressed a stick between Nelay's teeth. "My eyesight's not what it used to be, so this won't be pretty. But it should hold."

"What?" Nelay cried.

"Hold her," Scand said to Rycus. The old man moved to where Nelay couldn't see him, but she felt him leaning close to her wound.

Rycus gripped her hands. "Look into my eyes. Don't look away."

She did, whimpering and sweating as the needle pierced her skin again and again and again. When Scand was finally done, they wrapped her ribs and she couldn't look at either of them for the embarrassment of being naked from the waist up in front of them.

Finally, Rycus helped her put her shirt on. She puffed on the pipe until the pain eased off enough for her to rest.

Nelay woke the next morning to Maran coming in with a steaming bowl and cup. "I thought you might be hungry," the pregnant girl said.

"Yes, but I could also use the pipe."

Maran set the food on the floor before helping Nelay sit up. "Scand left it for me to give you. Start eating and I'll fetch it."

Nelay lifted the bowl with her right hand; moving her left still stretched the muscles in her back too much. "Where are Rycus and the others?"

Maran paused at the doorway. "He is trying to convince the remaining villagers to flee for Dalarta. The rest of his men are trying to scrounge up some supplies to take with them to wherever they're going.

Relieved, Nelay let out a breath. Rycus hadn't left her. He'd said he wouldn't, but a part of her had been afraid. He'd been nothing but loyal, yet sometimes fear wasn't rational.

"Did you convince your husband to go?" Nelay asked.

Maran gave a tight smile, her hands fluttering nervously. "We're loading our cart. It will take a couple days."

Nelay met the woman's gaze. "With your condition—" she waved at the woman's belly "—you should go now."

Maran took a step back. "We have to pack up our livelihood. If all of the Hansi Province is already in Dalarta, there probably isn't food to speak of." She gave another tight smile and stepped out of sight.

Nelay lifted the steaming bowl. Mashed grains with dried dates and a cup of hot goat's milk. She ate hungrily, and the food tasted better than anything she could remember eating in a long time.

Maran returned long enough to give her the pipe and promptly left again. Once Nelay's thoughts went fuzzy, the girl brought a large clay bowl filled with steaming water. "I thought you might like to clean up."

Thrilled, Nelay let Maran remove her clothing. She studied her body distantly. Her skin was ashen and her wrists chafed from the manacles. Bruises and lumps covered her. And she'd have a nasty scar from the arrow wound.

She held still while the girl scrubbed away a week's worth of grime and blood. Once, Maran's huge belly pressed up against Nelay's arm and she could feel the baby squirm. She started and looked down to see Maran's stomach writhe through her tunic.

"The baby's always wiggly after I eat breakfast," the girl said.

Nelay glanced up at her beaming face. "Does—does it hurt?"

"Sometimes, if I get a foot to my ribs or a fist in my bladder.

Nelay stared at Maran's belly in fascination.

"You're a priestess?" the girl asked.

Still staring at what was surely triplets, judging by the amount of movement, Nelay nodded.

"That must be frightening—always being in front of all those people."

Nelay's gaze snapped to Maran's. "I like being in front of people."

The girl studied her as if trying to decide whether she was serious or not. Finally, she helped Nelay dress in new Idaran robes in midnight blue. Then she left to fetch clean water. When she came back, she helped Nelay lie face down, her head hanging off the edge of the bed. Then Maran massaged soap into Nelay's scalp, rinsed it, and rubbed expensive oils into her damp hair. The soothing scents calmed her.

"Why are you doing all this for me?" Nelay asked. It wasn't like she could pay for any of it. The Clansmen had taken all her coins.

"Rycus paid for it," Maran said.

Instantly Nelay felt more awake. She'd become more of a risk than she was worth. The businessman in him had to realize that.

Maran disappeared for a while and came back with a platter of lamb chops cooked with almonds and dates. Nelay ate eagerly. The flatbread was especially tasty.

Once Nelay finished eating, Maran gathered up her things and left. Nelay stared out the narrow window, watching as the trees began swaying to the ovat, which blew a little gentler here due to the proximity to the desert. It still drove everyone indoors.

Nelay turned toward the door when Rycus appeared, sand in the creases of his clothes. He brushed it off and removed his headscarf. He must have washed himself at some point, because most of the grime was gone.

He pulled out her baldric and slipped in a new set of throwing knives. "You look almost like a priestess instead of a beggar."

"Why did you come back for me? It can't be for the money—though you remind me of it at every turn. The risks far outweigh the rewards. And you're too savvy of a businessman to be ignorant of that."

He took a deep breath, shut the door, and pressed the back of his head against the rough wood. "Did you really think I'd leave you to become a Clansmen slave?" The anger in his voice surprised her.

"It's the logical thing to do."

He took a step toward the bed. "As logical as you coming after your family?"

Suddenly it was hard to breathe. "I couldn't live with myself if I abandoned them—believe me, I tried."

Another step. She felt the tug in her belly again. She wondered if he felt it too—if that was what drew him closer. "So you care about them?"

"Of course." Now he was close enough she could reach out and touch him.

"Even though it defies all logic?"

"Yes," she whispered.

He knelt beside her, his entire body leaning forward as if anchored to her, yet he did not attempt to touch her. "Some things defy all logic." His gaze was soft.

She breathed deeply, taking in his scent. And she realized it was familiar to her, that it brought her comfort. Somewhere along the way, Rycus had become a part of her. Part of her as her family was part of her. She reached out, cupping his cheek. "This wasn't supposed to happen." She might kiss a few men here and there, flirt and tease, but she was always very careful not to form attachments. She was to be the high priestess. There wasn't room for anything else.

He stroked her cheek with one long, lean finger. He came in closer, his mouth hovering over hers. "If it makes you feel better, my high priestess, I didn't mean for it to."

She felt the words touching her skin. And then his lips claimed hers, a light brushing. Again and again and again. Nelay had never been kissed so sweetly. No passion, just tenderness.

Fire and burning, it had taken him long enough.

CHAPTER SIXTEEN

N elay stirred to the sound of silence—the ovat had died out. Something had woken her, but she wasn't sure what. She sat up slowly, testing her back. The pain was less but she was very stiff and still weak. After listening for a moment and hearing nothing, she looked down at Rycus, his thick lashes fanning out across his cheeks. In his sleep he looked innocent, almost boyish. And he was sleeping beside her. What was she doing? There was no room in her life for a man—especially not one who was a criminal. She was going to be the next high priestess, burn it!

She was considering how to get out of the bed without waking him when she saw a spider—the same kind she'd burned to a crisp in the fire. She had to resist the urge to find a knife and kill it as it scurried across the floor and up the wall. It paused at the windowsill, one of its eight legs tapping against the glass.

A sick sense of foreboding washed over Nelay. The fairies' help never came without a steep price, and they'd helped her numerous times over the past few days. She dreaded the day of reckoning, even as she knew she would take the help. She didn't have a choice.

The spider turned back to her, waving its legs before disappearing altogether. Nelay gasped and shook Rycus. "Something's wrong." He sat up and squinted at her. She rolled out of bed and grimaced in pain as she bent down to pull on her own boots.

Shouts sounded outside. In an instant, Rycus was wide awake. He bolted to the window and threw it open. "Their fore guard has attacked!"

He ran to the bed and dropped his cross baldric over his shoulders, then jerked on his boots.

"Where are my swords?" Nelay asked.

He scooped up her baldrics from the chair they were draped across and tossed them to her. She caught them, wincing as her back seized up.

Scand appeared at the doorway, sword in hand. "We've got to move!"

The three of them ran down the hall and burst into the main room to join Bahar, Cinab, Ashar, and Delir. The door had already been bolted. The parchment-covered windows were too small to worry about.

Maran burst into the room from the kitchen, fingers caked with dough. She took one look at the swords in Rycus's hand and said, "The cart is already loaded out back."

He headed in that direction, but not before footsteps sounded outside. The door shuddered and then shattered. A dozen Clansmen poured through. Ashar killed the first, Delir the second. And then the battle became so mixed up Nelay couldn't tell who was who. There were just swords and axes and arms and legs and men rolling around on the ground.

For a moment, Rycus's gaze shifted to her. "Go with Maran!"

"No, I—" Nelay began, hurt and angry at once.

"You're a liability and you know it. Go!" He charged forward, ducking a swing, his swords twisting around him.

Nelay's mind spun as she tried to force the players into a position where she could help Rycus. But he was right—she was slow. He'd spend more energy trying to keep her from getting killed than fighting his own battle. She had to run, to leave him to face this without her. Ignoring the pain, she forced herself to move.

Frozen, Maran stared, horrified and open-mouthed at the Clansmen with their axes and shields fighting against Tribesmen with their twin shamshirs.

Nelay grabbed her arm. "We have to go!" They stepped into the kitchen to find an Idaran man hiding on the other side of the fireplace. Nelay shot him a look of disgust. "Get a weapon," she said to Maran. "A sword. A knife. A big stick. Something."

Maran snatched a ridiculously ornate sword from above the doorway and a knife from a tub of soapy water. Taking the knife for herself, she passed the man the sword. "Sedun! We have to go!"

The man jerked as if suddenly coming awake. Without a word, he lumbered to his feet after them just as the fight moved to the kitchen.

Rycus had downed one of the Clansmen, but he and his men were still outnumbered two to one. It was only a matter of time before one of the Tribesmen was struck down.

"Help him!" Nelay shouted at Sedun.

He jumped as if her words had slapped him. "How do I know what to do with a sword?" He disappeared outside, pulling Maran behind him.

Nelay forced her mind to come up with a solution. She pulled one of her throwing knives, but she could feel the tension in her back and didn't trust herself not to hit one of her friends.

"Nelay," Rycus said through gritted teeth when he saw her.

Growling in frustration, she went out the door and jogged toward the stables, her wound throbbing with each step and her muscles feeling watery and slow. Sedun pulled open the stable door. Inside waited a water buffalo hitched to a cart full of huge wine pots and reed baskets of food. The animal lowed nervously at them, but Sedun was already untying three saddled horses that had been tethered to the back of the cart.

He and Maran climbed on two of them. Nelay took the reins of the remaining horse and heaved herself up. By then, the battle had moved behind the inn, with the six Tribesmen fighting ten Clansmen. Sedun and Maran took off, abandoning the agitated ox and the wine. Nelay held back. "Rycus!"

A dozen more Clansmen rounded the inn, angling to cut the Tribesmen off. Rycus saw them, saw her. "I won't leave my men. Go! I'll catch up!" He ducked a wide swing from an enormous man with an enormous axe. "Full retreat!"

The six of them ran, their path a thirty-degree angle from Nelay's, their strides long. The Clansmen split up, most going for Rycus and the others, the rest headed for Nelay.

Maran and Sedun were already far ahead of her. The players of the game spun, and once again, she had no choice. Nelay kicked the horse after them. The animal started climbing a worn path up the side of one of the mountains. The Clansmen were on foot, so it wasn't long before the horses outdistanced them on the steep slope. They passed an active mine, pickaxes and ore carts abandoned at the entrance.

The horses breathing hard and covered in sweat when Nelay, Maran, and Sedun emerged onto the top of the table mountain. Nelay looked back. Sopora was burning. She studied the road leading from the village toward the city of Dalarta. She could make out people moving, but she was too far away to determine whether they were Clansmen or Idarans.

How would Rycus find her? Had he and the others even escaped? Nelay turned away, forcing her questions and fears back inside the dark pit deep inside her. "You better find me, smuggler," she muttered.

Keeping a hard pace, the trio wound down the mountain. Sedun knew the back roads, which they followed, fearful of the

Clansmen. They rode long into the night, letting the horses pick their way with their superior night vision.

The journey took its toll on Nelay. The pain had returned with a vengeance, her wound so tight she couldn't speak. It took everything she had to keep herself from falling out of the saddle.

At one point, her horse bumped into Maran's and staggered to a halt. Nelay looked up. She hadn't even realized the girl had stopped. "Sedun," Maran said.

The man glanced back at her. "We need to put as much distance between the Clansmen and ourselves as possible."

"I can't go any farther," Maran said. "And neither can Nelay. We both need to rest."

Nelay looked closely at the girl and saw the strain on her face as she hunched over, obviously in pain. "You're in labor!"

Sedun jerked the reins and brought his horse around. "Maran, we can't stop. The Clansmen—"

Her eyes were pinched shut. "Sedun, the baby is coming."

His face went slack. Only then did Nelay realize he was Maran's husband. If she'd had half her wits about her, she would have noticed earlier.

In the moonlight, Nelay could make out Sedun glancing around. "There's an abandoned mine about a mile from here," he said. "Can you make it?"

Maran gave a tight nod. "I can make it."

When they finally arrived at the mine, he tossed his reins over a branch and dismounted, then motioned for Nelay to give him the sword. She complied and he pulled aside the brush in front of the entrance and entered sword first. Sometimes leopards or hyenas took over the abandoned mines, though she saw no tracks or scat of either.

She heard the murmur of voices coming from inside. Seconds later, an old Idaran woman emerged, striding straight for Maran. "Havva," Maran cried in relief.

"Who are you?" Nelay asked as she looked between the two. "Why are you here?"

"Come inside," the old woman hissed. "Before the Clansmen see you." She helped Maran down and the two shuffled back in.

Not long after, children, led by a girl who looked about twelve, surrounded Nelay and helped her down. Maran must have sent them. Nelay managed to walk into the cave and turned to see Sedun wrap his robe around the eyes of one of the horses and lead it after her.

Just past the entrance, the space opened into a natural cavern. A river churned through the far end until it disappeared under a natural bridge of rock just wide enough for a mule and small cart. Beyond that was the entrance to another tunnel. Nelay could smell the minerals used to make luminash. Against the wall to the right, a small fire burned well back from the entrance. Havva settled Maran beside it, and the children sat there as well.

Sedun removed the jacket from the horse's eyes and stepped back outside, presumably to bring in another.

"We thought you were Clansmen," Havva said.

Maran panted. "I'm glad to see you."

Nelay moved toward the light of the fire. Bracing herself against the wall, she slid down next to Maran. Soon, Sedun brought in the last horse and squatted on the other side of the fire.

"Is she really in labor?" Nelay directed the question to Havva.

Havva pressed her hands to Maran's belly as the girl's face screwed up. "Her pains might stop if she rests."

Nelay looked around. "Where are the children's parents?"

"Not here," the old woman said with a pointed look.

Nelay clamped her mouth shut.

The oldest girl poked the fire. "When the Clansmen came to the village, I ran with my parents and my brothers and sisters. I thought we'd gotten away, but they caught us in the dark. Father said to run and hide." The girl's haunted eyes met Nelay's. "Havva found us. Brought us here."

This would have been what, a few hours ago? Chances were, the parents had been captured or killed. "How far away from here were the Clansmen?"

"Not far," Havva said softly.

Sedun wiped his mouth with his hand and started for the exit. "Where are you going?" Nelay called after him.

He paused but didn't turn back. "I'm going to keep watch. If the Clansmen find us here, we'll be trapped." Then he was gone.

Havva was still pressing on Maran's stomach. "How long have the pains been coming?"

Maran tensed up, the cords of her neck standing out. After a long moment, she let out her breath. "They've been building since we left Sopora."

"Can you stop it?" Nelay asked. "This is a bad time to be having a baby."

Havva shot her an amused look. "Children have a knack for bad timing." The old woman began squeezing parts of Maran's stomach. "Head down. This is good."

Nelay let out a relieved breath. "You know what you're doing?"

The old woman didn't turn to her. "I have daughters and sons' wives, plus a few grandchildren." She grabbed a homemade torch of pitch and bark and lit it. Murmuring reassurances, she helped Maran to the mouth of a tunnel on the other side of the moving water.

Nelay studied the children, who only looked back at her. She couldn't help but feel they needed something from her, but she had no idea what it was.

Maran whimpered again. As much as Nelay didn't want to go back there, all these children staring at her with broken gazes was worse. She took a few steps toward the tunnel. Before she got there, the old woman came out. "Maran will have the baby this night. And you will help me deliver it."

Nelay backed away, but the woman caught her arm. "Men go into battle to kill, but women go to battle to bring life. There are casualties and wounds, but our sacrifice leaves the world a better place when we are gone. And we will not allow her to go through this battle alone."

Nelay took a deep breath to steady the trembling inside her and stepped around the corner.

CHAPTER SEVENTEEN

Nelay held the tiny bundle in her arms. Gently, she wiped away the gore, revealing perfect, soft skin. The baby, a boy, squirmed and cried in protest.

Long ago she had held her dead brother in much the same way. She'd sworn then she would never be a mother. Never sacrifice the way her mother had, burying so many of her children along the way. Never be dependent on a man the way her mother had.

But as Nelay held Maran's tiny baby, something in her softened and an ache formed. Some instinct within her . . . wanted a child of her own. Unsure what to do with such foreign emotions, Nelay finished drying the infant, then swaddled him in a ripped tunic and handed him to his mother.

Maran, her face pale and her body shaking, burst into a radiant smile. Nelay rubbed her glass pendant as she watched, feeling something swelling inside her. Joy and pride in womankind. She was part of this sisterhood. Part of something bigger and more complex than she'd ever imagined.

Havva helped Maran uncover her breast and began teaching her how to feed the baby. Nelay hadn't known it was something that needed to be taught.

Someone suddenly pushed past her from behind. Sedun took in the scene before him and his face paled. "Clansmen are coming. At least a dozen of them. We must go now."

Havva pushed herself stiffly to her feet. "She cannot ride, not yet! She'll surely bleed to death!"

Maran was trying to sit up, but she was shaking too much. Havva gently held her down. "There are only three horses. We won't all fit."

Sedun motioned the way he'd come. "There are over a dozen of them. We must go."

Maran was panting, her face gray. "Maybe if we're all silent they won't find us."

Sedun pressed his palms to the top of his head as if to keep it from exploding. "Why else would they come this way if they didn't know about this mine? We go, now!"

Maran's face was white, her fresh blood flowing onto the rocks around her. "You must fight," Havva said to Sedun. "You must protect us."

He backed away. "I can't fight over a dozen Clansmen!" His gaze landed on Maran, his expression torn. "You have to understand. If I stay here, I'll die."

"Sedun, please," his wife begged. "Please don't leave me."

He pivoted on his heel and fled. Nelay shot Havva a look. "Look after Maran. I'll be back."

Trying to ignore the pain of her wound, Nelay followed him. Sedun grabbed children from the ground and deposited them on the horses' backs. "This way," he muttered, as if to himself. "I'm saving the children."

"You really think the guilt of abandoning your wife and child will ever leave you?" Nelay said.

His head whipped around but he quickly looked away. "What do you want me to do? If I fight them, I'll die."

"Let them take you both." Nelay couldn't believe she'd suggested it even as the words left her mouth. "You might be slaves, but you'll be together. When the time comes, you can try to escape, like I did."

Sedun gave the oldest child the reins. "Ride for Dalarta. Don't look back and don't stop." He slapped the horse on the rump and it disappeared into the tunnel that led out.

"Come with me," Sedun said. "Take this horse. Get the children to safety."

Nelay shook her head. "I can't just leave them."

His face tightened. "If she stays still and hidden, perhaps they won't find her. If not, perhaps they'll take pity on her and let her live."

Nelay's fingers itched for her swords. "Do you know what they do to women they take pity on?" she choked out, thinking of Kalla.

Sedun refused to look at her. "I won't be their slave."

Nelay took a step toward him, barely containing her anger. "We fight! And if we die, at least we'll die well!"

He sent off the second horse, loaded with five children. He pushed the remaining children on the last horse and climbed up behind them.

He looked down at her, his face hardened. "You want my advice? Run and hide." He spared a glance into the dark tunnel and then kicked the horse.

Nelay chased him out into the predawn gray, trying to grab at the reins, to force him to stay and fight. But he quickly outdistanced her, and she dared not shout for fear she might be heard by the Clansmen.

Heart knocking against her ribs, she hugged the edge of the mountain and moved to where she could see down the path. Clansmen slunk forward, their multitudes of colors and dull skin looking dirty in the dimness, their axes dark with blood. They would arrive at the mine within minutes.

Nelay darted back to the entrance and tugged the brush over the opening. She backed into the shadows. Her mind spun with the players and objects she could use to her advantage. She cast aside the ideas that didn't work and latched onto those that did. She grabbed the few items the children had abandoned. The air was heavy with the scent of smoke, but there was nothing she could do about that. She could only hope the Clansmen didn't search the back tunnel.

After crossing the open cavern, she stepped into the tunnel and deposited the items she'd gathered. She and Havva exchanged a glance and without a word took hold of Maran under each arm and dragged her deeper into the tunnel, as far back as Nelay could go before the pain forced her to stop.

In the all-consuming darkness, Nelay crouched for a moment, letting the agony ease from her body as she listened to the heavy silence. She reached for her swords, but she couldn't lift her left arm over her head. "Havva, give me my swords," she gasped out. The old woman searched in the darkness and pushed the weapons into Nelay's hands. With the familiar weight of her blades in her hands, she felt a familiar calm seeping into her. "Don't come out for anything," she said quietly.

Nelay slid forward, Havva's voice following her. "Let's feed him again. It will keep him quiet."

At the branch where the tunnel met the cavern, Nelay peered at the ashy, early morning glow from the entrance. As she watched, the brush shifted. She jerked back, her heart thumping. Firelight touched the sides of the cave with tongues of gold. Her back against the tunnel wall, she took a deep breath and concentrated on centering herself.

She might die. It was fairly likely at this point. She accepted that, and her fear settled and her pain receded like a viper slinking back into its pit. She took the players and objects she had and began arranging them.

Obviously, their best chance was if these men simply moved on. In the probable event that they didn't, she would use her only advantage—surprise, which meant her knives. With only five, she would have to be judicious in their use. Then she would defend the entrance to the tunnel for as long as she could.

Easing her swords down tip first, the handles resting against the cave wall, she slipped her knives into her hands and twisted a little to loosen her back. She peered out to watch about ten Clansmen enter the mine with their torches held before them and their voices thick with their tumbling language.

"Keep your shields up," ordered a man with a pockmarked face.

Ducking out of sight, Nelay tightened her grip on her knives and listened as they carefully placed their steps and examined the cavern. Soon they noticed the tunnel she hid inside. Their steps shortened as they came closer, the torchlight growing brighter.

She darted into the opening and launched her first knife at the nearest man's middle. When he looked up, she realized he was more boy than man. The knife struck true. A gut shot. He stumbled back, as good as dead. The man to the boy's right shifted to catch him before he fell. Enough to expose his left side.

Nelay let her second knife fly. It sank hilt-deep and he shouted something unintelligible. When the man next to him straightened, her other knife found a home in his thigh. Hunched over, the three wounded men staggered out of range of her knives. "I told you to keep your shield up!" the pockmarked man barked. Two knives left.

Nelay took out her sling, loaded it with a rock from her pouch, and aimed for the men's legs, which weren't protected by their shields. Her first stone struck a man's leg, her second his other leg. "We need bigger shields!" he cried.

"Codin and Ven, see to them. Darvy and Marb, on me. Shield wall," the pockmarked man said. When the Clansmen hesitated, he growled in exasperation, "She's just a woman."

He yelped when Nelay's stone struck his leg. Cursed when she struck his other leg. He gestured to two more men—the natural bridge only allowed for three abreast. "Use your shields to push her against the wall and we'll tie her hands."

She dropped her sling, picked up both her swords, and assumed a classic defensive position.

"Careful, she looks like she knows what to do with those swords," one of the remaining four Clansmen said as they formed up. Three hefted their round shields and charged her. Nelay waited until the last possible second before dropping. She slashed both swords across their bare legs, carving deep cuts across the fronts of their shins.

Clearly well trained, the men didn't panic. Instead, they fell on her, the pockmarked man pinning her under his shield. They scrabbled for her hands, trying to jerk the swords free. But then they gave a shout and the man on top of Nelay went still. She shoved him off and clambered to her feet to find Havva launching rocks as fast as she could. Nelay whipped around, bringing out her knives. The Clansmen were dragging away their pockmarked leader, who blinked as if trying to bring his senses back.

Her first knife struck hilt first. It would leave a nasty bruise, but little else. Nelay didn't draw the remaining knife, not when her injury made her aim so poor. Instead, she pulled out her sling again and sent more rocks at them.

"Should have kept your shield up," the boy commented sarcastically. He'd been laid on the ground, her knife sticking up from his belly. The pockmarked man flashed him a rude gesture and then struggled to his feet. He shook his head again and lifted his shield.

"They're not going to come quietly," said a man with an enormous bulbous nose. "The girl is too dangerous to capture, and the old woman probably won't survive. It's kinder to kill them both."

Nelay's heart beat painfully in her chest and part of her wished she could go quietly, but it just wasn't in her.

The pockmarked man gestured to two more men, who joined his side.

"If you don't fight, they might let you live," Nelay said to Havva without looking back.

"I'd rather be dead," the old woman replied flatly.

Nelay braced herself, knowing she probably wouldn't survive a second charge. They rushed her, axes raised. Unable to raise her left arm, her solitary option was to drop down again.

This time, they anticipated the move, shoving their shields into her so she fell back on the ground. She reached around to slash with her sword. The other two men snatched her arms, pinning them beneath their knees while raising their shields to protect themselves from Havva's flying rocks.

Nelay couldn't breathe with their weight on top of her. The leader knelt on her chest and lifted his axe. She glared at him, wanting her face to haunt his nightmares.

A shout made him turn. At the mine entrance, men stood silhouetted in the morning light. And these men carried swords. Hope flashed through Nelay, for the Clansmen didn't wield swords.

The pockmarked man turned toward her as if to finish her off. But his distraction had already been his undoing; he just didn't know it yet. For a brief moment, one of the Clansman flanking him had dropped his shields, long enough for Havva's rocks to find their mark.

Stunned, the leader shook his head. Nelay wrenched her body to the side, managing to free one arm, snatch her last knife, and swing it, smashing into the man's neck. He collapsed in a heap. She pulled the blade free, twisted, and stabbed at the man holding her other arm. It bit into his back and he arched up and screamed.

Nelay sensed more than saw an axe swinging toward her. She tucked the knife to her chest and rolled. The axe bit into the rocks below her with a loud crack. Using the momentum from her roll, she shot to her feet, the knife slippery in her bloody hand.

The stunned Clansman had come around. He squared himself behind his shield and leveled his axe at her. She couldn't defend herself—not with just a knife. She had no choice but to drop, scramble back, and roll to the side to grab a fallen shield. Just in time, for his next swing nearly knocked it from her hands. She struggled to her feet and danced back, nearly tripping over something. An axe! She snatched it, then righted herself and swung again. The axe glanced off his shield. He hit her shield, sending a painful shock that made her arm go numb.

Burn it, he was strong. She tried to go on the offensive, but his swings came too fast and hard. A rock glanced off his shield. When their shields locked, the Clansman shoved so hard Nelay stumbled back and fell to one knee. Instinctively, she brought up her shield and caught his downward stroke.

She started to stand, even as she knew she wouldn't recover from another swing. But that swing didn't come. She peeked over her shield and saw her enemy's shocked face. He fell to his knees and then tipped forward.

Behind the Clansmen stood a man dressed in desert robes. Wincing, Nelay let her shield fall to her side. "Smuggler?"

He hurried toward her and gathered her in his arms. She winced in pain and he pulled back and glanced at the blood on his palm. He spun her around. "You're bleeding again."

As soon as he said it, she felt the pain, deep and sharp. "You all made it?" she asked in disbelief.

"What kind of smuggler would I be if I couldn't sneak a half dozen men out of an occupied town?" Rycus' heart didn't seem to be in the joke though.

"How?"

"We followed the same owl—Nelay, you know better than to bargain with such creatures."

"I didn't, but someone did."

His gaze moved past her. "How many more are in that tunnel?"

Scand took one look at her wound and set down his bag.

"Two," she said without thinking.

"Three now," Havva reminded her. "The girl's just given birth. I need someone to carry her."

Rycus nodded for Delir and Cinab to go. Scand pulled out wide sheets of linen and wrapped them tightly around Nelay's middle. "It's a miracle you haven't bled to death."

She rolled her eyes. "How many times do I need to say it, Scand?" He grumbled a response she ignored. "How are we going to get out of here?" She directed the question to Rycus.

"Luckily for us, these Clansmen left their horses nearby," he replied.

Nelay let out a breath of relief. She turned at a sound and saw Delir carrying Maran, and Cinab carrying the baby. Scand had finished with Nelay's bandage.

Bahar, his expression grim, brought her knives. He'd tried to wipe them off, but there was still blood where hilt met blade. She winced before taking them and shoving them into their sheaths.

"Get her to the horses," Rycus said.

Havva turned to him, her eyes flashing with anger. "She'll bleed to death. I know some herbs to restrict the flow. She'll be ready to go by tonight."

"That might be better anyway," Ashar commented. "These mountains are crawling with Clansmen patrols."

Rycus gave a curt nod. "All right." He motioned for Nelay to sit down. "Both of you get some rest."

She couldn't help but glance at the bodies. The boy was dead, crumpled in a heap, which suggested he'd died fighting. He was too young to be in a war. Then there was the pock-marked leader and the man with the bulbous nose—she'd killed them herself.

A flash of regret tore through her. They had seemed so human, teasing and working together. They'd even tried to spare her life. Yet they had attacked a village, killing who knows how many. They were monsters. And they were not. She didn't know how to reconcile the two in her head.

"I'm not staying here," she said, her voice trembling.

Rycus glanced at her in surprise. "Nelay, we can move the bodies—"

Her panic sprang up. "I'm not staying here!"

Still in Delir's arms, Maran shook her head. "Me either."

"Where the Clansmen hid their horses—it's secluded," Bahar said quietly. "Let Ashar and me go ahead and take care of it."

Rycus sagged. "All right."

Nelay left that horrible mine and stepped into the blood-red dawn. She glanced back and saw Maran holding her hand out to shield her eyes. Even in the weak light, she looked ashen.

They moved down the road and found the agitated horses tethered inside a crevasse. Bahar and Ashar were hauling dead men out of sight behind a rise.

Nelay cringed. She didn't want to be here either, but at least it was better than the cave where she'd killed so many men.

Delir set Maran down, and Cinab handed her the baby. Rycus looked the animals over with a critical eye. "Go through all the saddlebags. Take anything useful. Ashar, keep watch."

Nelay and Maran settled down while the men sorted through the saddlebags. Havva went in search of a plant.

Nelay didn't think there was any way she could ever sleep, but she did. Hard and dreamless. She woke when Delir offered them food from the Clansmen's packs. Then she fell asleep again. She spent most of the day like that, getting sleep and nourishment—both things her body desperately needed. When dusk settled over the land, Rycus crouched in front of her. "Nelay, I'm sorry, but we can't afford to rest anymore. We have to go"

"I'll be all right," Maran insisted.

Nelay wasn't convinced. She leaned toward Havva and said under her breath, "You said Maran couldn't travel last night. How is tonight any different?"

Havva shot a worried glance Maran's way. "Last night she was bleeding, more so when we moved her. As long as she doesn't start up again, she should be all right."

Nelay still wasn't convinced. She sought out Scand. "Are you sure she can travel?"

He looked affronted and horrified at the same time. "What do I know of birthing and women?"

The men had already loaded their spoils into the saddlebags of the animals they had chosen. Cinab and Delir hurried over to help Maran into the saddle, while Havva took the baby.

When Maran was situated, Havva handed the baby carefully to Delir. "You have to support his head."

He held the infant away from him as if it might bite. "What . . ."

Havva wagged her finger at him. "Maran needs her strength. Nelay is hurt. And—"

"You're old," Delir finished for her.

Her eyes narrowed dangerously. "I'm tired. You will hold the baby until he needs to be fed."

Delir opened his mouth to argue. At the look on Havva's face, he seemed to think better of it. He stuffed the swaddled baby down his shirt and wrapped his sash around the bulge three times. Then he held still while Havva inspected the arrangement.

Satisfied, she motioned for him to mount his horse. "Be careful with him," she admonished. "He's fragile."

Rycus helped Nelay onto a horse. Without the need for communication, Ashar took one of the finest horses and started off immediately. Each leading two pack horses, Bahar and Cinab positioned themselves at the rear. Rycus took the front, with the women directly behind him and Scand behind them. They climbed the road. At a break in the brush, Nelay had a view of a ranch farther north. A couple of buildings were burning. Even from this distance, she could see bodies around the yard. Farm animals wandered, their pens empty.

"How did you all really escape?" she asked Scand.

The old man studied her with his one good eye. "Sedun's desire to keep his wine saved all our lives. Probably saved most of the village as well."

Nelay leaned forward in the saddle. "I don't understand."

Scand let out a breath. "Most of the Clansmen were more interested in those jugs of wine than chasing after the villagers. It's the reason Rycus let you all rest. Today, they'll be hungover. Tomorrow . . ." His words trailed off.

Nelay glanced back at Maran, wondering how she would react to the mention of her husband. The girl's gaze was fixed on the ground and she would not look up.

All throughout the night, Nelay listened for pursuers. Her neck grew stiff from constantly looking behind them. They rode all through the next day. That evening, Rycus called for a halt. They hadn't found any sources of moving water, but Bahar had located a wet patch of sand. Bahar and Delir went to digging it out while the other men started setting up camp.

Nelay's back was so stiff she was unable to dismount. Rycus held his hands out for her and she practically fell into him. He helped her to the flat face of a tabletop mountain, where Maran collapsed beside her. She had started bleeding more heavily a couple hours before, soaking through every spare scrap of fabric they could find.

Havva had wanted them to stop and rest, but Maran had insisted she could go on. Now, the young woman was pale and listless. Havva went in search of more herbs while Nelay and Maran huddled together for warmth from the tavo.

After he'd started a small fire, Cinab brought Maran her son. The infant didn't even stir from being passed from one set of arms to another.

"You best try feeding him now, or he'll be up all night," Havva said tiredly as she started preparing a tea from the herbs she'd found.

Nelay studied the baby's round little face, the squinting eyes and the fluff of hair on his head. She couldn't resist reaching out and brushing three fingers across the softness of it. "What is his name?"

"It would have been Sedun after his father. But now I will call him Concon, after my father," Maran said.

Havva helped her unwrap her baby to wake him up. He started squalling as the cold night air touched his skin. Maran bared her breast, obviously too exhausted to care about covering herself. She had difficulty getting the child to suck, and her arms were so weak she could barely hold him. Bahar brought them stolen Clansmen blankets. Havva and Maran tucked one under him to help hold him. When he was finally sucking, Maran eyes grimaced in pain.

She grabbed Nelay's hand and held it tight. "What am I going to do?"

She didn't seem to expect an answer, but Nelay gave one anyway. "You'll stay with us." Going back to her coward of a husband was obviously out of the question, even if they could manage to find him.

When the child finally finished eating, the three of them wrapped up in the blankets, which were surprisingly warm and soft.

With Maran's body curved around Nelay's, suddenly all the barriers she'd built up between herself and the events of the last week came crumbling down. She saw the dead Clansmen in the mine, their empty eyes shining in the torch light. She felt her knife pop through muscle and bone to stop Dobber's black heart. She heard the plopping of the wet dirt as it fell on Kalla's body.

Nelay hugged herself. All that was left of her parents were bones and ashes. Her brother was missing. She might have failed to protect Kalla, but she swore then she would not fail these women, nor the men. She would see them all to safety, or she would die trying.

CHAPTER EIGHTEEN

The next day they reached the main road, which was clogged with terrified Idarans fleeing the approaching army. Rycus gathered their group in tight, with the women in the center and his men on the outside.

Nelay would have resented being herded around like a sheep, but her body had been pushed past its breaking point for days, and each step the horse took brought fresh pain. Even though Nelay healed more quickly than most people, it still took time and rest. She would be no good to her brother in the shape she was in, so she determined to let Rycus take care of her.

As he did, she noticed how good he was at this sort of life. He talked of his family—of brothers and sisters and cousins—with the other men. Once she overheard him talking with Cinab about missing home. She began to realize she or Rycus would have to leave everything to be with the other. And she didn't think either of them was the leaving type.

Over the next few days, Rycus discreetly handed out their extra provisions to other travelers who needed them most. A few times, men approached their group in the night, obviously intent on thievery. But whoever was on watch always caught them, and Rycus and his men responded with such a show of force and skill that the would-be robbers gave up almost before they'd begun.

Everyone took turns holding Concon as they pressed forward. On their fifth night, a ripple of fear came up from behind them. An advance guard of Clansmen was marching forward, taking Idarans to serve as tiams, and killing anyone who fought back.

Rycus studied Maran, who was still bleeding, though not as heavily. And Nelay, who did her best to hide her exhaustion, couldn't disguise her bloodshot eyes. It seemed he could barely unclench his jaw to ask, "Are you two going to make it?"

Nelay gave a sharp nod.

"I will," Maran managed.

Nightfall came, and with it the cold tavo wind from the mountains, but Rycus pressed forward. Concon cried frequently; it was hard for Maran to feed him while she rode. They pressed forward in the dark. The men watered the horses at every well and river they passed, letting them grab a few mouthfuls of scrubby grass where it grew in the shade.

Sometime in the night, Nelay made out a smudge of golden light. It grew in size by the hour until, in the darkest hour before dawn, she recognized the city of Dalarta, so far away she could cover it with her hand. It was the third largest city in Idara, its golden dome towers and white walls rising out of the most fertile fields in the Hansi Province. Two wide rivers flowed from the nearby mountains, and the Dalartans were experts at irrigation.

As the group drew closer they passed fields of grain, and orchards full of every kind of fruit and nut. People worked frantically in the fields, trying to bring in unripe crops before the Clansmen arrived and destroyed the country's food supply. A few army patrols could be seen, offering assistance where they could.

Nelay's gaze shifted back to the city. All the surviving residents of the Hansi and Shutar Provinces were fleeing here. If Nelay's brother still lived, she would find him somewhere inside the gleaming walls of this city.

By midmorning, she was so tired she could barely sit in the saddle. Maran didn't seem to be doing much better. The exhausted horses didn't even twitch their tails at the flies anymore.

Nelay was shaken out of her stupor when Maran said, "Look." She pointed behind them, her face ashen.

Twisting around, Nelay stood in the stirrups and covered her eyes to shade them from the sun. Far in the distance, she could make out tall towers rising toward the horizon. But they were moving.

"Siege engines," Rycus said grimly.

"How far, do you think?" Delir asked.

"Half a day's ride." Ashar responded.

The men were unusually quiet, their faces void of their easy smiles.

Rycus pulled his horse to a stop, and the others followed suit. "Where are the rest of king's armies? They could meet the Clansmen on open ground. Give the populace time to flee from the city so they're not trapped if it falls."

Scand growled his agreement, but no one had an answer.

Rycus leaned closer to Nelay to say, "We should press on to Thanjavar. It will be safer."

"If my brother is alive, he is here. I have to try." She glanced at Havva. "Besides, I promised Havva I would help her find her family."

"I can't risk my men in this war," Rycus said grimly.

"Some of us are going to have to go back to the cistern and round up those people," Scand added. "They'll be out of food soon."

Nelay considered telling Rycus to leave her. But her mind automatically tallied all the players on the field. Without him, her chances of success were dismal. And if she was being honest with herself, she couldn't bear for him to go, not yet. "As soon as we find Panar, we can leave the city," she said.

Rycus set his jaw. "Ashar, Bahar, ride ahead and let the people at the cistern know we haven't forgotten them. Cinab and Delir, slaughter some of the scattered flocks closer to the border for food."

Nelay's heart rate kicked up and her palms began to sweat. He was leaving her. She should be relieved to say goodbye, since he didn't fit in with any of her plans for her life. But she wasn't relieved. She was heartbroken.

"Offer sanctuary with the tribes to any who want it," Rycus went on. "The rest, lead to Thanjavar and collect your payment from Jezzel."

Ashar twisted in the saddle and looked toward the desert, then turned back to Rycus. "You're not coming with us?"

Rycus pursed his lips and shook his head. His five men grew very still.

Wait . . . he was staying? Nelay exhaled quietly.

"Rycus, you need to come with us before she gets you killed." Scand's voice practically vibrated with anger.

Nelay wanted to take Scand off his horse and shove sand in his mouth, but she kept still, knowing this needed to happen.

Leaning forward in his saddle, Rycus said, "You think I should just leave her to face this alone?"

Scand nodded toward the Idaran soldiers in the distance. "All she has to do is tell them who she is and she'll be escorted back to that temple in her own personal caravan."

"I'll go back when I'm ready," she ground out.

Scand made a cutting motion. "Your brother isn't a quarter of the man Rycus is. He's not worth dying over."

"Maybe not. But I have to try—he's my brother," Nelay said, her voice hard. "He's all I have left."

"You can't force me," Rycus growled to Scand. "I'm going."

Scand sat back in his saddle, seething silently. The other men exchanged looks before each of them rode even with Rycus and embraced him in turn. Delir rode close to Maran, and they stopped so he could hand her the baby. "I'm going to miss the little one." He gave a sheepish smile before loping away.

Bahar paused beside Nelay. "It didn't break you."

She was tempted to ask whom he had lost, but she realized it didn't matter. He'd loved the person. That's what mattered. "Not yet."

He nodded goodbye. They headed out in their familiar formation, Ashar taking the lead, with Bahar, Delir, and Cinab behind him. Scand made no move to follow them.

"Scand," Rycus said in a warning voice.

He settled deeper in the saddle. "I've guarded you since you were a boy. I'm not leaving you now."

"You have Sash and her children to look after," Rycus said gently. "If you die they have no one."

Scand dropped his head, but not before Nelay saw the tears filling his eyes. "Rycus . . ." he began.

"I'm not asking, Scand."

The old man scrubbed his face with his hands and rode even with Nelay, his gaze searching. "The thing about men with power—they're not used to being defied. And they're not very forgiving. Let him go."

Nelay stiffened, knowing he meant King Zatal and wondering how much Scand knew and how long he'd known it. But as she looked into his eyes, she saw genuine fear. And she realized he was right—Rycus wouldn't survive long when the king found out about him, whether she was high priestess or not.

She gave an almost imperceptible nod.

Scand's head came up and he rode past Rycus. "Remember what I said." The old man turned back one last time. "Nelay, change your bandages as least once a day. And you need a few days of rest. Maran too." He sniffled loudly. "Take care of yourself, Priestess."

Nelay gave him a small smile. "You really are like a cactus."

He grunted, jerked the horse around, and rode after the others. Rycus watched them go before whirling his horse around and nudging him into a trot. Nelay kicked her horse into a lope to catch up.

Riding beside him, she wanted to thank him for not leaving her. She wanted to tell him to go—that this wasn't his battle. That they weren't meant to be. But she didn't know how, so she asked, "Who's Sash?"

Rycus wiped his nose on his sleeve. "His brother's wife. Now his. If he'd ever scrounge up the courage to take her."

Burn it, trotting hurts my back. Nelay gritted her teeth. "What does that mean?"

"It's a Tribesman custom that when a woman's husband dies, her marriage contract shifts to one of her brothers-in-law or close kin. That way the women and children are always taken care of."

Nelay thought it a strange custom, but then she remembered her family's fear when her father had almost died during her childhood. Without him to provide for them, they could have easily starved. "What if the brother is already married?"

Rycus shrugged. "Doesn't change his responsibility."

"So the men have more than one wife?"

"Sometimes. And sometimes the men just provide for them, which is what Scand has been doing."

Glad she wasn't a Tribeswoman, Nelay looked back to see Scand and the others, who were now so far away she couldn't tell them apart. Without these men, she felt exposed. She had come to trust them, for they were gentle and witty, and very handy with their swords.

When she and her small party finally approached the city gates, her apprehension continued to build. They were firmly back in Zatal's territory. If the fairies had saved her life to turn her over, this was where they would do it.

The guards took one look at Rycus, still wearing his battered desert-tribe robes, and blocked his entrance. "What need has a Tribesman of the safety of Dalarta's walls? We're already crowded beyond capacity. Head east, into your own lands."

Rycus motioned to the women. "I bring three Idaran women."

"They may pass. You may not," the guard said.

"I have sworn to see them to safety."

"They are safe."

"But—" Rycus began.

The guard folded his arms. "You're not getting inside."

Rycus hesitated before leaning down. "One of them is a priestess."

The man's gaze swung to Nelay. She shot Rycus a glare—if the fairies didn't give her away, the smuggler would. She unclipped her veil and tipped her head to the side to reveal the tattoos on her face. "He is my personal guard."

The man's eyes widened, and he bowed.

"The other priestesses—" she began.

"They have already fled to Thanjavar, Priestess, as should you."

Hopefully, that meant the fairies would have no one to communicate with in Dalarta. "The Immortals, are they within the city?"

"As of yet, they are still with the king in Thanjavar."

Relief flooded through Nelay. If they hurried, she could be out of the city before the king or Suka could reach her. "Let us pass," she said with authority.

The guard moved out of the way, his eyes averted.

Nelay kicked her horse until she caught up with Rycus. "My identity is supposed to be a secret."

"Do you want to get inside or not?" he shot back.

They crossed under the thick stone wall, which gleamed from regular whitewashing. The view of the wealthy city slowly opened up. An enormous fountain pumped clear water from the underground cistern. This was strictly a drinking fountain, as evidenced by the carved stone tree at the center. Bathing fountains had statues of either men or women in the center.

Behind the fountain, the whitewashed buildings bore terracotta-tile roofs and wide porches to protect their inhabitants from the relentless sun. But this close to the main gates, there were mostly inns, with markets stalls in the wide spaces between buildings.

The king's soldiers were everywhere. A team of horses strained against their harnesses as they maneuvered a ballista into position at the wall. Thousands of arrows were being hauled up to the battlements.

Just past the gate, crowds of people waited to be admitted into the city streets by several men and women on hastily built platforms. Nelay was glad for the horses, which kept people from pressing too close. She cast a glance at Rycus, who looked positively ill. "Are you all right?"

"This is why I hate Idara. Too many people in too small a place. But I'll live."

Holding her baby tight, Maran leaned toward Nelay. "Who are they?" She gestured to the people on the platforms.

Nelay pointed. "See their long tunics? They're university students." Children of the upper class who could afford to pay for specialized training in government service, medicine, arithmetic, engineering, geography, music, and astronomy. "The city lord must have conscripted them to keep track of people."

Maran's eyes widened. "I didn't even know universities were available."

"They're not for poor people like us," Havva said.

The new mother straightened. "I'm not poor."

Havva shot her a look. "Compared to Nelay we are."

Nelay snorted. After she was done paying for this little adventure, she'd be the poorest one here.

Finally, it was their turn to stand before one of the platforms. A student, his tunic suggesting he studied astronomy, looked over the small group without actually seeming to see them. "What province and city?"

"Sopora of the Hansi province," Havva said eagerly.

He asked for their names. Only Maran and Havva gave him real ones. He finished writing them down. "All Soporans are asked to stay in the library courtyard. There is a fountain, but mind you don't contaminate it. Latrines have been dug. Use them. And you are required to relinquish your horses."

Nelay straightened. "But—"

"Absolutely not," Rycus said over her.

The student blew three short blasts on a whistle hanging from his neck. From Nelay's higher vantage point, she could see soldiers working their way toward them.

The young man pressed his pen to the scroll, his face one of long-suffering, as if he'd had this argument a thousand times before. "There is no fodder available inside the city. And our men need the horses. I've already made a notation beside each of your names indicating that you've given up a horse. When the war ends, you will be recompensed."

"This war will never end," Havva said.

The man shot her a look. "This is the price for entering Dalarta. If you refuse to pay it, you will be turned away."

Rycus leaned close enough only Nelay could hear. "You want a means of escape, we need these horses."

"Then you'll just have to steal them back," she whispered.

Three soldiers had gathered around them, waiting for the horses. Rycus shot Nelay a pleading look, which she met with a stubborn one. Grumbling, he dismounted. He removed his saddlebags and threw them over his shoulder. The rest of their party followed suit. Nelay figured they had enough food for a couple more days if they were careful.

"Come on, Havva," she said. "We'll help you find your family and get settled before we move on." She had every intention of taking Maran with them when they left.

The press of people forced them toward the western side. The farther into the city they went, the worse the smell became—human waste and human sweat. Obviously the city was filled past its capacity.

Breathing through her veil, Nelay searched the face of every person she saw. She had to find her brother. But something was wrong. She turned to Rycus, who said angrily, "The boys are in uniform. Everyone over the age of twelve." He glanced about suspiciously. "I'm surprised I haven't been conscripted yet."

A new sort of fear started in Nelay. What if Rycus was taken from her? How would she escape the city without him? She was shaken out of her dark thoughts when they approached a tall building and domes gleaming golden against the blue sky. The courtyard was jammed with refugees in a makeshift city of tents.

"How are we ever going to find anyone?" Nelay wondered aloud.

Maran suddenly darted forward and rested a hand on a woman's arm. "Ivet?"

Recognition dawned in the woman's eyes. "Maran? But you were killed!" Her gaze rested on the girl's flattened belly, and then at the baby in her arms. A shadow seemed to pass over Ivet's face.

"Why would you think that?" Maran said haltingly.

Ivet seemed at a loss for words. "Well . . . because that's what I was told."

By Sedun, no doubt, Nelay thought.

"Have you seen my family?" Havva asked quickly.

"I've seen them, but I'm not sure where they're staying," the woman responded.

Havva sagged in relief.

"What about a man?" Nelay interjected. "He looks like me." Or at least he had. "His name is Panar Favar Denar ShaBejan."

The woman shook her head. "Never heard of him."

"I told you, if he'd have lived in our village, I would have known," Maran said softly.

Nelay's head and back hurt, plus the overpowering smell of the city made her nauseous. "How can I find him?"

"All the names of the refugees are taken to the university. You could try there," Ivet said.

Maran wet her lips. "Ivet, have you seen my husband?"

The woman smiled. "Everyone's seen Sedun—he's a hero for saving all those children." Her face fell. "But he was conscripted with the rest. The men of our province have taken over the West Wall Inn—that's their barracks. I'm going to go visit my husband and sons tomorrow, when I have the time."

A child pulled on Ivet's skirt. She batted her hands away and looked at Havva. "If you come with me, we can ask around for your family."

Grinning, Havva started after her. Nelay felt conflicted. She'd grown attached to the woman and appreciated her wisdom and toughness.

Havva paused and looked back at them in confusion. "Aren't you coming?"

"I have my own brother to find," Nelay explained.

"Well, you'll need somewhere to stay while you look, won't you?"

"I should seek out Sedun," Maran finally said.

Nelay's head snapped up. "Why would you want to see him?"

Ivet glanced back and forth between them. "Women aren't allowed to stay at the barracks."

Nelay cast a questioning gaze at Rycus, who said, "It's clear we won't find Panar today."

Havva threw up her hands. "Ashes and burning, we're all exhausted and you two are injured. Eat, sleep, and for the Goddess's sake, bathe. Then you can go traipsing around after these foolhardy men of yours."

Without waiting for an argument, she took hold of Nelay's and Maran's arms and marched after Ivet. Nelay wanted to argue, but she was stumbling over her own feet. And she couldn't find it in herself to turn down a bath.

Havva robustly greeted many of the people. Maran seemed reserved, even more so after several of the villagers stared after her in shock.

Not far from the fountain, Havva gave a cry and ran forward, calling a woman's name. That woman dropped a basket and looked around wildly. As soon as she saw Havva, she cried out and ran to her. Her cry brought a dozen other people. Then a dozen more. Soon, it seemed half the refugees were hugging Havva.

Nelay watched in amazement. She'd never seen such wanton displays of affection. Maran hung back with her, patting the baby's back. No one came running forward to greet her, and she didn't seem to be looking for anyone. "Don't you have any family besides your husband?" Nelay finally asked.

"All dead," Maran said curtly, clearly unwilling to discuss it. That was fine with Nelay—she didn't want to talk about her family either.

Eventually, Havva seemed to remember them. She extrapolated herself from someone's arms and ordered a bath and food for everyone. Nelay almost pointed out that there would be bathing fountains in the city, but she was too exhausted to search them out. They were probably crowded anyway.

Nelay looked back as a young man led Rycus away. She gave a little wave, and Rycus mouthed, "I'll see you later."

One of Havva's granddaughters, who was only a little younger than Nelay and Maran, led the women to a tiny square of space between four tent walls, blankets strung in the gaps. There were already buckets of water. Havva's oldest daughter took Maran's baby and stripped off his soiled garments and started scrubbing them, while another daughter did the same to him. Concon wailed in indignation. Nelay wanted to run and hide from the sound, but the other women didn't seem bothered in the least. Maran tried a few times to get her infant back, but they only shooed her away.

The air was already unbearably hot, so it felt delicious when Nelay stripped out of the robes Rycus had purchased for her and ladled water onto her head. She scrubbed herself with soap and let Maran clean her wound. Maran's body was hard and lean, but for the soft sag and purple lines of her belly. Her breasts were heavy with milk, which dripped from her nipples, faster the more Concon screamed.

Havva nodded sagely. "Good. You will have plenty to feed him." The old woman's skin looked as if it had been cut two sizes too big and left to dry in a crumpled heap before being draped back over her knobby joints.

Nelay couldn't help but compare her body to the bodies of these women. Aside from the scars of weapons practice and the recent battles, Nelay's body was still in its prime. Still strong and beautiful, with large breasts and curving hips. But these women—their bodies had seen and done so much, and caring and nourishing life had left their marks. Nelay remembered what Havva had said, that women's battles were fought and won by bringing about life, not death. And they bore the scars of those battles.

When Nelay was done, Havva inspected her wound and exclaimed in surprise that it was practically healed. Nelay didn't comment.

They retreated from the ovat into one of the tents. They ate, the food simple and scant but hot. Nelay lay down on the soft wool skins, noting that Maran was feeding her baby again. She only had time to think how glad she was not to have an infant to care for, before she fell asleep.

CHAPTER
NINETEEN

Nelay woke much later than planned. But for one of the first times since she'd been shot, the pain had been mild enough for her to sleep deeply. Maran was still passed out, the baby in her arms. Most of the other women were gone.

Nelay stepped into the too-bright morning. Havva crouched beside the fire, stirring something in a big black kettle. The older woman slept very little and ate even less. Everyone else seemed gone. Nelay stepped in front of the tent Rycus had shared with about a dozen other single men and called out for him.

"He left in the gray hours," Havva said.

Nelay strode toward her, eager to start her search for Panar. "Did he say where he was going?"

Havva dished up a small bowl of cooked grains and held it out to Nelay. "To look for your brother."

"Why didn't he wake me?"

"You need rest if you're ever going to heal."

Nelay grudgingly took the bowl and watched the steam rise from it. They were safe. Her pain had started to fade. She would find her brother, then make her bid for high priestess. So why was she so miserable?

"Maran was up with the baby most of the night," Havva said conversationally, but Nelay couldn't help but think the old woman saw more than she wanted to reveal.

"I don't know much about babies, but this one seems to cry a lot." Nelay slurped some of the thin gruel, which almost tasted good. She must be hungrier than she'd thought.

"Some cry more than others. Didn't seem to bother you last night."

Nelay swallowed some water to wash down the hulls sticking to her throat. "I learned to sleep through the temple noise, so not much bothers me." She gestured around the immediate vicinity. "Where is everyone else?"

Havva hesitated before answering. "The first of the Clansmen's army arrived sometime in the night. The women and children all went to see their men before the battle starts."

Nelay's hopes sagged under the weight of the coming assault. For the briefest moment, she considered asking the fairies for help finding Panar, but she quickly pushed the thought aside. Deals with them always cost more than they were worth.

"Nelay," Havva said.

When she looked up, the older woman gestured behind her. Nelay shifted to see Rycus coming toward her, and she felt the familiar tug in her lower belly. How had she ever found him anything but handsome?

Before she could ask any questions, he held up a hand. "Where's Maran?"

"Have you found her husband?" Nelay slurped the last bit of gruel from the bowl.

Rycus nodded, his jaw tight.

"And Panar?" she said hopefully.

"I've bribed some officials. We ought to hear something by midday."

Nelay tried to push down her irritation. The longer they were in Dalarta, the harder it would be to escape.

"Let Maran sleep," Havva said softly.

Nelay crossed her arms over her chest. "Are we sure she should even see him? He left her for dead." And Nelay wasn't sure she could see Sedun without killing him.

Unfortunately, Maran chose that moment to leave the tent, her baby over one shoulder. She looked from Nelay to Rycus. "That's my decision, not yours."

Nelay worked to keep her voice calm. "You'll come with us when we leave the city."

Maran met her gaze with the most determination Nelay had ever seen. "If the battle truly is to begin soon, I need to see him." She let out a long breath and faced Rycus, hitching her baby up higher on her shoulder. "Lead on."

Havva stepped toward her with arms extended. "Leave him here, Maran. You don't know how this will go."

"But he might get hungry before . . ."

Havva pried the baby loose. "One of my girls with a baby can feed him. After you find your husband, come stay with me and my family."

Maran nodded, tears shining in her eyes. "I will. Thank you."

Havva met Nelay's gaze. "You're always welcome, Nelay. After all, you saved my life."

"Thank you, but I still have my brother to find." Her lips pulled in a tight line at the thought of finding a single person in this overflowing city.

They took water from a fountain they passed as they moved through the crowded streets. Weaving through the crowd made the going incredibly slow. Nelay knew Rycus felt uncomfortable with the press of bodies, but he kept it mostly hidden.

Frustrated with the delay and still reeling with disbelief at Maran's decision, Nelay asked, "Why would you go back to him?"

The girl wouldn't look at her. "My mother died when I was twelve. My father killed himself last year, after his mine failed. The debt collectors took everything we had. I had no other family. I was starving. Sedun was charming. He was my prince, and I his princess."

Maran dodged out of the way of a cart pulled by a water buffalo. "But after we were married, I couldn't seem to do anything right—I was too slow, too fast, too foolish."

The words Nelay wanted to say practically smoked in her throat. "He left you and your baby to die."

"You don't understand!" Maran sped up.

Nelay trotted to catch her. "You're right. I don't understand."

"I'm still in love with him!" Maran shouted. Then she seemed to notice people staring at them and hurried on. "Or at least with the man he used to be," she said more softly. "Maybe he can be that man again."

Nelay opened her mouth to argue, but Rycus squeezed her arm. "It's her choice," he whispered.

Huffing, Nelay hurried after Maran. It took every ounce of restraint Nelay had to keep her mouth shut.

It wasn't hard to spot the inn. Hundreds of weapons leaned against the wall, and the small courtyard was marked off like a training ground.

"Maran!" a man coming out exclaimed in disbelief. "You're alive." She barely spared him a glance as she stepped up to the dark inn with its tiny, deep-set windows. She paused just inside the entrance, her hands gripped in fists.

Nelay stepped up beside her. The smell of unwashed bodies, smoke, and sour food hit her hard. She blinked, waiting for her eyes to adjust to the dimness.

Maran cast a frantic glance about before whispering to Nelay, "Do I look all right?"

Maran looked terrible. She smelled of sour milk, her hair was dull and matted, her clothes faded of all color. But Nelay couldn't say any of that. "You are beautiful." That at least wasn't a lie—you just had to look beneath the exhaustion to see it.

They stepped farther into the room packed full of tables that were packed full of men. Most were gambling or playing a game with sticks and stones.

Maran seemed to shrink in on herself. She started to slip behind Rycus, her head down and her hair hanging like a curtain over her face. Nelay suddenly hated Sedun even more. And before she knew what she was doing, she'd grasped Maran's hand and pulled her up to stand beside her. The other girl gripped back tightly but didn't look up.

They started weaving around the tables, looking for Sedun.

"Hey boys, two lovelies have come for a visit," Nelay heard a voice call out. Another man said something crude. Nelay shot the speaker a glare that melted the grin off his face.

From behind them, Rycus spoke low. "You don't have to do this, Maran."

"Yes, I do," she whispered back.

Someone laughed, long and loud, and Maran's head came up. Nelay followed her gaze to see a man's profile. That thick build could only be Sedun. He had a woman on his lap, her arm draped possessively around his shoulders. She giggled at something he said, leaning forward so her bosoms showed.

Nelay reached for her sword, but Rycus gripped her wrist and said simply, "Don't."

Sedun laughed again, and someone slapped him on the back. The back slapper turned toward them and his laugh melted away. "Maran," the man gasped.

At that, Sedun spun around in his chair. His gaze locked on Maran and something like horror crossed his face.

The back slapper hooted. "Sedun's good deeds have been rewarded by the Goddess. His wife has survived!"

Men shouted and cheered. The back slapper-shoved Sedun out of his chair, nearly knocking the woman out of his lap. Sedun smiled at his wife, but even Nelay could see the warning behind it. He crossed the room and gripped Maran to him. Only Nelay was in a position to see her wince as he squeezed too tight.

The men kept cheering, calling out Sedun's name like he was some kind of hero, while the woman looked on with something akin to fury in her gaze.

Nelay's anger was strong enough to choke on. Rycus caught her gaze and she saw the same simmering anger reflected in his eyes. The same helplessness.

"The baby?" Sedun said.

Maran smiled, but she didn't look at all happy. "He's fine. I left him with Havva while I searched for you."

Sedun turned to face the crowd, his fist raised in the air. "I have a son! Sedun the Younger!"

"His name is Concon!" Nelay didn't mean to shout it. It just came out.

Sedun spun around and locked his gaze onto hers, a dark promise in his eyes. "Maran, why don't you and I go somewhere private."

Nelay smiled a dare at him. "They call you a hero?"

He stiffened.

"Nelay, don't," Maran said.

"He saved ten children," one man declared.

Nelay stared at her friend. "Maran, he left us to die. And now he's letting everyone call him a hero for it."

Sedun shifted to backhand Nelay. She stepped back to dodge it and use his momentum to take him to the ground. But Rycus got there first, slamming his fist into Sedun's kidneys.

Though Nelay was perfectly capable, she let Rycus handle him. After all, what use were all those glorious muscles if he didn't exert them once in a while?

The men in the room rose to their feet, protests on their lips. But they must have recognized that Rycus was a tribesman, for no one moved against him.

Hunched over and red-faced, Sedun glared up at Nelay.

This time it was Rycus who spoke, raising his voice to address the crowd. "Maran was giving birth and couldn't ride for safety. So he left her and his son to die."

Sedun slowly straightened, his arm wrapped around his side. "There were twelve Clansmen. Fighting them would have only sealed my death. I did what I had to do to save those I could."

Maran was crying now. "And if there hadn't been any children?" she asked quietly. Her gaze strayed to the woman, who was still glaring at her. "Would you have stayed with us then?"

Sedun stepped toward Maran, who backed up. He reached for her, but Rycus moved between them.

Sedun glared at him. "Who are you, Tribesman, to interfere in the business between a husband and wife?"

"I killed the Clansmen who attacked them." Though Rycus's voice was soft, it cut across the room. "And then I got her here safely. I don't see why I should stop protecting her now."

"Men, always taking all the credit," Nelay mumbled.

Rycus rolled his eyes and tipped his head toward her. "She helped." Nelay grunted.

Sedun shifted his gaze back to his wife. "Maran, my love, come with me. We need to speak alone."

She crossed her arms. "Answer me."

"Of course I would have stayed." Maran still wouldn't look at him, but he continued. "I've heard of this before—women who become hysterical after giving birth. Why don't you come back after you've rested and feel more like your old self?" He turned his back and stepped toward his table.

Nelay gaped at him. "Are you always this good at making all your mistakes Maran's fault?"

Sedun stiffened but didn't stop moving. Rycus cut Nelay a look and glanced meaningfully at Maran, whose face was filled with so much hurt it made Nelay's middle ache.

She gently gripped Maran's arm. "Come on. Concon probably needs to be fed again."

CHAPTER TWENTY

Nelay watched as Maran took her fussy baby and cradled him against her, making shushing noises as tears streaked down her face.

"Maran, I'm sorry," Nelay said, reaching for her. "But I've considered all the players, and there's no scenario that involves Sedun and happiness."

"What gives you the right?"

Nelay stepped back as if she'd been hit. "I saved your life."

The young mother's face went a splotchy, angry red. "Sedun saved me once and spent the next two years telling me what to do. He thought that gave him the right to. So I say again, how are you any different?"

Anger rose up inside Nelay where pity had been. Maran pivoted on her heel and stalked off.

Rycus spoke gently. "She's just lashing out. Give her some time."

Nelay sat down on the dirt under an awning and took a long drink from her water skin. Rycus was an amazing man. And she was going to send him away. "You should leave me," she warned. There was nothing but heartache in store for him if he stayed.

Settling beside her, he gave a half grin. "Don't think you're getting out of your payment that easily. All this is adding up, trust me."

Burn it, she loved that smile. She sighed as she imagined all her sparkling rings, all her bracelets and coin-wrapped skirts sliding into Rycus's hairy hands. "I don't even know if Panar is here, or if he survived."

"I'll be back." Rycus stood and walked toward a man who was obviously looking for someone. The two spoke briefly and some coins changed hands. Nelay growled low in her throat. She had agreed to recompense Rycus any additional expenses he incurred, and she was certain his bribes counted.

He jogged back to her. "Panar's name wasn't on the lists of refugees. Every man in this city has been conscripted. If he's in Dalarta, he must be in the barracks somewhere."

Nelay let out all her breath. "All right. Then that's where we'll start."

Rycus accompanied her to the university headquarters, which was packed with people searching for loved ones. Nelay took one look at the line and mumbled, "This is going to take days."

Rycus wiggled his eyebrows at her. "Not if we're smart about it."

"What do you mean?"

He smiled. "We go to the inn."

"The inn?" She would have been exasperated, but his eyes were gleaming the way they did when he had some clever plan.

She followed him into a crowded inn; they were always packed just before the ovat. Inside were mostly soldiers, many of whom sent appreciative glances Nelay's way. That is until they saw Rycus's piercing glare. He elbowed his way to the bar and called the woman serving drinks. She ignored him until he flashed a silver coin. She made her way over to them, annoyance clear on her face even as she pocketed the coin. "What do you want?"

Rycus held up a second coin and tipped his head toward the door. "I want to sit at the table by the window."

She snatched it up and went to the table. A few seconds later, the two burly men sitting there arose.

Rycus took Nelay's arm and steered her through the crowd. By the time they got to the table, the woman was busily wiping away the spills. "You eating?"

He slipped her a few more coins. "Best you've got," he said with a wink.

The woman gave him a conspiratorial smile and disappeared into the crowd of customers, many of whom were calling for their drinks.

Nelay leaned forward. "How many coins did you give her?"

"It pays to be rich."

"That's my money!"

He nodded sagely. "And if you can't be rich, it pays to have friends who are."

Nelay fought to keep her expression stern. "Why didn't you just pay the men sitting here to move?"

"Because more hands means spending more money. You would know this if you actually had to barter."

She stiffened. "I barter."

"Priestesses don't have to barter. You always get the best price because of who you are. Now, a lowly Tribesmen" —he gestured to himself— "he must scheme for every coin he spends."

"My coins," Nelay mumbled.

The woman plopped down some kind of fruity wine in ceramic cups, a plate of flat bread, and curry chicken and rice. Nelay's mouth started watering in earnest. She hadn't eaten a decent meal in so long she'd almost forgotten how good real food could be. She forced herself to savor every bite instead of simply inhaling it. When she looked up, Rycus was watching her, amusement in his eyes.

"All right, Tribesman, what's your plan?" she tried to sound gruff.

He motioned her closer. His breath smelled of sweet wine. "You'll spoil the surprise, High Priestess."

She rolled her eyes and sat back to finish her meal. When they were done, Rycus passed over more coins, and the woman came back with a platter of fruit. Nelay was already stuffed to overflowing, but she bit into a pear. Juice ran down her chin. Before she knew what was happening, Rycus leaned forward, his gaze locked on hers.

Laughing, she wiped her chin with her hand. He caught her wrist, staring at the droplets on her fingers. Slowly, he sucked gently on each finger, taking great care to remove all traces of juice. Nelay froze, unable to move as jolts of pleasure shot up her arm and warmed her lower belly. She should stop him, stop this thing between them before it grew into something she couldn't control. But she couldn't seem to move.

When Rycus had cleaned off every finger, he leaned into her. "If you hold very still, I'll take care of those lips for you."

Despite her brain screaming at how unfair she was being, Nelay tipped her mouth toward his. He sucked gently on her lower lip. And Nelay forgot about the press of bodies, the packed room, and the worry over her brother. Forgot about Maran and her traitor husband. Forgot about war and pain and loss. There was only this. Her lips on Rycus's mouth, the gentle press of his teeth, nipping her just enough to send another jolt that lit her up all the way to her toes.

He pulled back suddenly, and she blinked her eyes open. She was aching with want and need, and he wasn't even looking at her! "Take the pear with you, Nelay. I have plans for it later."

"What?" She tried to rearrange her scattered thoughts, but he was already up and out the door.

Another man immediately plopped down in the seat he'd vacated. "I'm more than happy to take his place, flower."

She barely paid him any attention as she snatched both pears and hustled out after Rycus. He had already intercepted an exhausted-looking soldier.

"They have us working from sunrise to sunset. I'm sorry, but I'm hungry and . . ."

Rycus slipped him a coin. The man looked at it. "I'm sorry, but I'd rather sleep—"

When Rycus slipped him another, the man hesitated, wavering. Another coin, with two more promised when he returned, and Nelay knew she was going to be starting her career as the High Priestess as a pauper.

The man disappeared back inside the teeming building. Nelay and Rycus tried to go back to the inn, but their table was now occupied and she refused to see more of her coins spent on getting it back. They found a spot of shade between buildings that was already packed with people who'd set up some kind of temporary shelter. Nelay ate her pear, barely tasting it now and disappointed Rycus didn't try to make good on his promise to make use of it later.

The ovat came in from the desert, parching her already-dry skin and making her eyes burn. She tied up her veil to protect her face.

The streets promptly emptied of any remaining people. Almost everyone napped to make up for the sleep they missed by working from first light until full dark. Nelay was exhausted, her body still recovering from her ordeal. She rested her head on Rycus's shoulder.

The next thing she knew, he gently squeezed her arm. "He's back."

Rubbing her numb hip, Nelay blinked her eyes open and looked around. It was the tail end of the ovat. Her clothes were clammy with sweat. She rose to follow Rycus out of the ally.

The man approached them, his uniform rumpled and his red eyes framed with puffy circles. His hands were stained with ink, which he'd carelessly smudged around his eyes, making him look like a badger. "I found no record of a soldier named Panar Favar Denar ShaBejan."

Denar was Nelay's father's name. She shuddered, the image of her his bones haunting her. "Did you check all records? For every branch of military?"

"I checked them all for all variations of his name. There are a few men named Panar ShaBejan, but none with Favar or Denar."

Nelay felt her hope fall out from under her.

"Thank you," she heard Rycus tell the man, who was already walking away, more of her coins in his hand. Rycus took her arm and steered her down the hot, packed-dirt street.

No trace of Panar at Sopora or Dalarta. "He must be dead," she heard herself say as if from far away. "The army has recruited all the other men."

"Not necessarily," Rycus said, but even he didn't seem to believe it.

She was hanging by her fingertips on the edge of something dark and irrevocable—being completely without family in the world.

Rycus rested a hand on her shoulder. "Not all men were recruited. Invalids, officials, surely some of the rich bought their way out."

Nelay halted in the middle of the street. "My parents—I sent them money. Enough to live very well. Yet they never even fixed that blasted door."

Rycus took a step closer. "What do you mean?"

"What if Panar took it?"

"How much did you send?"

"All my recruitment money—ten darics, and a daric every year thereafter." A daric was the largest of the Idaran gold coins, so large it covered most of her palm.

Rycus's gaze widened. "You've been holding back on me, high priestess."

She gave him a dirty look and pushed past him.

"So . . ." He drew out the word. "He has perhaps seventeen darics, if he took all of them. That's enough to buy his way into wealth."

Nelay picked up her pace so Rycus wouldn't see the anger and hurt she couldn't hide. "I gave that money to my parents."

"It was theirs to do with as they pleased," he said gently.

She closed her eyes. He was right, and yet Panar's actions were selfish. And by the time she was done rescuing him, she would have nothing. "When I find him, I'm going to throttle him."

Rycus chuckled softly. "I wouldn't believe he was your brother if you reacted any other way." Nelay made a noncommittal noise in her throat before Rycus added, "With that many darics, he could buy his way into anything he wanted."

Nelay forced herself to examine the field. She felt her gaze drawn to the palace in the center of the city. "Panar wanted to be a leader. Always has." It's why they'd fought so badly. Both of them thought they were right, and the other needed to fall into line. Nelay couldn't help it that she was actually right and Panar was wrong.

She and Rycus crossed through the city, avoiding the squares overloaded with refugees. People moved about hastily, their eyes darting toward the outer wall, where the Clansmen were setting up for the siege. Tonight, the first of the catapults would exchange fire.

Nelay loved the close quarters, simply because the fairies hated cities. In the midst of the chaos, she felt at safer than anywhere else. She reached the inner city, the lord's white palace walls gleaming under the relentless sun. The smell of human waste was behind them, along with the overcrowding and the noise. The inner city's gates were still open, though men were digging trenches around the outside, as if they already knew the city would fall and this would be their last resort. Nelay stopped to watch them work. "If we can't hold the Clansmen here . . ."

Rycus turned his eyes toward Thanjavar. "If the city falls, I'll get you out."

She studied him, wondering how she was going to say goodbye.

He took a half step toward her. "You've been quieter than usual. Are you all right?"

She couldn't answer that honestly, so it was best to say nothing. "Come on." Once past the inner wall, she began asking soldiers and shop owners. No one knew her brother. No one had seen him.

As evening fell, they stopped at the market and paid an outrageous sum for basil rice. Nelay ate her food and then tried to rub out the soreness around her arrow wound. Rycus batted her hands away. He gently began massaging the muscles, and she rested her elbows on her knees and let him.

"What if we don't find him?" she asked.

"Then you did all you could."

"Why didn't he come visit me? Dalarta is only five days from Thanjavar. At least he could have written. My parents could have written."

Rycus didn't answer. Instead he stood up and offered her his hand. She sighed, rolling her neck and wincing when it popped. After he pulled her to her feet, she saw someone walking toward them. A mangy-looking street rat, his clothes tattered and filthy. He stopped just out of range. "I hear you're looking for someone."

Nelay nodded for Rycus to answer—he'd already proven himself the better negotiator.

"Panar Favar Denar ShaBejan," Rycus said.

The boy nodded. "Doesn't go by that name anymore. He's Panar Hazeem now."

Nelay narrowed her gaze. "How do you know?"

"I saw it on the letters he throws away—I resell the paper."

Nelay winced. The only people who'd write Panar were her parents. How could he throw their letters away?

"I know where he lives," the boy went on.

The only thing to keep Nelay from crying out in relief was Rycus's warning hand.

"How much?" he asked.

The boy eyed them. "An attalic." Small silver coins, but more than this child would see in a year.

Rycus folded his arms. "How far is it?"

The boy shrugged again. "Not far."

"Then you ask too much. Surely, we can find someone who knows the area and will point us in the right direction for free." Rycus motioned for Nelay to follow him.

"Three bavaz!" the boy countered.

Rycus held up one bavaz. The copper coins were still too much, but he was just a boy. "One now." Rycus pushed the coin into the boy's palm. "And the other two when we know you've taken us to the right place."

The coin disappeared down the boy's front; no doubt he had a purse of some kind under his threadbare robe. "This way." He darted into a narrow street and led them closer to the palace. They passed three-story homes, built with shared walls. Each home had a porch with pots filled with sweet-smelling herbs. All the doors were fancily carved and hinged—Idarans took great stock in their doors, which showed the owners' wealth and artistic sense.

The boy stopped in front of a door painted turquoise, with brown hinges curling decoratively around the front. He stepped back as Nelay lifted the knocker shaped like a leaping fish—

ironic for a home in the desert. A few moments later, it was pushed open and a very pregnant girl stood before her.

"Why are there pregnant women everywhere?" Nelay said in exasperation.

The girl blinked at her. "Excuse me?"

Rycus tipped back his head and laughed, only calming himself with visible effort. "We are looking for one Panar." He waved his hand dismissively. "Something something ShaBejan. Does he live here?"

The girl eyed them. "And why are desert Tribesmen looking for him?"

Nelay leaned forward. "Then he is here? He is alive?"

The girl put her hand on the door, and Nelay knew her next step would be to slam it in their faces. "He's a respectable man," the girl said. "He has nothing to do with Tribesmen!"

"You forgot 'dirty' Tribesmen," Rycus said in a hard voice.

Nelay rested her hand on his arm.

"You see!" the boy cried from behind them. "It is his house. Now can I have my other bavaz?"

Rycus turned and flicked them to him. "I always have use for those who know things, boy. Where can I find you again if I need you?"

The boy grinned. "Same fountain where I found you." With that, he scampered off.

When Nelay turned back, the pregnant woman had already shut the door. So Nelay pushed her way inside and closed it behind her. The woman backed away, clearly terrified. "My husband is an important man! A treasurer for the lord! You cannot hurt me without reprisal!"

Nelay rolled her eyes. It was kind of fun playing games with this woman, but probably not very nice. She pulled off her headscarf, revealing the short hair above her ears and the tattoos on the side of her face, something only priestesses were allowed to wear.

The woman gasped, and Nelay could almost see her mind working toward the obvious conclusion. "You're Nelay." The woman made an elaborate bow. Suddenly, she was all sweetness. "But I thought the acolytes were never allowed to leave Thanjavar."

Nelay made a noncommittal grunt in her throat as she wandered around the home, admiring the things her money had bought—potted plants, upholstered chairs, two layers of drapes, one sheer to keep the bugs out, the other heavy to keep out the heat.

"Are you his wife or his servant?" Nelay asked.

The woman rose up indignantly. "I am his wife! My name is Atusa."

Nelay pressed her lips together to keep from smirking. She knew this woman was Panar's wife—she was too well-dressed to be otherwise—but seeing all this finery, all stolen from Nelay's parents, made her angry. "And where is my dear brother?"

Atusa narrowed her gaze. "At the palace. He will be home for supper."

Nelay draped herself across one of the chairs. "Good. I'll wait here."

Panar's wife shifted her weight from one foot to the other before bowing. "Priestess, I would be honored. And who is your . . . guard?"

Rycus leaned against the wall with one leg cocked, watching Atusa as if he couldn't figure her out. She dropped his gaze immediately.

"Call me Hunter," he said.

She tipped her head. "I have orray and banal bread, if you like."

Rycus's face lit up.

"He prefers it strong," Nelay warned.

"How strong?" Atusa asked.

"So strong it will make your tongue shoot out of your mouth to try and escape it, and then stronger still," Rycus retorted.

Atusa's hand fluttered to her chest and she shot Nelay an uncertain look.

"It's a mark of toughness or some such thing," Nelay said dryly.

As Atusa sidled into the kitchen, Rycus grinned at Nelay. "Your brother's alive."

She made a face. "And when he gets here, I'm going to kill him."

They ate banal bread and drank orray while Atusa went about fixing supper over a brazier in their small back courtyard. Just as evening came on, the front door pushed open and Nelay found herself staring at a man who was somewhere between what she remembered of her father and what she remembered of her brother.

"Nelay?" he said uncertainly.

She rose to her feet, stalked over to him, and punched him in the jaw. He flopped like he always had when he took a hit. Only now it was worse, because Nelay had been trained to stun someone.

He spit blood onto Atusa's perfectly scrubbed floor while his wife ran over to him and helped him up. She glared at Nelay, who was already seated in the very comfortable upholstered chair.

Panar wiped blood from his chin. "And I suppose you think I deserve that."

It took years of Nelay's training to keep her tears back. "You took every daric I sent them. Every one. And you bought yourself a life in the palace, with a wife who is either a wealthy merchant's daughter or else some distant nobility fallen from grace."

Atusa glared at her with a hint of shame. "The latter, then," Nelay went on, and she couldn't bring herself to care about the venom in her words. "They were five days' journey away, and you couldn't be bothered to bring them to safety."

Panar dropped in another chair. "They're dead?"

That was all he could say? Their parents were dead! Where was his grief?

Atusa still glared at Nelay. "Something is burning, Atusa," she spat. The woman huffed and retreated to the back courtyard.

Panar gingerly touched his jaw. It was already starting to swell and turn reddish black. He was lucky she'd pulled the punch or the bone would be broken. "I tried to get them to come to the city, but you know how Father is with the flock and our land. He refused to abandon either."

"He could have brought the sheep."

"The army doesn't have enough feed for them. They would have been slaughtered, and he would have had a pittance in return. He chose to stay behind and hope Arcina would hold."

Nelay stood up, the chair clattering to the tiles behind her. "Then you should have forced them to come! You work in the palace—you had to know Arcina would fall."

Panar glared up at her. "You didn't go after them either!"

Suddenly she felt boneless, as if her legs had melted. She sank onto the floor. "Actually, I did, but I was too late. I burned them."

Panar winced as she glared up at him. "But then you already knew that. Any refugees who haven't already arrived are dead or captive." She leaned forward. "What's the matter, Panar? Would two rough, uneducated shepherds not fit in with your wife and new status?"

He finally looked up at her, defeat written all over him. "Why did you come, Nelay? To insult my wife? To strike the only family member you have left?"

Tears burned her eyes. "You threw away their letters."

He sighed. "I was angry when Father refused to come."

Nelay couldn't bear to be in the same room anymore. She stormed up the ladder in the center of the house, having no idea what was at the top. She only knew if she stayed in that room one more moment, she'd hit Panar again. And this time she wouldn't pull back.

At the top was an entire floor. It was open, with a large bed and a small box for the baby. Cushions and books and blankets. Even some carved wooden toys—seeing them made Nelay think of her father.

"Believe it or not," Rycus said from below, "she's been searching for you for days. She nearly died looking for you."

"You don't know my sister as well as I do. She came here to make me suffer."

"No," Rycus countered. "She's just angry because her parents are dead, and it appears you didn't care enough to do whatever it took to save them."

Nelay obviously hadn't gone far enough. She climbed the ladder to the third floor. This part of the house smelled musty. There were broken bits of furniture and a couple old trunks covered in a thick layer of dust. Her brother was probably waiting for her next daric to pay for the repairs.

She climbed the ladder again, finally coming to the open roof, a large square with a half wall surrounding it. The mud bricks beneath her feet held the heat of the day, and the wind off the desert tasted like hot glass. She closed her eyes, feeling the breeze against her sweaty face.

When a person died, the last breath left his or her body in a puff of wind. That last breath joined the thousands of others that had gone before. That was how the ovat and tavo were born.

Nelay knew her parents were with her still. Every time the breeze brushed against her face, it was her mother caressing her cheek. Every time it tugged on her clothes, her father was reminding her to be gentle and always care for those who had less.

She took a deep breath and held it. But eventually, she had to let it go and draw another, for though her parents had exhaled their last, she had not.

Having found her center, she smoothly drew her shamshir, her body gliding from one motion to the next.

CHAPTER
TWENTY-ONE

Sweat soaked Nelay's skin, her breath coming hard and fast. She felt someone watching her and turned. Braced against the ladder and the top of the roof, Rycus stood with his arms folded.

"Nelay, take the advice of a person from a big family," he said. "Sometimes it's better to love someone from a distance."

She sheathed her swords and wiped her brow. "Is that why you're here instead of with your family?" Burn it, Panar was the only family she had left. And she'd lost him all the same—lost him ten years ago. If she'd ever even had him at all. *Just like I'm going to lose Rycus.* Tears threatened so she averted her gaze, refusing to let him see.

He sighed. "Forgive him. He's all you have left in the way of family."

"How can I?"

"If you don't, it will tear you apart from the inside out."

"How can I ever trust him again?"

"I'm not saying you should. I'm not even saying you ever have to speak to him again. Only that you must forgive him."

In the distance, a flash of orange caught Nelay's attention. She watched as a ball of flame arced through the sky and slammed into the city wall. She felt the reverberations through her feet. A beat later, she heard the crash. The whole world was falling apart—burning to ashes and charcoal all around her. Rycus took hold of her hand. She turned away and wiped her cheeks.

Nearby roofs quickly filled with the city's highest-paid workers. As everyone watched, the king's army retaliated, throwing glowing balls of their own. Other things were launched, but the darkness made it impossible to identify them.

"Nelay, we need to get out of here before the Clansmen completely surround Dalarta," Rycus said, his tone urgent.

"Are you really so certain the city will fall?"

"All of Idara is going to fall."

Startled, she looked at him. There was only compassion in his eyes, but her anger spiked nonetheless. "Then why are you here?"

He reached out to cup the back of her head in his hand. "You know why," he said softly.

Burn it, she liked hearing those words.

He leaned in and rested his forehead on hers. "Come with me? We can leave Idara and start a new life in the desert."

Breaking up inside, shattering like glass, Nelay started crying again.

"No, don't do that," Rycus pled. "I can't stand to see that."

She shook her head and tried to move away. Then his mouth crashed against hers. She wanted to pull back—she couldn't do this to herself, to him. But the tug in her lower belly shifted to a hard yank. She was melting, every hard edge she'd honed over the years going soft. Rycus pressed her up against the half wall, and her body yielded to his.

Suddenly his kisses slowed. "What's wrong?" she panted. She didn't want him to stop. Ever.

He chuckled. "Because we have an audience."

Nelay shifted her head and saw people from the other rooftops watching them. Her cheeks went hot. "I can't do this."

Rycus ran his hands up and down her back. "That's why we stopped."

She closed her eyes and slowly started shaking her head. "No. I mean you and me. We can't do this."

He pulled back to look at her face. "Is this about Zatal?"

"It's more than that." She moved out of Rycus's arms. "I swore a long time ago I would be no man's wife. No child's mother. You want those things—I know you do."

His jaw tightened, but he didn't deny it. "I've seen you with Concon. I know how you are with me. I think you do want those things. You just won't admit it."

"I've worked my whole life—"

"To be a high priestess, I know," he interrupted, his voice rising. "But Nelay, there isn't going to be an Idara left. Come with me. Start over in the Adrack. You can have everything you want, be a priestess and my wife and—"

"I can't abandon Jezzel!" she cried. "And . . ."

"And what? What else can't you leave? Because it seems to me you've already lost just about everything. And you're setting yourself up to lose more."

She crossed her arms over her middle, trying to hold herself together. "The priestesses—they're my family." But even to herself, the words sounded hollow.

"And they turned you over to the king without so much as asking." Rycus turned away, breathing hard. "I'm going to check on Maran and let Havva know where you are. It's time to start planning our escape."

Nelay's heart dropped. She didn't want him to leave, but she didn't know how to stop him. And then he was gone. She moved to the edge of the roof and looked down. He slipped out of the house a moment later and trotted in the direction of the library. She thought of going after him, but she wasn't ready to face her brother. So she watched the city walls take blow after blow and hold strong.

CHAPTER TWENTY-TWO

Pacing back and forth over an intricate rug in Panar's house, Nelay felt her sister-in-law's glare. "Do you know how much that rug cost?" Atusa asked tersely as she lit the last lamp.

With the city under siege, and Rycus gone all last night and all day, Nelay couldn't make herself care about a silly rug. "No, I don't," she said, "which is pretty ironic, considering the fact that I paid for it."

After blowing out the stick she'd used to light the lamps, Atusa went to the table and started scrubbing the dinner pots in a tub of soapy water. "Panar used that money to pay for his schooling at the university and his apprenticeship. He makes his own money now."

"Good. Then he can buy you a new rug."

Atusa slammed the rag down, sending water sloshing over the sides of the tub. "You don't know anything about him."

Nelay thought of the mean-spirited boy she had lived with as a child. She could still feel his fingers around her neck as he tried to choke her. But she had come searching for him all these years later, partly because she'd hoped he had changed, grown up. Partly because she longed for her family. And partly because Panar was simply her blood.

She stopped pacing and rested her hand on the wall. "I almost died looking for him, and all this time he was only a few days away. My parents would have told me where he was unless he asked them not to. He knew exactly where I was. He could have written at any time, could have visited. And he chose not to. So forgive me if I'm not overjoyed to see him again."

Atusa stormed over to Nelay. "He was ashamed! He had dreams, too. Your parents wanted a better life for him, so they gave him that money. It was theirs to do with what they wished. He's a good man, a good husband!"

"Then why can't he tell me that himself?"

Atusa stepped back, trembling. "Because he's a man, and they have their pride." She sagged as if suddenly exhausted. She ran her still-wet hands over her hair, smoothing a few stray strands, then jerked open the front door and stormed out.

Nelay collapsed in the chair, her elbows braced against her knees and her head hanging low. Moments later, the door swung open. Nelay looked up, expecting to see Atusa coming back for something she forgot, but Rycus stood in the doorway.

They stared at each other as if afraid to break the silence. Finally, he shut the door. "Why did Atusa just storm out?"

Unwilling to discuss it, Nelay crossed her arms and studied him, wondering where they stood after their fight.

He glanced around. "Panar's not home yet?" Nelay shrugged, knowing they were both dancing around what had been said last night.

Rycus crossed the room, sniffed at the orray pot on the table, and poured himself a cup. He took a sip and pulled a face, half disappointment, half disgust, but it didn't stop him from drinking the stuff. "You Idarans don't know how to take your orray."

Nelay rolled her neck, cracking her spine. "How bad was the damage to the city?"

"Come on. I'll show you from the roof." He set the cup down. "You should take a blanket. The tavo's particularly bitter tonight."

They borrowed a couple of thick wool blankets from Panar's room, and then Nelay followed Rycus up to the roof. The first of the stars were beginning to peek out, but the mud bricks felt pleasantly warm from the heat of the day. Other people sat on the nearby roofs, watching the bombardment.

Rycus was right—the breeze was chilly. Nelay wrapped a blanket around her shoulders and watched the army, which looked and moved like an infestation of ants.

"The outer wall held up remarkably well," he said. "Their catapults haven't managed to do more than surface damage so far."

Nelay spread her hand across the half wall. "Can we expect this every night?"

"Right now, they're just attempting to weaken Dalarta's walls while their soldiers try to cut us off from Thanjavar. After that happens, they'll start charging the walls, trying to get in." Rycus spoke gently as if to soften the blow of his words.

"And will they cut us off?"

"They outnumber us five to one—there are five hundred thousand men out there from the nations we've defeated—all led by Clansmen."

"How many days do we have?"

He shrugged. "A couple."

"Won't the king send more of his armies?"

Rycus looked away. "He's sent as many as he can spare without risking Thanjavar."

She sighed. "What about Havva and Maran?" He paused long enough for Nelay to figure out that something was wrong. "Just tell me," she said in exasperation.

He leaned over the edge as if seriously contemplating the distance to the street. "Maran went back to her husband."

"What?" Nelay blurted out.

"And what would you do if you were in her place?" Rycus asked, now looking off into the distance.

"I wouldn't be in her place," Nelay scoffed.

He met her gaze. "And what would you have done if the priestesses had never come for you? If both your parents were dead and you had to survive and tend your flock alone?"

"I would have run it myself." That wasn't true. Her father had planned to marry her off the moment she turned fourteen to a man more than twice her age.

"And when bandits came? Or when you were hurt and had no one to help you? What would you have done then?"

Nelay's nostrils flared. "I would have killed them. I—"

"You wouldn't know how to fight," Rycus interrupted.

"I would have found a way to take care of myself." She knew even as she said it that she was lying to herself.

"The truth is, we can't always be strong, and we're not meant to be alone. People need each other." Rycus let out a long breath. "Maran needs Sedun—or believes she does. And until she changes her mind about that, she won't leave him."

The siege engines lobbed their projectiles over the wall. Nelay watched as the king's armies scattered, shifting to repel attacks and firing their bows and catapults. From this distance, it was almost pretty, in a twisted, horrifying kind of way.

She watched until the cool shifted to cold. Shivering in earnest, she barely registered Rycus leaving and coming back with more blankets for both of them. He settled another around her shoulders and wrapped his arms around her from behind. "You should rest. You're still recovering."

She glanced around to see the other rooftops had been deserted. "About what we said last night . . ."

He rested his forehead on the back of her head. "Come with me, back into the desert. Leave behind this dying country and live with me."

Nelay studied his hands—a Tribesman's hands. She'd watched him for weeks, watched him keep his men's spirits up. Watched him care for her. Watched him love her.

She thought of the life she would have if she left him. She imagined herself sitting in Suka's dais surrounded by the pool of water and floating prayers. She imagined the people bowing before her. She imagined leading the nation. And she realized she no longer wanted it. Not if it meant being without Rycus. "Yes."

His head came up. "Yes?"

She took a long breath and let it out, testing herself. She felt relieved, like she'd just cast off a huge burden. "Yes."

He brushed his cold nose along the crook of her neck, and she found herself tipping her head to the side to give him better access. He trailed kisses behind her ear all the way down to her shoulder, leaving sparks in their wake. "You can still have everything. We'll go back for Jezzel, convince her to come with us. You will have a family again. My family will love you like their own."

His lips were making it hard to think, but she imagined herself in one of the canyons Rycus had told her about. The pools of bright-blue water deep within the cliffs. Then her smile disappeared. "And wait at home with your babies while you smuggle?"

"I won't always be a smuggler."

"What?" She tried to turn around to face him, but he held her in place. "What else would you be?"

He tugged her robe sleeve down and kissed her bare shoulder. "Being a smuggler is sort of a hobby—because I'm very, very good at it. And I wanted to experience more than just the Adrack Desert before I settled down."

A low burn started in Nelay's lower belly. "And now you're ready to settle down?"

He whispered against her ear, "I've found everything I was looking for." His hands ran up and down her sides, then slipped around her stomach. One finger brushed along the base of her breast.

A wave of heat burned through her and she melted against him. He sucked on her ear, a gentle pressure that ignited her. She maneuvered his hands, putting them where she wanted to be touched. He groaned and cupped her, kneading her body and sending her heart racing. Breathless, she pivoted in his arms and her mouth found his. His kiss was all heat, his tongue tasting her mouth. She tasted him back, her hands spreading across his chest, around his shoulders, down his back.

He made a sound low in his throat and eased her onto the warm stones that made up the roof. Everywhere he touched her, his fingers left trails of fire in their wake. Their bodies intertwined like twin flames—growing brighter and hotter with every stroke, every breath.

CHAPTER TWENTY-THREE

Nelay pulled back, the fire burning under her skin. Rycus continued to kiss her throat, her collarbone. "No, stop."

He paused, groaning. "Nelay—"

She held out her hand. There was a rushing sound, like dozens of footsteps. Another sound—one only someone who'd trained for hours under the grueling sun would be familiar with. The unique sound of boiled leather bouncing against skin. Armor.

Rycus and Nelay bolted apart at the same instant, the cold tavo a slap to her exposed skin. She peeked over the half wall to find the streets swarming with Immortals. Their helmets bore raised markings that mimicked their intricate scalp tattoos. Those helmets told Nelay two things: first, they were here to fight; second, they were the king's personal guard.

Fire and ash, Zatal found me, Nelay thought, knowing the fairies must have revealed her location. But how had he arrived at the city so quickly? Her mind spun, discarding and choosing players at random. In a stride and a half, she grabbed her baldric and slipped it over her head. Then she vaulted over the half wall separating the roofs, Rycus right behind her. The landing made her feet sting. This roof had chairs and tables and even a brazier, but thankfully, no people.

Nelay and Rycus kept leaping over roofs, glancing back carefully each time for any sign of soldiers. When they reached the end of the block, they paused behind a potted orange tree.

"How did they find me?" she asked breathlessly.

Rycus didn't answer as he tried the trapdoor. It opened with a groan of hinges, and she winced at the noise. He surveyed the shadows doubtfully. "I don't like it."

Nelay glanced around, trying to rework the field into something more useful. They couldn't jump down from the building—three stories was simply too far. "What else can we do?" she whispered.

They descended into the shadows, both of them holding their breath, waiting for any sound to reveal they'd been discovered. This room was empty, though there were sleeping pallets on the ground.

Rycus shook his head and pressed his ear to the trapdoor beneath them. Slowly, he eased to his feet and pointed back up.

There must be Immortals waiting below! Nelay thought with a gasp. They had to go back. Find another way down.

She silently climbed the ladder, but when she peeked over the edge, she came eye to eye with the sword of an Immortal—the whole rooftop was covered with the king's guards. She sucked in a sharp breath as this guard stuck two fingers in his mouth and let out a long, shrill whistle. The trapdoor beneath her shot open, and Immortals flooded into the room. Nelay looked down at Rycus and knew he also realized they were trapped. When she glanced back up, King Zatal had just climbed over the roof line.

Bone-deep trembles shook Nelay. The king could have her killed, have Rycus killed. Her mind spun to find a solution as she climbed the rest of the way up and stood by the ladder. Rycus moved to follow her, but the Immortals leveled their swords at him, forcing him back. Nelay kept one hand on her sword hilt—after all, she was still a priestess.

Zatal studied her, his expression revealing nothing. "Did you save them—your parents?"

Nelay's jaw worked as the memory temporarily robbed her of speech. "No," she finally managed.

He inclined his head. "I am sorry." Nelay kept quiet. The king motioned below. "Who were you with?"

"The smuggler I paid to find them." She wasn't going to reveal his name.

Zatal's gaze hardened. "And I suppose this is the man who helped you escape Thanjavar?"

Nelay kept her back straight. "Yes." There was no point in lying—Zatal would have guessed as much already.

"Take his weapons," Zatal called down.

Nelay was relieved when she didn't hear a struggle—that would be suicide. She desperately wanted to see Rycus, feel him near her, but she didn't want the king to know of her deep worry.

Zatal made a sound low in his throat. "Give me your weapons, Nelay. I swear no harm will come to you."

She didn't believe him, but neither dared she provoke him. She drew her shamshirs and held them out, hilt first. The king passed them to one of his Immortals without taking his eyes off her. She handed over her throwing knives as well, feeling a sharp sense of vulnerability without them.

"Some privacy," the king said to the soldiers around them. A man shouted a command. An Immortal climbed partway up the ladder and shut the trapdoor, cutting her off from Rycus. The rest of the guards moved to the edges of the roof.

Zatal circled Nelay, his gaze pausing at her loose sash and disheveled robes—she hadn't even thought to straighten them. He stepped so close she could feel the heat of his skin against her own. "How long have you and this smuggler been lovers?"

Nelay sucked in a breath. "We are not lovers."

The king discreetly tightened her sash, as if he wanted to shield what he did from view. "Not long," he said, as if completely disregarding her denial, "since I suspect High Priestess Suka's spies would have noticed." He shook his head. "This would have been easier for both of us had you not formed attachments."

"You have a mistress and children," Nelay shot back, then immediately regretted the outburst.

"Don't be an idiot. It's easy to discern the mother of a child. Not so easy to determine the father, and that man's sons will not sit on my throne. And if you already are, well, we'll take care of it."

Nelay felt a keen sense of relief that a baby wasn't a possibility. "You still want me as your queen?"

"No," Zatal replied simply. "But it will be done nonetheless."

"If you don't want me, why are you doing this?" Her voice rose with each word.

The king's face flushed with anger. "For the good of Idara."

She narrowed her eyes. "You see the whole world as yours, as something to be conquered and controlled. But I am not yours. I never was."

Zatal laced his hands behind his back. "The world is a place of chaos and inefficiencies. I bring order. The lands we conquered went from places of lawlessness to stability. They are better, stronger for being adopted into Idara."

"Is that how you see yourself?" Nelay asked. "As some kind of benevolent father? Forcing people—forcing me—into your idea of perfection, regardless of how many you cut down in the process?"

Zatal's gaze hardened. "You're a shepherd's daughter. Is it not true that you must cull the flock to keep it strong?"

"Those are animals. I'm a person!"

"People are animals too, Nelay. Wild and untamed. I teach them how to be civilized."

She huffed. "Is that what I am? Some kind of animal to be tamed?"

He studied her. "You see it, don't you? How the Game of Fire is life. Everything is just moves and countermoves. That we are all players, and if you can nudge people this way or that, you can control the world."

She had never known anyone to look at the game the same way she did, but she wasn't sure she liked being so similar to the king. "And yet you lost it all."

He gave a bitter laugh. "That's because I didn't plan on going up against a goddess."

Nelay wet her lips, wondering if that was true. "So I'm just another of your players?"

"Unfortunately for you."

"And you won't tell me what my role is?"

Zatal tipped his head to the side. "You must realize your vast potential, which is being squandered on chasing after people who should be taking care of themselves. You have the chance to be a great and powerful queen. And you would give that up for what?" He gestured, unseeing, toward Rycus. "Some smuggler?"

"No." She threw her shoulders back. "A high priestess has more power than a queen." She could still be high priestess of the Tribesmen. Being with Rycus didn't change that.

The king took a step closer. "I'm afraid that is impossible now. But I can make you a queen. You have to admit, that's more powerful than a smuggler's wife."

She would find a way to escape the king and go with Rycus. After all, she'd escaped Zatal once, so she could do it again. She lifted her face to find him watching her with a knowing expression. "I see that you will not be dissuaded by mere words," he said. "That leaves me no choice but to cut off your other options."

He motioned for his guards to open the trapdoor. "Long ago I learned you cannot leave any other option but surrender. For if you do, the conquered will find a way to rise up against you. He must die, Nelay. But I will make it quick. We will give him an honorable funeral."

"No!" she cried, charging toward Zatal. Three Immortals snatched her arms and held her back.

She looked down as the Immortals surrounding Rycus moved closer, awaiting the final order. He took a defensive stance and spared a single hopeless glance her way. Though emotions twisted inside her, Nelay forced herself to reset the field, only with a new objective—saving the man she loved.

"Give the order," Zatal said to one of his guards, who walked toward the trapdoor.

"You harm him," Nelay said to Zatal, "and I swear upon the goddess, I will kill you. No matter how many guards, no matter how many precautions, I will find a way around them." She knew she had given him every reason to kill her, but she didn't care. The Immortals tightened their grip on her until it hurt.

Zatal held out his hand, halting the Immortal who would pass on the order. The king's eyes flashed, and Nelay realized he loved this—this life and death bargain. Conquering those he thought beneath him.

"But if you let him go," Nelay went on quickly, "I'll stay with you. I will bear you three sons. And then our bargain will be fulfilled and I will be free to do as I wish. These are the terms of my surrender."

Zatal stroked his chin. "How do I know you won't find a way to see him behind my back?"

"I'm sure you're already planning to have me watched day and night."

"Bring him to me," Zatal called down below. Two Immortals motioned for Rycus to move.

A guard came up first while another shoved Rycus from behind. Zatal put a hand on Nelay's shoulder and pushed her a half dozen steps back. He put his face right before hers. "I will show you that I can be merciful."

Rycus slowly raised his head, his expression defiant, even as Zatal turned to face him. The king's reaction was instantaneous. He swore violently and drew his dagger, charging Rycus and knocking him down. He tried to drive his dagger into Rycus, but Rycus held his forearms, not giving way.

"Did you know she was meant to be mine? Did you?" Zatal screamed, spit flying from his mouth.

Not understanding his sudden rage, Nelay struggled against the men holding her, but they held firm.

Rycus glared at him. "Not everything is about you, O great king."

Nelay looked between the two men. Did they know each other?

The Immortals converged on Rycus and pinned his arms against the rooftop, leaving him defenseless.

Nelay writhed against the Immortals holding her. "Stop it! Leave him alone!"

Zatal pressed the tip of his knife to Rycus's neck. "I should kill you now."

Rycus's jaw hardened—an expression Nelay was all too familiar with. Mercifully, he kept his sharp tongue still.

She went still. "If you do," she said, her voice quivering, "by the Goddess, I will kill you."

Zatal punched Rycus in the eye. Then he shook out his hand, pushed himself off the floor, and turned to Nelay. "Very well, I accept your terms. On one condition." He pointed down at Rycus. "He must swear it as well."

Rycus rolled to his side, covering his rapidly swelling eye with his hand. "I'm not much for promises, King."

"Then you will die." The rage had left Zatal's face, leaving hard, cold hatred. "I don't care who you are."

Nelay looked between the two of them, wondering again if they had met before. Perhaps Rycus had smuggled for the king at some point . . . She shook her head. Whatever was between them didn't matter. What mattered was that Rycus lived.

Suddenly he staggered to his feet and swung, his fist dropping one Immortal. He head butted the other. Nelay took advantage of one guard's slack hold, twisting free. She kneed one between the legs and shoved the other.

She ran toward Rycus—to do what she wasn't sure, but before she got there, a third guard held a sword to Rycus's throat. "My king," the guard said, "would you have me kill him?"

She froze as a line of blood ran down his neck. "Rycus! Stop!"

His gaze flashed to her. His eyes were wild, the veins in his face bulging. In that moment, she knew he wouldn't stop fighting until he was dead. She couldn't let that happen.

The players of the game fell into place effortlessly. She stepped forward and placed her palm on the edge of the blade, pushing it away from Rycus's neck. It was sharp enough that it slipped inside her skin. She was betting the Immortals wouldn't risk harming her, their future queen. She was right. As soon as the man saw the blood running down her hand, he withdrew his blade.

Nelay glanced at the wound at Rycus's throat. He would have a scar, but it would heal. She looked into his eyes and saw the determination—the dauntless will. There was only one way to save his life. She tipped forward and kissed him. She could taste tears on her lips—whether hers or his she wasn't sure. She pulled back and rested her forehead against his. "Do you love me?"

"Yes."

Her heart ached at how quickly he'd said it, so full of conviction. "Then don't make me live in a world you're no longer a part of." He stiffened. "Please, Rycus. I could not bear it."

"Nelay . . ." There was so much hurt in his voice.

Her eyes welled with tears, but she fought to keep control. If she gave in to her emotions now, she was certain to lose this game. "Swear to me, Rycus. Swear that you will go into the desert. I'll come to you when I can." She had no intention of keeping her promise to the king.

Rycus's body shuddered beneath her. "I can't."

"If there is any way out of this, I will find it. You have to trust me."

He was silent for a long time. "Remember the stars?"

His question caught her off guard. She remembered the stars above them last night—a scattering of jewels and dust. She remembered the stars around them the night he'd bound her wounds. And before that, the stars he'd shown her in the desert. The map he'd taught her. "I remember."

"I'll wait," he said. "If it means we won't meet again till the next life, I'll wait."

Nelay couldn't hesitate—her emotions were too raw. If the king saw her waver, he would know her weakness and would not keep his promise. She kissed Rycus again, holding his cheek in her bloody hands. And then she stepped around him and marched past the king, who watched her with a sad gaze, past the Immortals jamming up a dozen or so roofs. She vaulted over the low wall and crossed the roof. Five times she did that. Then she descended the ladder into her brother's musty-smelling top floor.

The king came down behind her. Nelay refused to look at him. "I choose two handmaidens, Maran and Havva. Acolyte Jezzel will be the head of my personal guard." Nelay would need her friends if she was going to survive this. "Your men will find Maran and Havva in the square before the library. I will have them brought to me before we leave the city."

Small concessions, ones she knew Zatal would be willing to give. He nodded. "Of course."

She descended the ladder to the first floor. Atusa was wringing her hands and pacing by the table. Panar stood at the entrance, his hands behind his back.

At the look of satisfaction on his face, Nelay suddenly knew. The fairies hadn't turned her in—her brother had. He'd sought out the king and brought him to her. She marched up to Panar and looked him in the eye, making herself go still as stone.

He glared down at her, as if this was her fault. "You are a priestess! Not some Tribesman's whore!"

She kneed him in the groin, so hard his face went white, and he collapsed to his knees. Choking, he coughed and groaned.

Nelay crouched before him, seething with hate and anger. "You are no longer my brother. If I ever see you again, I'll kill you myself." She stood and backhanded his face.

He crumpled in a heap. Atusa screamed and collapsed beside him. Nelay couldn't bring herself to care. Without looking back, she strode out onto the street.

CHAPTER TWENTY-FOUR

I n the private worship room of the Temple of Fire, Nelay knelt on the cushions before the pool that reflected the glass idol of the goddess. Her body felt numb as she wrote her prayer, but her fingers remembered the folds, tight and perfect. She creased and twisted and curved until her hand held the perfect form of a flame flower. Inside, her prayer asked for love. For passion and hope and freedom. That her fire—her will—would never be consumed by another.

Then she touched the tips of the petals to the embers. They ignited in a flare of orange, the myrrh-soaked paper giving off a heady fragrance. With the flower resting on the tips of her fingers, she sank her hand into the pool, sending ever widening ripples across the perfectly still water. The flower spun slowly and the petals burned as her prayer was carried into the air, where it would join thousands of others, as well as the souls of her parents.

Hand dripping with water, Nelay stood as the highest-level temple priestesses draped her in robes the color of fire—red and orange and amber. Over her head they draped a veil that brushed the floor. To display the king's wealth, every hem of her clothing was lined with gold coins, which tinkled whenever she moved.

After shaving part of her scalp, the acolytes loosely braided her hair so her tattoos would show. Then they lined her eyes deeply with kohl and added a slash of red to her lips. One of the girls brought a mirror. Nelay studied her dusky skin against the color of her bodice and thought she looked like a combination of fire and ash.

As one, the priestesses inclined their heads to someone behind her. Nelay turned to find Suka standing at the doorway, glaring at the burning paper as it sank. With a dismissive wave, she motioned the other priestesses out. Nelay did not bow. She would never bow to this woman again.

Suka circled the room and stopped before the statue of the goddess. "I wish I could say I'm sorry—but that would mean I wish I could do things differently, and this is the only way. I am a mere mortal caught in a game of the goddesses."

The high priestess's words were like a gust of wind against the coals of Nelay's anger. "What does forcing me to marry the king have to do with the goddesses?" she scoffed. "I don't know what game you think you're playing, Suka, but forcing me to become one of your players will cost you—I swear it."

The high priestess turned to her with a resigned and sad expression. "I know. I've always known. I have made a play, one that will cost me my life."

"What do you mean?"

Suka gave a bitter smile. "Every time you have written a prayer, every time you have knelt on the cushion, has been a lie."

Nelay took a step back, her body feeling suddenly cold. "What?"

Suka rested her hand on the beautiful glass statue of the goddess. "She hates us," the high priestess said so softly Nelay could barely hear her. "The goddess hates us and loves winter. She has betrayed us." Suka's face contorted in rage and she gave the statue a hard shove, sending it toppling. It hit the ground and split in a half dozen pieces, all stained with smoke on the inside. Incense and ash plumed and scattered, some pieces shattering the stillness of the prayer pool.

Nelay gasped and jumped back. "You can't possibly know that!"

"The fairies told me, and the proof is all around us. Has been for decades." Nelay shook her head, but Suka went on ruthlessly. "It started the day our army perished in the clanlands. It continued every time we lost one of our vassal kingdoms. The storms that savaged our ships. The famine that weakened our lands. The speed with which the Clansmen have routed us from our cities."

Nelay clapped her hands over her ears. "Stop!"

Suka stared at her, and for a moment, Nelay saw the absolute fury that consumed the woman. There was no question in Nelay's mind now. Suka was insane.

"I don't believe you." Nelay's voice trembled.

At the sound of running steps, shutters seemed to come down over the high priestess's anger.

"High Priestess!" someone gasped.

Suka turned calm eyes on the priestesses rushing into the room. "Every statue—every single one—is to be replaced," she declared. Stunned silence met her command. "Break them. Break them all."

The women hesitated—as acolytes, each evening they had washed the soot from the statues. They'd bowed to them and reverenced them since coming to the temple.

"Now!" Suka cried.

The priestesses scrambled away, and soon the sound of breaking glass filled the temple. Suka turned dead eyes onto Nelay. "Only one more move, and then my game is finished."

Nelay froze, filled with a sudden fear.

Suka moved past her and stepped into the corridor. "Come, your king awaits."

Nelay wanted to fight, wanted to run, but she'd seen Zatal's Immortals surrounding the temple, five men deep. She would not endure the indignity of being forced.

So she lifted her head high and stepped through the corridors into the public bethel, her garments a cloud of fluttering and tinkling around her. Seven priestesses stood in the pool around the idol, their robes damp past their knees. They tied ropes around the goddess's head. Just as Nelay stepped into the archway that led outside, she heard a groaning and turned to see the three sections of the glass statue come apart before they splashed into the pool, sending a wave of water through the hall.

Nelay shot Suka a disbelieving look, but the woman was already halfway down the stairs. Hurrying to catch up, Nelay stepped into the courtyard that defied the dark night with hundreds of golden lamps. They crossed the wide square, skirting the fountain with the burning ashes of folded prayers coating the bottom. Behind Nelay, Maran and Jezzel took their places; Havva had refused to leave her family.

Nelay and Jezzel used to be the bitterest rivals, as the two strongest, fastest, and smartest acolytes. Until they learned they had different goals. While Nelay wanted to be high priestess, Jezzel wanted to be commanding priestess of the Goddess Army, the high priestess's elite fighting unit.

By asking Jezzel to be the captain of her guard, Nelay was asking her to put her lifelong dream on hold. Still, Jezzel had accepted. "I'm sorry," was all Nelay could manage. "But I need people I can trust around me."

Now, Jezzel glared at the Immortals as they converged, forming a box around them five men deep. The tattoos on their scalps identified them as high-ranking Immortals. "Who does this king think he is, ordering a priestess around like she is some commoner?" Jezzel asked.

Nelay felt a rush of relief that Jezzel's anger wasn't directed toward her. "Suka masterminded it."

Jezzel growled low in her throat and tipped her head toward Maran. "Who's the timid one?"

"I'm not timid," Maran murmured.

Jezzel shot her an incredulous look. "You're about as scary as a thunderstorm in the Adrack."

Maran blinked, clearly not understanding. Nelay sighed. "Because it doesn't rain in the Adrack." She shook her head. "This isn't important. She's someone I trust—that's all you need to know, Jez."

The procession marched toward a speckled-gray horse—the color of ash just as Nelay had requested. The animal was a fine-boned mare of the Adrack breed, whose stamina was renowned the world over. Nelay's choice was another message, however small, for the king.

"You couldn't have picked a stronger ally?" Jez scoffed.

Her expression tight, Maran stepped forward to hold Nelay's veil so she could mount. Nelay shot Jezzel a sardonic grin. "I have you, don't I?"

Jez smiled. "That's true." She took her position in front of the horse while Nelay grabbed the reins, which matched her wedding attire. The brass temple gates leading to the palace courtyard opened on silent hinges.

Thousands of people filled the courtyard, holding oil lamps and unlit silk lanterns. The way was kept clear by stone-still Immortals, who stood twelve men deep between Nelay and any chance of freedom.

The priestesses spread out first, the burning ends of their staffs a blur of gold around them. They beat the staffs to the ground, pounding out a fast tempo. Stretching up, the priestesses just in front of Nelay touched the tips of their fire staffs to channels built on suspension bridges. The channels held a special blend of luminash that burst into a rainbow of colors and filled the air with intricate patterns of fire as she passed. The people cheered, for the spectacle was beautiful and a little terrifying.

The Immortals around Nelay marched out, forming a barrier between her and the enormous crowd. She rode her mare through, her gaze locked on the palace. She didn't not wave or smile. She refused to pretend to be the jubilant bride.

Finally, the palace entrance loomed before them, the doors made of intricately carved wood with beaten gold overlays. The palace itself was a blinding white with plated gold domes rising out of the tans and oranges of the desert. At the base of the steps, the procession halted. This was supposed to be the king's winter palace, so it was not nearly as grand as his summer palace by the seashore. Or so Nelay had been told.

Maran helped arrange Nelay's robes so she could dismount. As she faced her future, her thoughts betrayed her with an image of Rycus's crooked grin. The feel of his mouth on hers. The way he smelled of hot sand. She couldn't bring herself to take another step.

Maran discreetly squeezed Nelay's hand. "It's going to be all right."

She shuddered. "I'm to become the queen of a dying kingdom, Maran. All to fulfill the purposes of some mad high priestess."

Maran didn't have a response for that.

Jezzel shot Nelay a grim look and entered the palace. Taking a deep breath, Nelay marched after her, crossing the threshold at the exact same moment the acolytes lit the luminash. Multicolored flames flashed around the frame.

Her guard of Immortals didn't follow her inside. Here, there was only one row of Immortals between her and the people—and these soldiers were the highest officers in all of Idara. She walked through the enormous throne room, past hundreds of lords, advisors, and professional guild leaders, who presided over their representative trades. Each of them held a lit lamp. Nelay approached the throne, above which was crafted into a phoenix, wings spread and plated in gold. Standing below it was the king.

It should be Rycus she was walking towards. Rycus who would stand beside her to face the hardships and joys of life. Rycus who would hold her and comfort her.

Nelay's gaze locked on Zatal, but his gaze wasn't on her. It was on a woman standing beside the doorway to his left and a little farther down. Even from this distance, Nelay could see the woman was beautiful, with large, expressive eyes and a petite nose. The woman turned and their gazes locked. Nelay saw sorrow and anger, but no hatred. She wondered what the woman saw in return—an interloper who was taking her rightful place, who would have power over her?

Nelay could hate this woman, treat her as a rival. But she didn't see the point. She dipped her head in a show of respect. The woman's eyes widened in surprise. After a moment, she bowed back. When Nelay turned back to the king, he was watching her. Her whole body stiffened. She lifted her airy robes and stepped onto the dais beside him, aware of Jezzel taking a step closer to her than was technically appropriate.

Suka shot Jezzel an icy look—which Jezzel expertly returned—and slipped past the king until she stood directly before the throne, facing them. Her officiating robes were a golden white, the color of the hottest flame.

Facing Nelay, Zatal leaned forward and spoke low. "Neither of us want this, but perhaps we can view it as a business arrangement."

She pulled back half a step. "But for the fact that I lose the man I love, while you get to keep your mistress. But for the fact that I am required to share your bed and bear your children."

Suka cleared her throat loudly, and Nelay caught her fierce glower. The king nodded for the high priestess to begin. She looked to her side, and two highest-ranking priestesses carried forth a huge vessel of clear glass filled with golden oil.

From a breast pocket in her robes, Nelay removed a vial of oil dyed such a deep red it looked like blood. The colors of passion and battle. The king held a similar vial—he'd chosen blue. The color of cunning and precision. Both of them poured their vibrant oils into the vessel. The liquids curled and danced like colored ribbons. Slowly, they combined into a pale lavender.

"Ah," Suka said loudly. "The king's cunning softens the queen's temper."

Nelay resisted the urge to roll her eyes.

Three priestesses, the Holders of the Prayers, came forward and reached out their hands for the long rolls of cotton fabric on which Suka, Nelay, and Zatal had written their prayers. Despite the huge length of fabric stiffened with salt so it would burn slower and hold its shape, Nelay's prayer had been short—that she would be free of this marriage as soon as possible. That Zatal would never touch her.

Judging by the amount of ink on his paper, the king's prayer hadn't been much longer. But Suka's paper was filled on both sides with characters crammed so tightly Nelay could only pick out a few—binding, her people, and war.

As the Holders of the Prayers set about braiding the prayers tightly together with deft fingers, Suka lit a sheaf of dried, fragrant herbs. She waved the smoke around Nelay and Zatal, close enough Nelay could feel the heat. The smoke was to cleanse them of apathetic emotions, leaving them with only the most powerful of passions for their marriage and wedding night.

"For as long as a flame burns, these two lives are connected. In the blazes of passion, might they spark new life. And may that spark carry on from generation to generation until the great and last day when the world is consumed and turned to ash."

The women had finished braiding the wick. One end had been attached to a piece of jewelry chosen by the husband-to-be—in this case a headdress with a sapphire for the forehead. After the oils were gone, the headdress would be Nelay's to keep as a token of their promises.

She wondered what Rycus would have given her. Probably some throwing knives. She would have berated him for it. And he would have teased her until she laughed and forgave him. At the thought of him, a sad smile touched the corners of her mouth.

The headdress dropped in the oil, pulling down the wick and anchoring it in place. More priestesses lit the marriage channels behind the throne. Flames shot up the walls and then toward the golden phoenix. The flames started in the bird's chest before exploding outward along its spread wings.

Four priestesses raised the vessel of oil in time to touch the first flames from the bird's burning beak. The wick burned in a rainbow of colors, everything from green to magenta. Then the women placed a silk shade around the vessel to keep it from being blown out and hurried off to place it in a windless room in the temple, where they would stand guard over it through the night. It was said a flame that went out before morning meant the marriage would end badly.

Nelay was half temped to trip one of them just to make it official, but it would only incense the people.

Zatal held out his hand, and she rested hers on top of his. He led her to a door to the side of the throne, with Suka, Maran, and Jezzel directly behind them. Behind the throne and to the left was a corridor, a length of curling stairs off to one side, which they climbed, coming above the phoenix and crossing a bridge that bisected the throne room from above.

They came out onto a balcony, where the rest of the populace was waiting. Suka came to stand beside them. "I give you Zatal, King of Kings, and his wife, Queen Nelay."

The people cheered and lit their silk lanterns. The flames caught and the lanterns rose up into the night in graceful, twisting waves of gold and red.

And with that they were married.

Nelay watched the crowd, wondering if somewhere Rycus was watching this spectacle. If his heart was breaking as hers was.

Zatal took her hand. Nelay raised her eyes and looked into the eyes of her husband. His gaze was soft with compassion and pleading, as if he was asking her to at least try. It was then that the horns sounded—the blaring warning horns of the outer gates. The Clansmen had come.

CHAPTER TWENTY-FIVE

Z atal whirled around and cut through the entourage, crossing the corridor and calling as he went, "War Council, to the observation tower! Immortals, to the wall!"

Immediately, the soldiers tucked their spears under their arms and marched double time from the throne room as noblemen backed away, clearly distressed.

Jezzel dropped in next to Nelay. "Bet you wish they'd let you wear your swords."

She didn't answer as she ran after her husband. At the bottom of the steps, Zatal turned and leveled his gaze at someone just past Nelay. She turned to see Suka close behind them. "This better work, High Priestess, or we're all dead."

Suka's gaze was distant. "Let us hope so, my king."

Zatal hustled away, his war council falling into step behind him. Suka turned to Maran. "Go prepare her rooms. I'll bring her up shortly." Then she gazed flatly at Nelay. "Come with me."

Nelay and Jezzel exchanged glances before following Suka across the throne room, which was still packed with panicked nobles. The high priestess didn't speak as they traversed a corridor, passing great dining rooms, sitting rooms, and a gaming room. Finally, she approached the south side of the palace.

Two priestesses dressed in the armor of the Goddess Army stood at the door. Nelay knew what was beyond that door, though she'd never been there herself. The gardens over the old luminash mines.

"Did you clear the garden?" Suka asked.

They both bowed. "Yes, High Priestess. We checked it twice."

"And Siseth?"

One of the priestesses wet her lips nervously. "She's there."

Nelay froze. She hadn't heard that name in nine years, not since she'd been taken from her family. Not since the snake fairy had warned her that the price of asking for a fairy's help was always too high.

"Is that the fairy who bit you?" Jezzel asked.

Nelay nodded.

Jezzel palmed one of her knives, but Suka turned, her eyes narrowing. "You will wait for Nelay in her rooms."

Jezzel glanced at the priestesses then back at Nelay, her gaze asking if she wanted her to kick the high priestess's teeth in.

Suppressing a smile, Nelay gave a slight shake of her head. "I want answers."

Jezzel relaxed, slipping her knife back into its sheath and leaning against the wall, right next to the door, with one foot cocked.

"I said, back in Nelay's rooms," said Suka tightly.

Jezzel ground her teeth, obviously wanting to argue, but Nelay knew there was still a big part of her that wanted to be the Priestess Commander someday. Talking back to Suka was a good way to never see that happen.

"Go," Nelay said. "I'll be fine."

Jezzel pushed off from the wall. "I'm supposed to be your guard. You're not even armed."

"One of my priestesses will escort her to her rooms," Suka said with a tip of her head toward the two women still standing at the doorway.

Nelay nodded encouragingly to Jezzel, who made a sound halfway between a growl and a hiss and handed Nelay one of her throwing knives. Nelay nodded goodbye to her friend before she took off down the corridor.

Suka pushed the door open, just enough for them to slip through. Beyond was a garden the likes of which Nelay had never seen. Trees so heavy with fruit they bowed to the ground under the weight. Flowers growing in a purple carpet of lushness. But what shocked Nelay the most was the lake. She'd never seen that much water. It moved even though it had nowhere to go, lapping against the shore. And so blue! Not a bit of brown anywhere. She felt herself drawn to it, aching to feel the cool touch against her skin, wishing Rycus was here to share it with her.

But then she realized Suka was crouched beside a bush heavy with clusters of red berries, the blackened remnants of petals covering the roots. "Are you certain?" she whispered.

The high priestess was conversing with fairies.

"How long?" Suka asked. At the answer, her face went grim. "Good. Good. She'll be weak, and battles to the north grow in pitch. She'll be distracted."

Nelay stepped closer and peered into the thorny bush. She gasped and stumbled back, for a viper was inside. It wasn't very large, only about the length of her hand, but even a newly hatched viper was deadly.

"It's not what it appears," Suka said.

That didn't make Nelay feel better. "I know." Nelay hated snakes, but she was more afraid of the fairies. As her mother had always said, they were tricksy and cruel.

"It is time for you to have your Sight back," Suka said, her expression rapturous as she gazed at the snake.

Nelay's gaze jerked from the snake's beady eyes to Suka's. There was something in the other woman's gaze, the lengths she'd gone to bring Nelay back to the temple—to even find her in the first place. It all came down to this. The thought sent a cold shiver of dread down her spine. "What have you asked of them? And what did they promise in return?"

"You'll find out soon enough," Suka replied.

Nelay slowly shook her head. "Whatever they have promised you will cost more than you are willing to pay. I should know, for I've paid their price before." Nelay had asked the fairies to save her father's life, and in return her infant brother had died. And then she had been taken from her family, never to see them again.

Then there was the promise she had made. A promise to grant the fairies a favor—anything they asked her. She had lived in dread of the moment that cost came due and had a feeling that moment was now.

Suka's eyes flashed with challenge. "I will pay any price."

A month or so ago, Nelay might have been thrilled to finally be the perfect acolyte with the perfect Sight. But now, she didn't want it—didn't want any of it. "I swear, I'll go somewhere you can never find me," she announced.

"That place does not exist. Haven't you realized that yet?" Suka looked down at the snake that was not a snake. "I suppose we'll have to do this the hard way then."

The snake shot forward so fast Nelay could do little more than tense. It sank its fangs into her leg, shooting barbs up her calf and the back of her knee. She threw herself back, trying to get away before the snake bit her again. But it was only staring at her with an intelligence that belied its form.

Then the creature's outlines became hazy and distorted before they melted, shrinking in length and growing in girth. Round eyes became almond-shaped. The face flattened, the slitted nostrils turning round and shifting into place on her face. The fairy's eyes were solid pools of black. Thick coils of hair spread from a knot in the top of her head. The snake's scales spread and split, becoming wings with sharp points. Her dress was made of scales, as were her boots over her long, pointed feet.

Nelay had not seen a fairy since she was nine years old—and this fairy in particular since she'd given her a gift that had turned out to be a curse. Hate welled up inside Nelay. She had thought herself incapable of forgetting their cruel faces, their expressions void of any emotion besides cunning. But she'd been wrong. They were far more terrible than she remembered.

She gasped as the pain left her. She looked down at her ankle and discovered two puncture marks dripping fluids. This was not the first time this fairy had envenomed her. "You took away my Sight—the first time you bit me."

Siseth grunted. "And now I've given it back."

"Why?" Nelay panted.

The fairy didn't answer at first. "Because the fairies notice those with the Sight. I couldn't risk the Summer Queen finding out what you are."

"Summer Queen?"

"I used to call her Goddess of Fire," Suka answered. "But that is not what the fairies call her, and not what I call her anymore." She took a long breath. "Her real name is Leto. Did you know that?"

The high priestess didn't seem to expect an answer, and Nelay didn't give one. She was having difficulty thinking of the goddess as a queen; it was simply too human.

She looked around the garden, knowing what she would see. Fairies were everywhere. What had looked like a bird crouched in a tree was really a fairy with feather wings. What Nelay had thought was a branch was really a fairy's lithe brown body with leaves and poison-white-berry-colored eyes with black pupils.

"If I'm part of your plan, why did you keep all of this a secret from me?" Nelay asked.

"Leto's spies are always listening. Had she known what you were, she would have killed you as a child," said a soft, feminine voice, her tongue smacking stickily to the inside of her mouth. "But the queen is no match for the eyes we have everywhere."

The speaker, another fairy, scuttled from the undergrowth. In addition to the eyes in her face, six black, bulbous orbs protruded from the mane of hair piled atop her head. Her wings were woven of spider silk, and she wore what looked like a fur collar and a short, thick fur skirt.

As she came closer, Nelay realized it wasn't fur but spider hair. She shuddered in revulsion. "You," she gasped. This was the spider she'd impaled and thrown into the fire. The same fairy who'd tapped on the glass the day Sopora was invaded.

"Ah, Tix," Siseth said. "What have your spies found?"

"We may speak without Leto's spies listening," Tix replied. "And that hurt." The fairy shuddered. "It hurt very badly."

Nelay glared at the fairies as her memories rose up. One in particular started the wheels of her mind spinning. The fairies always cleared out when she lit a fire. "The incense—all through the temple?" She directed her words to the high priestess.

Suka tipped her head in acknowledgment. "I was trying to keep any enemy fairies away from you. Away from our plans."

Nelay glanced at all the fairies in turn. "Why me?"

Siseth flew back and forth, almost hypnotically. "Because you have more than the Sight, Nelay. You have the gift of life."

"Doesn't everyone?" She couldn't help the sarcasm that dripped from her mouth.

Siseth hissed, her black tongue flicking out of her mouth. "No. It is the rarest of gifts. It is why you have never been sick. Why you are stronger, faster—why you survive wounds that would kill any other mortal. And why we searched for twenty years before we found you."

So they'd been searching for her before she'd even been born. Nelay thought she'd known fear before, but she was wrong. For she felt it now, down to her very core. Whatever Suka had promised them, Nelay was to pay at least part of the price. "I don't understand."

"Not everyone can be a Summer Queen," Suka answered. "Only those with the gift of life—those who've tasted a petal from an elice flower. Only they are strong enough to survive the transformation."

"As those who become the Winter Queen must be touched by death," Tix mused.

"There used to be dozens of them to choose from—three every year," Siseth said. "But not anymore. For Leto gives the elice flower to the Winter Queen—Ilyenna—to prevent her daughter and husband from aging. The other petal Leto gives to her own husband. This goes against the Balance!"

"Why do you call them queens when they are goddesses?" Nelay asked.

"They are not goddesses to us," Tix answered.

It had all begun when Nelay's mother had bargained for a flower from the fairies. Had she known the price of that bargain then? The lengths she'd gone to keep Nelay's Sight hidden indicated that she had.

"What do you want from me?" Nelay asked.

"It's really very simple," Suka said. "I promised that you would kill Leto. That you would become the next Summer Queen."

They couldn't mean what she thought they meant. "That's impossible!"

"I assure you, it is not," Tix said.

"She's a goddess—I'm a mortal!" Nelay protested. "And I've worshipped her since I was a child!"

"She was once mortal, just as you are." Nelay watched as another fairy flew toward them and landed in a crouch on a boulder. Her unnaturally blue eyes matched her liquid hair. Water dripped from her body. Everywhere she touched, vibrant green moss grew.

"Leto killed the previous Summer Queen," the moss fairy said. "As you will kill Leto."

"Nos," Tix said to the moss fairy, "you risk breaking the web."

Nelay had no idea what that meant. "I won't be your player in this sick game."

Siseth opened her black mouth in a wide smile, her white fangs standing out in sharp relief. "You don't have a choice."

The promise Nelay had made, to do a favor for Siseth someday. Nelay's mind whirled, sorting through players and surveying the field. "I lied."

Siseth hissed. "It's not a promise you can break, fight it as you may."

Nelay shook her head as she backed away. "No," she said with certainty. "You can't force me, and you can't harm me. I'm too important to your plan."

"You act as though this promise is something I must enforce," Siseth said, "something you can escape. But when the time is right, you will keep the promise. The Balance will see to it—if you survive long enough."

Nelay whirled around and started off, but Suka ran to her and gripped her shoulder. Nelay swung her arm around, trapping the high priestess's hand. She drove Suka and pinned her against a palm tree, her forearm wedged against the older woman's throat. Suka clawed uselessly at her grip. "So I kill their queen and take her place," Nelay growled. "And what do you get? More wealth? More power?"

Suka's eyes bulged and she struggled to speak. "They promised to save Idara."

Stunned, Nelay let her go. The woman crumpled to the ground, gasping for breath. "Even if they did," Nelay said, "Idara would be blighted and broken beyond repair. That's how their promises work!" She glanced at all the fairies in turn. "Their price is too high. It always was. My life is my own—my choices my own. And I will not do this. I will find another way."

Nelay whirled and started toward the palace, but the snake fairy was suddenly before her, fangs bared. Nelay staggered to a halt.

"Ilyenna is helping the Clansmen," Suka gasped. "She's behind the blizzard that destroyed our army when they invaded the clanlands twenty years ago. The storm that sank our navy earlier this year. She's the reason for your parents' deaths."

Suddenly unable to get enough air, Nelay turned slowly to face Suka. "Did they tell you that? The fairies?"

Suka's mouth tightened. "Leto and Ilyenna are friends. Leto is letting Ilyenna and her army invade Idara and destroy her people and the temples where she is worshipped. She cares more for the woman who should be her enemy than her own subjects!"

Nelay stormed back to Suka, who recoiled, but Nelay simply crouched before her. "They will tell you anything—anything—to get what they want."

"Then how do you explain the clanlands invading the most powerful nation in the world within a few weeks? How do you explain the way they topple our cities, our strongholds?"

Nelay's resolve faltered a little, but she braced herself and stood back up. "Because they have some weapon we don't understand."

"You're letting fear blind you," Suka said, the fight seeming to drain out of her.

Nelay frowned. "Why would the Goddess of Fire—Leto—betray us? We worship her!"

"Because of what Idara did," Suka replied. "They call us Raiders in the clanlands. Our kingdom has killed hundreds of thousands of people. Enslaved others, forcing them to let go of their traditions and beliefs in favor of ours."

Nelay remembered Dobber calling her a Raider not long after she'd been captured.

"Leto thinks Idara deserves to be punished—to be crippled so we can never harm the world again. She refuses to see that Idara is simply the dark side of the Balance, bringing destruction and chaos to offset peace and order."

Nelay gaped at Suka. "We brought order and civilization." Even as the words left Nelay's mouth, she wasn't sure she believed them anymore. She rounded on the fairies. "And why should we believe you? You've already proven yourselves traitors, and all traitors are liars by necessity."

Nos took to the air, her wings beating furiously. "It is Leto who has betrayed summer!"

"Why would we lie?" Siseth asked.

Nelay studied the fairy whose interference in her life had changed it irrevocably once before. She would not make the mistake of letting it happen again. "You don't want what's good for Idara. You want what's good for yourself. And I will not be used."

"Our interests align!" Suka insisted as she arose to grasp Nelay's forearms.

Nelay shook her off. "You are a fool to trust them." She heard the city horns in the distance, calling the soldiers to the wall and urging Thanjavar to defend itself. Stand up or fall, a fall from which Idara would never rise again. And Nelay realized all her plans to run away and find Rycus would have to wait. She could not leave Idara on the brink of collapse, not when there was a chance she could help save her people. The realization left her heart broken all over again.

She pushed open the doors and fled down the hall and into the throne room, one of the priestesses falling in behind her. The jangle of gold announced Nelay's presence, her silk robes flaring out behind her. The veil slipped from her head and puddled on the floor in a pile of silk and gold.

She passed servants, soldiers, ladies and lords. Her hair came loose, streaming behind her as she flew up the grand staircase through hundreds of delicate arches. She entered her rooms and slammed the door shut on the priestess guard. Nelay flew passed the large table, the sitting area, and the fireplace to her bedroom.

At the sight of her, Maran jumped from a chair. But it was to Jezzel that Nelay went, for she stood on the round balcony, her hands behind her back as she looked out over the city. Nelay followed her gaze, heart in her throat. She was too far away to make out anything more than squares of Clansmen that were more texture than shape. The mass went on as far as she could see.

"What did she want?" Jezzel asked.

In as few words as possible, Nelay told her. Jezzel listened without interruption, her eyebrows climbing higher and higher. Nelay considered telling her friend about Rycus, but wanted to save that conversation for a happier time.

When she had finished, they stood quietly for a moment before she asked, "Do you believe Suka?"

"No," Jezzel answered softly. "If for no other reason than the ridiculousness of the Goddess of Fire freely giving up her lands to her mortal enemy."

Relieved, Nelay felt herself relax.

"In a couple days, they'll have us surrounded," Jezzel said matter-of-factly, but inside Nelay knew she was angry and terrified.

Nelay covered her mouth with her hand in an effort to keep her emotions from spilling out.

"They're setting up their siege engines now. They'll attack tonight."

"And will we hold them?" Nelay asked in a small voice.

Jezzel didn't answer for a long time. "I don't know."

CHAPTER TWENTY-SIX

Nelay sat straight up in bed, her heart pounding. At first she feared Zatal was somewhere in her rooms, but then she heard the distant crashes. She pushed her way through the lake of blankets on her bed, stumbling when one refused to let go of her leg, and ran to the balcony. She got there just in time to hear the distant sound of a boulder slamming into the wall.

From her vantage point, she could see hundreds of torches along the balustrades, and tiny figures running to and fro along the wall. She rested her hands on the top of the banister. Another round hit the wall. Though Nelay could not see where it struck, she could guess, for the torches shook and men scrambled along that portion of the wall.

Idaran soldiers let loose their arrows. Nelay lost the shafts in the dark, but she imagined them striking the Clansmen. Above all of this was the moon, blood-red from the rising smoke. Remembering what Rycus had said about the moon being the soul of a woman, she couldn't help but think that woman must be weeping now.

"You can stop this—your people dying."

Nelay jumped and turned her head, coming face to face with Tix, who hung upside down from an invisible thread of spider web. "As if I would trust anything you say," Nelay replied.

She'd had more time to process what had happened in the garden and was even surer she was right about the fairies.

Tix chuckled darkly. "It isn't about trust. It's about what you must do and what you must not do."

"Do you think I'm a fool? You would have me end this war only to start another with the Goddess of Winter—one that would consume every kingdom and land the world over. How many would die in that war?"

"You can choose not to fight."

Nelay crossed her arms over her chest. "You didn't turn me over to Zatal when I was in Dalarta. Why?"

The fairy sniffed. "Zatal is an extraneous part of our plan."

Which meant Panar really had turned Nelay over. She shot the fairy a haughty glare. "My mother said whenever goddesses and mortals mix, mortals always lose. I'm not a fool. You're asking for more than my taking a goddess's life. I'll lose mine as well, won't I?"

"Very clever," Tix responded after a while.

"I've had time to process."

"Yes. As queen, your soul will burn and you will arise from the ashes reborn."

"One thing I don't understand. Why did you marry me off to the king?"

"That was Suka's condition. The queens who are bound to a consort are protective of them, and by extension, the people that consort loves. The consorts also help them regain their humanity."

"Even when I hate my consort?" Nelay huffed.

"Ilyenna hated her consort too. My spies heard her say it. Yet because of him she retained a measure of her humanity." The fairy flicked her wings in annoyance. "Personally, I like the wars."

Nelay ground her teeth. "That's because you cannot die."

"I can die," the fairy reminded her.

Nelay threw up her hands in exasperation. "Only to be immediately reborn."

"Well, it is painful. Especially when one is stabbed and then burned to a crisp."

Nelay wasn't sorry. "And what makes you think I won't turn on you the moment I'm made a goddess?"

The fairy's wings stiffened. "You will need allies. You won't remain our queen long if you kill all of them."

Nelay knew, deep in her heart, that if she accepted this, she would change beyond recognition, and not for the better. The wars that would follow, with two goddesses with armies of fairies bent on killing each other—how many thousands would die? "Thanjavar will stand—and we will stand without your interference." Her voice shook as she said it, but she could not trust the fairies. Of that she was absolutely certain.

Tix watched her with an unreadable expression. "The web has already been spun, Nelay Arel Mandana ShaBejan. Every spider worth its eyes knows to stay out of sight while we wait for you to fly into that web."

Nelay's brows went up. "So you're going to leave me alone."

"We have never really left you alone. Yet you did not know it."

Furious, Nelay stepped forward and blew hard on Tix, sending her spinning over the balcony. She snapped her wings out, catching herself, and glared at Nelay with her eight eyes. In response, Nelay slammed her balcony doors. She stepped to her wardrobe and fumbled about in the dark for her boots.

Maran must have heard her rummaging around, for she shuffled into sight, a terracotta lamp in hand and her robes twisted awry. "May I be of assistance, my queen?"

"Just bring the light closer." Nelay pulled on a pair of silk bell-shaped trousers, tied the drawstring at her waist, and added a long tunic with slits up the side for movement. All the while, she was aware of Maran watching her. "I'm—I'm glad you're here, Maran. I need friends about me."

Maran set the lamp down and helped her strap on her scabbards—Nelay's back was still stiff and it was difficult to lift her arm over her head. "I'm just grateful you got Concon and me out of Dalarta before it fell."

"And Sedun . . ." What Nelay really wanted to ask was why Maran would ever go back to that selfish coward. But she hesitated, not wanting to start another fight.

Maran didn't answer for a moment. "He made it out before the city was overrun. He's in Thanjavar now."

Lovely, Nelay thought.

"And Rycus?" Maran said, her eyes downcast. "Did . . . did the king let him go?"

Nelay froze, her longing temporarily robbing her of strength. She started moving again slowly. "He's alive."

"Are you going to escape and go to him?"

Nelay gave her a small smile. Of course she would. As soon as she could manage it. But secrets are only secrets if you keep silent, even with those you trust.

When Nelay didn't answer, Maran said, "Do . . . do you really think I'm timid?"

Nelay sighed. "Do you want me to be honest or do you want me to make you feel better?"

Maran looked away. "It's not fair for you to judge me. You haven't been through what I have."

Nelay laced her boots. "I suppose that's true. But Maran, what do you think? Do you like who you are? Because if not, start changing it."

The girl wouldn't look at her. "I don't know how."

Nelay stood. "If you want to change who you are, surround yourself with people who make you better. Then work on yourself one day at a time." Taking the lamp, she started out the door.

"Go back to bed. I'm sure Concon will keep you up enough for the both of us."

Nelay stepped into the halls. The pair of guards at her door snapped to attention. Both were about the same age, both bearing the scars of war. One had an ear that was grossly deformed and twice the size of its mate—it was a common enough malady in soldiers. And he was ugly. Very, very ugly.

The other had a nose that appeared to have been broken so many times it had given up any hope of keeping its shape and had flattened to a lumpy mass. She wondered if Zatal had chosen these men so as not to tempt her, or simply for their skills. Knowing her husband, probably both.

Jezzel was nowhere to be seen—she was probably asleep.

Ignoring the soldiers, Nelay held her lamp out before her. It only lit about five steps on all sides. She moved through the corridor toward the stairs, dismayed when the guards followed five paces behind. A sense of loss washed over her. A maid and now guards. Not to mention her new husband. How was she ever going to slip away from all of them and go to Rycus?

Nelay stood at the banister and rested her hands on the cool marble as she looked down at the throne room, the phoenix gleaming darkly below her. Before her, the suspended bridge led to the public balcony. Every few steps there were four marble pillars bracing up an intricate almost lacy arch. The banister beneath her hands was a fine miniature of the larger pillars and their decorative arches. All the cool beauty seemed at odds with the explosions she could hear, and the pitched battle she could not. Idarans were dying.

Nelay turned toward her guards, acknowledging them for the first time since she'd left her rooms. "What are your names?"

The men seemed taken back that she could even speak. "Hazar," said the uglier of the two, the one with the bloated ear.

The other didn't reply at first. "Ahzem," he finally said grudgingly, his voice sounding every bit as nasally as Nelay imagined.

"Where are the king's rooms?"

Ahzem hesitated. "My queen . . ."

"Show me."

Hazar made a sound low in his throat, but then he tipped his head to the left. "That way."

She hesitated, uncertain in the dark. "Can't you just show me?"

"We are not allowed to proceed you except in your defense, my queen," Ahzem said.

"Oh." What a stupid rule. She strode forward until she could see a corridor. She cast a glance back at Hazar, who gave a slight nod. She turned to enter the hallway, but froze at the sight of a hunched form scrambling over something, a lamp sitting to one side.

Nelay first thought was of assassins and thieves and any number of nasty things. Her guards started past her, but she held out her hand as realization washed over her. The shape was too small. No bigger than a child. This was one of Zatal's children—who else could it be?

She forced her wooden legs to stir and came upon a girl scraping the last of a scattering of sweets into a basket. She turned as she heard them, the light from her lamp casting harsh shadows across her face. Nelay saw her husband in the child's jaw, her nose, the spark of intelligence in her deep-set eyes.

The girl's face darkened. Nelay knelt beside her, picked up the last pastry, and set it carefully in the basket. "You don't deserve to be queen!" the child blurted.

"If it makes you feel better, I don't want to be."

The little girl stood, the basket slung over her arm. "It should be Mother—he loves her, not you."

"Yes," Nelay said simply.

The child deflated and then took off at a run, abandoning the lamp where it lay. Nelay watched her stop at a door and push it open. The sounds of a child crying emerged from within. Nelay wondered how many children Zatal had.

"I brought the treats," the girl said, then shut the door behind her.

If listening to the distant sounds of battle frightened Nelay, she couldn't imagine how terrified the children were. The girl must have been sent to the kitchens for something to keep the younger ones happy. These people—these strangers—loved each other.

Nelay closed her eyes, missing Rycus so much in that moment and wishing he was there with her. He would tell her a story or tease her. And she would forget her fears and worries, at least for a moment.

She cast a pleading look back at the guards. Hazar pointed to the door across the hall from the one the girl had just entered. "There."

Zatal's rooms were right next to his mistress's, while Nelay was in a separate corridor. She didn't want him as her husband, so why did that sting so much? She stood, her knees popping, and approached the door, her limbs heavy and hopeless. She forced herself to knock. But there was no sound from inside. She rested her forehead against the richly carved wood.

"My queen?" Hazar said. "He's probably with his war council."

"Where?"

The two guards shifted their feet but didn't speak.

Nelay raised an eyebrow. "Did the king forbid me?"

"No," Hazar finally said.

She a hard smile slipped over her face and tipped her head to the side so her tattoos showed. "I am not just a woman. I am a priestess of fire." And if Suka had her way, she'd be murdering the woman they worshiped. "And I am a queen."

CHAPTER
TWENTY-SEVEN

Nelay stared her guards down, waiting for one of them to crack.

"The observation dome is the highest tower." Hazar blurted. Ahzem shot him a dark look.

After blowing out the lamp left by the child, Nelay hurried downstairs to a corridor behind the throne room. There were doors all along it, but she instinctively headed for the heavy one at the end. She pushed it open and came into a wide, round room.

In the center was an enormous, circular table surrounded by chairs and cluttered with maps and scrolls. Men looked up at her as she entered, their faces registering shock. The king was not here, but there were two more doors. "Which one?" Nelay asked her guards under her breath.

Hazar tipped his head to the door on the left. With shoulders thrown back, Nelay marched through the open door and was met by a set of spiraling stairs that went on and on above her. Taking a deep breath, she started up them. They spiraled tighter the higher she went. Her thighs ached and sweat beaded her brow, but she refused to slow down.

At the top of the stairs, she emerged onto the highest tower. There were no walls, only four wide columns to hold up the gold-plated dome roof. In the center of the space sat a huge marble brazier filled with burning embers. Nelay could only assume it was there to ward of the nightly chill. Immortals were everywhere, all wearing scale armor at their chests and leather armor skirts. Their helmets bore the embossed designs that mirrored their scalp tattoos.

Nearest the stairs, she passed nearly a dozen wiry boys, each wearing a simple tunic and a messenger tube. As she walked into the tower, conversations stilled one at a time. She moved to one of the framed arches and felt the heat of the flames as she stared out over the city.

The city's outer walls were thick and high—easily ten stories. Inside were homes and shops, growing in size and grandeur as they neared the palace's walls, with the temple nestled inside.

If the city wall fell, the only retreat was within the palace. And those walls were scarcely five stories tall, made to keep citizens out more than an army, though someone with forethought had built in seize engines. Still, they wouldn't hold long.

Nelay prowled the perimeter of the tower, realizing with dismay that the Clansmen had the city completely surrounded. Their armies extended for as far as she could see. There had to be at least five hundred thousand of them to Thanjavar's one hundred thousand. Even if she had an opportunity to escape Zatal, there was no way she could move past those armies.

The king suddenly appeared at her side. "What are you doing here?"

She spared him a quick glance. "Did you know about Suka's plan?"

He glanced around and stepped closer. One little push, and he could send her toppling past the railing and into oblivion. "Why do you think I agreed to marry you in the first place?"

She looked up at him. "Why not tell me?" He leaned closer, and she couldn't help but compare him to his daughter.

"Because they are always listening," he said, his words full of meaning.

Nelay sucked in a breath. Thinking of Tix, she knew he was right.

"I don't have time for this now, Nelay. Get—"

"King Zatal!" shouted an older man with a neatly trimmed beard. The tattoos on his helmet marked him as the high commander, leader of all Idara's fighting forces. He pointed toward the west wall.

Zatal hurried toward him, raising his telescope. "What is it, Nashur?"

Forgotten, Nelay followed close behind. Passing a small table with more telescopes, she snatched one. She extended it and brought it to her eye as she stepped even with the men, one step from falling into the dark night. It took her a moment to get her bearings, but when she did, she understood the men's reaction. One of the city gates had fallen. Clansmen fought hand to hand with Immortals, their bodies highlighted bizarrely by flashes of torchlight.

So quickly? It hadn't even been an hour. Nelay's thoughts went to Suka's warning, the fairies' predictions, but she quickly pushed them out of her head.

"They're going to be overrun," Zatal said as if to himself, then ordered loudly, "Send in the reserves—Dubha's division!"

A man standing at attention to the side of the brazier scooped a cup of luminash from one of a dozen or so bowls on the table and scattered the contents across the embers. Blue-green flames shot up, washing everything in a strange glow. The man lifted the ram's horn he wore around his neck and blew a long, trilling note that rounded out at the end. Then he paused and blew the same note again.

Nelay peered through the telescope again. Reserves had been strategically positioned between each gate. One group was marching double time, their torch flames nearly horizontal for their speed. "How do they know where to go?" she asked.

Nashur, the man who'd called for the king, was scanning with his telescope. "Ever heard of a color wheel?"

"Like a rainbow but in a circle?" She couldn't see what that had to do with anything.

"Each division has a melody the horn calls out," he said without looking at her. "Each compass point has a color—north, yellow; east, red-orange; south, purple; west, blue-green. The quadrants between them are gradients of those colors. Twelve colors in all. The melody calls up a division, the color tells them where to go."

Nelay read over the color-labeled bowls. "And no one ever mixes up blue-purple, purple, and red-purple?"

"Our Immortals are well trained," Nashur replied.

"King Zatal!" a general shouted. Nelay didn't need her telescope to see that another gate had fallen.

"Send Hozer's division!" the king roared.

Another burst of color. The horn sounded again, a long blast followed by four bursts.

"How are they getting through the portcullis and gates so easily?" Nelay quietly asked Nashur.

He looked at her then, a gleam of grim fascination in his eyes. "They freeze them."

She reeled back, wondering if Suka could be right. But the Goddess of Winter couldn't be behind this. The Clansmen must have some weapon, something like luminash, only instead of fire, it brought cold. "Freeze them? How?"

"If we knew that, we'd be able to stop them," Nashur answered. "But it always follows a pattern—they only hit one or two gates. And they always wait about two or three days before they freeze them again." Before Nelay could question him further, he cried, "The Borz Gate is about to fall!"

Three gates had fallen, all next to each other. The reserves were busy fighting back the encroaching Clansmen. If another gate fell, they wouldn't have any reserves to plug the hole.

King Zatal ground his teeth. As he hesitated, another gate came under siege, and then another. "Bring them in from other gates."

"But King Zatal, if they breach one of the gates that doesn't have reserves, they'll enter the city unmolested," said a man Nelay didn't know.

"If we don't do something, they're going to enter the city now!" Nashur roared.

Zatal pointed to one of several wiry men lined up near the stairs. "Go to the woodworker's guild and have them start on new doors—now! Thick and strong. I don't care what they look like." As the man turned to go, the king pointed to another. "And have the iron workers see if they can't reinforce them."

Two young men took off at a sprint.

Zatal pointed to another man. "Round up the palace guards. Send them to the Avarta Gate." Even as that man left, the king was speaking to a third. "Go down every street—call for every able-bodied man or woman and have them report to the nearest gate with whatever weapon they can find."

The man next to Nelay spoke up. "It would take hours combing the streets to round them all up. Avarta needs soldiers now."

"What do you want me to do, Nashur?" growled the king. "I'm running out of men!"

"Send the priestesses," Nelay blurted. She didn't mean to say anything, but they were missing key players that were at their disposal.

The king whirled toward her. She met his frantic gaze with a steady one. "Send the Priestess Army."

"But . . ." Nashur couldn't seem to finish the thought.

"The Priestess Army only marches at the high priestess's orders," Zatal said.

The wind picked up, sending smoke straight at Nelay. "If you ask, they will fight, Suka's order or not. They aren't called an army for nothing. And we'll die with the rest of the city if those gates fall."

The king paused for a moment, then pointed to another messenger. "Go! Beg them on your knees if you must. Tell them their people need them at the Borz Gate!" When the man hesitated, the king shoved him. "Go, man!"

The soldier took off and the king shrugged into his cross baldric.

"Where are you going?" Nashur asked.

"My guards are the finest warriors in all the world. You're in charge until my return." Nelay realized Zatal meant to fight with his men.

"You can't risk yourself, my king," Nashur said darkly. "Not like this."

Flames of anger seemed to burn behind Zatal's eyes. He gripped Nashur's chest armor and shook him. "Idara—the strongest nation in the world—falls to the Clansmen in a few short weeks. We can't even hold our last city for a night! I'll not stay here, sniveling like a coward while they take everything we are!"

He shoved Nashur away and spoke to Nelay, "If the city is breeched, seal the palace gates. The defenses won't hold up long—not against five hundred thousand men. Your best chance is to outlast the pillaging and rape. When they offer you surrender, take it. And hope they don't murder you the moment your weapons are gone."

He started down the stairs. Terror buffeted Nelay, leaving her raw from the inside out. "Call for the Tribesmen!" she shouted to Zatal when she could see only his head and shoulders. "We need more players on our side—allies! If the desert tribes attack from without, we might survive this."

"I already asked." The king met her gaze. "They will not come." He trotted out of sight without waiting for her response.

Which was for the best, because she was struck speechless. Rycus and his men would have come. And she'd come to think all the Tribesmen were like him. Gathering her wits about her, Nelay pounded down the stairs after the king, squeezing past generals, messengers, and soldiers. Finally, she caught up to Zatal.

He glanced askance at her. "What are you doing?"

"I'm coming with you."

"No."

"I can fight."

"No."

"But—"

He whirled on her. "If I am killed, who rules Idara?"

She froze, all the blood draining from her face. He must have seen the recognition in her eyes.

"Suka says you are important, Nelay—the only person who can save Idara. You will stay back, where it is safe. And if the city falls, you will beg the Clansmen to spare what remains."

With a start, the king seemed to remember himself, gazing around at his entourage of Immortals, who had come to a standstill. "Now, don't make me waste resources making sure you obey."

"If you go, you will die." She was certain of it.

"I'd rather die in battle than be crucified by Clansmen later," Zatal said. He pivoted and rushed away, his Immortals following him.

As soldiers streamed around her, Nelay stood frozen in place, unable to think past the ringing in her ears. When everyone had moved on, she climbed the stairs like a forgotten ghost. Immortals called out colors that appeared in flashes of smoke. The horns rang out again and again, a combination of bursts and long, wailing notes.

Nelay turned to one of the messengers. "Find the head of my guard, Jezzel, and bring her to me."

The messenger hesitated as if unsure he should obey her, but then he pivoted and took off. Realizing she still held a telescope, Nelay brought it to her face to search for the king and his men. She was starting to wonder if the messenger had obeyed her at all when she heard a voice behind her.

"You've already infuriated the king?"

Nelay turned to see Jezzel, arms crossed over her armor. Judging by how rumpled her clothes were, she'd slept in them.

"I seem to have a talent for it."

Jezzel glanced around, then snatched a telescope. "What's going on?"

"Several gates have fallen. Zatal sent in the reserves. He's sending out the priestesses and calling for any citizens who haven't already been drafted."

Jezzel inhaled sharply. "Fire and burning!"

Nelay adjusted her telescope to see what her friend saw. In the pale morning light, soldiers in multicolored tunics streamed past the gates. The Immortals fought like dragons, slaying the tide of Clansmen who broke across them. And for a moment, Nelay was sure the line would hold. But the Clansmen just kept coming, washing over and past the Idarans and streaming into the city. They were met by a rabble of Idarans, carrying sharpened sticks, clubs, knives, axes—weapons they dropped as they died. They didn't fight with the finesse and order of the Immortals, but they did not run as they tried to keep the Clansmen from advancing farther. The Immortals—those who had survived the initial onslaught—dropped back, adding their numbers.

"The line won't hold," Jezzel said.

The citizens were dying too fast, and the well from which the Clansmen drew was insatiable. On the side street, a big Idaran wielding a club went down. Clansmen broke past him, streaming into the streets. The Idarans and rabble tried to close the gap, but it was already too late.

"By the Go—" Nelay stopped herself from invoking the woman she had once worshiped. If what Suka had said was true, the Goddess of Fire was letting this happen.

"What . . . what if they were right? What if the goddess really has abandoned us?" Thanjavar—the strongest, most powerful city in all the world—had fallen in one day.

Jezzel slowly lowered her telescope. "No. I won't believe it." It came out as a half gasp, half whisper.

Nelay braced herself against one of the columns, wondering what would happen to them now. Would the Clansmen kill them all?

"Wait," Jez murmured. She brought the telescope back up. "Look! Look!"

It took Nelay a moment to find the gate again, but when she did, she saw guards from the palace, and she caught sight of King Zatal's shining helmet with red feathers at the crest. His swords whirled around him, carving a path through the Clansmen. Behind his men came the priestesses in their glorious armor. Slowly, the Idarans regrouped, pushing the Clansmen back towards the gates.

More citizens came. Zatal began rotating soldiers, giving those who'd been fighting on the front lines a break. Nelay watched the men at the back exchanging broken pieces of wood for more swords. Axes were taken from Clansmen's bodies. Steadily, the invaders were forced back. And then came the new doors, roughhewn planks hastily bound together. The Idarans pushed most of the Clansmen out and held them past the gates as craftsmen quickly ripped out the broken-down doors and installed the new ones.

The battle became sore, so much that bodies—lifeless or writhing in pain—were pulled out of the way. Finally, the craftsmen ran back, and the Immortals pulled back from the gap. The Clansmen pressed forward, but the Idaran archers let loose wave after wave. The huge doors swung shut, trapping numerous Clansmen inside, which the Immortals quickly dispatched.

Nelay searched for the king. "I can't find Zatal."

"We pushed them back!" Jez crowed. "Our Priestess Army pushed them back!"

Nelay scanned the wall. "The reserves and priestesses are moving to the other gates, but that was the worst one. The others are holding." She set the telescope on the table and hurried toward the stairs. "I'm going down there."

"What? You can't—"

Nelay was already running down the stairs, Jezzel hard on her heels. "The battle is over, Jezzel. I'm going."

"You go down there and you'll end up a dead woman's ashes!"

"We've been in worse."

"We have not! And that's counting the time we tried to sign up at that brothel."

Nelay whipped around. "Shut it! We don't need that story getting out."

Jezzel dropped her voice as low as she ever went, which wasn't very low at all. "Well, how else were we supposed to get Big Ozozo to tell us where the tunnels were?"

Nelay let out a snort of laugher before reining herself in. "Be quiet. That man has more spies than we do. And he's still looking for whoever drugged him and tied him up."

"It's the donkey he's mad about. Started all kinds of nasty rumors." Jezzel started giggling. Nelay shot her a dark look, but at the sight of tears building in Jezzel's eyes, Nelay started laughing too.

It was a little manic, a little hysterical, but it released the tension. Still, the looks the two friends got from passing commanders weren't appreciative.

Jezzel clapped Nelay on the shoulder. "There. Now you're loose enough to fight."

Nelay quickly hugged her friend. "Come on."

At the base of the staircase, the war room was nearly empty. Nelay crossed it and opened the door to two walls of very furious men, their mouths tight with anger. Fire and ashes! She'd forgotten the guards. The king must have berated them for letting her come to the observation tower before he plunged head first into suicide.

"Move," Jezzel commanded. They didn't obey.

Nelay glanced at her. *So my title is in name only. Insulting, but good to know.* She rested her hand on her sword hilt, ready to draw. "Do you really think you can stop us?"

The men's eyes widened—surely this was the first they'd ever encountered a queen eager for battle. A silent exchange passed between them and Nelay, and they backed away. She and Jezzel practically ran through the palace, the slap of their feet the only sound to break the stillness. The servants must have fled; perhaps they feared what would be done to them should the city fall.

CHAPTER TWENTY-EIGHT

Nelay only paused at the stables long enough to grab a magnificent black stallion—it was one of the king's, but she didn't really give the stable hand a chance to argue. Horses were also saddled for Jezzel, Ahzem, and Hazar, and they all left the palace at a dead run. The closer they came to the gates, the more people they passed, some of them recognizing Nelay.

"It's the new queen!"

"Has she come to fight?"

"Fool woman, get back where it's safe!"

"Hush. She's gone to see if the king is dead."

"Is he?"

Nelay pretended she couldn't hear them. Finally, she reached the Avarta gate. The streets were soaked with blood and covered with bodies. Some of the unmoving figures didn't even look dead yet, with color still in their cheeks, but their empty eyes, awkward positions, and wounds spoke the truth.

Many of the wounded cried out in agony. Women went among them, treating their friends and loved ones. Nelay recognized more than one of her fellow priestesses lying among the soldiers. The sight of their familiar faces tore at her chest. Meho was there—the girl who'd almost caught Nelay the day she fled the temple. The girl's chest was practically shredded. She reached toward Nelay and the others. "Help me!"

"Fire and burning," Jezzel said, tears choking her voice as she dismounted and ran to kneel at Meho's side.

Nelay watched her best friend. Jezzel hadn't yet learned how to recognize someone who was beyond helping.

"Jez," Meho said in a strained voice. "It hurts . . . so bad."

Trying to staunch the blood flow, Jezzel looked back to Nelay. "We have to get her to the healer!"

Never had she missed Rycus's steadying presence as much as she did at that moment. "Moving her would only cause her more pain."

"Please!" Tears streamed down Jezzel's face.

As much as Nelay wanted to help her friend, she couldn't go down there. She couldn't have memories of another Kalla to deal with. "She's bound for the wind," Nelay said softly. She felt Meho's gaze on her but refused to meet it. Then the girl's breathing turned to choking, and she died.

Jezzel stared down at the girl's still face. "She shouldn't have even been here. She was still an acolyte."

Nelay led Jezzel's horse to her side. She decided not to point out that they were technically still acolytes as well. "We need to go."

Jezzel wiped her face, obviously unaware that she was smearing blood on her cheeks, and climbed into the saddle. They rode out, Nelay sticking close to her friend, whose eyes were dull, all mischievousness gone. Is that how Nelay had been the first time she watched a friend die? "Sometimes it's better not to look," she told Jezzel. "You must let yourself go numb." What had Rycus said? "Take what you've seen and lock it up tight, and never look at it again."

Jezzel didn't respond, her eyes darting from one face to the next.

"We won't be able to do what has to be done if you look at them like that," Nelay said quietly. "Let the horses pick their way through. Keep your eyes on where you're going."

Nelay turned to Ahzem and Hazar, whose gazes were filled with empathy. Nelay wondered how many friends these men had watched die—if they even bothered making friends anymore. "We need to find the king," she said.

"Ask him." Ahzem pointed to an Immortal closer to the gates. His embossed helmet showed his high rank. He supervised the men gathering up the injured and laying them gently in carts pulled by water buffalo. For now they left the dead where they had fallen.

Nelay guided her nervous stallion toward the commander. At the sight of her, he gave an exhausted bow. "Queen Nelay."

"My husband . . ." she began, though it felt wrong to call Zatal that. "Is he alive?"

The commander pointed toward the wall. "He's there."

Nelay smiled. She didn't really like Zatal, but in that moment she realized she didn't hate him, either. She reined the horse toward the stairs built into the side of the wall. After tying their mounts to posts, she and Jezzel and the two guards climbed the stairs. Seeming to shake herself out of her daze, Jezzel insisted on taking the lead. At the top of the wall were dozens of soldiers. Zatal stood in their midst, looking out across the Clansmen's armies with his telescope.

The relief Nelay felt left her breathless. He hadn't consigned her to face this alone. She worked her way through the men toward him. "You're alive."

He jerked at the sound of her voice and looked her over before his accusing gaze fell on her guards.

"You really think they could have stopped me?" she said softly.

Zatal pursed his lips. "Apparently you're too selfish to consider that Idara needs one of us to survive. If the clanlands suddenly attack this wall, we could all die." He went back to his telescope.

She crossed her arms. "More selfish than you?"

"Why are you here?" he growled.

"I wanted to see if you'd killed yourself."

The king spoke to one of his commanders. "The Borz Gate is shut. They managed to hold them off during the installation. That's the last of them." He headed back down the stairs, his own personal guards following him.

Jezzel stepped up beside Nelay. "He's alive. Can we go look for our friends now?"

"Not yet." Nelay followed him and watched as he paused in front of the hastily built gate. This close, she could see the gaps between the boards. She crouched before a chunk of broken gate, stunned at the carnage. Four feet of solid wood reinforced with sheets of metal had been broken to bits as small as her fingers. "How did they do this?"

Zatal bent down, sorting through pieces. He tossed one her way. "See for yourself."

Nelay nearly dropped it. It was cold, so cold it burned her skin. She stepped in closer and felt cold radiating from the remnants of the door. She caught sight of a dead man half-buried in debris. His body was blue and ringed with what looked like jagged fur.

"Fire and ashes," Jezzel breathed. "What is that?"

"I'm told it's called hoarfrost," Zatal said.

Jezzel asked, "Is it a weapon?"

The king rubbed his bald head. "They pour a liquid on the gates. It looks like water, but it freezes so hard the Clansmen can shatter a gate with one swing of their battering rams."

Nelay looked up only to find Nos beating the air before her. "They did this," the fairy said. "Ilyenna's fairies."

"You're lying," Nelay retorted.

"You dare accuse me of lying," Zatal barked.

Jezzel stepped up beside Nelay. "She's not talking to you. She's talking to a fairy."

Nelay felt a rush of affection for her friend. Both of them knew not to attract the attention of fairies, but Jezzel wasn't letting Nelay face this alone.

The fairy looked at Jezzel, who expertly kept her emotions hidden from the creature.

"You will see, Nelay," Nos said dryly. "I have forever to wait. You have until your city falls." She beat her wings hard and was gone from sight in an instant.

"What did the creature say?" Zatal asked.

Jezzel rested her hand on Nelay's arm. "You know you can't trust them. They're just trying to manipulate you for their own purposes."

"But what if we're wrong?"

Jezzel tightened her grip. "We're not."

Nelay turned to face Zatal. "What has Suka told you?"

He kicked at some of the broken gate. "The high priestess believes the Clansmen are using the Goddess of Winter's powers."

Nelay was incredulous. "And you believe her."

"You don't?" Zatal said. "You're the priestess."

"Not anymore."

Zatal gestured to the gate. "At each of our cities it has been the same. The gates explode and the Clansmen come pouring in, and my Immortals and soldiers die holding them back. Every few days this happens, until I don't have the soldiers to hold the gates. Then we are forced to abandon the city."

His shoulders hunched. "I have commanded armies since I was thirteen years old. Whatever is driving these Clansmen, it isn't natural."

"What else did Suka tell you?" Nelay said quietly.

He looked at her then, his gaze sad, and Nelay realized he knew everything. "More I will not say. Not out in the open like this."

Jezzel came level with Nelay and remarked under her breath, "But after Thanjavar, we don't have anywhere else to retreat."

Another sliver of doubt pierced Nelay's resolve. But even if the high priestess was right and Ilyenna was aiding the Clansmen, turning to the fairies would only make things worse. Nelay knew that for certain.

Zatal grunted and rose to his feet, but he swayed, his face suddenly ashen. Nelay saw blood seeping around his scale armor. "What—"

He turned away. "Leave it."

She hurried to his side. "You need a healer."

"I've already had one." He moved away from her to speak with one of his generals. The two conversed briefly before the man took off at a jog.

"Why is the Goddess of Fire allowing this to happen?" Jezzel asked, her voice sounding small.

Nelay had a sudden urge to break a few of the glass idols in the temple herself. "I don't know."

Though Zatal was surrounded by Immortal commanders, Nelay realized he wasn't moving with his usual purposefulness as he started toward the stairs. He was hunched over, his back curving around pain. Nelay followed him, a terrible knowing growing within her. He stood looking out over their enemy. Just as she reached his side, the man gate opened and a boy slipped through carrying a pristine white flag edged in gold. Across the no man's land between the city walls and the enemy army, the boy strode across the field of dead and paused. Nelay's gaze swept over the massive armies of the Clansmen.

Her heart sank, pulling her hopes down with it. There was no escape for her, no way to reach Rycus. Would she ever see him again? Ever feel his touch, listen to his stories? Ever enjoy the peace of his arms?

"How bad is your wound?" Nelay asked Zatal.

His gaze flicked to the growing bloodstain before he stiffened and pointed across the field. "They're coming."

Another white-flag-bearing man separated himself from the Clansmen armies, the flag snapping smartly in the wind. The air tasted of baked sand, for the ovat would be upon them soon. Nelay wondered how it could possibly be after midday when she had left the palace shortly after sunrise.

The boy and the Clansman conversed, and the Clansman headed back to his lines. The boy ran back toward the city.

"What are you doing, Zatal?" Nelay asked.

"Requesting a parlay."

Nelay's mouth parted in shock. "Why? You can't mean to surrender."

The king rested his hands atop the wall, his head bowed. "We lost upwards of ten thousand men today, and the Clansmen already outnumbered us five to one."

"But we have the city wall. We—"

"They breached our wall in one day, Nelay. One day." His gaze met hers and she saw the hopelessness sitting like a stone in his eyes.

A man jogged up the stairs. "They've agreed to meet," he said breathlessly.

Zatal straightened his shoulders. "Then we go." He turned away from Nelay without another word.

She exchanged a glance with Jezzel before running after him. "You mean to go yourself."

"The Clansmen are honorable fighters. I'll be fine."

"If they're so honorable, I'll go with you."

He frowned at her before his gaze fell to her guards trailing beside her. "If the queen crosses the wall, I'll crucify all three of you."

Nelay felt them take a step closer to her, but his words had stopped her as surely as if he'd bound her. She wouldn't forfeit any of their lives, especially not Jezzel's.

"I think he means it," Jezzel said.

Nelay didn't bother responding. Zatal donned his king's robe, and the phoenix mantle was settled over his chest. She considered telling him to be careful, but with no love between them, such sentiment would be false.

He barked a command and ten Immortals surrounded him. Nelay leaned over the wall, watching as they emerged, one by one from the man door, the king last of all. He strode across the field of dead, diverting his path only to circumvent a cluster of bodies. A similar-sized contingent of Clansmen strode out to meet them, their tunics in ten different colors.

Nelay watched as they spoke, desperately wishing she could hear what they said. The ovat began as a low wail, whipping the flag to stand at attention. The Idarans reached for their veils and covered their faces, their headscarves already providing some protection. The Clansmen had no such covering. They tipped their heads and turned their backs to the wind.

Nelay imagined how they would breathe in the sand and cough. How gritty their hair would feel, left in the open like that. How the sand would coat their skin and sift down their strange boots that gaped at the top instead of being tied closed.

"They don't belong here," she ground out.

"No," Jezzel agreed.

Finally, the two groups turned away from each other, and Nelay rushed down the steps two at a time. Zatal was the first one through the man door. He glanced at Nelay before speaking to his generals. "I have given the Clansmen permission to collect their dead. We will not fire upon them as they do so."

He called for his horse. Nelay asked Jezzel with a meaningful shift of her eyes to fetch their horses. With an exasperated sigh, she moved to obey.

Nelay stepped closer to the king. "Why did you go out there?"

Ignoring her, Zatal mounted the horse, his gritted jaw the only sign of his pain. Jez brought the horses, and Nelay swung up beside the king, a well of dread spilling over inside her. "You didn't surrender, but you offered them something."

He turned weary eyes to her. "You're a clever woman—I don't think I like that about you."

Affronted, she straightened.

He gave a low laugh and said under his breath, "I wanted to know their terms of surrender."

Nelay gasped. "You can't. We can brick off the gates. The walls will hold. The men—"

"The walls will not hold." Zatal said. "They will fall and the Clansmen will raid our city, and we will be completely at their mercy."

Nelay swallowed her retort. "What did you offer them?"

"Peaceful surrender. They choose their own king. The people stay free."

Zatal had offered to step down? That didn't seem like him. "And they refused?"

"They want to make slaves of us all. Send us to the lands we occupied as servants to repay the wrongs we committed. Yet they take no responsibility for doing the same to us." His gaze was haunted. "Curse them and their cursed reparation." He laughed bitterly. "But after five years, they said we could be free."

Nelay grabbed his arm. "You didn't agree!"

"No." His gaze was distant, as if he was looking at something she couldn't see. "Idara is breaking, crumbling like a palace of sand. I cannot hold it together—not against a goddess-driven army. But I will make them pay for trying to take us."

He spurred his horse forward, the animal's hooves ringing against the flagstones.

With Jezzel beside her, Nelay passed through the palace gates at the height of the ovat, sweat pouring from her body. Her black horse was covered in dirty foam. She dropped to the ground just behind Zatal, who strode toward the palace almost frantically. Nelay cast a worried look back at Jezzel before rushing after him.

The guards swung open the heavy doors just enough to let them pass, then pushed them shut again. The cool air of the palace cleared Nelay's muggy thoughts. She caught sight of Zatal hurrying past the throne and ran after him. He stepped into a side room she'd never been inside of before. She kept the door open with a slap of her palm and slipped through.

Standing in what appeared to be a council room, Zatal wavered before her—all his hurry collapsing. Sweat dripped from his fingertips.

"Zatal?" Nelay gasped.

"I tried to trade myself to save my city. I'd hoped their hatred toward me would be enough. It was the one thing I had left to give."

She took a step toward him. "It's not just you they hate—they despise all of us."

He turned his head to the side. Nelay stopped, for his dusky skin looked like old ashes, cut by lines of running sweat. "What's wrong with you?" she blurted.

He shuddered, bracing himself over the table. Nelay took a step closer and became aware of a putrid smell. Unconsciously, she lifted her hand to cover her nose as he turned to meet her gaze.

"I had to get away before my soldiers saw—before the people saw." He was panting now. "I was so strong. My army, our weapons, our tactics, my rule—all were stronger than any other. But I was wrong." His haunted gaze met hers. "I meant what I told you the day we met. A good leader is both strong and selfless. You'll have to learn that fast if you're to be a better queen than I was a king."

She took a step toward him even as his legs folded beneath him. "Guards!" she cried. She wasn't fast enough to catch him. She knelt beside him as the door shoved open and their personal guards flooded the room.

"Nelay?" Jezzel sounded frantic.

"Get the king's healer. Now!" A guard ran to do as she'd commanded. Nelay didn't know how to comfort this stranger. She rested her palm awkwardly on his shoulder. "It's going to be all right."

"No," Zatal said, his voice resigned. "The axe pierced my bowels. I will have an ignoble death."

That explained the smell. "You knew," Nelay said in a whisper. "And still you went out to meet them."

He grunted, his lips white. "It would have been a good trade. They didn't need to know they'd be killing a dying king."

Speechless, Nelay stared at Zatal, knowing he was not the monster she'd thought he was.

The healer came running, her brown robes flaring around her. Her assistants were a step behind, and then there was no more room for Nelay. She stumbled back, her knees aching and numb; she must have dropped harder to the ground than she'd thought. Jezzel was suddenly beside her. Nelay had forgotten she was there at all.

The king was carried from the room. In a daze, Nelay realized she should follow, but she didn't want to—didn't want to watch the man die whom she'd come to grudgingly respect. But Jezzel gave her a little push and her legs seemed to move of their own accord, sending her following after the frantic entourage of a dying king.

CHAPTER
TWENTY-NINE

I n the sickroom, there was a flurry of motion. The healer and her helpers forced foul-smelling liquids down the king's throat, even though he commanded them to let him be. Then there was the sweet aroma of opium smoke, and the king stopped commanding anything.

When they cut into him, Nelay looked away from the flowing blood. Her gorge rose in her throat. The room felt tight and hot, the scent of blood combining with that of the offal. She shoved open the door and spilled into the hall, where she braced her hands on her knees and panted, trying not to pass out.

"Nelay?" Jezzel had followed her.

"I don't belong here. I barely even know the man. They're butchering his body in hopes of saving him. And it won't—no one survives a bowel wound."

"Does his mistress know?"

Nelay groaned and pressed the heels of her hands into her eyes. "If she knew, she would be here. What's her name, anyway?"

"Ziyid."

Nelay took a deep breath and met her friend's gaze. "Will you tell her?"

Jezzel nodded and swept past Nelay, who slumped on the floor, imagining how she would feel if it was Rycus in there. A while later, the healer came through the door, wiping blood from her hands onto a rag made from the same brown cloth as her robes. She bowed. "Queen of Queens, we have stitched his bowels together and closed the wound."

"Why?" Nelay asked. "Why not just let him die?"

"Because he is the king," the woman said simply.

Nelay pushed past her into the room. Zatal seemed groggy from the smoke, but his gaze sharpened when he saw her. "Did you know?"

She froze at the accusation in his voice. "Know what?"

He watched her with sharp intelligence before settling back. "No. I don't suppose you did." He reached for a cup of water and took a small sip. "There are others better suited to take my place. But I have seen things—things that cannot be explained any other way but by the Goddess of Winter's interference. And Suka swore you were the only one who could stop her, that making you my queen was the only way to save Idara." The king let out a long breath. "So I won't sign an edict naming someone else to rule in your place, on one condition. Ziyid and my children. You must swear to me that from this day forth she is your sister, my children your niece and nephew."

"You forget," Nelay said softly, "I don't want to be queen. I never did."

"What you want doesn't matter to me."

She took a deep breath and let it out slowly. "Ziyid was your wife. I was your queen. I don't envy her role, and I doubt she envies mine."

"Swear it!" Zatal roared.

Nelay jumped. "I swear!"

He sank back down in the bed, and for a moment seemed unable to speak. "I've already called for Nashur. He's the high commander, the best there is. Where he leads, the others will follow. Trust in him."

Each of the king's words fell like a heavy stone on her shoulders. "I don't know how to fight a war," she said.

He grunted. "But you do know how to fight an opponent. Moves and countermoves. This is just a bigger scale."

She met the king's gaze and saw sympathy there. "You're not what I thought you were," she said.

"I was, once. And worse."

She didn't have the strength to argue.

Zatal chuckled to himself. "When I saw you in the temple, trying to seduce me, I knew you would do whatever it took to save those you love." His eyes seemed to bore into her soul. "The question is, do you love Idara and her people enough to make those same kind of sacrifices?"

Nelay thought about it. "Suka's information is from the fairies—you can't trust them, and therefore, you can't trust her," she finally said. "They don't care about us."

"But do you trust yourself?"

Her head came up. "This isn't about me."

The king's expression said he didn't believe her. "You have to trust yourself—that you can hold on to love. That when the time comes, you won't lose yourself to apathy. That you will remember who you are and where you came from."

She looked away. "And if you're wrong? If I can't save anyone, or if this is all a trick and the Clansmen breach our walls?"

"I would rather have our people live on as legends than as slaves."

Nelay sighed. The physician held a pipe to the king's lips and he inhaled deeply, holding the smoke in his lungs before letting it go slowly.

Behind them, the door flew open. There stood Zatal's mistress, her eyes frantic and watery. The guards grabbed her arms, restraining her, then looked at Nelay as if awaiting her instructions. She wasn't sure why at first, but then it dawned on her.

They had heard Zatal's words, and their allegiance had already shifted from the dying king to her.

Nelay stared at the woman who should be her rival. What did the king's mistress see when she looked at Nelay? Did she consider her calm and cold, uncaring? The enemy? Then Nelay caught a gleam of fear in Ziyid's eyes and understood. Once the king was gone, his mistress would be completely at Nelay's mercy. "Let her pass," she said to the guards.

Ziyid took it as permission to dart to the king's side. She grasped his hand. "Zatal? Zatal! No!"

Nelay couldn't bear it. She didn't belong here. She strode from the room but paused outside. The guards had blocked the children from entering, a nurse holding the younger of the two in her arms. Nelay studied the girl, who returned her gaze warily. Then Nelay told the guards, "When the king and their mother are ready, let the children go in." Not wanting to frighten them, she didn't mention that they would be saying goodbye to their father.

She strode toward her rooms to clean up. At a choking sound, she looked back to see tears streaming down Jezzel's face, her shoulders ridged with emotions she was trying to hold in. Nelay knew her friend would never want the men under her command to see her lose control, so she picked up her pace and hurried them to her rooms, then hauled Jezzel in and shut the door on the other guards. Jezzel stumbled a few more steps before collapsing at the table and burying her head in her hands. Silent sobs shook her whole frame.

Maran stood uncertainly after settling her baby in a little box lined with blankets. "What happened?"

Nelay crouched by her friend. "Jezzel? Is it the king?"

She shook her head. "Meho, the others . . ."

Maran looked between them. "I don't understand."

Nelay collapsed beside Jezzel. "We lost many of our sisters today." What else could she call the women she'd spent every day with since she was nine years old? She rested her hand on

Jezzel's back, surprised she wasn't crying herself. But Nelay's grief was distant, unreachable. "It's my fault," she said quietly. "I sent them there."

Jezzel's sobs hitched and she shook her head. "Without them, the gate would have fallen. You had to."

"But they're still dead."

Maran fetched a basin of water and some clothes, then knelt before Nelay and started to unlace her boots. Nelay looked down at her, not really seeing her, and said, "The king is dying."

Maran stilled for a moment before she slipped off the boots and washed the blood from Nelay's feet—Nelay had forgotten about the blood soaking through the soles—and replaced her soiled boots with clean ones. Then Maran went about doing the same for Jezzel.

Nelay kept seeing Meho die over and over, hearing Ziyid calling out the king's name, felt the king's daughter's accusing stare. Nelay stood, not sure where she was going. Jezzel started to follow her, but Nelay held out her hand. "No. You're not ready yet."

"I'm supposed to—"

"Maran, don't let her go until she's ready."

The girl stood, her expression determined. Her baby had started crying, so she picked him up and settled him in Jezzel's arms, saying, "Here, you need something to love."

When Nelay stepped out of her rooms, her guards silently took up positions on either side of her. There was only one place to go. As she passed through the observation tower, the men went silent. She looked out over the Clansmen armies.

Nashur came to stand beside her and said, "He wants me to support you."

She remembered what Zatal had told her. If Nashur followed her, the other commanders would fall in line. "And do you?" she asked him.

The commander was silent a moment. "For now." Facing the men gathered around them, he declared, "The king is dying. We now answer to his queen. Now back to work. We have a city to save."

A hard silence followed his pronouncement, and Nelay noticed some of the commanders glaring at the Clansmen armies. Others looked at the ground. Some watched her.

She turned away so they wouldn't read the fatigue and weariness in her face. Her gaze strayed toward the desert and she suddenly realized she would be a widow soon, that her wedding prayers had been answered. If she survived this, she and Rycus could be together.

But only if the city stayed strong.

Steeling her resolve, she turned to face Nashur. She needed more information in order to hold all the players in her head. "The king said the city will fall. Do you agree?"

Nashur turned back to look at the gates, but not before Nelay saw moisture gleaming in his eyes. He cleared his throat. "Our armies are the finest in all the world."

"Yes, but we are outnumbered more than five to one."

"We have our walls."

"The gates were breached in one attack." Nelay didn't like that she was parroting Zatal's words, but she found she agreed with them. "If you can't change the players, change the field," she murmured to herself. "It's the only way to shift the game in our favor."

Nashur blinked at her. "My queen?"

She looked into his face and saw the battle within him. He was experienced and strong—she was an upstart queen. Would he try to unseat her? Lock her up and run this battle as he saw fit? He had men enough to do it.

Her mind whirred, as it always did, and she saw what Nashur needed to hear. "High Commander Nashur, I need your help. You have experience where I have none. But I have a knack for strategy."

His expression softened a little. "And what would you suggest?"

She motioned toward the armies. "That we fight dirty." She studied the city, her gaze sweeping over each section. "The brickers—have them block off the gates with mud bricks. Let's see if our enemy can freeze that."

"Unless they change their battle plan, they won't try it for a few more days. Plenty of time for the mortar to set," the high commander declared.

Nelay nodded. "We'll force them over the walls or not at all."

"That will destroy any chance of escape."

She faced Nashur again. "Escape? The entire city? With a surrounding army? And where would we all go? No. Block them all off."

"We should leave one unblocked."

"Why?"

He scratched his ear. "The entire city doesn't need to escape. Just you and what remains of the army."

She gaped at him aghast. "And abandon the people?"

"I know you were born alongside the Adrack Desert, so perhaps you do not understand. But I am from Mubia and a shipwright's son. When a ship is sinking and you only have one boat, do you let it go down with the rest, or do you save those you can?"

"The gates are a liability—you don't fix that, you lose everything." Nelay tamped her anger down. "Block the gates."

"I will leave one," Nashur said stubbornly.

She gritted her teeth, knowing he wasn't going to budge. "Fine. One stays open."

He took a deep breath and gave the order. Nelay gaze's landed on the temple, or more specifically the black smoke rising from it in great, bilious clouds. They were burning the bodies of the dead with a blend of luminash meant to consume any fuel until none at all remained—not even the bones of the dead. Was Meho's body among them?

Nelay forced the thought away, burying it in the sand like Rycus had advised her. "It won't be enough," she mumbled as she peered through a telescope. It was the height of the ovat, and the Clansmen were not to be seen. They must have huddled under their tents for whatever scrap of shade they could find. They did not have cool stone buildings to retreat into.

As she went to withdraw her telescope, she caught sight of wavering lines. She looked closer and realized it was heat rising from the glassmaker's quarter. "Why do the glassmakers still work?"

Nashur looked back at her from a map spread in the center of the table. "I don't know."

"The man who makes the glass idols is a cripple," Jezzel spoke up from behind her. The girl's eyes were red and swollen.

Nelay thought of the time she'd visited the glassmaker's shop, watched as they'd poured the sand into the cauldrons and added the other ingredients. She remembered how the sand had glowed red hot before finally melting into slag.

Her mind latched onto a part of the field they could use to their advantage. "What's the one thing we have plenty of in the desert?"

Nashur looked blankly at her. "Heat?"

"Sand," Jezzel said.

Nelay felt the winds dying, the last of the ovat choking out. "And wind."

CHAPTER THIRTY

Nelay rode the stallion through the city's streets, with Hazar and Ahzem following her. Nashur was at her side, Jezzel led them, and a handful of messengers Nashur never went anywhere without trailed behind.

Nelay had her swords strapped to her cross baldric, her knives in their sheaths, and her sling at her hip. She also wore armor she'd "commissioned" from the Priestess Army, and she had to admit she felt more herself than she had since arriving in Thanjavar.

When they reached the glass shop, Jezzel held the stallion by the bridle while Nelay dismounted. "Stay here. I'll be right back."

"How am I supposed to protect you from out here?" Jezzel called after her.

Nelay motioned for Nashur to join her. "Kidin isn't fond of priestesses at present." Or so she had been told.

"You're going?" Jezzel protested, but Nelay ignored her.

With Nashur beside her and Hazar and Ahzem following, Nelay strode toward the open doors of the glassmaker's shop. The moment she stepped inside, sweltering heat blasted her, and she found it hard to breathe the heavy, smoky air. The shop was run by crippled men, all hired by Kidin, himself a cripple. And

Nelay realized why the shop still operated—the army wouldn't have wanted these men. No one but Kidin did.

Wearing only their dhotis and thick leather aprons, the workers stopped to stare as she passed. Rivulets of sweat ran down their bodies, their hair plastered to their heads.

Nelay glanced at some of the partially finished idols, which wore a priestess's ceremonial bodice and skirt. The attire struck her as odd, but she didn't have time to ask about it. "Where's the glass master?" she questioned the first person she came to, a boy with a muscular body except one arm, which was shrunken and deformed.

He took a dipper out of a bucket of water and tipped his head farther into the shop. "Working on the main sculpture."

Careful of the hot glass everywhere, Nelay eased past him. She'd only been inside a few minutes and already she was soaked through with sweat. She wiped her forehead with the back of her hand, her skin feeling feverish with heat. "How do they stand working here all day?" she said to Nashur.

He shrugged. "I guess you'd have to get used to it."

After questioning two more people, Nelay finally found a man who was much younger than she remembered, with an eye-patch over one eye, a peg leg, and a hard body covered in melted-looking burn scars. "Are you the glass master?"

Kidin didn't even glance at her as he motioned to three other cripples to help him heave a huge square into the billowing oven. They limped and shuffled, their faces red and straining. He stepped back, picked up a large stick, and used it to push the blocks in deeper. "I am."

She squared herself. "I am Queen Nelay. And this is High Commander Nashur." She didn't introduce her guards.

Kidin turned a glare on her that would have melted marble, but that look quickly shifted to one of astonishment before he turned to assist his men.

"I need your help," Nelay announced.

He ignored her as he strained to push in another block. It slid partway in, and the men picked up long sticks and pushed it in the rest of the way.

"Fascinating as this is, I need your help now," she said.

"Unfortunately for you," Kidin replied without looking at her, "it takes hours and unholy amounts of combustibles to heat our ovens to the right temperature. And these molds are all ready to go in now. You can wait."

Nashur growled low in his throat. "The safety of Thanjavar is more important than the idols."

Kidin ignored that. Nelay waited, her patience growing thinner and thinner by the moment. Finally, Kidin used the stick to shut the door, then locked it in place with a lever. He pushed past Nelay's guards and went directly to a bucket of water, where he dunked himself in to his shoulders. He came up blowing and dipped a cup into the bucket he'd just vacated and drank.

Without even looking at Nelay, he strode past her, weaving through men painting wax onto what looked like a black sculpture. "What are you doing?" she called as she hurried to catch up to him.

"Glass casting. It involves sand and heat, plaster and molds, and a lot of general good sense. Something you priestesses lack by the bucketful."

Nelay tried to take a deep breath to calm herself, but only ended up coughing as the heat scorched her lungs.

"Don't you care that our city is about to fall?" Nashur asked incredulously.

Kidin spun, water and sweat spraying from his hair and splattering across Nelay's face. "My father and I spent years making the statues in the temple. Years! They were his crowning achievement. And your high priestess has a fit and breaks every last one." Tears shone in the man's one good eye. "And then said high priestess demands more sculptures. Now."

He wiped his nose on his arm. It was hard to tell with all the water and sweat running down his cheeks, but Nelay was fairly certain he was crying. "So no, I don't care if this blasted city falls. Good riddance!"

He turned and stomped away, or at least as best he could stomp with his peg leg. Wiping her face with her sleeve, Nelay started after him. She passed a wall that protruded halfway into the shop and froze as a life-sized cast of a woman came into view. She wore ceremonial robes. The sides of her scalp were shaved, her hair braided. And her face—it was Nelay's. That explained Kidin's astonished expression. "She's a priestess!" Nelay gasped. "You're . . . she's me!"

"The high priestess was very specific," he replied dryly. "I suppose you should be flattered to be the model."

Nelay was definitely not flattered. Rather, she was angry that her willingness to become the Goddess of Summer was a foregone conclusion.

Kidin plopped down before a door that opened to the outside, letting in a cool breeze. He poured himself something to drink and slumped in the chair. "What do you want? Why are you here?"

She tore her gaze away from the statue. "Sand. Very hot sand." By the time she finished telling him the beginnings of her plan, work all around them had ceased.

Kidin watched her, the corners of his mouth seeming weighted down. "By the goddess, you're heartless."

His words wounded her, but she refused to let that show. "If you want to win a street fight, you have to fight dirty."

He slipped his hand under his eye patch and rubbed at whatever was beneath. "I thought the Immortals had a code of honor."

"Not anymore," Nelay said, her voice hard. Nashur shifted uncomfortably beside her.

Kidin grunted. "All right, but I'm going to need hundreds of men and every cart you can round up."

She turned questioningly to Nashur. He tugged at his beard. "I can't pull soldiers from the wall."

"We can ask for volunteers," Nelay suggested.

"We have already drafted every able-bodied man within the city."

She began pacing. "What about the women?"

"You're a priestess, so you don't understand," Nashur said carefully. "The women who aren't already fighting have little ones to take care of, or old ones. They're all that's left to keep the city running."

Kidin finished his drink and poured himself another. "What he is trying to say is most of them cannot be spared."

Nelay scowled at him. "Where do you suggest I find hundreds of men sitting around with nothing . . ." She froze and slowly faced Nashur, who began to look distinctly nervous.

"My queen—" he began, but she was already rushing away. She ran through the shop and then outside.

"How'd it go?" Jezzel asked sarcastically, but one look at Nelay's expression and she turned off her attitude and jumped into the saddle.

Nelay mounted her horse, Nashur only a few paces behind her. "Queen Nelay?"

"I have another player to add to the field."

"What does that mean?" When she didn't answer, he turned his questioning gaze to Jezzel.

Not waiting for either of them, she took off toward the leatherworking section of town, where she'd met Rycus the first time. Only the poorest and meanest citizens lived on the southeast side, due to the reek of urine and feces used to treat the raw leather. She had to slow down as the streets grew cluttered and decrepit.

"Queen Nelay, this is a very unsafe area," Nashur said.

Jezzel grumbled, "Unsafe to our sense of smell."

"I know." The smell of the tanneries made Nelay's eyes water. She held her sleeved arm over her face.

Nashur took shallow breaths, his face contorted with disgust. "I must insist—" He broke off suddenly as they turned a corner and rusted gates came into view. Confusion vanished from his face, replaced by apprehension. "This is a bad idea."

Nelay looked up at a gray-clad jailer watching them from atop the battered walls. He called out to someone on the other side. "The only ideas we have left are bad ones," she countered as the gates opened to admit them.

More jailers met her, their heads bowed in respect. "I will speak with the man in charge," she said.

"I have already summoned him, my queen."

For once, Nelay was glad for the palace guards, whose presence announced her identity without the need for time-consuming introductions. She dismounted. "Take me to him."

The men hesitated before one of them led her through the guard house, some kind of barracks, and to a door. Just as she was about to knock, it swung open.

A bald older man started when he saw her. His hair was mussed and his eyes heavy lidded. Behind him, a young woman pulled on her boots. She gave a quick bow and fled. Nelay turned her attention back to the man.

"My queen," he huffed as he tucked his shirt in.

"Who was that woman, and why was she here?" Nelay cut in.

He passed a hand over his bare scalp. "She's a dear friend." Nelay raised an eyebrow. "She just came for a quick visit."

"As prostitutes often do." Nelay turned to the cluster of officers who had followed her. "I need a new commander. Which one of you would like the position?"

The men exchanged glances before two of them stepped forward. Nelay looked between the two. "All for him" —she pointed at the younger man— "raise one hand." She pointed to the older man. "All for him, raise both hands."

Most of the men raised one hand. Nelay turned to the younger man, whose ears stuck out straight from his head as if his mother had given them a hard tug one too many times. "Your name?"

"Awan."

"I need all the prisoners gathered where I can safely speak to them. Can you arrange it?"

Awan bowed. "Right away." He called out orders and men started moving.

The man Nelay had just sacked stepped toward her. Jezzel blocked his path. "My queen, you don't understand," he said. Nelay turned to leave the way she'd come. "My queen, please, have mercy upon me."

She didn't pause. "I don't have time for mercy. We are at war, you fool." He reached for her, but Jezzel kneed him in the stomach and Hazar drew his sword. Hunched over, the man gasped. "Please, my queen."

Nelay glared at him in disgust. "Nashur, it seems this man is no longer needed here. Perhaps you can find a place for him with the soldiers."

Nelay followed Nashur as he gripped the man's arm and hauled him outside. He spoke to one of his messengers. "See he's put in Uzah's unit. If he tries to take off, kill him for desertion."

The seedy little man shot one last, desperate look at Nelay, but she was already turning to face Awan. The messenger mounted his horse and motioned for the man to precede him.

Directing Nelay to follow him, Awan climbed the ladder leading to the top of the mud-brick wall. Jezzel moved to go next but paused and said to Nelay, "Last I heard, Ozozo was in here. Let's hope he's forgiven us." She flashed a grin before hustling up.

A moment later, Nelay stood on the wooden walkway and surveyed the many plain buildings in perfect rows. Men were emerging from them. She couldn't tell the color of their hair from their skin—or their clothes, for that matter. It was all covered in the same greasy grime. "Do they not bathe?" she asked Awan.

"No, my queen."

"This is a bad idea," Nashur grumbled as he hauled himself up beside her. "These men are criminals—they are dangerous. You cannot arm them and turn them loose on the city."

She leaned forward. "Of course not, High Commander. I'm arming them and putting them under your command."

He took a step closer. "I don't have time to play nursemaid to a pack of wild dogs."

Jezzel nudged Nelay with her elbow. "Remember that time with the elephant dealer?"

Immediately she realized what Jezzel was hinting at. Nelay straightened her shoulders. "Commander Nashur, I want you to loudly disagree with me at every turn."

He grunted in disbelief. "You do?"

"Absolutely." She and Jezzel locked gazes for a moment. Jezzel grinned, her arms folded over her chest.

That's what she loved about Jezzel. No matter how bad things got, she always made Nelay smile. Fighting a chuckle, Nelay faced the throng and spoke loudly. "Prisoners of Idara, I am Queen Nelay. No doubt you have heard the Clansmen at our gates. They broke through only yesterday, killing ten thousand people—men and women whom I cannot replace." She paused and swallowed against her dry throat. "You are here because of something you have done in your past—some crime."

Nashur wasn't disagreeing with her. She discreetly elbowed his side. He shot her an incredulous look before seeming to understand. "They are not to be trusted!"

She let out a tiny breath in relief. "They are still Idarans."

He looked out over them. "Are they?"

"They are men who would rather die fighting than be slaughtered when the wall falls. And it will fall."

There was a gleam in Nashur's eyes that said he'd realized what she was doing and he was even enjoying himself. "What are you going to do? Pardon them?"

"Yes." Nelay let the word hang in the air before she turned back to the criminals, who watched her intently. "If you will fight—if you will protect those you once harmed—your debt, your shame will be turned to honor."

"And what's to keep them from running at the first sign of battle and disappearing in the masses?" Nashur spat.

She blinked at him. But then her eyes strayed to the tattoos of rank on his scalp. "We will tattoo a curving line across their left cheek. After they have served faithfully and true, we will add another curving line, creating a simple flame, a mark of restored honor."

"A tattoo—you think that will stop them?"

"I will put a bounty on their heads that will leave no safe landing place—no place of rest," Nelay declared, an edge to her voice. "Their prison will be the entire world."

"This city falls, and you will be dead. Who's to carry out your threat?" growled Nashur.

"They cannot kill us all. The truth of the mark will survive and follow them wherever they go." She paused, looking out of the gathering of filthy-faced men. "What say you? Shall I call you criminals, or soldiers?"

There was a beat of silence, and Nelay's heart almost stopped in her chest as she waited. Then the first man roared his willingness to fight. Another joined him. And another. Until the entire prison was shouting, "Fight, fight, fight!"

She held her hand up and waited until they settled enough to hear her. "Will you swear your allegiance to me? Will you swear to serve me?"

They shouted their assent, some dropping to one knee as if already speaking their oaths to her. Nelay stepped back from the wall and out of sight.

Jezzel slapped Nashur on the arm. "And that, O Great Commander, is how we got a dealer to donate an elephant to the Temple of Fire." She started down the ladder, calling out to Ahzem to get the horses.

Nashur shook his head and started after her. "Is she always like this?"

Thinking of earlier that day, Nelay sobered. "Trust me, she's better like this."

"Did you get to keep the elephant?" Awan asked.

Nelay remembered its gentle eyes with long lashes, and its rough skin. "For a little while." She forced herself back into the here and now. "I don't want any mass murderers. Or rapists."

He shrugged. "All those are hanged. These are just thieves and smugglers, for the most part."

Nelay's heart skipped in her chest. When this was all over, she was going to pardon her own smuggler.

"Make them swear an oath of fealty to me," she told Awan, "and a pledge to obey their commanders. Then get them washed up and send them to Kidin." She turned her attention to Nashur. "You have men assigned to do the Immortal's tattoos?"

"Yes."

"Send for them."

Nashur called to another of his messengers, who departed immediately.

"See that they have uniforms," Nelay went on. "And assign them as you see fit."

The high commander's gaze was unreadable. "I'll get things started, but the main tasks will be delegated to one of my men."

Nelay started walking toward the horses. "Fine."

"It would be better if they had one of their own to answer to, if there's anyone who can be trusted," Nashur said.

She hesitated. "There's a man named Ozozo. He's crafty and has more connections than anyone. But don't let him touch the wine. He's a fool drunk."

"My queen?" Nashur called after her.

Nelay situated herself in the saddle and then looked down at him. "Yes?"

"That was brilliantly done. In the space of a few minutes, you secured those prisoners' loyalty and gave them a taste of pride—a taste that will leave them hungering for more."

"I wouldn't ask this of you, Commander, if I didn't know you were equal to the task."

He watched her with a slightly amused expression. "Campaigning for my loyalty?"

"I want more than that. I want your best."

"I'm giving you that."

Nelay smiled at him. "No, Nashur. You are the best tactician alive today—but you could be more. You could be the most brilliant tactician to have ever lived."

There. She'd given him a goal, lit a fire beneath him. She could see the sparks of it dancing in his eyes.

She turned her horse, ready to leave, when another horse barreled past the open gates. The man's helmet bore the markings of a high-ranking Immortal. As he came closer, Nelay recognized him from the war council, though she couldn't remember his name.

"My queen." He bowed over his lathered and puffing horse. "You are needed at the palace."

She spun, her eyes locking on Awan. "Get them ready. I'm leaving you in charge for now."

She rode out after the Immortal, and several others flanked her. "Is it the king?" she asked, even though she already knew the answer.

The man had switched his beleaguered horse for one of the messenger's animals. "The healer says it will be soon."

CHAPTER
THIRTY-ONE

Head pounding and mouth dry, Nelay strode into the dark room, its windows shuttered against the ovat. Ziyid rose from the side of the bed, her face haggard and eyes puffy. She swallowed hard, then fled without turning back.

Nelay stood beside the bed, looking down at the king. With his eyes closed he looked as if he was made of wax instead of real flesh. Panic shot through her. *Is he already dead?* "Zatal?"

He stirred and slowly opened his eyes, then stared at her without recognition.

"Nelay, your queen," she reminded him.

His gaze sharpened, as if her words had cut through the haze. "Death stalks me. I can feel it whispering in my ear." He studied her a moment more before he winced, his face screwed up in agony. He didn't make a sound. Nelay turned to the healer, who was already coming forward with the smoking pipe.

Zatal pushed it away. "No. I will not die witless." The woman bowed and moved to the corner of the room.

"Send for my scribe."

Nelay gasped. The king would only call for a scribe if he wanted to issue an official mandate. "What do you mean to do?"

He breathed hard for several long moments. The scribe appeared as if he'd been waiting just outside the door. "My king?"

When Zatal spoke, his voice was raw and glinting, "I enact the ancient custom of my mother's people. Nelay's marriage will not be voided at my death. Instead, the bond will transfer to my closest kin."

"What?" She staggered back. "Even now you will take away my freedom?"

He looked at her without seeming to see her. "My closest surviving kin lives among the Tribesmen. This creed will in effect make him king of Idara. That might just be incentive to get them to join the war."

Nelay considered killing Zatal then and there. "Haven't you forced me through enough?"

"Strong and selfless, Nelay. Remember? Besides, it just might work out for the best."

She couldn't see how. Burn it, she'd started to hope that if she survived this, she'd be able to find Rycus again. "We won't be Idara—not after this. And I will no longer be Nelay."

The king shifted and the smell was so strong Nelay could taste the rot in her mouth. Fighting the urge to gag, she covered her mouth with her arm.

"Get out," Zatal ground out. "Yours will not be the last face I see."

She whirled on her heel and rushed out of the room, then shut the door behind her and stood panting in the hall.

Jezzel took a step toward her, arms raised as if to embrace her, and then seemed to think better of it. "What did he do?"

Ziyid took a step toward the door, but Nelay was in the way. The woman looked like she was moments away from choking on her grief. Nelay stepped aside and started down the hallway.

"What will you do with us?" Ziyid called after her.

"Nothing," Nelay said without pausing. She only wanted only a cool bath and a long nap.

When Nelay woke, it was eventide and the king was dead.

Maran had already laid out her white robes—white like old ashes and pale corpses. Nelay put on her trousers and short robe, then wrapped herself from head to toe in a sheer veil so only her eyes showed through the obscurity of grief.

Jezzel was waiting for her in the antechamber.

"I feel like a fraud," Nelay said. She'd only been married to Zatal for a few days, and he was barely more than an acquaintance.

"Is there a chance . . ." Jezzel trailed off, sending a pointed look to Nelay's belly.

Nelay scoffed. "We never shared a marriage bed. He knew I didn't want him, and to be honest, he didn't want me either."

"And now he'll never have his heir on the throne," her friend answered.

Nelay's thoughts flashed to Zatal's steel-eyed daughter. Jezzel might be wrong.

"It's just like any other funeral ceremony. Only this time you're leading the procession instead of dancing at it." Jezzel took up her position beside Nelay. "Ready?"

Nelay let out a long sigh. "Ready."

Jezzel pushed open the door to reveal a corridor lined with officials, all of them holding oil lamps to stave off the shadows. Nelay walked between them and they converged behind her. Not for the first time, she thought of the similarity between the wedding and funeral marches. One marked a beginning, the other an end. Weddings always started at the temple and ended at the home. Funerals always started at the home and ended at the temple.

Zatal had been laid before the throne on a bed of sweet-smelling herbs over a litter of woven reeds. He was dressed in his finest, the phoenix mantle gleaming from his chest, his head freshly shaved to show the dizzying pattern of tattoos.

Nashur stood at one corner of the litter, a guild leader at another, and two men Nelay didn't recognize at the other two. Hanging back in the hallway behind the throne were Ziyid and her children. They would have to follow in line with the palace servants.

"Jezzel, you have served me faithfully and been a great friend for many years. Walk beside me." Nelay said, giving the place of honor to her dearest friend. Then she met Ziyid's gaze. "Will you follow and carry my veil?" The veils hadn't been long enough to drag on the floor in decades, but it was still customary to have someone carry it. It was the only polite way Nelay could think to let Ziyid walk with the man she loved.

Gratitude crossed Ziyid's face as she bowed and came out to gather the long train of the veil. Nelay said, "Your children may walk beside you. I do not wish them to be left alone."

Then she nodded for the procession to begin. The men carrying the litter, Nashur among them, moved out at a stately pace. Nelay followed directly behind them. They stepped into the darkening night, the generals and dignitaries falling into step after the queen. Immortals fell in next, and then guild leaders and wealthy merchants, until all the most powerful men and women of the city trailed Nelay down the palace steps into the courtyard.

In the distance, she heard the sounds of battle and smelled the smoke from the fires that never seemed to cease burning. To the east, the temple gates stood open, the priestesses waiting in a long line, each holding a single lamp. As the litter carrying Zatal's body passed them, the priestesses—all of whom Nelay considered her sisters—blew out their lamps a pair at a time, leaving darkness behind them and light before.

When the procession passed the fountain, the flames went out. Suka headed toward Nelay, taking the side opposite Jezzel. "Had you listened to me, the king might not be dead. Thousands of our people, my priestesses . . ." Suka's voice choked off.

A series of painful memories flashed in Nelay's mind—Meho's face, Jezzel's nearly silent sobs, and the blood welling between Nelay's toes. *Was all this my fault? Could I really have stopped the Clansmen? Saved Idara if I'd just done what Suka wished?*

But then Nelay remembered the promise she'd made as a child. The blanket parting to reveal her brother's lifeless face. "Their price is always too high."

"When are you going to realize we don't have currency left for them to take?" Suka said coldly. "When the city has fallen? When everyone you love is dead?"

"The fairies don't care about us," Jezzel interjected, her face rigid.

"Of course not!" Suka glanced around as mourners shot her disapproving looks. "But you—you could have cared," the high priestess said in a lower voice. "That's why I married you to the king, so you would find your humanity again and save us. And now, all my years of careful planning, all of it is for naught."

Nelay was shocked to see tears streaming down the woman's round cheeks. The procession stopped on the east side of the temple, before a large chamber set deep into the ground. Only Suka and the men bearing the litter moved forward now, the high priestess leading them down into the chamber. They laid the king in the center, and Nashur removed the mantle. Suka sprinkled the funeral luminash on his corpse.

They backed away, careful not to disturb the luminash powders circling the dead man. The four pallbearers climbed out of the chamber. With the last remaining lamp, Suka bent down and let the flames touch the powder.

Instead of an outright flame, the luminash lit a thin line of red-orange fire, like an ember creeping around Zatal in an intricate pattern that matched the tattoos on his scalp. They told his life story as he had lived it—a moment of burning that would not stop as life never stopped until the end, when his ashes burned away on the wind.

Surrounded by the glow of intricate luminash patterns, Zatal's body caught fire. The luminash burned bright and hot, so hot Nelay had to resist the urge to step back. The priestesses tossed more sweet-smelling herbs to cover the scent of burning hair and melting flesh. The funeral luminash worked fast, consuming Zatal in moments. In reverence to the king, he alone would enter the flames this day, for there were thousands of dead still to be burned.

When the blaze had died to smoldering remains, Nashur placed the phoenix mantle across Nelay's collarbone. The weight of it seeming to pull her down almost instantly. She turned and the entourage reversed itself, Immortals moving back into position so that she walked through a tunnel of the living on her way back from the dead.

As she reached the palace, the colors flashing from the observation tower painted everyone in a weird glow. Nashur jogged passed her. "I can't be away any longer, my queen."

"Go," she said, but he was already headed for the observation tower. Nelay hesitated. She felt heavy and tired and wasn't sure she could bear another moment of turmoil.

Jezzel touched her arm. "You don't have to go."

Nelay pulled the veil off her hair and handed it to Ziyid. "You were his true wife."

She left the mantle. It was heavy and awkward, but it was a burden Nelay would never be released from. Not while she lived, anyway.

Free of most of the trappings of death, she rushed to the observation tower and wound her way up the gradually narrowing flight of stairs. At the top, the commanders glanced at her, then turned back to the walls and towers under siege. She ignored them and scanned the walls.

"The northern wall is on fire," Jezzel said.

Nelay hurried to her friend's side. "How is it burning? It's plaster and mud bricks."

"The wall isn't burning," Nashur answered. "It's some kind of oil—or maybe pitch."

She snatched a telescope, making a mental note to ask for one of her own, and studied the flames. There were three bucket lines surrounding it, trying to stop the flames from spreading to the city.

"Are they trying to burn down the city?"

"Since we've blocked off the gates, they have to find another weak point. The heat will damage the walls. I imagine they're digging tunnels as well."

Nelay watched a building catch fire. The walls were stone or mud brick. They wouldn't burn. But the roof beams lit up, catching everything inside on fire as well. From this distance, it looked no bigger than a tinder flame.

At a shout, men began pointing. Nelay swung the telescope around. She wasn't sure what she was seeing at first. In the dark, she could make out moving shapes—Idaran soldiers running. There was an odd shine to them, reflected by the torches.

"It's some kind of oil," Jezzel cried.

Nelay gasped as fire arrows lit up the night. They flashed orange and brilliant yellow before finding their mark. Immediately, the wall lit up. There were shapes—men who looked as if they were made of fire. But they weren't, for they fell, succumbing to heat. Nelay insides tightened like a fist.

Nashur was signaling for more horns, more luminash, calling for Immortals to respond, ordering buckets. The Idarans stationed at the wall fought back the flames with cloaks and handfuls of dirt.

As Nelay watched, another building went up before the Idaran soldiers could get there. Motioning for Jezzel to follow her, she turned, her white trousers spinning around her legs like a shower of falling petals.

"Where are you going?" Nashur called after Nelay.

"To find Kidin and Awan."

"It's the middle of the night—he won't be at his shop."

"Then send one of your messengers. Have them meet me at the Borz Gate."

Nashur swore and called after her, but she shot him a dangerous look and he ordered one of his messengers off with a flick of his hand before turning back to protecting the city.

Surrounded by her guards, Nelay trotted down the stairs. She reached the ground level and called for someone to ready the horses.

CHAPTER THIRTY-TWO

Nelay swung up onto a new horse, her backside aching from the hard riding earlier that day. Jezzel, Hazar, and Ahzem mounted up around her. And then they rode through the shadowed city, which was eerily deserted and silent. Occasionally, residents peeked out of the windows, but no one came to pay homage to their new queen.

Before the northern wall, Nelay rode out to the Borz Wall. There were torches everywhere, revealing some faces and casting others in shadow. She found Awan first, working among his criminals. "Where's the master glassmaker?" she asked.

He led her through the throngs of Immortals and prisoners. Each of the latter wore the new tattoo that marked him as a prisoner—a curving line across one swollen red cheek.

Nelay moved past them as if she wasn't afraid, as if their superior numbers didn't guarantee they could easily overpower her guards, who pressed close to her. She imagined the guards' hands twitching towards their swords at any sudden movement.

Jezzel scanned the crowd. "You know when we do things and afterward realize we were fools? This is one of those things."

"We'll be all right." Or so Nelay hoped.

Her friend snorted. "We crossed some of these men."

291

Nelay spotted Kidin, arguing with a woman who stood beside a catapult as it was cranked down with a loud *clack, clack, clack*. "Queen's orders," he barked.

"I don't care whose orders you have—you get this sand away from my catapults and these criminals back to the prison where they belong."

Nelay studied the woman's helmet. She was the catapult commander. Nelay nodded to Jezzel, who cried out, "Bow before your queen!"

Immortals stopped what they were doing and stared at her. "Bow!" Jezzel shouted again, her voice threatening.

The soldiers dropped their faces, their backs curving. "You may rise," Jezzel called. "Back to your duties."

Nelay urged her horse forward a few steps. "What's your name?" she asked the woman. "Why aren't you obeying my orders?"

The woman grimaced. "Yavish. We're under attack. I haven't time to listen to your foolish schemes."

The catapult stopped cranking, and soldiers used a pulley to position what looked like a round mud brick packed with sharp shards of rock into the catapult bowl. It released with a *thwack* that made Nelay jump.

She opened her mouth to berate Yavish, but Jezzel had already dismounted and leveled her weapon at the woman's chest. "You will obey orders or be run through for sedition!" Jezzel believed swords spoke better than words.

Yavish glared at Jezzel. "Fine. We can't hold them off much longer anyway." She turned to her soldiers. "Do as the queen says."

Wearing lots of cumbersome-looking leather, Kidin opened the door to a portable kiln. Awan directed the criminals to remove an enormous pot filled with piping-hot sand, which he capped off with a soaked cork.

The same pulley was used to maneuver the pot into the catapult bowl. "Careful," Kidin directed, hovering beside them. "Drop it and we'll all wish we were dead."

The soldier manning the pulley shot him a glare.

"What if the tavo changes directions?" Yavish asked.

"It never changes directions." Nelay's voice was low, but it carried.

Kidin backed away from the catapult, nodding worriedly. "This should work. The pot shouldn't break from the force of being thrown. And even if it does, it probably won't kill anyone."

"Kidin, that isn't helpful," Nelay hissed.

Jezzel started toward the wall. "Come on. Let's watch."

Along with the guards, Kidin, Awan, and Yavish accompanied Nelay and Jezzel as they climbed the steps to the top of the wall.

Kidin rubbed his hands together nervously. "Right. Let it go!"

Yavish nodded, and an Immortal released the lever. The pot shot into the air. Cringing as it passed over them, Nelay waited for it to shatter from the force. But it did not; instead it twisted end over end before smashing down in the midst of the clanland armies.

A red glow plumed and spread. The Clansmen screamed. Wind caught the sand, shifting it through the soldiers, who were already running, trying to get away from something that was all around them. A fire started and was quickly snuffed out. Then another one. And another. Busy running from the sand and putting out the fires, the Clansmen were no longer attacking the walls.

Yavish stared down her telescope for a minute before snapping it shut. "Right then. Get me more of that sand. Now."

Kidin gaped at her. "I can't produce that much. Nor that quickly."

"You'll have to." Yavish was already moving away, calling for the catapult to be shifted.

"I don't have enough kilns—" Kidin mumbled and hurried after her. Nelay followed to see what happened.

"What about blacksmith forges?" Yavish said. "Clay-pot makers . . . surely there are other kilns in this city."

Kidin held his hands out in exasperation. "Not portable ones."

"What if we heated the pots and brought them here?" Nelay piped in.

"If we could find a way to insulate them, keep them hot . . ." Kidin scratched under his eye patch. "If one of the pots breaks, there will be fires. And horrible burns."

"Clear the streets around you," Yavish directed as if it would be easy. She gestured to the criminals wearing nondescript brown vests that were supposed to pass as uniforms. "Find more of that protective leather for these reprobates, like what you're wearing." She walked toward her catapult. "Release!" she called to her men.

The catapult jerked beside them, making Nelay jump even though she knew it was coming. She rested her hand on Awan's shoulder and gave him a little push. "You heard what she said." He started off as well. "And have them ask nicely," she warned.

Awan shot her a grin, then turned and trotted through the criminals, ordering some of them off. Nelay watched him, surprised the men he'd guarded would listen to him. When he finished he came back to Nelay, clearly expecting more orders. "Why aren't they slitting your throat?" she asked.

His expression hardened. "The man you sacked was horrible to the prisoners. Said the faster they died, the less he'd have to feed them. I was helping them, and they knew it. Plus, Ozozo said they had to."

Jezzel looked around nervously. "Where is old Ozozo, anyway?"

Awan shook his head. "Died in the fires earlier."

Jezzel blew out and nudged Nelay with her elbow. "Well, that's one comeuppance we won't have to pay."

Nelay felt equally relieved, and then somewhat guilty for that relief.

Despite Jezzel's disapproval, Nelay stayed at the wall, observing as the Immortals coordinated with Kidin and his criminals. It took almost an hour to get one pot of sand, but when they dispatched it, the effects on the enemy were devastating.

Watching the carnage unfold through her telescope, Nelay sighed in frustration. "It's not enough. We need another player." There had to be a way to capitalize on the sand—a way to increase its effect. "Yavish, would it be possible to fill jars with oil?"

"We've done it before. Unfortunately, you'll run out of oil fairly quickly."

Nelay studied the Clansmen as they fought to put out a dozen or so small fires. And suddenly, she was seeing Zatal's body burn again. Breathless, she bent over. And then an idea came to her. Her head came up and she stared at Awan until he shifted uncomfortably.

"Oh, I don't like that look," Jezzel muttered.

Nelay couldn't answer. She was too horrified with this piece of her plan to put it into words. "Awan, take twenty carts to the temple and requisition as many pots of luminash as you can carry from the storerooms."

Jezzel stared at her, horror in her eyes. "Nelay, the luminash is sacred. It's for ceremonies. And it won't burn if you throw it at them anyway—it'll be too scattered."

"Go," Nelay snapped at Awan.

Jezzel's fists tightened, and Nelay knew it took everything she had to keep the words she wanted to say behind her lips.

Awan glanced uneasily between them, bowed, and left without a word.

With him gone, Nelay didn't have anyone else to carry out her orders. Nashur's messengers were a brilliant idea. She needed to get her own. But for now, she stepped up to the wall and shouted, "Does anyone know where to find the leader of the Potters Guild?" She paused. "I assume there is one?"

Criminals, Idaran soldiers, and Immortals paused, but no one answered.

"There's a guild for every trade," Jezzel said helpfully.

Someone cleared his throat behind Nelay. She turned and saw a mid-ranking Immortal. "I know the man," he declared, "though I'm not sure what the no-good, lousy, cheating—"

"I want every pot from every shop," Nelay interrupted. "And as many more as the potters can make."

"They've probably been drafted with the rest of the men," the Immortal said.

"Well, undraft them!"

He backed away from her. "I'll try to find someone with the authority to have them released from their units, my queen."

"Take some of my . . ." She couldn't call them criminals, not if she expected them to continue to follow her. "Take some of my Redeemed with you. They will help transport any pots you find."

Jezzel shot her an incredulous look. Nelay met it with a glare. "If the king can have his Immortals, I can have my Redeemed."

"You get mean when you're tired. Do you know that?"

Jezzel was right, which infuriated Nelay more. "I'm fine."

"You most certainly are not. It's going to take hours for everything to be in place. In the meantime, you need to rest."

Nelay set her jaw stubbornly.

"I haven't slept either," Jezzel went on quietly. "And neither have Hazar or Ahzem."

Nelay looked over her guards, whose exhaustion was plain to see. Just thinking of rest made her body feel heavy. Her head hurt, and her eyes were dry. "All right," she said, but she made Yavish promise to send for her when everything was finally in place.

When Nelay arrived at her rooms with Jezzel, Tix was sprawled out on a spider web on the balcony, as if waiting for them. "All this work," she said in her sticky voice. "All these clever tricks, and you're only moving closer and closer to my web."

"Then why don't you force me now," Nelay hissed.

"Approaching the prey too soon risks breaking the web. We will let you tire yourself out in the struggle before we take you."

Nelay drew her sword.

Tix pushed herself off, tugging a strand of the web so it vibrated. "Save yourself the trouble and stop fighting." She flew lazily away.

Jezzel cursed and stormed forward to slice through the web in one swipe. "How do you like your web now, you flaming bug eater?"

A laugh burst from Nelay's mouth as she remembered Tix on fire. She slapped her hand over her mouth. Jezzel turned blazing eyes to her. Nelay's laugh bubbled up harder, but her hand prevented it from coming out of her mouth so it sounded more like snorts.

She cleared her throat. "I'm sorry."

Jezzel's shoulders slumped. "Do you mind if I stay here like we used to? I don't want to be alone."

Nelay sobered. "As long as you want."

When she returned to the wall that evening, the Redeemed had deposited hundreds of pots and every transportable kiln they could find to the catapults in the northwest and southwest corners of the city. They busily filled the smaller pots with luminash. The bigger pots were reserved for the sand.

By nightfall, Nelay and Jezzel stood with her two guards at one of the wall towers, telescopes in their sweaty grips. The

Clansmen roared, calling out a garbled war cry. Her body tingling with anticipation and fear, Nelay watched as soldiers cracked their whips and horses heaved against their harnesses, moving their siege engines into place.

The Clansmen also deployed their breaching towers—rectangular rolling towers filled with men. When a breaching tower came close enough, a plank with cruel hooks would be lowered, allowing the Clansmen to breach the city wall.

"Kidin," Nelay called down to the glassmaker.

"It's not hot enough yet," he growled as he pumped the bellows, sweat pouring from his skin even though the tavo blew hard from the cool mountains.

Resting her hand on the wall, Nelay could have sworn she felt the cracks running just below the surface. Her ribs were like too-tight bands around her racing heart.

When the horn sounded to signal the charge, Nelay watched the Clanmen rush toward their walls, their battering rams inside rolling huts draped with soaked moss so they wouldn't burn.

Immortals shot fire arrows at the battering rams, while soldiers launched stones from slings. Yavish called down for her men to shift the ballista, like a crossbow three times the size of a large man. When she had it where she wanted it, she ordered the enormous string cranked back. "Fire!"

The bolt shot out, the coiled rope behind it snaking forward with a hiss. The bolt hit true, the barbed ends smashing into a joint in the Clansmen's breaching tower. Clansmen immediately started hacking at the enormous rope that stretched back over the wall, attached to teams of oxen.

"Take out the slack!" Yavish shouted.

Soldiers standing behind the oxen cried out a command to the oxen. As soon as the slack was gone, Yavish hollered, "Pull!" The drivers cracked their whip, and the oxen heaved against their harness. "Stand clear!" Yavish shouted to a pair of Idarans who'd strayed too close.

The Clansmen's breaching tower tipped, lurching forward with a groan and dragging forward to crush the men who couldn't clear out fast enough. Yavish called a halt long before the mangled remains reached the city walls.

Gaping at the smashed bodies, Nelay sank to her knees and vomited. Soldiers scattered, cursing under their breath. When Nelay was finished, Jezzel handed her a handkerchief. She wiped her mouth and nose, determined not to feel humiliated, and only halfway succeeding. Yavish rolled her eyes and ordered one of the men to dump dirt on the vomit and sweep the mess up.

"The sand is ready," Kidin called from below. Nelay's Redeemed opened the doors and began easing out an enormous clay pot.

"Raise our flag," Yavish called.

An orange flag came up. Nelay swung her telescope around and checked the catapult flags within her range. As she watched, two more were raised.

They were all watching the palace tower when it flashed in a rainbow of colors. "Luminash," Yavish ordered.

Dozens of men gently set dozens of smaller clay pots in the catapult's cup. Some of the pots were dark with age—obviously they'd been used for years by families who'd given them up the night before. Others had the dusty look of freshly potted clay. When Yavish deemed the cup full enough, she ordered everyone back. When they were clear, she cried, "Launch!"

Even as the clay pots spun through the air, the catapult crew was already twisting the catapult and cranking the arm back down. The unwieldy pots dropped first, while the slimmer ones flew farther out. The pots shattered on impact and the tavo caught the luminash powder, spreading it out like fine dust. Clansmen were already crying out, for while luminash was harmless when handled, it burned the eyes.

Horses twisted the catapult, moving it to the side. Another round of luminash went flying. Like the first round, these pots spun and dipped and careened until they crashed into the Clans-men, who must have known what was coming, for they turned and ran. By now, Nelay could smell the powder, and though most people found the scent sharp and unpleasant, it reminded her fondly of her time as an acolyte.

One more time, the catapult launched the luminash. And then Kidin was ready with piping hot sand in an enormous pot, which, judging by the soil clinging to the bottom, had been used for some kind of potted tree. As soon as the crew had moved out of the way, Yavish ordered the launch. The pot didn't make it much farther than the city wall before shattering in a plume of red hot sand that lit the luminash, which had thoroughly coated the Clansmen.

Now it flashed hot and bright, nearly pure white. Nelay's eyes were stained with the afterimage of living pyres, but she forced herself to watch, glad she'd already emptied her stomach.

All the Clansmen who could walk retreated immediately, obviously assuming more was coming. The catapult was cranked back again, this time with smaller pots of sand pulled directly from the kilns and settled in the cup. These pots went farther. The Immortals sent a barrage of fire arrows which went farther still. More luminash caught fire, until Nelay worried her plan had worked too well, for the fire soon spread to the base of the city walls.

"They won't burn," Jezzel assured her. Still, Nelay watched them carefully.

Unnoticed by the dying Clansmen, and even by most of the Immortals, an Idaran slipped out the main door, sprinting into the burned-out fields. He was dressed as a Clansmen. Nelay had watched as his hair was painted and his skin smeared with ash to hide his dark skin. In the deepening twilight, she knew if her tel-escope slipped off him for even a moment, she would never find him again. He made for a gap in the Clansmen's lines. He darted between two soldiers and then was lost to her. No matter how hard she looked, she could not find him again.

But she did find something else. A man, his face contorted in a scream she could not hear. It was one of the men who'd captured her. Memories tore through her—Harrow's many kindnesses culminating in him risking his life to free her. Surely there were others out there just like him. And Nelay had killed them, by the thousands. She felt something inside her crack, breaking off and leaving jagged edges that cut her with every breath. Her heart pumped erratically in her chest, and she couldn't seem to get enough air.

Jezzel was suddenly before her, her voice sounding far away and muffled. "Nelay? What is it?"

She couldn't answer.

"Hazar, Ahzem, help me!" Jezzel cried.

They converged on Nelay. Hazar lifted her into his arms. They carried her back to the palace, where Maran closed all the drapes and set a sleeping Concon on the bed beside her before helping Nelay out of her clothes. She lay in bed with Maran running a cool cloth over her skin, while Jezzel stood in the doorway. Nelay closed her eyes and breathed in Concon's sweet baby smell as Maran hummed something soothing and rubbed her back.

Eventually, Jezzel climbed into the bed as well, lying in front of Nelay, the baby between them. Nelay thought of Rycus then—of all the times he had helped her simply by telling a story. And she realized Jezzel, her dearest friend, didn't even know Nelay was in love. "Jez, do you remember Rycus?"

"The smuggler?" Jezzel said softly.

Nelay smiled, remembering all the times she'd mocked him with that name, all the times he'd mocked her by calling her high priestess. And somehow, the mocking had been replaced with teasing, and then tenderness. "He's more than that."

They whispered together, sharing it like a secret. And they giggled and got a little bawdy.

Concon had eventually fallen asleep on his mother's chest. Maran played with his tiny fingers. "Nelay?" she said hesitantly, then wet her lips nervously. "I thought about what you said. About liking myself. I realized you were right. I don't like myself." She trailed off into silence. "I know it's not important. All of Idara is falling apart, and it's just my silly—"

Nelay reached out and snatched her hand. "You're important. And that's the first thing you must begin to change—knowing you're worth kindness, and always demanding respect."

Maran nodded. "I . . . thank you."

Jezzel took Nelay's other hand. "Love is important. Friends are important. More now than ever."

Later, Nelay was aware of someone coming in, but she wasn't sure who until he spoke. "The Clansmen have all retreated," Nashur said. "They've stopped their assault. And I do not believe they are stupid enough to try it again."

When Nelay didn't answer, he leaned down and rested a heavy hand on her shoulder. "You were wrong, my queen. I'm not the most brilliant tactician alive. You are."

CHAPTER THIRTY-THREE

With the tavo brisk and cool against her left side, Nelay stood at the top of the observation tower, the smell of burning all around her. Five days had passed. Days that began with death and ended in fire and ashes.

The Clansmen had learned the tavo and ovat well, and they now attacked only when the wind was in their favor. But with the gates sealed shut, each attack cost them much and Nelay little.

Nashur rubbed his hands along the thin bristling of hair on his scalp. The fact that it wasn't perfectly shaved revealed how exhausted the commander was. "Our food stores are holding out, but the luminash won't last forever," he said. "Though I suspect that fool high priestess is hiding more somewhere."

"Our man got through," Jezzel reminded him.

Nashur turned his full focus on Nelay. "Have you considered what you'll do if the Tribesmen won't heed your summons?"

"They will heed it," she said simply, because if they didn't, the game was over. The Clansmen would win. The fairies would win. And Nelay was determined to be the victor here.

"They didn't heed Zatal's summons, and he was half Tribesman himself." Nashur's gaze narrowed. "What did you promise the desert tribes that has you so sure they will join in this war?"

"I didn't promise them anything. Zatal did," Nelay responded bitterly. Looking through a telescope, she scanned the horizon toward the Adrack Desert, as she had for days, only leaving when she could no longer stay awake.

Nashur made a sound low in his throat and walked away.

When Jezzel burst into the queen's bedroom just before dawn, Nelay was sound asleep. "The Tribesmen have been spotted."

Nelay jumped to her feet and buckled on her weapons— she'd taken to sleeping fully clothed—and sprinted to the observation tower. Her two guards, Jezzel, and a shiny new messenger trailed behind them.

By the time Nelay climbed the last stair, she was out of breath and dizzy. She snatched the nearest telescope from the table.

"Clear that blasted gate!" Nashur shouted to one of his men. It was the one gate he had refused to block off, even after she'd harassed him about it numerous times. Instead, he'd had the ironworkers build in a portcullis and an enormous gate studded with sharp points.

Even with the rays of the rising sun in her eyes, Nelay could tell Tribesmen were everywhere, attacking Clansmen who'd been asleep in their tents.

"Look toward the desert," Nashur said.

She swung her telescope to where he pointed. There the Tribesmen were thickest, thousands of them fighting like lions. A group of a few hundred had broken off and were battling toward the gate Nashur had refused to block off. Behind a few hundred mounted cavalry, there appeared to be hundreds of wagons.

The gates finally swung open and the Immortal cavalry shot out, clearing a path for the Tribesmen. The two groups met in the middle and then punched their way back to the city, the Immortal archers providing cover from above.

Jezzel crowed in delight, and bursts of applause and congratulations spread through the commanders.

Nelay handed her telescope to Nashur. "See that their delegation is brought to the palace with as much pomp as you can manage." She turned and headed for the stairs, Jezzel and Hazar talking animatedly behind her.

"My queen," Nashur said, hurrying after her. "What did Zatal promise them?"

She paused before saying so softly only he could hear. "Idara."

He let out all his breath at once. "What?"

She turned to see his shocked expression. "My marriage to the king shifts to the nearest male relative." She'd asked around, and apparently, it was an old man—an uncle or something.

Nelay battled back against her frustration and helplessness. "Zatal was right. It is best for Idara, so we will honor that contract."

The high commander halved the short distance between them. "But you are queen."

"And I will be queen still. After all, you and your Immortals are loyal to me, not some unknown Tribesman."

"Yes. But we need them, not the other way around," he said slowly.

She blew out. "I know."

"As king, he will outrank you. You will only have the power he gives to you."

"I know!" Nelay turned and pounded down the steps, her head aching from lack of sleep. When they'd reached the empty corridor that led to Nelay's rooms, Jezzel trotted to catch up and walk beside her. "Burn it, Nelay, they can't keep marrying you off like this."

"Shut it, Jez."

Nelay was suddenly against the wall, Jezzel's arm across her collarbone. "I have done everything you have asked me, and more. I have been there for you through all of this. So stop snapping at me!"

Nelay thought of a dozen different ways she could break her friend's hold. She did none of them. "It's not you the fairies, the Tribesmen, and Idara are all piling pressure on—it's me! And it's not you who's to blame if Suka is right and everyone's deaths are on me."

Jezzel backed away. "We can beat this on our own. You know we can."

Nelay rubbed at her headache. "I'm not so sure anymore."

"We're going to the healers to get you a sleeping draft. That or I'll knock you out."

Nelay smiled a little. "I'll take the draft." She knew from experience how hard her friend could hit.

Grumbling, Jezzel took up the lead. When they entered Nelay's chambers, Maran straightened from where she'd been playing with Concon on the floor. "My queen?"

Nelay scooped the child up and held him so his head rested on her shoulder. He squirmed and settled his face into the crook of her neck. Nelay pressed her nose to his forehead, breathing in his sweet smell. When had she become so attached? "He's the only one who doesn't care that I'm queen," she murmured. "The only one who doesn't want anything from me."

She glanced up as Maran gave Jezzel a concerned look. Jezzel rolled her eyes. "She's forcing herself to marry another old man. She's touchy and weepy, and I'm probably going to kick her teeth in before the day is through."

Maran's mouth came open. "Have you considered showing her some kindness?"

Jezzel shrugged out of her baldrics and dropped down on a rug, then rolled her neck until it popped. "That's your job— you're the nice friend. I'm the one who makes her laugh and tells her she's an idiot." Jezzel stayed on the rug, stretching her back and legs.

Tears sprang to Nelay's eyes. She loved both of these women so much. She cleared her throat, hoping Jezzel wouldn't notice how emotional she was. "I need to look like a queen, Maran. And quickly."

"I'll lay out your clothes." The girl disappeared into the other room and Nelay heard the water running.

"She's not so bad." Jezzel chuckled quietly. "She was scary-fierce the day I lost it. Wouldn't let me go. Helped me get myself together." Jezzel glanced up. "I wasn't very nice to her."

"She's forgiving. Perhaps too forgiving."

Jezzel studied Nelay. "I'm sorry. This isn't fair."

"I know."

"Well, I'd better go get myself cleaned up too. Be back soon."

Maran appeared at the doorway. Nelay reluctantly handed over Concon, who fit himself to his mother's arms and stuck a fist in his mouth.

Nelay disappeared inside the bathroom. The water was cool, just as she liked it. She scrubbed herself twice and let the oils soak into her hair. Maran entered and her clothes over the sink. Nelay stepped out of the water and toweled herself off. She slipped into her fanciest clothing—bell-shaped trousers and a fitted bodice that bared her stomach. Coins hung from every hem, and the color went from pale blue at her shoulders to midnight below her ankles.

She stepped outside and Maran fastened the bodice. Then Nelay sat on a chair as one of the servants from the temple shaved the sides of her scalp and styled her hair to show off her tattoos. They painted her skin with gold markings and bedecked her in so much jewelry she couldn't move without something clanking or tinkling—including gold chains across her stomach.

Last, they rested the golden phoenix mantle across her collarbone. She stared at the phoenix for a moment, wishing she didn't have to leave this room of friends to face one of strangers. Wishing it was Rycus she was going to. What she would pay to see him again, even for a moment.

Maran handed Nelay the veil, which she draped over her head. Jezzel returned, and the two of them left her rooms without looking back. Nelay descended the beautiful staircase to the throne room. Waiting for her was a group of Tribesmen—an even mix of men and women. Their swords were gone, though their veils were still up.

Her parents, Panar, and now Rycus. A pang shot through Nelay's chest, longing wrapped in the beginnings of bitterness. Would she always be fighting for the people she could never have anyway?

Nashur was already beside the throne, most of the commanding Immortals spread out behind him. He gave Nelay a nearly imperceptible nod. Everyone turned to watch her as she crossed the room, so she was very careful not to trip. She stood before the throne, deciding not to sit in it.

The man at the head of the Tribesmen unfastened his veil, revealing a face weathered by decades of wind and sun. He gave a short bow. "Queen Nelay, I am Bathzar, a chieftain of the desert tribes and Zatal's uncle."

So this was the man she was to marry. Nelay bowed back, steeling her face to remain expressionless. "I watched your attack on the Clansmen earlier, Bathzar. It was very well executed."

He tipped his head in acknowledgement. "Do you often watch the battles?"

"Sometimes she leads them," Jezzel reported.

Bathzar blinked at Jezzel before he looked back at Nelay. "How so?"

"It was her idea to use luminash to light their armies on fire," Nashur said.

The corners of Bathzar's mouth turned up. "Ah, a brilliant move. They will hesitate to attack your walls again. And I see you have the loyalty of those under your command. That speaks to your leadership."

An involuntary sigh left Nelay's mouth. "But the Clansmen haven't given up yet."

"Which is why you agreed to marry a Tribesman," Bathzar said.

Nelay forced herself not to wince. "Which is why I agreed to marry you."

He bowed. "It is a fine offer, one that affords many benefits, but I am afraid I must refuse."

Nelay stood in stunned silence, humiliation sliding from the top of her head down her whole body. "Why?"

"Because I am already a powerful leader of the tribes, and I will not leave my position or my people to be trapped within these walls. Also, my wife is rather fierce. Only a fool would cross her, and I am no fool."

"Then why did you come?" Nashur asked.

"Because my nephew has no such compunction. And as the contract shifts to the closest kin at my refusal, it is his to refuse or accept."

Another veiled man stepped up beside Bathzar. Nelay recognized those eyes. But her mind would not believe, even as he lowered his veil. "Rycus?"

It took every bit of self-control she'd learned in the temple to keep from running into his arms.

He gazed at her with a smoldering expression. She took in the men around him and realized one wore an eye patch.

"Scand?" She shook her head, desperately trying to dislodge a thought or two.

Four more men unfastened their veils: Cinab, Bahar, Ashar, and Delir. Tears sprang to Nelay's eyes. She blinked rapidly in an effort to disperse them before they betrayed her. "And the boy and the others you went back for?"

"All safely in the Adrack," Delir answered.

Nelay nodded to Rycus's friends. "I'm very glad to see all of you." She paused, trying not make herself a fool in front of all these people. "Rycus, I will speak with you in private."

She turned on her heel, her Immortals parting so she could pass. With Rycus following, she entered the first vacant room she came to, the library, and shut the door in Jezzel's face. Then Nelay turned and threw herself into Rycus's arms, breathing in the baked-glass smell of the desert and something that was manly and him.

"Nelay," he whispered, squeezing her harder.

And then she was sobbing. He was here. He was hers. After all the hopelessness and defeat and heartache. He pulled back and took her face in his hands, then kissed the tears from her cheeks.

"Did I ever tell you the story of how flowers came to smell so sweet?"

She laughed, dizzy with happiness. "Does it have something to do with a great Tribesman?"

Rycus grinned. "Don't all the best stories?"

She tipped forward, fisting his robes in her hands and holding them against her face, breathing deep. "Yes. I think they do."

He drew her back into his arms. "It involves a woman who loved a man, only she he was taken captive in battle."

Nelay shook her head. "I don't think I want to hear this story." Instead, she went up on her toes and kissed his mouth, pulling him to her with a desperation that exploded inside her like a pot of hot sand. His lips met hers, and her mouth yielded to him.

She was melting, every hard edge she'd honed over the years going soft. He sucked gently on her bottom lip.

She felt her mouth curve into a smile. Someone knocked on the door behind them. Nelay broke the kiss, and Rycus cradled her head against his shoulder. "Just a moment," she called. "We are discussing our union."

"Is that what this is called?" Rycus chuckled, deep and low. The sound brought a tug in Nelay's lower belly.

She sighed. "It's what we're supposed to be doing." She stepped back, knowing she couldn't touch him like this and think straight. "You're Zatal's cousin?"

Rycus nodded. "Yes."

That was why Zatal had reacted so badly when he'd seen Rycus's face—the king had felt betrayed by his own family. Now Nelay understood what Zatal had meant when he'd said it might all work out. He'd hoped Bathzar would allow the contract to pass to Rycus.

"And you will be chieftain of the desert tribes?" she queried.

"My grandmother chose me years ago."

Another reason Zatal let Rycus live, because he was family and a prince in his own way. Nelay shook her head. "Why didn't you tell me?"

Rycus looked sheepish. "I couldn't, not until I knew you weren't going back to Thanjavar. It wouldn't be safe for me in Idara otherwise. I was going to tell you that night, but—"

"But Zatal came and nearly killed you," she said. "Because you're his family." Rycus nodded. Nelay cast her eyes heavenward. "We're not going to do this thing where you make me drag everything out of you. Tell me what's going on, smuggler."

He leaned against one wall, his arms folded across his middle and one leg cocked. "Oh, we're not, are we?"

"Rycus," she said in a warning voice, but there was an undercurrent of laughter. She was eager to disperse the heaviness that seemed to be growing between them.

He tipped his head to the side and waited with mirth in his gaze. Rycus and his stories. She blew out hard. "How are you related to Zatal?"

"Remember the story I told you? Of King Kutik and Queen Marif?" Nelay nodded. "Marif was my aunt, the oldest daughter. My mother is the youngest."

Nelay bit her lip. "So you helping me escape Thanjavar, and what came after . . . was that some kind of family rivalry between you and Zatal?" Because if it was, she swore right then that she would throw Rycus to the Clansmen herself, and burn the consequences.

Rycus shot her a dark look. "I'm a smuggler. Being paid to move goods without being caught is what I do. As for the rest, I tried to keep my distance from you. But you are hard to ignore."

They hadn't exactly gotten along. Nelay tried to remember when that had changed. It was the stories, she realized. He'd told them for her. "So why didn't Zatal inform me who you where? Why the secret?"

Rycus dropped his gaze to the floor, his first sign of weakness. "Because I humiliated him. I'm surprised he didn't kill me outright for it." He looked at Nelay. "I didn't mean to fall in love with you."

She let out a long breath. "Where does this leave me?"

"According to my cousin's edict, your marriage contract comes to me if we both agree."

Nelay crossed her arms to keep from fiddling with the jewels on her bodice. "So you accept it?"

"It's not quite that simple," Rycus said softly. "The tribes have certain requirements." She stiffened, but he held up his hand as if asking her to withhold judgment for a moment. "It's not like Idara. I can't just command an army of Tribesmen. They have to agree. And there are terms that must be met first." He tried again to smile. "Looks like you'll be starting out our marriage in debt to me again."

She couldn't exactly command the armies either, not without Nashur. She shook her head. "We're going to have to go back out there. I can't agree to anything without the high commander."

Rycus took a step closer, and then another, until he stood in front of her, close enough to touch. "Before we do, I want you to know that by our customs, you would be my equal—except for the fact that you still owe me eight darics."

When she didn't smile, he reached toward her cheek. "Stop," she chided. "Now is not the time to be cracking jokes."

He tipped his head to the side. "When someone is sad, that is the best time to make them laugh."

She studied him. She loved him. He would be a good king. So why did it feel like she was about to betray her people? "Very well."

His hand came up and cradled her face. "I'm not sorry. About any of it. Are you?"

She looked into his eyes, remembering the way she had fit next to him like she was meant to be there. "Some of it. Kalla, my parents, my brother." Even Zatal, though she didn't say it.

Rycus leaned forward and pressed his lips to her forehead. "It's going to be all right."

Nelay melted into him. And the weight she had carried for so long seemed lighter because he was there to share it with her.

"Well," said a voice. "I suppose it's good to see you two getting along."

CHAPTER
THIRTY-FOUR

Nelay pushed Rycus back to find Jezzel in the doorway, one eyebrow arched and amusement flashing in her eyes. Nashur stood behind her, his expression dumbfounded.

"Nashur, meet Rycus. He's the man who smuggled me out of Thanjavar," Nelay said.

"Hello, Rycus," Nashur said, recovering quickly. "It's good to see you again."

Nelay looked between them. "You two know each other?"

Nashur nodded. "Zatal's family visited sometimes."

Rycus held out his hand for her. "Shall we?" Nelay studied his hands, calloused and rough. If she had any say about it, they would be her husband's hands.

"You have a room full of people waiting for you," Jezzel reminded them dryly.

Nelay straightened her shoulders and strode back into the throne room, still filled with dignitaries, Immortal commanders, and Tribesmen.

She stood before the throne with Nashur and Jezzel beside her. Rycus headed up the Tribesmen, with Bathzar at his side.

"Queen Nelay," Rycus said, all the levity gone from his voice. "You have proposed an alliance between our nations, but this alliance affords us little and you much."

He paused and took a deep breath as if to steel himself. Nervousness bubbled up in Nelay, making her feel numb. "You will give us everything," he continued.

Nashur straightened up beside her, his nostrils flaring. "That is ridiculous! Idara is a nation of wealth and power. The Tribesmen don't even have a name to call themselves!"

Rycus's gaze narrowed. "We are Tribesmen. That is enough. But as an act of generosity, you will be allowed to keep the name of Idara."

Nashur flung his hand out. "Idara has ten times the citizens of the Tribesmen. Our cities flow with gold and silver. Our harbors are some of the richest in the world. And you think—"

Nelay laid a hand on his arm. "Let him finish."

Nashur turned furious eyes to her. "You don't understand! You've not seen the wealth of Idara. The power and majesty. To give it—"

"Commander!" she said sharply. He cut off abruptly, his mouth pressed in a hard line. Nelay took a deep breath to calm herself. Nashur was the Immortals and the armies. In all reality, he was more powerful than she. "Please, just let them finish."

Nashur held his hands behind his back and stared at the ground for several seconds before looking up. "Continue."

"Idara will be grafted into the Tribesmen," Rycus went on. "Not the other way around. Your lords and ladies will be replaced with Tribesmen of our choosing. Your laws will be rewritten, your coffers drained. In short, Idara will become an extension of us."

Nelay's jaw hardened. How could he do this to her? To Idara? "How would you be any different from the Clansmen?"

Rycus leveled her with a gaze. "Your people will be free."

Silence pierced the room, punctuated only by the muffled sounds of battle.

"You didn't think we would agree to help you for nothing," Bathzar said.

"No," Nelay replied, working to keep her voice from shaking. "But I did not think to lose everything."

"All great stories begin thus," Rycus said softly.

Nelay shot him a glare. He stepped closer, close enough to reach out and touch her. So softly only she and those near her could hear, he said, "It took everything I had, and everything Idara has, to get them to agree to come this far."

"I don't want to lose Idara," she finally said.

"You already have," Rycus said quietly. "This way, at least you will keep as much of your country as possible."

Nelay studied him, wishing for a time when things had been simpler, when it had just been the two of them and their allies had been clear, and their enemies even clearer.

She motioned for him to step back and then turned to Nashur. He took her shoulder and led her back into the library. Jezzel managed to slip inside just before he slammed the door behind him.

He immediately began pacing. "That man is either very stupid or far too clever."

Nelay held her hands out helplessly at her sides. "Nashur, what choice do we have?"

"Bowing down to those desert scum like they're our betters, when they should be bowing to us. Taking our gold and fighting—"

"They're not mercenaries," she interrupted.

He rounded on her. "And don't you take their side! Just because you were stupid enough to—"

"Don't," she warned.

Nashur ground his teeth. And Nelay went silent, watching as he paced. She went over the field and every player in it a half dozen times. And even with the Tribesmen, she came out behind more than ahead. But Nashur was a smart man. He would come to the same conclusion on his own in his own time. It would do no good to push him.

Suddenly, he ripped a dozen scrolls from the wall and hurled them across the room. Then he stood looking at the carnage as if surprised by the sight of it. Nelay and Jezzel exchanged glances and then went back to waiting. Finally Nashur's shoulders slumped and he muttered, "After this is all over, we're going to stage a coup."

It would be a very, very bad idea to argue with him at this point, so Nelay kept silent. Nashur let out a long breath. "But for now, we need them."

They filed back into the throne room, where Nashur asked Rycus, "And if Idara falls?"

"The Tribesmen will melt back into the desert," Bathzar replied. "Safe from the Clansmen, as we have always been."

Nashur dropped his head, his fingers tapping against his leg. "We can't say no." Even as he said it, he shook his head.

Bathzar rubbed his hands together. "Excellent. Then we shall have a wedding, Tribesman style. You Idarans take too long."

Nelay didn't trust the gleam in his eyes. The Tribesmen started forming a circle. "And how do the Tribesmen marry?" she asked. There was too much bitterness for her to taste the sweet relief of being with the man she loved just yet.

"Oh, I've heard of this," Jezzel said. "I've always said I should have been born a Tribesman."

Nelay shot her a look. "You've never said that."

Jezzel shrugged. "Well, I should have."

Nashur looked like he was considering smacking some sense into her.

Nelay glanced around. "And what exactly is a Tribesman wedding?"

Rycus grinned. "I told you from the beginning I wouldn't mind dancing blades with you."

"You can't be serious," Nelay scoffed.

Jezzel chuckled lightly. "I need to find my own Tribesman." Several Tribesmen shot her looks of open invitation and she waggled her eyebrows at them.

Rycus bounced on the balls of his feet and windmilled his arms to loosen up.

All right. He was serious. Nelay blew out and started slipping off her jewels with Jezzel's help. It took forever, hundreds of eyes watching her the entire time. Finally, Nelay wore only her bodice and loose trousers. Starting to stretch, she asked Rycus, "So am I supposed to let you win?"

He winked at her. "Nope. In fact, you win, I'll be considered lucky. If I win, you'll be considered lucky."

Nashur moved closer to Nelay and said under his breath, "Show these sand fleas what it's like to be at the receiving end of Idaran anger, eh?"

She stalked into the circle, her mind whirling with Rycus's strengths and weaknesses.

He gave a lopsided grin. "I won't pull back."

She circled him. "What's the objective?"

His grin widened, showing his slightly uneven teeth. "First one pinned or forced out of the circle."

Shouldn't be too hard. The priestesses had trained Nelay how to fight bigger, stronger opponents. She took a deep breath, finding her center. She'd have to drop him fast and not let him get his hands on her.

Rolling to the balls of her feet, she waited. Rycus leaned toward her, his longer arms reaching.

"Begin!" Bathzar called.

Rycus lunged for her. She twisted, stepping to the side and shoving him past her. But she didn't let go. Nelay landed on his back, knowing she'd have to lock his joints—there was no way she could hold him by sheer force. She tried to wrench his arm up his back. He was already twisting, attempting to lock her arm so he could flip her and pin her.

She tried to trap his arm and roll, forcing his elbow the wrong direction. But he was too fast. He flipped her and pinned her arms to the floor. She wrapped her legs around him and locked her ankles

"This is going to be a fun marriage," he grinned from above her.

Nelay jerked one arm free, pinned one of his hands to the floor, dropped her opposite foot, and reared up, pinning his upper arm with her elbow. Then she leveraged Rycus up before dropping him down and wrenching his elbow in the wrong direction.

His face contorted, but he didn't concede. Fool, stubborn Tribesman. She pulled harder. "All right," he gasped. "I'm the lucky one."

Nelay let him go, hopped to her feet, and inspected her silk robes for damage. A little wrinkled but otherwise intact.

The Tribesmen cheered her and loudly booed Rycus, who grinned. "I let you win."

Nelay laughed. "Want to go again?"

He winked at her. "Later, high priestess."

And with that, they were married. As Nelay's anger began to fade, an overwhelming gratitude rushed over her. She'd thought her opportunity to be with this man had been snatched from her forever. Rycus stared back at her, the same joy in his gaze.

Jezzel elbowed Nelay and murmured, "If you two are finished making moon-eyes at each other, I'd like to point out that this was much more straightforward than the last wedding." She helped Nelay back into the veil.

Rycus's face went blank and he turned away.

"Say something to them," Nashur grumbled.

Nelay took a deep breath and announced to those present, "This union will provide Idara with the means of conquering the Clansmen!"

The people cheered. Nashur shot Rycus a look that demanded he say something.

"Idara is a great nation," Rycus declared. "And she already has a great queen. I will stand beside her, and together we will rid the lands of the Clansmen."

"And then Idara will rid the lands of Tribesmen," Nashur said under his breath before he stalked off.

"As a dowry," Rycus went on, "I have brought a thousand Tribesmen to Thanjavar, all of them ready to fight. The rest of our men will harry the enemy throughout Idara."

The Immortals broke into cheers again, and Rycus leaned toward Nelay. "I've asked Scand to be one of your personal guards. He's too old to be on the front lines with the rest of them, but I trust him with your life."

"I'm sure Jezzel will be happy to have him," she said, not really sure at all. She looked around until she found Scand and smiled at him. He nodded to her.

"Well," Rycus called over the cheers, "let's go see what to do about winning this war."

Nelay led the way into the war room, the Tribesmen and Immortal commanders trailing her inside. Nashur waited there for them.

Rycus stood before a huge map of the city. "What have you done so far?"

As if he'd been waiting for this question, Nashur launched into a tactical presentation that impressed even Nelay.

Rycus cast her an approving glance. "I must say, I'm amazed at what you've accomplished so far." He looked back at the map. "But the worst is before us. Thanjavar is in the most danger now."

Nelay dropped into one of the chairs. "How so?"

"My tribes will cut off the Clansmen's supply route, starve them out, and molest them throughout Idara. The Clansmen have to do something now or nothing at all." Rycus folded his arms.

"But if we can just survive a few weeks, I believe they will be forced to retreat behind one of their captured city's high walls."

"We might not last that long," Nashur said. "The Clansmen don't attack when the wind is in our favor. And the luminash won't last forever—we've already used half of it."

"But the Clansmen don't know that," Rycus replied.

"They do not," Nashur said a little grudgingly.

"What about the sand?" Rycus asked.

Nashur nodded. "That we have plenty of. And we can make more pots."

Rycus studied the map. "If we can make them think we'll never run out of luminash, this just might work."

Nelay felt hope for the first time since the siege had begun. She had all the players to win this game. They would save the city. They would save Idara.

As Jezzel instructed Scand on his new guard duties, Nelay opened the doors to her rooms. Maran stood up from where she sat in a chair at the table, nursing her baby. She gestured to a covered tray on a table before the hearth. "I've had food brought for you, my queen. I'll see no one disturbs you."

Nelay blushed furiously as Rycus stepped up behind her. "Unless the wall's breached."

"At which point, I'm sure you'll hear the horns," Maran said with a smile. She shooed the others out and slipped outside, then shut the door behind her.

Nelay turned toward Rycus, expecting him to hold her, to want to be with her as much as she wanted to be with him. But he strode out of sight into her bedroom. A little flustered, she lifted the lid from the tray to reveal fresh fruit, sliced cheese, and bread. She wasted no time taking a bite of cheese and bread, then popped a handful of pomegranate seeds into her mouth. "Want something to eat?" she called toward the bedroom.

"Give me a few minutes," he replied.

She heard water splashing and decided he'd just wanted to clean up first. She settled herself down to eat while she waited.

When he emerged a short while later, he wore a pair of loose trousers and nothing more. Nelay stared at his lean body as he sat down beside her and devoured the bread and cheese in a few bites. He wiped a bit of mango juice off the side of his mouth, then sucked it off his thumb.

He caught her watching him and reached out to unclip her silk veil, which he pulled off and let slide onto the floor. Nelay closed her eyes as the hot breeze from the window wicked over her sweaty skin.

"You don't bear this burden alone," Rycus said gently. "Share it with me. Between the two of us, it won't be so over-whelming."

Tears burned in Nelay's eyes. She realized she was exhaust-ed, body and soul. "I don't know how."

"Let me help you."

She looked up into his eyes, so dark they were almost black. "I'll try."

The back of his fingers traced her jaw and moved down her neck to rest on her collarbone. "I'm in no rush, Nelay. It's all right if we take things slow." He pulled back from her. "Where would you like me to sleep?"

Her body cried out at his absence even as humiliation slid across her skin. She shot to her feet and turned her back on him. "I thought that would be fairly obvious, but perhaps not."

She heard him stand up and come up behind her. He wrapped his arms around her from behind, but she pulled away. He raised his hand in a placating gesture. "I just . . . I don't want to push you."

She whirled around to face him. "Push me?"

His gaze locked on hers. "I know you were with Zatal only a few days ago. I don't know what happened between you, but I don't imagine it was pleasant."

She softened. "Oh, that's what you're worried about?"

"I just want you to know we don't have to hurry things."

"Zatal never touched me," she said. A look of relief washed over her new husband. "Would it matter if he did?"

Rycus shook his head. "I just want to be gentle."

She stood before him and looked into his eyes. "I want you to kiss me."

He pressed his lips softly to her forehead. "Like this?" he said, a dull hope in his eyes.

She pulled back and tapped her lips. "No. Not like that. Here."

He grinned before leaning in and obliging, a soft gentle kiss that spread through her like warm honey, sweet and slow. It wasn't nearly long enough. "Like that?"

She licked her lips, tasting him. "Let me show you."

And she did.

CHAPTER
THIRTY-FIVE

The breeze stirred across Nelay's skin, and she shivered in her robes and curled closer against Rycus. But then she remembered he had shut the patio doors before they'd gone to sleep. She shot up just in time to see two forms slip inside.

"Rycus!" was all she had time to say before a man was on her, his knife plunging toward her chest. Her training kicked in and she blocked with her wrists, wrapped her legs around his waist, and rolled him under her.

She pinned his knife hand to the bed and punched him in the throat. Gasping for breath, her attacker cuffed her on the side of the head with his free hand. Nelay ignored the ringing in her ears and chopped down on his hand, aiming for the spot that would make his fingers numb. He released the knife.

Before she could grab it, he rolled under her, taking her with him. They both fell to the floor, her back taking most of the impact. She heard a crash and knew Rycus was fighting a battle to the death against at least two men. She had to finish this and help him!

Had anyone heard her initial cry? Nelay wanted to scream—needed to scream for help, but the effort would cost her, and she was barely holding him off.

And then another figure cast a shadow from her balcony.

She and Rycus would not win against so many. She let out a scream. It cost her, as she'd known it would. The man pinned her on her stomach, his other arm wrapping her in a headlock. Stars cascaded across Nelay's vision.

She threw her head back and felt his nose break. She flung her elbow into his gut. A knife hit her arm instead of her vitals. There was no pain, only the sensation of her flesh parting and something sharp and foreign inside her. He drew away to stab her again. Nelay threw her weight back and twisted to get on top of him. They rolled on the floor, fighting for the knife.

The door banged open, sending in a shaft of lamplight. Someone darted into the room, but Nelay couldn't see who. She was aware of flashes of metal and clanging steel, but that was all.

Scand suddenly appeared above her. He drove his blade into the man on the ground, mortally wounding him. Nelay wrenched the knife from his failing grip. Instinctively she wrapped a hand around her bleeding arm and staggered to her feet. Rycus had managed to fend off his attackers and find his swords. He was fighting two men, also bearing swords.

Scand started toward him, but another attacker jumped the old man from behind. They fell to the floor. The attacker clearly had the advantage as they grappled, trying to choke one another.

Nelay couldn't decide whom to help, Scand or Rycus. Then a fourth man landed on the balcony and sprinted for Rycus from behind. Nelay took a step closer to get the rotation right and threw. The knife hit the attacker in the chest, right where she'd aimed. He glanced at her and she was shocked to see blue eyes. Clansmen. In her city. And wielding swords.

"Nelay!" Maran stood at the door, Concon nowhere in sight. She motioned for Nelay to come toward her. "Quick!"

Nelay's fingers searched for the swords she always kept beside her bed as she scanned the fights. Rycus was holding his own. And in the dark Nelay couldn't tell Scand from the Clansmen as they rolled across the floor.

Jezzel suddenly darted into the room. Unable to find her swords, Nelay snatched a vase and threw it at one of the Clansmen fighting Rycus. He stumbled back and Jezzel swung, her sword sinking into his abdomen. He glared at them and tried to thrust again, but Jezzel pulled her sword free and he sank to his knees, one hand pressed against his belly. He struggled to stand again, but only managed to fall on his back.

Jezzel whirled around. "Where are your swords, Nelay?"

A flash of shame tore through Nelay. "I don't know!"

Jezzel grabbed Nelay's arm and tried to haul her out of the room, but she planted her feet. "No! What about Scand and Rycus?"

"Without a weapon, you're a liability!" Jezzel said.

Hating that her friend was right, Nelay allowed herself to be dragged into the antechamber as the city's warning horns sounded.

"Maran, hide," Jezzel whispered loudly.

She backed them up to a corner and passed Nelay her throwing knives. Hearing quick footsteps in the hall, Nelay tensed, preparing to throw.

Hazar and Ahzem came running through her doors wearing only their dhotis, swords clenched in their hands. Nelay relaxed her grip on the knives. Jezzel barked orders. The three of them formed a half circle, with Nelay in the center.

More Immortals darted into her bedroom. They came back out moments later, dragging a half-conscious Clansman between them.

"Take him to the dungeon for questioning," Jezzel said coldly.

Rycus burst into Nelay's antechamber, looking around frantically. The moment he saw her, he sagged in relief. "Have the palace searched. Give no quarter," he said to Jezzel.

As she barked out orders, Rycus nodded to Nelay and disappeared back in her rooms. An Immortal left her chambers at a run, presumably to round up whomever he could find, as most of the guard had been sent to defend the city.

"On me," Jezzel said to Hazar and Ahzem. "We're going to search every corner of her rooms, then search them again."

Maran emerged from behind a wall hanging. Hazar spun around, his sword out. She gave a little scream and he scowled before moving past her. She ran to a drawer, pulled Concon out, and tucked him to her chest. The baby was sound asleep.

"You did the right thing, coming to get me," Jezzel said.

Maran nodded, and something seemed to pass between the two, something that looked like the start of a friendship. Then Maran glanced at Nelay and a soft cry left her lips. "You're hurt!"

Nelay felt it then, the distant pain. Her left side was soaked with clammy blood from the wound in her arm, warm drops dripping from her fingers. "It won't kill me," she said dismissively. "I should go to the observation tower—see what's going on."

Jezzel moved to stand between her and the door. "Not until the palace is secure."

Delir, Bahar, Cinab, and Ashar burst into the room, along with more Immortals. Jezzel ordered one of them to fetch the healer. At Nelay's request, she ordered the Tribesmen to stand guard at the door. The Immortals she sent to search the palace.

Then she and Maran knelt beside Nelay and looked at her arm. After a quick inspection, Jezzel relaxed. "It's a flesh wound. You'll have a nasty scar, but you'll live."

Maran tore off a strip of cloth from a towel in the cupboard and handed it to Jezzel, who wrapped it so tightly around Nelay's arm that she hissed through her teeth.

An Immortal returned and began reporting to Jezzel. Nelay looked around the room, scanning to make sure everyone was accounted for, and suddenly realized she'd never seen Scand come from her bedroom—the room Rycus had disappeared in the moment he'd known she was safe.

"Scand?" Nelay's voice sounded small. She took off at a run. No one made a move to stop her as she entered the bedroom. Scand lay crumpled beside her bed. Rycus knelt beside him, pressing Nelay's balled-up sheets against the old man's chest. The sheets were soaked in blood.

She rushed to kneel at Scand's other side. He gave a slight shake of his head. "Ten years ago, I'd have bested him easily." The old man tried to laugh, but it came out as a wet, gurgling cough.

Nelay wiped the blood from his mouth with the corner of a sheet.

Scand gripped Rycus's hand. "My wife . . ."

Rycus nodded. "I'll tell her. And I'll see she wants for nothing."

A lump formed in Nelay's throat. She hadn't even considered Scand's wife, and now he was dying—no one survived an injury to the lungs.

"You saved our lives," she choked out.

Scand grunted. "This wasn't the first time—just the last."

A tear slipped down Nelay's cheek.

"The Clansmen are in the city," Jezzel cried from the other room.

Nelay's head snapped up and she rose to her feet. She started for the door before pausing to look back. "Thank you, Scand." Such a trivial thing, those words, but it was all she had to offer.

Scand lifted a hand in farewell. Rycus caught her gaze, and she tried to convey her sorrow. Just as she crossed the threshold, she heard Scand say, "Give me your knife while I can still do it."

Her steps stuttered, knowing the old man meant to kill himself quickly rather than die slowly. Should she go back, be there for Rycus? But then Jezzel swore, and the fear in her voice drove Nelay to the other room.

She spotted Rycus's cousins. "Go to him. Now," she said. The men exchanged looks before moving to obey. Pushing away the thought of what would greet them, she strode to Jezzel, who stood at the open window. Nelay took the telescope her friend handed to her and peered through it to see Clansmen fighting inside the city walls. She sucked in a breath, temporarily losing her bearings before she located one gate after another. "They're all intact?"

"As far as I can tell," Jezzel responded.

"Then how did they get inside?" But then she saw the wall itself had collapsed. Clansmen streamed over the rubble.

Nelay touched the glass idol at her throat. "Jez, the Goddess of Fire has betrayed us."

"I know," Jezzel answered softly.

"I don't think we can beat this."

"I know."

Nelay's grip tightened and she pulled the necklace over her head to stare at the idol's worn body. She opened her fingers, letting the idol fall with a small clink on the ground. Then she brought her heel down on top of it and broke it into pieces. As she looked at the bits of glass, a feeling of loss shot through her, like the last connection with her father was gone.

"What's that?" Maran asked from behind her.

"Just a piece of glass," Nelay replied.

CHAPTER THIRTY-SIX

Nelay needed her armor and weapons. She turned, intending to get them. But Maran was coming from her bedroom, her face ashen and her arms full of Nelay's things. Nelay didn't know whether to say thank you for thinking ahead or sorry for what she'd had to see. In the end, Maran met her gaze, tears streaming down her face. Nelay nodded and Maran seemed to understand.

She helped Nelay into her armor while Jezzel helped herself to a couple extra knives and strapped them to her ankles.

A messenger burst into the room. "Commander Nashur sent me, my queen. The palace is secure. You are to come with me."

Rycus approached the door, his face blank. Without a word, he started out, taking the lead as the rest of them followed.

"How did they get inside the city?" Jezzel asked.

"They collapsed the wall," said the messenger.

"How?" Nelay burst out.

"I'm not sure," he replied. They hustled through the war room and up the winding stairs to the observation tower. At the top, the Immortal commanders were running and shouting, the luminash flashing and horns sounding.

Nashur stood before the brazier, holding a map down. He glanced at them and began talking before they'd even reached him. "They infiltrated the palace before attacking the city."

"But how did they get inside the palace?" Jezzel demanded. "How did they know which rooms to target?"

"We don't know that yet," Nashur said.

Nelay rubbed her throat. "One of the men who attacked us survived."

"I know. My men are questioning him now."

Rycus leaned forward. "And if he doesn't talk?"

"He will," Nashur assured him.

Nelay swallowed. "Is there anything else we can do?"

Nashur stared at the map as if the answer might reveal itself at any moment. But he remained silent.

Nelay covered her mouth with her hand, not sure if she was going to cry or vomit or both. Just yesterday, victory had been days away. She stared out over the falling city. "I had all the players. All of them." Her gaze sought out Jezzel's. "Maybe . . . maybe I should go to Suka."

Jezzel shook her head over and over, but she said nothing.

"Go to Suka?" Rycus said. "What's that supposed to mean?" When no one answered him, he stepped closer to Nelay. "What does that mean?"

Jezzel took him aside and spoke in low whispers.

One of the palace guards strode up to Nashur and said something too soft for Nelay to make out.

"My queen," Nashur began, "the populace has gathered at the palace gates. They want inside."

"Let them in."

"I must caution you, there may be assassins among them."

"Let them in," Nelay said more firmly.

Nashur inclined his head and called for a flag she'd never seen, a centurion standing before a set of gates. Nelay stepped to the banister to watch as the palace's heavy gates heaved open and Idarans spilled inside. She studied them through her telescope. None seemed injured. Most had arms full of bedding and food.

She shifted her focus to the city. Jezzel and Rycus came to stand beside her. Morning wasn't far off now, and Nelay could make out men fighting in the streets. The fighting was concentrated around the collapsed sections of wall, all clustered fairly close to each other and a gate.

"You can't do it—what Suka's asked you," Rycus said from behind her. "We'll find another way."

"Everything we try fails," Nelay gasped out. "No matter how many times I rework the field and the players, more of my people end up dead." The Idaran soldiers were fighting for their lives and the lives of their families. And they were dying.

"Northeast wall," Nashur said. "Look! Look!"

Jezzel shoved a telescope into Nelay's hand and she swung it around. The Clansmen from without had managed to push a breaching tower to the wall. The hooks swung down, embedding themselves in the mortar.

Clansmen spilled from the tower onto the wall, swords and hammers chopping and slicing. Men rolled to the ground, knives and fists coming out. And the soldiers held them. But they were spread too thin. Clansmen managed to break through to open the last gate that wasn't bricked over. Others were using the Idaran's own pulley system to open the portcullis.

"If they break through, the city will fall," Jezzel said.

"Nashur!" Nelay called.

He hurried to stand beside her. "The Immortals won't reach them in time."

"Look!" Rycus cried.

Nelay watched as a group of archers on the wall ignored the Clansmen mowing them down, lit their arrows, and pulled back their wicked recurve bows. The arrows flew free, their fires temporarily disappearing as they sailed through the air.

Nelay winced when they hit their targets. Clansmen and Immortals alike were pierced, some dying immediately, others contorting in agony. It was the archers' final act, for the Clansmen killed the last of them and kicked their bodies from the wall. Yet their arrows had flown true, striking the scaffolding of the pulley system. It was burning. But the Clansmen were still able to use it.

The portcullis inched upward, just enough for dozens of Clansmen to fit under it. They were quickly dispatched by the Idaran army. But then it crept up a little more. Then a little more, until Clansmen could fit through simply by crouching down. More Clansmen poured through. Faster and faster they came, a tide that was simply too great for the exhausted, dwindling Idarans to fight off.

"We can't stop this," Nelay said.

"My queen!" It was Nashur again, his normal calm underlined by a panic she'd never seen before. "The Market Gate has collapsed."

She swung her telescope to her right to see Clansmen pouring through the broken bricks, quickly overpowering the Idarans. The telescope was suddenly too heavy for her to hold. "Sound the horns for retreat."

For the smallest moment, everyone around Nelay stilled. She looked up to find Rycus, Nashur, and Jezzel watching her with grim faces.

"Am I wrong?" she asked.

"No," Nashur said, defeat weighing down the word. "We've lost the city."

He motioned to one of his men, who ran to a column. A small pipe Nelay had never noticed before stuck out the side.

"Cover your ears," Nashur said even as he followed his own advice.

Nelay pressed her palms to her ears as the man blew. The whole tower seemed to vibrate with the sound of the massive horn. As it slowly tapered off, Nelay lowered her hands, her ears ringing.

The soldiers began steadily retreating.

"And they will all come to the palace, soldiers and citizens?" Rycus asked quietly.

"How will they all fit?" Jezzel asked incredulously.

Nelay took a deep breath. "Have you seen to the palace's defenses?"

"Weeks ago," Nashur stated.

"Sir," one of the Immortals cried. "We're trying to move the citizens to the gardens behind the palace, but the people are clogging up the palace gates."

Nashur wiped the panic from his gaze. "Send down fifty men. Keep them moving."

"We're trying, sir, but there's simply too many of them."

"Open the palace doors," Nelay said. Then they wouldn't be jammed up against the palace.

Nashur looked at her in surprise. "They'll loot and destroy."

She shot him a look. "Thieves are the last of my concerns at present."

He gave the order. As soon the palace doors opened, the citizens streamed inside. Nelay steeled her courage and looked back through her telescope.

Two more gates had fallen, and Clansmen streamed into the city in a constant wave. The Immortals, who were well trained, retreated in an organized fashion. Behind them, the general citizens fled toward the palace.

Taking a deep breath, Nelay swung her gaze back to the Clansmen. They were looting. Even as she watched, a little boy jumped from a second-story window and took off. A Clansman brought him down with a single swing of his axe.

She gasped and lowered the telescope. It fell from her fingers, clattering on the ground. "Nelay?" Rycus said.

She leaned against him, her eyes closed. "They're murdering my people—a little boy." She couldn't finish. It was her fault. Somehow, somewhere, she'd missed a player, and it had cost her people everything. Great shudders rocked her body. Her heart was racing too fast. She couldn't breathe.

Rycus half supported, half carried her down the stairs. The moment she was out of sight of her commanders, the sobs took over, until Nelay could no longer walk. So he carried her.

Halfway down the stairs, she managed to wriggle from his arms. "Rycus, I have to go to Suka."

"No. We can figure this out. There has to be another way."

Jezzel and the rest of their guards were silent behind them.

"I don't want to do this, but I don't see—"

Rycus took Nelay's face in his hands. "I just found you. I'm not going to lose you again. Give me a chance—give us one more chance to fix this. Please."

She looked into his pleading eyes and couldn't say no. He must have seen her acquiescence, for he turned to Jezzel and said, "You keep her from doing anything foolish. Swear it."

She gave a tight nod. It must have been enough, for he pressed a kiss to Nelay's forehead and bolted down the stairs.

CHAPTER THIRTY-SEVEN

The healer knelt before Nelay in the library. Though she could feel the pull of the bone needle and the thread, the stitching of the wound didn't hurt. When the woman finished, she bound Nelay's arm.

Jezzel pushed open the doors and stopped a good distance away, as if hesitant to approach.

"What is it?" Nelay said.

Her friend cleared her throat. "You're going to want to see this."

Nelay rose heavily from the chair and followed Jezzel down the long corridor, which was guarded by a pair of Tribesmen, to the crowded throne room. Hazar and Ahzem moved before her, clearing a path. Nelay had made it halfway across the room before the people began to recognize her. The crowd pressed in on all sides, so tight she feared they would crush her.

A little girl grabbed Nelay's left hand and begged her to send the Clansmen away. An old woman demanded Nelay send Immortals back into the city for her son and his children. An old man marched toward her, bent around Hazar, and spat in her face, screaming that the city falling was her fault.

Jezzel drew her swords and held them to his belly. "I will kill you." He looked down at the blades and back at her, but he held his ground. "As a priestess of the goddess, I swear I will kill you where you stand. Now move!"

His nostrils flared before he slowly stepped to the side. Hazar and Ahzem had also drawn their swords. Nelay was tempted, but she couldn't see her way to killing the people she'd tried so hard to save.

Suddenly, Cinab, Bahar, Ashar, and Delir were there, easing their swords from their leather scabbards. The people backed away, clearing a path for them.

"Where did you four come from?" Nelay asked in relief.

"Rycus sent us to fetch you," Bahar responded.

"Letting the people in the palace might not have been a good idea."

"Nashur tried to warn you," Jezzel said as she made eye contact with some injured Immortals and waved them over. Though battered, bruised, and limping, they came to their queen, putting another barrier between her and the mob.

The group stepped into the courtyard. Citizens still streamed inside the gates. The Immortals quickly shuttled them around the palace toward the back, to the expansive grounds.

"Thank you," Nelay said to the Immortals and Tribesmen.

One of the Immortals met her gaze. "They don't know what you've done for Idara. But we do." He nodded in respect and resumed his vigilance.

Jezzel glanced back as if making sure Nelay was still following her as she started up the wall's steep steps. At just over five stories tall, this wall was only about half the height of the city wall.

Rycus already stood at the top, as did hundreds of Idarans bearing some form of weapon. Nelay moved to her husband's side, looking out across their once-great city. Half of it was overrun by Clansmen. The Idaran line of defense had condensed as the distance between soldiers shrank, allowing for a more orderly retreat.

Jezzel pointed. "There, do you see it?"

Nelay didn't need a telescope. About a league from the palace gates, a pocket of a few hundred Immortals, soldiers, and citizens had become stranded in the midst of the Clansmen. Trapped between buildings, they fought on two fronts, desperately trying to hold the line.

They were faltering. Nelay took in all the players before her—the angry mob in her palace, the retreating Idarans, the people watching beside her, the hopelessness a physical presence all around them. Her mind spun, nudging the players this way and that until they all fit together. And then she had it. "Sally out and bring them inside," Nelay said.

Rycus turned to her in surprise. "Just as many men might be lost retrieving them as they will save."

She met his gaze. "We lost the Thanjavar. Thousands of our people have died. If I can give them one victory, their courage will not fail them."

She turned to go, but Rycus gripped her upper arm. "The only soldiers inside the palace walls are those who were injured. If you force them back into that and they don't return, you'll face a mob."

She deflated a little. "What do you suggest?"

"Volunteers."

Nelay moved to the edge of the wall looking down at the crowded palace courtyard and shouted, "Citizens of Idara! Immortals!"

"Don't forget us," Ashar grumbled.

"And Tribesmen!" Nelay added.

When the din didn't settle, Jezzel banged the flat side of her swords together. Once she had everyone's attention, she cried. "Queen Nelay!"

Nelay reached up and pulled the curving sword from her back. With it in hand, she looked at over the people clustered below. "Tonight, I have seen the majesty of Idara. When faced with the overwhelming waves of our enemy, any other army would have broken. Ours has not."

She paced before them, giving them back their broken pride one piece at a time. "I watched as they delayed the horde so that our people might flee. Even in defeat, they were not defeated."

She pointed behind her. "Even now, a cluster of hundreds of Idarans are trapped in the midst of the Clansmen. They are fighting—and I have a feeling they will fight to the last man."

Now she had to give them a goal—something achievable. "I cannot order you to save them. You are exhausted to the brink of collapse already, many of you injured. But I know my armies. I know my people. They will not leave their fellow soldiers and citizens stranded. And so I ask for volunteers."

Some of the people below Nelay straightened. She knew what she was—what she had to be. She was hope. And hope was a powerful thing. More powerful than an army. More powerful than the fear of death.

A woman stepped forward. She had to be in her forties, her hair gray at the temples and her body softened by children. "I was an Immortal once. And I would be proud to be one again."

More women came forward, by the dozens. The Tribesmen joined them. Priestesses streamed from the temple gates with armfuls of training weapons, which they immediately began passing out.

Nelay caught their gazes, one after another, tears shining on her cheeks. "You, each of you, are mine. And I am yours. I will fight with you. And perhaps some of us will fall, but not all of us."

They cheered and stomped their feet, creating a rumbling she could feel in her bones. "And our fellow Idarans will not fall, because we will not allow them to."

She turned to Rycus and Jezzel. They were tightlipped, their faces hard. "Have you lost your mind?" Rycus asked.

Nelay took a deep breath. "I know it must sound that way, but trust me when I say I have to do this."

"You can't," Jezzel said.

Nelay pushed the tears off her cheeks. "I am hope. If they cannot see me, cannot feel me, they will fall, and we with them."

Jezzel knew her well enough to know how methodical her plans were, but this had to go against every instinct she had. "If our queen falls, what do you think that will do to them?"

Nelay chuckled bitterly. "Then I will be a martyr and they will fight even harder." When Jezzel still didn't relent, Nelay stepped toward her. "I was almost mobbed earlier, Jez. I have to do this."

"I'm coming with you," Rycus said.

She met his dark gaze. "One of us needs to stay. They can't lose us both."

He pushed past her. "I'm coming."

Nelay knew that short of tying him up, there was no stopping him. Steeling herself, she turned back toward the crowd. "If this be the end," she said loudly, "then it will be an end to remember."

Those willing to fight gathered in front of the temple. Rycus ordered large rectangular shields and wicked-sharp spears be brought from the priestesses' arsenal. He briefly told the volunteers how the Tribesmen used shields to create a wall, spears piercing from above.

Nelay was not given a spear or a shield—she wasn't tall enough to use either effectively. Jezzel positioned her in the center of the volunteers, all of whom were angry or proud or simply past fear.

Ahzem and Hazar took up positions before and behind her, Jezzel at her side. Ashar, Bahar, Cinab, and Delir stood protectively around Rycus, who wore the robes of the tribes. Over the top of that he wore mismatched Immortal armor. He certainly didn't look like a king.

He wouldn't look at her, and anger pulsed from him in waves. She slipped closer and touched his back. He stiffened before turning to her. She stared deep into the blackness of his pupils and thought she caught sight of his soul in their dark depths. Tears filled her eyes. She loved him. As the sun loved the sky, she loved him.

He softened a fraction and leaned forward to kiss her forehead. They stood like that a moment, Nelay holding his wrists, he holding her head. Then he gave her a gentle push to take her place before turning to face forward again.

As she moved back to Jezzel's side, relief washed through Nelay. Even though Rycus disagreed with her, he hadn't withheld his affection.

"Fire and burning, Nelay, you are in love with him, aren't you?" Jezzel was aghast.

Nelay managed a watery smile. "Wasn't part of our plans, was it?"

"Just so we're clear, my plans haven't changed. I have my eye on a few Tribesmen. I figure if I play it right, I can rotate between at least three of them."

Nelay snorted. "Maybe just one at a time."

"Don't tell me what to do, woman," Jezzel said in mock anger.

From just in front of her, Rycus called out the signal and they jogged through the open gate in a spear formation, their shields forming a wall around them.

"We're both coming back from this," Jezzel said, all trace of humor gone.

Nelay knew if anyone could hold off an army with sheer stubbornness, Jezzel would be the one.

Nelay was shorter than most of the formation, so she could not see ahead or behind, only the bobbing heads and the two- and three-story buildings surrounding her as they traveled down the gradual slope. She nearly tripped over Delir's big feet and decided then to keep her eyes on the flagstones, glancing up only to see where they were.

At less than a half a league from the palace, the formation slowed. "What's going on?" Nelay asked Rycus, who was tall enough to peer over the heads in front of him.

"We've reached the Idaran line."

The Idarans parted to let them through. There was a brief, intense fight and then they broke past the Clansmen and behind enemy lines. They ran until Nelay's legs felt floppy and her breath sawed in and out of her throat.

A dozen streets past the defensive line, they reached the trapped Idarans. Their group staggered to a halt, the men at the front holding their shield walls while the men behind them stabbed at Clansmen from above. Their flanks were protected by the building's solid walls.

Nelay's hands were sweating on her grips, and her body itched to swing them. To do something besides being blind and trapped inside.

The fighting slowed and Rycus called for the formation to change. Their wedge-shaped head split into two, allowing the bloody and beaten Idarans to stagger behind their shields. The group was mostly women and children with a smattering of exhausted Immortals and soldiers, who became a flash of broken noses, blackened eyes, sweat, and fear. Nelay pointed back the way they'd come. "Stay together! Head for the palace!"

As they streamed past, Nelay caught sight of an old woman being carried across the back of a young man. Their gazes locked, and beneath the grime and blood, Nelay could have sworn she saw Havva.

"Fire and ashes," Jezzel swore beneath her breath.

Nelay whipped her head back around. Behind the fleeing Idarans, the full force of the Clansmen was coming, cutting down anyone in their path.

Rycus's gaze locked on the Clansmen, his face tense as he waited. Finally, he called for their formation to wield back together one measured step at a time.

The formation clipped back together. The men holding the shields let Idarans who were mixed with the Clansmen slip through while the Idarans stabbed down at the Clansmen from above.

"Retreat!" Rycus ordered.

The shield bearers took orderly steps back while the spear wielders continued stabbing from above. If the shield wall buckled, they'd be overrun.

They managed this for a few blocks, arriving at the place the original defensive line had been. They were gone, their steady retreat always taking them closer to the palace.

Rycus rotated soldiers so they didn't grow too tired. Finally, Nelay caught sight of the palace. The gates were closed. They were trapped.

Arrows rained down on the Clansmen attacking them. Nelay glanced at the wall to see archers doing their best to save them.

Someone cried out in Clannish, "Honor to the Shyle!"

A cluster of Clansmen sprinted at their formations from the side. The shield line buckled, and Nelay suddenly found herself on the front lines. She felt no fear, only a profound sense of relief. She wasn't useless anymore. Her body slipped effortlessly into rhythm, slicing and cutting. Jezzel fought in perfect rhythm beside her as they retreated.

When they were finally close enough to the gates, a formation of Immortals sallied out. They beat the Clansmen into their own retreat before turning and arrowing through the gates.

CHAPTER THIRTY-EIGHT

Once inside, Nelay had a hard time putting her swords away. She was still itching for a fight. Gradually that faded, leaving her tired, her injured arm throbbing in time to her heartbeat. Hazar and Ahzem, only a little battered, jogged up to her, relief on their faces. They took up positions at a respectful distance.

She found Rycus, alone. "Where are your men?"

"I lost them," he replied even as his eyes scanned the crowd for his cousins.

Someone called out, "Queen Nelay!" and she started, thinking of the man who'd spit on her. But as people broke out in a cheer, slapping each other's backs, she relaxed a bit. More citizens called out to Nelay. Her guards closed ranks around her as the Idarans who'd been trapped slipped by, grasping her arm or hand and tearfully expressing their thanks.

Rycus watched them warily and said, "I guess you were right." He and Nelay stood side by side, but neither of them made a move to touch the other. Her tender feelings for him seemed so far removed from the battles and the death that she couldn't reach out to him. Not yet.

"I could have just as easily been wrong," she told him.

Lines of worry etched his face. "I'm going to check on my men."

She moved to follow him but saw someone she recognized—one of Havva's granddaughters. Around her was a cluster of people Nelay recognized from her time with them in Dalarta. They were Havva's offspring, and they were crying.

The face Nelay had seen . . . Numb, she and headed toward the group, but a woman blocked her path. "Those soldiers saw us trapped. They stopped to help, knowing they would fall behind." Tears filled her eyes. "We thought we would all die or become slaves, but you saved us."

More came to speak with Nelay and touch her. She pushed them back. "Let me through!" Ahzem and Hazar made her a path. Finally, she reached the group of Havva's loved ones. The old woman lay in the midst of them, pain written on her wrinkled face. One of the girls looked at Nelay. "She saved my life—hit one of the Clansmen over the head when he tried to . . ." Her voice trailed off as sobs racked her.

Nelay leaned forward and pulled back part of the Havva's robes to reveal deep and bloody wounds in her abdomen. "Havva?" she gasped.

The old woman gripped Nelay's hand, her delicate bones standing out in her pale skin. She was dying, and they both knew it. Nelay remembered what Havva had told her about a woman's sacrifice. "You gave life, you saved life. The world is a better place because you lived in it. You won."

Havva managed a smile, even though her body was jerking. "Knife."

Nelay shook her head. She couldn't do this again. First Scand, and now Havva. "No."

The old woman's pleading eyes met Nelay's. Nearly choking on her tears, Nelay took one of her throwing knives and pressed it into the old woman's gnarled hand. Then she staggered back, unable to watch.

The family moved close again, and several seconds later their cries became screams. A boy turned and gave Nelay a look of betrayal.

She staggered away and practically collapsed on the palace steps. Jezzel sat beside her, resting her hand on Nelay's back. Nelay wasn't sure how long they sat there, but when she looked up, Nashur was storming toward her.

Jezzel jumped to her feet and stepped between them. "Now is not a good time, High Commander."

He shoved her away and shouted at the queen, "You didn't!"

"I did." Nelay scrubbed her face with her sleeve.

"And you let her," he barked, glaring at Jezzel.

She shrugged. "Queen trumps captain of the guard."

Nashur's glare returned to Nelay. "You could have been killed."

"I wasn't."

"What were you thinking?"

"I had to."

He took a deep breath and let it out slowly. "Why?"

Nelay wiped her nose. "Because it gave them back their pride. We were an army defeated, but even in defeat, we were strong."

Nashur rested his hand on his sword hilt. "I haven't the final counts, but it looks like we lost half of our Immortals. Roughly half of the army." Nelay's hand went to her throat—that was over fifty thousand men. "I've assigned men to count the Idarans, but those numbers aren't in yet."

Her arm throbbed harder. "How bad is it?"

Nashur folded his hands behind his back. "Our provisions won't last long. A few days."

Rycus came to stand beside them, his face hard. Nelay could tell he was grieving, and her heart sank. "Who is it?" she said.

It took him several seconds to respond. "Delir—he's missing. No one saw what happened."

Nelay swallowed. "Havva was with them. She had—" She couldn't continue.

"Her wounds were mortal," Jezzel finished for her.

"This has to end now," Nelay said. She looked at Rycus, asking him with her eyes to understand. To forgive her. To know she couldn't bear to be the cause of any more deaths.

"Give us some space," he said without looking at the others. They withdrew, their backs turned.

Rycus sat on the steps beside his wife. "I have to go to Suka," she said. "I have to try."

He took her arms in his hands. "Nelay, once you start plotting, you can get out of anything."

"And if more people die?"

"You just saved hundreds of people. The gates are already closed. It will be hours before the Clansmen try anything. Use those hours—that's all I'm asking."

The words she wanted to say got stuck in her throat. She looked down.

"You promised you would try one more time," Rycus reminded her.

She had a feeling they were just delaying the inevitable, but he was right—they were safe at present. Silently, she nodded.

Rycus helped her to her feet and walked with her toward the palace. After a moment, Nashur, Jezzel, Hazar, and Ahzem joined them.

"I want a list of every man who went on the charge with us," Nelay said to Nashur, her voice trembling with emotion. "And the names of the Immortals we saved. See that each receives a hero tattoo and an elevation in rank."

Nashur relayed her orders to a messenger, who looked around before approaching a woman dressed in the robes of a university apprentice.

Rycus cleared his throat. "Why weren't we more prepared for the outer wall to fall?"

Nashur motioned for them to follow him into the palace. The throne room, at least, had been cleared out. "To be blunt, we were as ready as we could be."

Nelay felt a headache forming in her forehead and knew she needed to eat. "And the palace's defenses?"

"We fare better there," Nashur replied. "One of the priestesses admitted they have some luminash left. And their armory is extensive. The food on the other hand . . ."

Jezzel leaned forward. "If it wasn't for the food shortages, how long could we hold out?"

Nashur looked back at the Idarans milling about beyond the palace doors before he stepped into the corridor. "Our numbers are reduced, but they're also highly condensed. The wall isn't as high or as strong as the city wall, but it was made by the finest engineers in the world. I'd say with a reliable food supply, and protection from that blasted weapon they use to knock down the gates, we could hold them off indefinitely."

They all looked at Nelay, apparently waiting for her to come up with some brilliant and unique solution. But she was empty, like a burned-out lantern. She searched the faces of her husband and her best friend. "Ideas?"

"Did they really tunnel in?" Jezzel asked as they arrived in the war room and Hazar and Ahzem took up positions at the door.

Nashur sat on a chair with a grunt. "They came up in an abandoned building. At some point, a signal was given. The tunnel's supports were burned, which collapsed the walls. Our gates were attacked from both sides. We hadn't the men to defend at that point."

"Did you ever find out how the assassins came to be in the palace?" Rycus spoke up.

Nashur shook his head. "Not yet."

"But there's a way we can find out," Jezzel said. "Unless you killed the man we captured."

"He didn't survive the questioning," the high commander said without emotion.

Nelay cringed at the implication, fighting back a wave of nausea.

"Someone must have helped him," Jezzel said.

Nelay could feel each of the stitches, feel the heat and swelling of her arm, pulsing, pulsing. "What Idaran would do such a thing?"

"One who does not want to become a slave," Rycus said tightly.

CHAPTER THIRTY-NINE

Maran sidled into the war room, Concon in her arms. Seeing her brought out Nelay's memories of Havva all over again.

Jezzel patted Nelay's back. "I'm going to go see if I can round us up some food. Don't leave this room until I come back."

"I'll go with her," Rycus informed Nelay, then fell in beside Jezzel. "I need to see one of the healers."

"Why?" Nelay said sharply.

He turned to her and lifted his trouser leg, revealing a gash on his shin. "It's not too deep—a few stitches and I'll be fine."

She moved to go with him but he held up his hand. "You need some rest and you need to be available if the Clansmen decide to attack. This shouldn't take long."

Nelay glanced at his wound again. It didn't look too bad—she'd had worse. "All right." She collapsed in a chair and rested her head on her folded arms.

"I tried to keep them out," Maran said in a rush as soon as the others had stepped away. "I really did. But they came inside anyway."

"Keep who out of where?" Nelay mumbled from within her arms.

"Your rooms," Maran wailed. "They've been taken over."

Nelay almost laughed. Of all the struggles she'd endured today, this was nothing. "It doesn't matter."

"But all your things—"

Nelay wiped her eyes and sat up. "They were never mine. They were Zatal's." She opened her mouth to tell Maran about Havva, then realized the telling of it would break her again. And Nelay couldn't afford to break.

She glanced around suddenly. "Wait, where are his mistress and children?"

Maran grunted. "Ziyid had better luck barring the doors than I did."

"Well, I imagine she's had more practice since I became queen." For surely the woman had barred them to keep Nelay out. "We'll be staying with her from now on."

"I don't think she's going to like that."

"I don't much care. Go to her rooms and demand that she let you in."

Maran hesitated and seemed about to say something, but Nashur trotted down the last few stairs from the tower. "My queen, the Clansmen have called a parley."

Nelay had an overwhelming urge to run. "For what?"

"To discuss the terms of our surrender."

"Surrender." She pushed to her feet, her jaw tight. Before she ever surrendered Idara, she would give herself over to the fairies. She looked around for her husband, needing his strength, then remembered he was with the healers.

"They're waiting, my queen," Nashur said.

Nelay sighed. "Very well." She started off and spotted Maran. "I thought I told you to go to Ziyid."

Maran pulled something out of her robes and thrust it at Nelay. It was the phoenix mantle. "I couldn't carry anything else and Concon. I'm sorry."

Nelay wished she'd left it altogether. "Thank you." She slipped it over her head, sure she didn't look very queenly. Her clothes were sour, her hair coming out of its braid, but with her swords, she would at least look fierce.

Maran nodded and left. Jezzel jogged back into the room, a basket on her hip. "I brought what I could find.

Nelay looked at Hazar and Ahzem, who had been following her around for hours like burrs on a donkey. "The Clansmen can wait."

They ate traveling food: dried meat, hard biscuits, fruit, and nuts. Nelay could have eaten more—she knew they all could have—but it was better to have a little now than none later.

As she strode through the palace to the gates, Idarans shifted out of her way. A guard opened the man door, and Nelay stepped outside with Nashur and her guards at her sides.

The Clansmen had set up a tent in the center of the road. She tried not to pay attention to the bodies she had to step over or their sickly sweet smell. She strode up to the tent as if she wasn't afraid, as if she didn't loathe the ten men waiting to greet her.

A man of about forty stood a step in front of the group, wearing an intricate belt over a linen shirt with embroidery around the hem. "I am High Chief Bratton of the Shyle. These are my fellow Clansmen, all chiefs of their own clans."

He motioned for another man, who began translating into Idaran. Unwilling to let on that she spoke Clannish, Nelay waited for the translator to repeat the words before she said, "I am Nelay Arel Mandana ShaBejan, Queen of Idara." She held out her hand toward Nashur. "And this is Nashur, high commander of the Immortals and the army."

Bratton raised a single eyebrow—she wondered how he did that. "Isn't there a new king?" he asked the translator.

The translator nodded. "The prince of the desert tribes who has given us so much grief."

One of the clan chiefs said under his breath, "Maybe we made her a widow again."

A few of them cracked smiles. Bratton frowned. "I do not find that comment amusing, Gregan."

The man's smile disappeared.

Bratton looked her in the eye. "Queen Nelay, your soldiers have fought bravely. You have defended your city bravely. But now it is time to end the fighting."

He waited while the interpreter translated.

"You would make us slaves," she said as soon as the man was done.

Bratton frowned. "Our laws of reparation demand a debt to be repaid."

"I have no debt to you or your people," Nelay said when the interpreter was finished. "I was not even born when King Kutik attacked your lands."

Bratton watched her impassively. "Raiders are not to be trusted. Murderers, conquerors, monsters, the lot of you." He growled in his throat and said to the interpreter, "Don't tell her that, I lost my temper." He rubbed his forehead. "Tell her that our dead demand justice."

She trained her gaze on this strange man as the interpreter finished. "You think yourself better than us? You who have invaded our lands, killed our people, destroyed our homes?" She scoffed. "Clansmen killed both my parents in their home. Neither of them had ever been soldiers. What of the boy I watched one of your Clansmen murder as he ran for his life? What of the girl whose grandmother died trying to save her granddaughter from your men's ravaging hands? What debt did they owe?"

Bratton's face had turned red with rage. "It was because of the conniving of the Raiders that my father became a cripple. That my Clansmen were murdered. I lost my sister and my best friend. The Raiders will haunt us no more, because they won't exist."

Nelay steeled her expression to remain neutral until the interpreter had finished. Then she said coolly, "The worst kind of liar is a hypocrite, for he is lying to himself."

She turned on a heel without another word and marched back to the palace. Once inside the war room, she slumped into the nearest chair.

"That did not go well," Jezzel said.

Nelay chuckled darkly. "No. It did not." She felt tears pricking her eyes. "I hate them. Truly hate them."

Nashur braced himself against the backs of one of the chairs. "We should accept."

Nelay's gaze jerked up. "What?"

He wouldn't look at her. "We don't have a choice. I can't watch our people starve to death."

Nelay's mouth hung open before she snapped it shut. "Idara will be gone. Our way of life, our cities—everything. We'll be a legend, a myth."

Jezzel said, "Not to mention the fact that they'll kill all of the leaders, which includes us."

"They didn't say that," Nashur replied.

"They didn't have to. You're too dangerous to be kept alive." Jezzel looked around the room. "We all are."

Nashur dragged his gaze to Nelay's. "Better a myth than a tomb, which is what this palace will become."

"Zatal didn't think so." She found herself wishing he were alive, that this burden was still his to bear. "Nashur, if I've lost you, I've lost the armies."

"My queen, it's over," he said softly. "I can't send my men to fight, not when there's no chance of survival."

But there was a chance. Nashur just didn't know it yet. Nelay considered telling him, then remembered what Tix had said about the goddess's spies always listening. "I won't let it come to that," she promised quietly.

He didn't respond, and the silence grew until it filled the room. Nelay glanced at her exhausted guards. "You three get some rest. Nashur can assign someone else to watch over me."

Even Jezzel didn't argue as Nelay pushed herself up from the table. "I will speak with my husband now."

Jezzel grabbed her arm. "You promised him you would try one more time. You can't give up, not yet. Not when the price might still be more than we can afford to pay."

Nelay closed her eyes. Of course Jezzel knew her well enough to realize when she had given up. "I don't see another option."

"That's because you're convinced there isn't one. You can't succeed when all you see is failure."

Nelay pulled away. Nashur motioned for two of his men to follow her as she headed toward the door. "Nelay." Nashur rarely called her by her given name. "This is the only option left to us. You must see that."

Her hands clenched to her sides, Nelay left the room and made her way to where the healers were treating the injured. In the shade of the palace gardens, people were packed in neat rows on the ground. The smell was terrible—waste and vomit mixed in with sweet opium smoke and herbs.

One of the healers looked up at her. "I sent your husband to Ziyid."

"You did what?" Nelay blurted, her thoughts flashing to the beautiful woman King Zatal had loved.

"He'll be better cared for by her—she's the best healer the palace has."

It was news to Nelay, who hadn't even known Ziyid was a healer. She turned on her heel and took the stairs to the second level two at a time, her harried guards right behind her. Upstairs, she took the first hallway down the crowded corridor and stopped in front of the familiar door. She tried to push it open, but it was bolted tight. She slapped it with the flat of her hand. "It's Queen Nelay. Let me in!"

After a moment, the bolts slid free and the door opened just enough to admit her. On the other side stood the oldest girl child—Nelay didn't even know her name.

"Parisa, bring her here," someone out of sight called.

The girl, Parisa, led Nelay through the receiving room, which was littered with high ranking Immortals and nobles. In the second room were more Immortals and nobles.

And Rycus. He was lying on his back, with Ziyid and Maran kneeling next to him. His leg rested in a bath of cloudy water. As Nelay watched, Ziyid ran her hand down his leg over and over again. His eyes were closed tight with pain.

Taking a deep breath, Nelay stepped up to them. Maran saw her first. "Nelay!"

Ziyid rubbed Rycus's leg harder, saying, "It's not too deep, but it wouldn't stop bleeding."

Worried, Nelay crouched beside him. His leg was cut in two places; he'd only shown her one. A chunk of skin hung off his knee, and there was a deep puncture in his shin.

"The warm saltwater flushes the wound," Ziyid said, then took a pair of scissors and trimmed off the skin. Rycus winced and kept his gaze locked on the ceiling.

Nelay was having a hard time catching her breath.

Ziyid showed Maran how to apply a compress of pungent-smelling herbs over the wound and tightly wrapped it. Then she washed her hands in another basin of water her daughter brought and wiped them on a clean towel. "He should be fine as long as he changes the wrapping."

"Thank you," Nelay said.

Ziyid looked her in the eyes for the first time. "Maran has a talent for this. Would it be all right if she stayed here and helped me?"

Nelay looked at Maran, who was blushing. "If she wants to."

Maran smiled. "Please."

Nelay nodded.

Ziyid studied Nelay. "Rycus is my children's cousin. He's family. And you've done nothing but shown my family and me kindness. You don't need to demand entrance. You are welcome here. Always."

Nelay felt tears burning her eyes as Ziyid's compassion chipped away at the hard shell she'd placed between herself and the emotions looming over her.

Without waiting for a response, Ziyid rose to her feet and moved on to the next patient.

"I'm going to be all right, Nelay," Rycus said.

"Why did you hide one of the wounds from me?"

He took hold of her hand, his skin rough. "I just needed it cleaned. Nothing to worry you about."

She let out a long breath. "Nashur thinks we should surrender."

Rycus pushed himself up on his elbows. "You're not considering it, are you?"

Nelay's pulse thrummed in her wrist. "Maybe he's right. The palace is overrun, and there's not enough food for everyone."

"Do you know what they'll do to you?"

She let out a bitter laugh. "Does it matter in the end?"

"It matters to me."

Nelay stared without actually seeing anything. *The Clansmen who tried to assassinate us—what if they came in through the mine?* Her mind grabbed hold of the thought as she remembered how enormous the mine had been.

An idea hit her suddenly with the force of a sandstorm. A move that could save them all. She was standing and moving toward the door before she'd made a conscious decision to do so.

"Nelay?" Rycus called. He stood and started limping after her.

"You should stay here," she chided him.

He settled his baldric over his shoulders. "We wouldn't have anyone left to fight if everyone who was hurt sat back."

At the door, Nelay turned to pin Maran with a stare. "Remain here unless I call for you."

The girl pushed herself to her feet. "Where are you going?"

Nelay held out her hand. "Just stay here."

Maran nodded reluctantly.

Nelay slipped out after Rycus, then told him her plan as they walked. Soon they entered the war room, where she glanced at the group of commanders. "Where is High Commander Nashur?"

After receiving four different answers, she held up her hand for silence. "Find him. Now. See that he meets me at the observation tower." Four solders split up to do her bidding. "Has anyone seen Yavish? Did she survive?"

"She is seeing to the palace's catapults now, my queen," a man spoke up.

"I need her as well." Nelay trotted up the steps and emerged in the burning sun. She looked out over her city—the ruined buildings, the smoke, the bodies scattered everywhere. And watching her from the center of every archway were the three fairies, Nos, Siseth, and Tix. "It won't be long now," Siseth said darkly.

Before Nelay could think of a reply, they turned and flew away. She closed her eyes for a moment to calm herself, then opened them and studied the catapults built behind her walls. She noted the placement of each one, as well as the distance to the outer walls.

Rycus watched her patiently. Perhaps he, like Jezzel, had come to recognize when she was maneuvering the players of the field. Making everything fit.

Nashur joined her, his eyes bleary and red-rimmed. Then Yavish appeared, saying, "Queen Nelay, the only thing standing between the clans' armies and ourselves is a handful of soldiers, a far-too-thin wall, and my catapults. You'd better have a good reason—"

"I have a plan," Nelay interrupted. "It's dangerous and terrible, but it just might work." As she and Rycus related everything, the group fell quiet.

When they had finished, Nashur broke the silence. "You remind me of Zatal. Had he lived, the whole world would have bowed beneath your combined cunning."

CHAPTER FORTY

From her seat by the fire in the war room, Nelay watched the council plan their defenses, speak of contingency plans, and briefly discuss how the armies would regroup, retake one of the other cities, and from there, retake Idara.

It was in that council that she saw the majesty of men. They would willingly shed blood—even die—to protect their people. They were not just strong of body, but also of soul.

As night wore on into morning, exhaustion took hold of her and she fell asleep. Maran's hand on her shoulder woke her. Nelay was in a strange bed, with sunlight streaming in from the window. She felt the heat of midday. "Where? How—" she began.

"You're in Ziyid's bed. And I'm pretty sure Jezzel drugged you," Maran said softly. When Nelay's expression hardened, Maran grunted. "You should thank her."

Groggy, she sat up and found some milk and banal bread, which she ate hungrily.

"Hurry," Maran said. "Nashur needs you."

Nelay finished it quickly, then took a moment to clean herself up before heading out. She located Nashur in the war room. His face was tired, but his eyes were as sharp as the blades at his back. He nodded. "We're ready. It will give the armies courage to see you."

Rycus held out her baldrics, then helping her put it on since her back was still stiff. "Did you sleep?" she asked him.

"Not as much as you, but enough," he said teasingly. He limped beside her as they left the war room. Jezzel, Hazar, and Ahzem took up positions around them.

Nelay shot Jezzel a look, which she returned with one of smug satisfaction. "You need me, Nelay. Remember that."

She rolled her eyes. "Like I need a bug in my eye."

Ignoring that, Jezzel studied Rycus's limp. "You're supposed to stab them, not the other way around."

He nodded sagely. "If only you had told me before."

Jezzel smirked. "I'm telling you now."

At the doorway to the throne room, Nelay paused, watching as the surviving Idarans moved in a steady stream down the corridor that eventually led to the dungeons, and from there to the mine. Scattered around the palace were the remnants of Idara's vast wealth—the precious gold pitchers and chests of coins, left behind in favor of blankets and food.

Jezzel nudged Nelay and she moved on, out the palace doors and into the bright sun and sweltering heat of the courtyard. Weaving through the soldiers, they climbed the wall's steps and stood looking down at what remained of Idara's armies. Their uniforms were no longer uniform, for their ranks had been forced to swell with citizens and Nelay's Redeemed. There was a contingent of priestesses as well, their armor and eyes gleaming with the hunger to be proven.

"Do you want to say something, or shall I?" Nelay asked Rycus.

"You've a knack for it," he replied.

She looked out over her army, her heart swelling with pride. She reached up and pulled free one of her curved swords.

"Here we go," Jezzel whispered in a playfully mocking tone.

"These past few days, I have seen the indomitable will of Idara," Nelay shouted, holding up the blade for them to see. "It is in your strength, true. But it is more than that. It is in your courage and goodness."

She paced before them. "I saw it as you gathered around me to free the Idarans trapped in the city, knowing some of your brothers might not live to see the next sunrise, knowing you might not live to see the next sunrise."

Nelay stopped and looked many of the soldiers in the eye. "I see it now. Though fear courses through your bodies, you do not stand down, you do not turn away."

She pointed beyond the wall. "The Clansmen will charge the gate when they realize what we're doing. They will try to stop us. We mustn't let them."

No one cheered—they couldn't even if they wanted to, for surprise was a large part of their attack, and they must not make too much noise.

After a few more words of encouragement from Nelay, Nashur dismissed the soldiers.

"That is why you give the speeches," Rycus commented from beside her.

"It's kind of scary how good you are at that," Jezzel said dryly as she handed Nelay a bucket of water.

Nelay dipped her veil inside, soaking it. More buckets of water were being passed around so the soldiers could dip their veils. Nelay tied hers up, the wet fabric feeling strange against her face. "And so it begins," she said to no one in particular.

Nashur turned to her and Rycus. "You two will be split up. That way Idara stands a better chance of one of you surviving."

Rycus straightened. "I'm not leaving her."

Nashur watched him steadily. "And what could you do for her that her guards cannot?"

"He's right, Rycus," Nelay said gently. When her husband ground his teeth, she added, "This is about more than just us."

"All right," he grumbled. He kissed her forehead, something she was growing to love. Then he turned and went where Nashur told him to go.

Nelay waited, Yavish at her side. The ovat picked up, gusting and blowing hard. Nelay glanced at Nashur for confirmation. He nodded once. She lifted her hand, holding it long enough to be sure it couldn't be missed.

Behind her, she heard the scuff of dozens of footsteps, the creak of the catapults, and the clack as the gears caught. She dropped her arm. The catapults thwacked and their load launched out, sailing over her city, beautiful still even after days of siege.

The boulders hit, causing an explosion of mud brick. Nelay was too far away to hear the chaos, but she raised her telescope and studied the broken buildings. There didn't seem to be Clansmen scurrying about. That far from the palace, the buildings must have been abandoned.

Yavish called out adjustments, one at a time, then ordered the men operating the catapults to reset them and wait for her command.

Below, Nelay watched as the Clansmen streamed out of the beautiful homes closest to the palace, shrugging into their armor, holding their axes and shields while they looked about blearily in confusion. She wondered how long it would take them to realize what she was doing.

Within minutes, the buildings were in rubbles. Behind her, Nelay could hear the flaming arrows catch fire. They hissed as they passed above her, going so fast it appeared the fire had gone out. But as soon as they hit, the luminash inside those buildings exploded, burning so hot there was little smoke. The other catapults launched, smashing another building to pieces, until there were thirteen burning buildings.

For a moment, inexplicable sorrow consumed Nelay. She was destroying her beautiful city, hollowing it out to rubble and ruins. But she would rather see it destroyed than home to her enemies.

The Clansmen's leaders were shouting their men into formations, but it was clear they didn't understand what was happening. Now it was time for the second part of Nelay's plan.

Yavish called for what little luminash they had to be unleashed on the buildings the Clansmen had taken as barracks—all of them just out of range of the Idaran bows.

There weren't any kilns inside the palace, and no one had seen Kidin. The next part wouldn't be as effective without the hot sand, but Nelay was betting it would work, for buildings burned easier than men.

Nashur ordered his soldiers to release their fire arrows. Driven by the ovat, the outer fires had picked up speed, smoke pumping from them in great billowing clouds. Now the smoke from the new fires chugged out, making Nelay's throat sting and her eyes water.

Her view of the Clansmen grew hazy, but she saw enough to know they finally understood. They were trapped between a fire and a wall. Even if the flames didn't kill them, the smoke would.

They charged, their battering rams slamming into the gates. But they didn't use the rolling shed to protect themselves, and the Immortal archers picked them off, one at a time.

The smoke grew thicker, and Nelay pressed the barely damp veil to her mouth and fought the urge to cough. Below her, Clansmen broke rank, snatching ladders and thrusting them against the wall.

One swung up in front of Nelay, the hooks at the top of the ladder biting into the mortar. Two Immortals tried to pull out the hooks, but they weren't budging. Jezzel pushed Nelay behind her and then stood shoulder to shoulder with Hazar and Ahzem, their swords drawn. An enormous Clansman launched himself up and over the wall, his axe chopping down, killing an Immortal instantly. He wielded his axe in short, inelegant, untrained chops that cut into her Immortals as more Clansmen vaulted over, pressing forward.

"Get that ladder!" Jezzel cried. "Or we'll be overrun!"

Nelay felt a surge of anger that such unrefined weapons would be allowed to harm her Immortals. The enormous Clansman, easily twice her size, locked gazes with her. He said something in Clannish, but she couldn't hear it over the blood rushing in her ears.

He charged toward her. Jezzel tried to block him, but she couldn't disengage from her own battle. His first swing was uncannily fast, too fast for Nelay or her blades to block it. She let her instincts and training take over, throwing herself back and slashing her blades under his shield, toward his soft middle.

When he let out a groan, she knew she'd hit her mark. She twisted her wrists to come back around, her eyes trained on his axe as he repositioned. He swung at her again, but his swing lacked the speed of his first two strikes. She stabbed his unprotected arm, her blade severing the tendons and spraying blood.

The axe fell from his fingers. He stumbled back from her, his badly injured arm held across his bleeding middle. In his other hand, he still held his shield. She saw the grim determination in his eyes. He was going to die, but he wasn't going to stop fighting. Nelay swung her blades at his side. He blocked with his shield and rushed her. Light on her feet, she sidestepped him, cutting into his other side. He fell.

She was already spinning for the next threat, but the Immortals had managed to remove the ladder. The last two Clansmen were backed against the wall, fighting a losing battle.

Nelay felt something wet on her face and wiped at it with the back of her arm. Blood. Her eyes shifted to the enormous man at her feet, who was watching her, his gaze full of bloodlust. He didn't try to block her as she thrust a blade down into his chest. The two remaining Clansmen looked at the half dozen Idarans and jumped from the wall.

"You all right?" Jezzel asked Nelay.

Trying to get the images of death out of her head, Nelay nodded, the smoke causing her to cough. Jezzel handed her a bucket, dripping with fresh water. After Nelay had dunked her veil again, she held it over her mouth and breathed through her nose.

Suddenly, she realized the battering ram had gone silent. Why had the Clansmen stopped trying to get out of the city? She peered between the parapets and squinted through the thickening smoke. The Clansmen were soaking the gate with liquid.

"What are they doing?" Jezzel asked.

"Their weapon!" Hazar cried.

Nelay saw a flash of silver and looked closer at the gate. Fairies. She grabbed a telescope from an Immortal and peered down. These were different from any fairies she had seen before—pale blue and silver, their wings like fine glass with angular, flower patterns trapped beneath.

Even as she watched, they held out their hands, touching the gate. White spread forth, bearing the same pattern as their wings. One fairy exploded like shattered glass, and Nelay knew she had died and would be taking up a body somewhere else. Nelay also knew why the Clansmen could only attack one or two gates and then had to wait a few days.

The fairies were dying to bring these gates down, then being reborn somewhere far away and traveling here again. These were the players Nelay had discarded as a lie—the players that changed the game entirely. And she'd had the knowledge all along.

"The high priestess was right," Nelay murmured. "It's my fault. It's all my fault."

"What are they doing?" Jezzel demanded.

Nelay backed up and started running. "To the gate! To the gate!" Her throat burned from the smoke, and the bottom half of the palace was lost to the haze. She reached the bottom of the stairs and faced the gate. A spot of ice bloomed across the gate's surface, the edges like ripped cloth. The gate cracked, loud in the sudden silence.

Rycus was already there. "More shields," he cried. "Stronger men in the front, taller in the back with spears."

Immortals, soldiers, Redeemed, and priestesses quickly obeyed. Shields were passed down the line, and Rycus shoved Nelay behind him. "You should get back. The front lines are no place for a queen."

She grinned as she sheathed her swords and took a spear. "But I was a priestess first."

"They're going to break through," Rycus cried. "We must hold them!"

Another loud crack brought Nelay's head up. The gate was now covered in a thick layer of ice. A cry rose up from the Clansmen beyond. Nelay imagined them gathering up the battering ram, rushing forward.

The gate shattered, large chunks that splintered into smaller ones on impact. Debris and smoke spewed out, and she ducked behind Rycus's shield.

When the gate was gone, she peeked out. The men who'd carried the ram were buried, killed by the falling gate.

Suddenly Clansmen roared and appeared through the smoke, trampling their newly dead. Rycus braced himself. They clashed in a tidal wave of shields, spears stabbing, axes hacking. Almost immediately, Clansmen broke through. Nelay launched the spear, dropped one, and jerked her swords free of her scabbard.

Thickening smoke made her cough on every other breath. It wasn't long before she could no longer see the other soldiers, could only hear their cries rising up all around her. She spun and realized she'd lost Jezzel and her other guards in the chaos and smoke.

A Clansman approached her through the smoke. Nelay ducked his swing and stabbed underneath his shield with one sword. As he buckled, she kicked him in the back, ducking a blow from another Clansman bearing a war hammer. She sliced his leg even as he brought his shield down toward her.

All she could do to avoid the blow was drop. So she did, knowing she wouldn't have a chance to recover before he smashed her with his hammer. She screamed as he swung toward her. But then he stiffened, his eyes bulging. A sword stuck out of his side, buried half the length of the blade. Even as he dropped to his knees, Nelay was scrambling to her feet.

She turned toward a dark shape, not needing to see his face to know it was Rycus. She wanted to scream at him, for he'd broken the first rule of combat—never throw your weapon.

Before she could, he lifted his shield to block a blow from a Clansman, caught the crook of the axe on the lip of the shield, and ripped the weapon from the Clansman's grip. The two soldiers bashed at each other with their shields.

Nelay yanked his sword out of the dead man's side. "Rycus," she called as she threw it toward him. She followed quickly after it.

He reached out to catch it. The Clansmen took advantage of the distraction, spinning to come up behind his opponent and swinging the edge of his shield toward his head. Rycus half turned, his sword arcing upward toward the man's ribs. He was too late. The shield connected with Rycus's neck, and he dropped into a crumpled heap.

Nelay arrived a few seconds later, swinging her swords and striking the man's vitals. After kicking his body free of her blades, she stood over Rycus, determined to keep him safe.

"Jezzel!" she cried. "Hazar! Ahzem!" Nelay coughed, her throat raw and her lungs aching from the smoke. The Clansmen were thinning out as if in retreat.

Jezzel finally appeared at her side. "They're seeking shelter from the smoke. We have to go."

Nelay collapsed beside Rycus and pressed her ear to his mouth, terrified he was already dead. His breath puffed against her ear. "Help me," he mumbled.

The two women wrapped his arms around their necks, lifted him, and rushed for the palace.

CHAPTER FORTY-ONE

Squinting against the smoke, Nelay stumbled over bodies on her way to the palace. But with all the soldiers trying to get through the doors at once, the retreat came to a standstill.

Her body heaving on every breath of poisonous smoke, Nelay waited her turn, listening to Nashur's voice calling out orders through his coughing. She drew a deep breath to shout to him, but the smoke choked her. They weren't going to make it. "Will the fire keep burning?" she asked the wheezing Jezzel.

"Nothing can stop it now. Half the city is burning. Even if the flames don't get them, the smoke will."

A coughing fit took over Nelay. She couldn't get enough air.

"Bend down," Jezzel said. "The air is clearer down here."

Nelay followed the advice, but her head grew light and her legs gave out. She and Rycus collapsed in a heap.

Flat on her back, she placed her hand on his chest, relieved to feel his heart beat beneath her palm. She squinted through burning, watering eyes and saw the sun, a red smear above them. Feather-light ash drifted lazily and landed on her skin.

Jezzel bent down and tried to pull Nelay up, but she was coughing too hard, fighting for breath. Then she too collapsed. All three of them were going to die, buried under ash. But it wasn't so bad—not if they'd died saving Idara.

Just as the blackness circled her vision, Nelay felt a cool breeze on her cheek. The smoke churned and the sun grew less red. Nelay took a breath and her lungs didn't seize in protest.

She took another breath and another, then pushed up on her elbows. Jezzel had collapsed half on top of her, and Rycus was still unconscious at her side.

Slowly, the soldiers nearest Nelay began to sit up. Those still trying to cram into the palace turned to the sky.

Nelay reached down and slapped Jezzel's cheek, smearing ash. "Jez?"

She groaned and sat up. "Just burn me now and end this."

If she was well enough for sarcasm, she'd be fine, Nelay decided. Bracing herself against Jezzel, she forced her legs under her.

There was no mistaking it. The wind had changed. But the ovat never changed. "What is this?" she asked.

Nashur jogged to them "We need to see what's happening." He tugged on her arm, pulling her toward the palace wall.

Nelay planted her feet. "Rycus."

Nashur looked down at the still body and drew in a sharp breath, then demanded they find the palace healer and bring her here at once. Then Nashur pulled on her arm again. She shook her head, refusing to leave her husband.

"You're a queen first, Nelay," he reminded her.

Tears burned her eyes. "Stay with him," she ordered Jezzel, and for once her friend didn't argue.

Nelay followed after Nashur. She stumbled at first, then moved faster as the dizziness passed. By the time she reached the top of the wall, the sky above her was blue, and Nashur was gaping at the cool wind blowing at them from the mountains to the northwest.

"The wind changed." Nelay stood beside him, dumbfounded. "It never changes!"

She stalked to the edge of the wall and saw Clansmen staggering to their feet, coughing and hacking. It wouldn't be long before they headed straight for the shattered gate.

"We're not going to be able to stop them." Nashur turned to his soldiers and ordered them inside the palace, instructing them to bar the doors after them.

"The city is still burning," Nelay said through numb lips. "There's still a chance this will work."

When Nashur didn't answer, she turned to him. He pointed behind her, his jaw hard.

She whirled around and her mouth fell open. Rolling toward them at an impossible speed was an entire citadel of clouds, billowing and churning, black with rain.

The wind gusted, blowing her hair back. Nelay shivered, her body locking up at the bitter feel of it. Within seconds, it had blotted out the sun. She stared above her, at what appeared to be more ash falling from the sky.

Moving slowly and delicately, the ash danced on the wind until it fell onto her outstretch palm. It was cold and it turned liquid against her skin. "What is this?" her voice came out breathy.

"Snow," Nashur said in disbelief. "But it has never snowed in Idara."

Nelay felt a flurry of the stuff, like ice against her face, falling harder and faster—the pieces nearly as big as Concon's fist.

Sluggishly, she turned to look at the burning buildings closest to her—the snow obscured her view of the outer wall. The fire was sputtering and choking to death on the snow.

"This isn't possible," Nashur finally said. "We won. The invasion was over."

Turning her face to the sky, Nelay saw something that sent her heart careening against her chest. On the wind, a poisonous green shimmer shifted and twisted like a lithe snake. She knew from the books what this was. An aurora.

In the shape of wings.

"It's the Winter Queen." Nelay whirled around to see High Priestess Suka standing there. "She's come to finish Idara herself."

CHAPTER FORTY-TWO

N elay opened her mouth—to say what, she wasn't sure. But Suka's eyes slid past her to their enemy gathering below.

"Quick," Suka said and then whirled around, her spotless robes swirling around her. "The palace doors won't stand long, but the temple walls haven't been breached."

Nelay didn't argue, just sprinted down the stairs and headed toward where Rycus still lay, Jezzel standing guard, the healer bent over him.

Nashur didn't hesitate; he simply scooped Rycus into his arms and started running. Nelay and Jezzel ran ahead of him, calling for anyone they passed—mostly priestesses and Immortals—to join them. They bolted across the deserted grounds, dodging the remnants of the Idarans' campfires and belongings, their sandaled feet leaving dark prints in the snow.

Nelay was shivering and wet, her feet already numb. "Where are Hazar and Ahzem?"

"Dead," Jezzel responded.

Nelay groaned. As they passed the massive temple gates, the changes inside made her breath catch. Gone were the perfectly oiled guards. The doors between the columns of the public bethel were closed tight. The fountain was shut off, the water at its base gray with soot.

Still running, Suka half turned. "If the Clansmen get inside, we're all dead. Hurry, Nelay. There is little time."

Nashur draped Rycus over Jezzel's shoulder. She staggered under the weight but held him. Then he met Nelay's gaze—there was so much in that simple gaze. Determination and respect and a final goodbye. Then he turned away.

"Bar the gates and get up the walls!" Nashur started shoving people in the direction he wanted them to go. "You priestesses raid your armory for anything that's left! Bring us everything we can use! If the Clansmen get through, we're all dead!"

Nelay started toward the temple, Jezzel and the healer behind her. Suka and some other priestesses dropped their shoulders to push open the massive doors. Nelay entered the dark sanctuary, coughing violently as the thick smoke from the incense burned her already raw throat. She crossed the floor, melted snow and soot dripping from her face.

At the center of the public bethel was the empty dais surrounded by the pool. The statues that had been there all of Nelay's life had been destroyed.

While the other priestesses headed to the armory, Nelay ran to the living quarters. At the first apartments she came to, she pushed the door open for the healer and Jezzel, who laid Rycus carefully down on the bed.

"What's wrong with him?" Nelay asked as she wiped dripping snow off his face. "Why isn't he waking up?"

The healer turned her sorrow-filled eyes toward Nelay. "His neck is broken."

Inhaling sharply, Nelay stood up to face the woman. "What?"

"My queen, there's nothing I can do."

Nelay had an overwhelming urge to hit the healer, but a broken voice made her stop. "Nelay?" Rycus called.

She dropped back to his side. His dark eyes focused on her. She stroked his damp, dirty hair back from his face. "Does it hurt?"

He coughed a little. "I don't feel anything."

Tears pounded the back of Nelay's eyes. "Rycus . . ."

"I heard what she said," he whispered. Tears spilled from his eyes—Nelay had never seen him cry before. "I can't—I can't grip my knives. I can't do what Scand did." His gaze shifted to the knives on her baldric. "I need you to do it for me."

Nelay reared back. "Never!"

Rycus choked on a sob. "Please don't leave me like this, listening while all of you die, helpless to stop them from murdering any of you."

"You can save him, Nelay," Suka said from behind her.

Nelay's anger immediately flared, but she strangled it into submission. "She was here—the Goddess of Winter. She saved the Clansmen. And the Goddess of Fire let her."

"Are you ready to do whatever it takes?" Suka said simply.

"Yes."

"Then come with me."

Nelay turned back to Rycus, who looked at her pleadingly. She hadn't realized she was crying too until she saw the drops land on his face. "I will come back to you. I'm going to heal you."

He looked deep into her eyes. "Hold on to yourself, Nelay. Come back to me."

That's what Zatal had told her—to hold onto love so she wouldn't lose herself. She bent down and pressed her lips to Rycus's forehead before she turned to look at the healer and said, "Keep him alive." Then Nelay darted from the room.

"Nelay," Rycus called after her, his voice sounding broken.

She kept moving, Jezzel falling into place beside her, as they had done since they were children. They crossed through

the corridors, through the private bethel, and finally into the outer courtyard.

Here, Nelay had spent the majority of her childhood. Coming back felt like coming home. But the courtyard covered in
snow and ice reminded her that even if they did win this war, her
home would never be the same.

"You are my sister," she said to Jezzel.

Jezzel reached out and took hold of Nelay's hand. "Until the
end."

"It's time," Suka said.

If Nelay hadn't been watching, she might have missed the
fairy with falcon wings shooting to the sky and disappearing into
the snow.

Suka crossed the training grounds, snow caking on her sandaled feet. "The Balance has shifted. Winter was never meant to
visit these lands, never meant to meddle in the affairs of men.
Because of that interference, thousands of our men have died.
Famines and storms have cost us thousands more. The Balance
will struggle to right itself, using whatever tools it can find. You
were made to be that tool."

Nelay lifted her gaze to meet the older woman's. "Made?"

Suka gathered weapons and pressed them into Nelay's
hands. "The elice flower—you alone in all the world have tasted
one of its petals."

That wasn't true. There was another. But perhaps the fairies
didn't know about Harrow.

"It is said the Winter Goddess steals the rest for herself,"
Suka went on. "It filled you with life, more than just your own."

That was why the priestesses were always rounding up
those with the Sight. "And if I fail?" Nelay said.

"Then we all die. Idara will be no more. And the Balance
will find another way."

A dark cloud caught Nelay's attention. She blinked in surprise to see an army of fairies approaching, wearing thick bark

and animal skins as armor. They bore spears made of sharpened wood sticks, leaves still trembling on them. Without a word to anyone, they took up positions around the perimeter of the courtyard.

"Why does it have to be me?" Nelay asked. "Why do I have to be the one to kill her?"

"Because only then will the fairies loyal to Leto fear you." Siseth emerged from the fairies' ranks, sporting armor made of glistening scales. Her fangs protruded from her mouth. "Those fairies have already fled before Ilyenna, leaving Leto alone and vulnerable like she has never been before and never will be again. You must strike before she has a chance to counter. It's the only way you will win."

"Why? Why would she abandon us? We loved her," Nelay said.

"Because she loves Ilyenna more." A second fairy had appeared, this one with brown, feathered wings and owl eyes.

"You—you're the one I followed all those times."

The fairy inclined her head. "I am Orawil. I was there when Leto saved Ilyenna. Both women were betrayed by those they loved. Both were victims to Idara's schemes, so they decided the world would be better without your people."

Nelay's hurt at the goddess's betrayal shifted into anger. "How do I kill her?" Nelay gasped as soon as the words left her lips, hardly believing she was seriously considering the fairies' plan. But every other idea and resource was gone.

Siseth scraped her needle-sharp claws against one another, the sound making Nelay cringe. "Quickly," the snake fairy said. "Though she is immortal, she can die the same as any other woman. If she has a chance to draw her power, it'll be too late."

Nelay should have been terrified, but her emotions had already been pushed past the breaking point. She simply felt numb. Suka, who had been quiet, informed her, "After she is dead, the fairies will transfer her power to you. They will do it quickly. It will change you, burn your soul. The power will be overwhelming and heady. But you mustn't lose yourself to it. For there is another battle you must fight this day. One even more important than the first."

"So you tell me I must kill the woman I've worshipped since childhood, and that isn't even the real fight." Nelay lifted her gaze. "You have to know there's almost no chance I will survive any of this."

Suka's eyes took on an almost maniacal gleam. "You will. And afterward, you will kill all of the Clansmen."

A bitter laugh left Nelay's lips. "You tell me my soul will be burned from my body, and you think I'm going to care about the Clansmen?"

Suka tipped her head back in a show of superiority. "The Winter Goddess, Ilyenna, loved a man, and it caused her to remember who she was. To remember her people and become protective of them. As you will remember Idara and protect her."

That was why Suka had forced Nelay to marry Zatal. "Rycus would have been enough."

Suka's jaw tightened. "A bond to the king would be a bond to Idara. Rycus was a Tribesman. I knew your thirst for power, so I thought you would welcome the marriage."

Ironically Rycus was the king of Idara, but only because Nelay had made it so. "You've thought of everything," she said in a soft voice.

"Yes," Suka agreed.

"If I become the Goddess of Fire and as heartless as you say, you know I'll burn you for it."

Suka didn't flinch. "I've always known."

Nelay turned to Jezzel, whose face was tight. "Jez, what do I do?" Her voice broke.

She thought her friend would fight her, demand she leave now, but instead, Jezzel lifted a hand to Nelay's shoulder. "We are all going to die today if you don't, Nelay—you included.

This is the only move left with any hope of survival. The only chance for any of us."

Nelay closed her eyes. "We've watched so many people die. What if this only leads to more death?"

"You have to embrace the fear, Nelay. Stop fighting it."

"I don't . . ." she faltered.

Jezzel eyes softened. "Embrace the fact that you might die. Make your peace with the life you've lived. Then the fear will fade."

Nelay closed her eyes, remembering her childhood, her parents. She had been a good child. As a priestess, she had worked hard. And when the time came to protect those she cared about, she had done always done what had needed to be done.

When she'd found love, she'd taken it. She had regrets, things she would have done differently, but she had always done her best. It was a life she was proud of. A calm washed over her. Death came to everyone. One way or another, it would come to her today. But she was no longer afraid. "Thank you," she whispered.

Jezzel pulled her in for a hug.

"So, will you fight for your people?" Suka asked.

Nelay searched her heart. Strangely, it was Zatal's words that came back to her. Something about things being broken before they can be rebuilt stronger than they were before.

She thought of her childhood, how she'd had to reveal her Sight in order to save her father. The revelation had broken her life, but she had rebuilt it better than before. The same had happened when the king came for her, breaking her hopes all around her.

Yet because of that, she had met Rycus. She had known real love. She had learned to be a true leader—to be selfless. Nelay took a deep breath and let it out. "Very well."

The snake fairy's tongue flicked out, tasting the air. "I will call her." She lowered herself to the ground and closed her eyes as other fairies took up positions around her.

"Nelay," Suka said from behind her, "send Jezzel away. All she can do is die here."

Nelay hesitated. But Suka was right. There was nothing Jezzel could do. "Go. Defend Idara. Defend our people."

Jezzel's gaze went from gentle to determined in a heartbeat. "You will not face this alone."

Nelay didn't argue, glad she had a friend through this. And she thought she would change what Zatal had said. "To rise from the ashes, first you must burn."

"Always giving speeches," teased Jezzel, drawing her sword.

Tix touched Nelay's shoulder. "Hide now." Her wings were a blur of motion behind her. "All of you, hide."

CHAPTER FORTY-THREE

The cold air turned warm and slowly began to smell of rich, damp earth and growing things. The snow melted, turning to puddles. Nelay tensed, not daring to move lest she give away her position, her every sense attuned to her surroundings.

The wind stirred, hot and humid, pressing against her in short gusts—almost as if stirred by wings. "Siseth, what is it? Why have you called me?" The voice was warm and full, nothing like Nelay had imagined.

Nelay didn't hesitate, for those who hesitated in battle died. She pivoted around the tree, taking in the scene before her in a glance. The woman with flaring wings like some kind of huge leaves, her charcoal skin, her close-cropped head. Nelay threw her knives, one right after another. The woman pivoted, her eyes wide with shock, three knives sticking out of her. She lifted her hand, and Nelay could see the fire building in her palm.

Nelay sprinted that last step, her blades swinging from low to high. The woman was still pivoting, still lifting her flaming hand. Nelay felt the warmth and humidity turn to ash, the heat searing her skin. Knowing she was seconds away from being obliterated, she sliced across the woman's middle.

And then the Goddess of Fire fell. Nelay stood over her, watching her convulsing, watching her wings go smaller. Ruby-red blood fanned out, curling patterns spreading across the puddles around her.

Nelay stared at the goddess she had worshipped since she was a child. Worshipped, and now killed.

The fire in the woman's hand slowly died, choking out as her black eyes landed on Nelay. She gave a bitter laugh. "They killed me because I was not cruel enough. They would rather have a murderer replace me."

Guilt and horror warred within Nelay, but her anger was stronger. "No. I killed you because you are a traitor."

The warm glow of the woman's skin was being stolen away. "You will learn. It is never as simple as that." Leto took a final breath, and when she let it out, her eyes became unfocused and she went unnaturally still, so still Nelay knew the heart no longer beat in her chest.

Nelay looked up as Siseth flew toward her, looking impassively at the body that seemed so much smaller. The fairy lifted her gaze to Nelay. "I claim you for the light side of the Balance, and make you Summer Queen."

With the speed of a striking snake, she darted forward. Nelay stumbled back, expecting to feel her bite, but there was only a brief pressure on her lips.

And then the world exploded. Colors bright and sharp enough to cut. She could see air currents, wrong and twisted, feel the black auras of death and suffering around the plants and animals.

Nos came forward, a crown of moss and twigs on her head, her hair the washed-out color of the morning sky. Her kiss was like a coal pressed to Nelay's lips.

Nelay shied back, but the fire was already spreading through her face, stabbing into her head like a lightning bolt, and running through her veins like liquid fire. She collapsed into a heap on her side, her head in her hands. Fire burned through her muscles, piercing her skin, and then flashed out, scouring her and burning away her soul.

A third touch, this time by Tix, and the agony grew distant, far enough away that Nelay knew death was close. She welcomed it, stepping away from the torture and toward the darkness. But before she could, Orawil delivered a final kiss, so terrible against the agony of Nelay's lips. That touch also spread, leaving a warm healing in its wake. Slowly, she uncurled herself, testing for pain as she did.

She found it. A too-hot spot in a line along her spine. She arched her back, groaning with the ache to stretch. With a whoosh, Nelay felt something break free, and the last of the suffering was over.

She opened her eyes to stare at the beautiful wings on her back, golden flames that danced and shifted behind her like a thousand molten ribbons.

"Nelay?" a feminine voice said.

She shifted her gaze to a woman kneeling before her, one arm held up to shield her from the heat. "Nelay? Is that my name?"

The woman's eyes widened. She stood and stumbled away. "There—there's fire in your eyes."

Nelay staggered to her feet and tipped her head back. She felt the power of summer within her, growth and light and heat. And then she looked around with her new sight and saw how wrong everything was. Nature had been wrenched out of balance. The flows of summer were distorted. Cold where heat should be. The urge to right it swelled deep inside her. But there was more. Nelay sensed something—a smudge of bitter winter. Her enemy! She stretched her wings, preparing to take flight, to defend what was hers.

"No," Siseth said, and Nelay felt the heat of anger gathering in her chest.

Siseth shifted slowly from side to side. "My queen, your enemy is near. It will not take her long to learn you have killed her friend. She will come."

Nelay's wing's flashed yellow. "Winter dares trespass on the lands of summer?"

"The Winter Queen's name is Ilyenna," Orawil said.

"And I am the Summer Queen." Nelay was glad to have a name for what she was.

The woman from before stepped toward Nelay. She wore weapons at her side, and Nelay's wings flared with streaks of red. The woman lifted her hands, palms out. "Nelay, don't you know me?"

Nelay looked her up and down, the desire to burn her for daring to speak making her hands tingle with beautiful heat. "Why would I know you?"

"I'm Jezzel—I'm your friend."

"I have no memory of you," Nelay scoffed.

The woman asked, "Then do you remember Rycus?"

At that name, Nelay felt a stirring in her breast. Her soul was gone, burned to ash, but there was a kernel, a seed of re-membrance. That seed was Rycus.

She closed her eyes and felt an echo of something she longed to hold onto. Tipping her head to the side, she nudged the knowledge to grow. Memories bloomed slowly within her, re-vealing themselves one petal at a time.

But Nelay was no longer the girl who had become a queen. The girl who loved a boy with midnight-sand eyes. Now she was a goddess to mankind and a queen to her fairies. And the fate of the man she had loved wasn't nearly as important as confronting the fool who dared invade her lands.

Fury flashed through Nelay. Her wings turned white hot, and women and fairies alike staggered back against the heat. With a burst, Nelay took to the skies, her wings leaving a melted circle in their wake. She felt her connection to the summer fairies, as numerous as the creatures all around her. She called for them, called them to arms. Called for them to fight.

No mercy. No hesitation.

Her rage bled over to them, until she felt them coming by the thousands. She pumped her massive wings, pushing back the cold, burning up the clouds.

Colors appeared against the velvet grays of the clouds. A poisonous green that shifted to purple and then pink. "Leto, what are you doing?" came a disembodied voice as cold as death.

Then the Winter Queen appeared. She was like a thousand glittering diamonds, her feet bare, her hair tangled and wild, her skin blue and silver. Her eyes took in Nelay, and her already marble-pale face lost any remaining color until she looked like death itself. "No."

"These are my lands." Nelay let the heat unfurl from where it rested inside her—the hottest desert wind blasting against the Winter Goddess.

More memories surfaced, more wrongs at the hands of this cold woman. "You have upset the Balance," Nelay said. "And you will pay for it."

"You killed her." Ilyenna's icy voice keened like the wind through a mountain pass, as if she hadn't heard Nelay's threats at all. "She was kind and good. And she was my friend. My only friend."

Nelay pressed forward, forcing the Winter Queen back. "She was a traitor and a coward."

Ilyenna's gaze shifted down to the city below. Nelay followed her gaze and saw the clanlands' armies, saw them streaming through the palace wall, breaking down the doors. These men did not belong here anymore than the Winter Queen did. With a sweep of Nelay's hand, the city was burning, the fire as white-hot as her wings.

"No!" Ilyenna roared. She held her hands out, ice and snow streaming from her palms. The clouds behind her gained strength, turning black and churning forward.

Nelay cut off the blast of snow with a ball of fire. Furious, she let out a battle cry and dove forward, her fairies at her back.

Something glittering and translucent shot toward her. Only the battle instincts from her past life saved her as she veered to the side. As she dodged another ice dart, Nelay realized she needed something of her own to throw.

"Call for a branch."

Nelay twisted around to see Siseth, her mouth opened unnaturally wide, showing her black gums against her white fangs. Siseth wrapped her arms and legs around a winter fairy and chomped down on her shoulder. The fairy's purple body shattered into a thousand shards of snow.

Siseth's tongue flicked out, tasting the air as she came to land on Nelay's shoulder. "You may have more experience in combat, but Ilyenna has had two decades to refine her powers."

One of the ice darts pierced Nelay's arm just above her elbow. She felt a flash of cold pain and watched as her blood spilled into the open air.

"Call for the branches—command them to grow."

Nelay wasn't sure what Siseth meant, but she tried it anyway. And suddenly a slim, green branch appeared in her hand. She darted above the clouds, caught sight of Ilyenna, and launched branches at her, one after another.

With a powerful thrust of her wings, Ilyenna shot out of range, but some of her fairies weren't fast enough. The branches imbedded in them and grew fatter, leaves sprouting from the fairies' mouths, and they wailed in agony before shattering into puffs of fur, snow, or ice.

Ilyenna let out a howl of rage. Hail and ice shot toward Nelay, but she sent out a wave of heat, melting them. Ilyenna called up a maelstrom of snow.

Nelay stirred her hand, creating a whirlwind of sand, which she flung at Ilyenna and her fairies. The two tornados met, both spinning off and sending out gales of wind. But Siseth was right. Here, Nelay was stronger.

Ilyenna's mouth tightened as she looked again at the burning city. She tucked her wings and dove. Nelay hesitated before tucking her own wings and giving chase. But despite how natural her wings felt, she was no match for Ilyenna's experience. The Winter Queen cut through the city, shooting ice on every fire, calling for the Clansmen to retreat. They stumbled through the city, their clothes and skin stained with soot, and spilled beyond the palace walls. Nelay let them go, concentrating on solely on Ilyenna as she darted and turned, making herself impossible to hit.

Still, Nelay kept shooting branches at her, calling up the sand to blind her. The woman's cold shriveled up before Nelay's heat, and still Ilyenna did not stop.

The Clansmen mounted their horses, what was left of them, and fled from the city. Ilyenna was helping them escape.

Nelay's nostrils flared in fury. These served the Winter Queen, and therefore they were invaders just as the winter fairies were. An invasion they would pay for.

With a thought, Nelay sent her sand-storm fairies, with wings of shifting sand, after them, commanding them to flay the flesh from the men's bones.

Determined to catch the Winter Queen, she flew faster, harder, and with every beat of her wings she came closer to Ilyenna—so close she could almost reach out and touch her wing tips. And then the Winter Goddess turned abruptly. Nelay shot past but flared her wings and rolled her body forward to stop. She reversed and charged back toward the alley at full speed, but then rounded a corner and slammed into a solid wall of ice. She crumpled, dazed, her fire wings going out and leaving nothing but a silhouette of charred earth. She blinked up through fire and dust to see fairies fighting above her.

If Nelay stayed here, she would die. She hauled herself to her feet, noting her wings had burned a perfect outline on the flagstones. She let the flash of heat along her spine unfurl once more.

More cautious this time, she flew above the city, her eyes searching. But it was not her eyes that told her where the Winter Queen was. Nelay could feel a pocket of cold radiating from her left, toward the palace. Sensing this was some kind of trap, she hid the light of her wings, forcing the white hot to fade to a deep red.

She saw a building roaring with fire. Growling low in her throat, she settled down in the midst of it, knowing it would hide her, that it wouldn't hurt her. Instead, the flames danced along her skin, feeling like a thousand strands of blowing silk.

She waved them aside and they parted like a curtain, giving her full view of the palace gates. Ilyenna was crouched there, clearly exhausted, her magnificent wings puddling around her.

Nelay gripped the handles of her swords, preparing to launch forward and end this once and for all. But just as she took her first step, she heard a soft sound. It brought with it an image of the wind howling through the crevasses of a blue glacier, something Nelay had never seen.

She took another step forward and saw crystal tears falling from Ilyenna's cheeks to land on the dirty, crumpled body of a man she held in her arms. Ilyenna hadn't collapsed in exhaustion—she'd collapsed in grief. But instead of a raging inferno of anger and pain, her grief was like a sharp point, cold and hard and poisonous.

Nelay called for her wings and rose enough to see the man's face. Bratton—the high chief of the Clansmen. He was dead. Nelay should go forward, kill Ilyenna. But she hesitated, not out of sympathy as much as curiosity. What power was so strong it had felled a Winter Queen?

A fairy suddenly appeared at Ilyenna's side. Feeling no connection to her, Nelay knew she was a winter fairy. She was obviously weak, her face flushed and wilted. Her wings were white and furry. "My queen, we must go," she urged Ilyenna. "We cannot win, not so deep in her territory."

"He is dead, Chriel. My brother is dead," Ilyenna said, her voice hard and broken.

Bratton is Ilyenna's brother?

"Ilyenna, you must make a choice now," Chriel said softly. "Stay and die, or leave and live."

Ilyenna looked up, the tears frozen to her white-blue face. "I do not care anymore."

"Not caring is choosing to die," the fairy said desperately.

Ilyenna rested her forehead on Bratton's. "Leave me alone."

"What of Rone? What of Elice? They will die without your protection."

At this, Ilyenna finally lifted her head. A sob caught in her throat. "I'm too weak to carry him."

Chriel fluttered forward. "He died a warrior in battle. It is an honorable death."

"He died because she burned him to death."

Nelay knew who that "she" was. She lowered her swords to her sides.

The fairy spotted Nelay and jerked back, pointing. "My queen!"

Ilyenna rose regally and faced Nelay, her wings drooping at her sides like fallen soldiers. "Murderer!"

Nelay stepped from the char and embers. "You call me murderer? You who have perverted the laws of the Balance?"

Ilyenna's eyes were like chips of dark water. "You Raiders are the biggest hypocrites of all."

Nelay's brows rose up, remembering that as the name the Clansmen used for Idarans. The two goddesses glared at each other, but neither moved.

"You have to kill her," a voice hissed. "Winter does not forgive." Nelay didn't have to look to know it was Siseth, hiding in her dark hair.

She was right. Ilyenna would never forgive. And neither would Nelay. She lifted her swords and surged forward. Ilyenna's wings snapped up and she shot into the sky, every pump of her wings an exercise in perfection. Nelay was stronger but less experienced, and soon Ilyenna had outdistanced her.

After chasing the Winter Queen for what felt like hours, Nelay pulled up alongside the border of winter, somehow knowing she was at the outskirts of her reach. If she went any farther, she would be in Ilyenna's domain, and she would lose every advantage.

"How?" Nelay asked Siseth as the fairy caught up to her.

Panting, Siseth landed on her shoulder. "She created an air current and rode it home. You'll learn to do it eventually."

In the distance, Ilyenna paused and looked back. They were too far away to harm each other, but both made silent promises that ended with the other dead. Not turning away, Nelay slowly retreated until she was far out of range. Then, she whirled around and flew back the way she had come.

When she arrived in Idara, her powerful wings stirred up a dust storm so thick it would be impossible to breathe, with winds strong enough to scour flesh from bones. Lightning flashed within its choking depths. She drove it toward the retreating army.

She didn't pause from one city to the next, but routed them all the way to the sea. Then she turned back, determined to find those hiding and finish them all.

She wasn't sure how long she flew, how many hundreds of thousands died, but she finally stopped at the sight of a face. He was young, close to her own age. And he was alive when he should have been dead, like the hundreds of companions around him.

A name formed on her tongue: Harrow. He had saved her once, at risk to himself. Nelay's anger cooled, shifting to something like apathy. As the sand and the wind settled, his gaze snagging on her. "Nelay?"

His face registered shock and then understanding. "Remember what I said, Nelay. Some laws are not meant to be broken. You have to stop before you pull the Balance so far out of alignment that you end up destroying us all."

Not answering, she spread her wings and shot to the sky in a flash of heat that left melted glass in her wake. She touched down in Thanjavar, in the temple courtyard. She wasn't sure why she came here, except that she remembered how important this land and its people had been to the woman she was before, and she was curious about the man whose name had unlocked her memories.

Certainly the temple and palace were grand for human buildings. The people were nothing, dirty and damaged. They spilled from the temple, their gazes locked on her in equal amounts of fascination, fear, and adoration.

They dropped to their knees, as they should before a Summer Queen. Nelay glanced up at the fairies lining the palace walls, their eyes trained on her. "Bring me the elice flower. Do it now."

Nos shot up and darted away.

Nelay glided forward, into the temple—her temple. Idarans scattered from her path, as was proper, then bowed as they should.

It was dark inside. With all the doors shut, her skin glowed, casting light and liquid shadows across hollow, haggard faces within. With a thought, Nelay formed a ball of fire in her hand and tossed it toward the ceiling, where it grew in size until the room was perfectly lit.

A woman hurried toward her. She wore robes the old Nelay recognized as ceremonial attire. She dropped to her knees, her forehead touching the ground. "I am High Priestess Suka, Goddess. I beg your forgiveness for forcing you into this."

Nelay tipped her head to the side. *Goddess. Yes. That's what they call me.* She decided it was a fitting title from a mortal. Her lip curled in distain. "Oh, I remember you." She hoped the woman would reach out to her—a single touch would turn her to cinders. But then Nelay caught sight of the corridor beyond the priestess. Her consort was back there.

She stepped past the high priestess, who jumped to her feet and hurried after her. "I meant to have the statues of your likeness finished before this day came, Goddess, but the limitations of mortality prevented it. I shall have them done as soon as a new glass smith—"

Nelay whirled around, her wings flaring beside her. "You dare speak to me? You dare follow after as if I am your equal?"

The woman dropped to the floor. "Please, I only—"

Nelay whipped her hand out, and the woman collapsed in a pile of smoking ashes. Then the Summer Queen pivoted and walked away from the mess, her sole thought for her consort.

The young woman from the courtyard came running. Nelay knew her now. Jezzel, who had been like a sister to the woman Nelay was before. When she saw Nelay, Jezzel's expression morphed into something like wariness.

"Where is he?" Nelay asked.

"Here." Jezzel gestured the way she'd come.

Nelay followed and was shown into a priestess's room. Jezzel came in after her and moved to a corner.

Rycus lay on the bed, his skin gray and ashen. He stared at Nelay, his eyes red and his lips purple. "Nelay?" He blinked and squinted up at her. "There's fire under your skin."

She knelt beside him, her body arcing over his. She wasn't sure why she felt the need to protect him. Except that he was hers. And no one else could have him.

Still, she dared not touch him, afraid she might burn him. "I have defeated the clans."

His eyes did not leave hers. "Did you hold on to who you are?"

She didn't know how to answer that. It appeared she didn't need to, for his breath caught in his throat and horror filled his eyes. "No," he whispered. "After all this, I've still lost you."

Nelay tipped her head to the side, wondering why it mattered. "I suppose."

Rycus closed his eyes. "I can't feel anything below my neck. I can't move. I—" His cheeks darkened with shame, and he took another breath. "And I've lost her. You have to let me go." He opened his eyes again to stare at her. "Let me die a man."

Nelay's anger rose, heat pulsing from her skin, her temper even harder to control now. "No. You will not die. I will heal you."

"Nelay . . ." he tried again.

"Silence!" she roared, her wings expanding, blackening everything they touched.

"Rycus," Jezzel said from where she was crouched in a corner. "You're going to get us all killed."

Tears slipped from his eyes, but he remained quiet. Nelay's anger slowly cooled. She turned as she felt Nos approaching. "This is Lila, my queen."

The new fairy had white blossom wings that turned burgundy where they attached to her body. Her eyes were solid yellow. In her hands, she held a flower that looked identical to her wings. With the fairy's erratic, labored wing beats, Nelay knew the incense was making her ill. Trembling, the fairy held out the flower. "My queen, the elice blossom."

Nelay reached out her hand and caught the fairy as she collapsed. Holding her gently, careful of her fragile wings, Nelay plucked one of the flower petals. Then she turned to the bed. "Open your mouth."

Rycus stared at her and then at Jezzel, who shot him a pleading look. He opened his mouth and Nelay laid the petal on his tongue. Even as she watched, it dissolved. He closed his mouth.

"I feel . . ." He didn't finish as his eyes rolled up in his head and his lids fluttered. Nelay tugged down his tunic and watched as the swelling and bruising around his neck began to fade. His gray skin turned dusky again and the purple faded from his lips. He took a deep breath and let it out, then shifted into a healing sleep.

Nelay studied this man, wondering at the devotion she'd once held for him. Curious, she reined in her heat, hoping she wouldn't burn him, and very carefully laid her hand on his head.

Instantly, her whole body flushed with joy. The seed of her memory blossomed and expanded, filling her with knowledge of the life she had lived, the woman she had been. Perhaps her soul had been burned away, but Nelay could grow a new one. One that loved Rycus. Loved Idara.

She bent closer to him, pressing her lips against his forehead, a reminder of how many times he'd done that for her. She stood and caught sight of Jezzel in one corner, the skin of her hands blistered and some of her hair melted.

"Oh, no, not your hair."

Jezzel jerked in surprise. "Nelay?"

Nelay smiled and opened her arms. Jezzel shot into them, sobbing with relief and joy. The new Nelay vowed to love this woman as the old Nelay had.

"I thought I'd lost you."

"Suka—oh, burn it, I killed her!" As well as thousands upon thousands of Clansmen. That should have filled Nelay with horror and self-hate, but it didn't.

Jezzel pushed back. "You were terrifying."

Nelay felt power surge through her body and knew she was terrifying still. But there was no need for Jezzel to know that.

"She was right," Nelay finished softly. "Rycus helped me keep my humanity." Though perhaps not as firmly as before.

Nelay plucked one of the petals and held it out for Jezzel, but she waved it away. "The blisters will heal. Some cold water, and the burning will fade—just promise you won't do that to me again."

Nelay made a mental note to mark the position of all her allies before she lost control of her anger again.

Jezzel looked over Nelay's shoulder. "How long is he going to sleep?"

The old Nelay would have stayed by Rycus's side, waiting for him to wake up. The new Nelay couldn't see the point. "With as bad as his injuries were, a long time." She took her friend's arm and steered her out of the room. "Come. We have much to do."

Outside stood a group of people, the healer among them. They watched the Summer Queen in awe and more than a little fear.

"Nelay, how . . ." Jezzel's words trailed off.

But Nelay paced toward the healer, who stepped back until the press of the crowd prevented her from going any farther. Nelay lifted her hand, and the woman flinched as if she expected to be blasted with fire.

Holding out the flower, Nelay lifted her brows impatiently. "A single petal will completely heal one person."

When the woman made no move to take it, Jezzel huffed in frustration, took the flower herself, and pressed it into the woman's hands.

The healer wet her lips nervously. "And what if I gave a little bit too many people?"

Nelay opened her other hand and blew a warm spring breeze into the fairy's face. She stirred and opened her heavy eyes. Nelay relayed the woman's question to her. When the fairy had given her answer, she passed out again.

"The whole petal will save one from death," Nelay explained. "Steep the petal in a tea, and each drop will heal a degree."

The healer pivoted, breaking off petals and ordering people out of her way.

Nelay strode through the crowd, toward the doors. Like her fairies, she found the indoors insufferable. She needed to feel the wind and sun and earth, see the sky, and smell life. She held her hand toward the light hovering over the pool and balled her fist, extinguishing the fire.

"Guard the king," Jezzel told one of the Immortals and took off after Nelay.

At the doors, Nelay blew again on Lila, who groaned and opened her eyes. She looked around and took a deep breath. Then she opened her wings, bowed deeply, and fluttered away.

"Tix," Nelay called. The fairy was at her side in the space of a blink. "Find any winter fairies that might have been left behind. Kill them."

The fairy bowed before disappearing.

Nelay arched her back, and her cramped wings sprung from her body. With a yelp, Jezzel jumped away. "Where are you going?"

Nelay spread her wings. "To heal the land from the damage Ilyenna has done."

CHAPTER
FORTY-FOUR

Nelay stood on the balcony of her palace, staring out over the gutted city. Smoke still rose in places. Buildings were broken, with empty doorways that reminded her of the people's hollow eyes. Hundreds of thousands of Idarans had died. And she'd burned their bodies all at once, the smoke from their pyre darkening the sky and turning the sun into a blood-red jewel.

Maran lay her silk shawl on the banister. "Are you sure you don't want me to braid your hair, Nelay?"

"No. I like the feel of the wind through it." Being inside these buildings was hard for her—it left her feeling heavy and itchy. She longed for the freedom of the sky. For the companionship of her fairies, for she was more like them now than she cared to admit.

Maran hesitated. The old Nelay knew why. Her bodice was scandalous in its lack of fabric. But her wings stretched from the tip of her shoulder to the middle of her back, and they ripped anything in the way. The new Nelay didn't care about something as silly as human customs, so Maran had made a collar that attached a panel to her skirt, leaving her back bare.

"Your husband . . ." Nelay began.

Maran hesitated. "He survived. But he's with another woman now."

"I'm—I'm sorry." The sentiment felt foreign on Nelay's tongue, but she knew it was something that should be said. "Would you like me to punish him for you?" That felt much more natural.

Maran gave a small smile and shrugged. "Really, I was more upset by Delir's death. But Bahar . . . he's lost someone too. He's a good friend."

Nelay was happy for her. Bahar was a good man, something Sedun had never been.

Maran settled the headdress on Nelay's head, straightened the jewel on her forehead, and sprang in for a quick hug. "Thank you for teaching me to love myself before all others," Maran said. Then she backed away, wiping the tears from her face, and left without another word.

When the woman was gone, Nelay rested her hands on her abdomen. Her powers as Summer Queen allowed her to sense the life growing within her long before any mortal. Soon, she would have a child of her own—a son. Her wings curled protectively around her body. Warm and happy, they tickled and licked at her flesh.

A shape caught her attention and she whirled around, a branch already forming in her palm. It was Rycus at the doorway, his mouth hanging open. "Nelay?"

This was why she had stayed. And why she would stay, for as long as she could bear it. Her joy expanded, her wings flaring and stretching. They crowded the enormous room, curving in on the tips. They didn't burn anything, because she didn't let them.

"Is it you? Really you?"

A smile broke across her face. "Most of me, I think."

He stepped hesitantly into the room, bracing himself as the wings brushed against him. When nothing happened, he let out a breath of relief. "Why isn't it hot in here?"

"Because I don't want it to be," Nelay responded.

He reached toward her wings and then hesitated. "Can I?"

She wondered what it would feel like. "I won't let them burn you."

He put a hand on one wing, and she felt the same sensation as if he had touched her skin, but more so, for they were sensitive. The fire in them darkened to a deep burgundy, sparks of gold dancing in their depths.

"It feels like silk, only richer, fuller." He turned to her, and she could see the fear and hesitancy in his gaze. "How much of you?"

She turned away from him, suddenly uncertain. "I'm not sure, but I feel different, and I think differently."

He stepped forward, looking her over as if searching for some sign of injury. Then he reached into his pocket and pulled something out. She took a step closer. It was the pendant her father had given her. The one she'd crushed. Her breath caught in her throat.

"So you remember this?"

Pain and betrayal and anger flashed through her in waves. She struggled to keep her emotions under control before she frightened or harmed Rycus.

But he wasn't looking at her and seemed oblivious to the danger. "I took it days ago, planning to fix it as soon as the war was over." He glanced up at her. "Things can be fixed."

She pulled her wings away. "Is that what you think? That I need to be fixed?"

"They've taken so much from you."

His words hurt. He wanted the old Nelay back, the one who was burned to ash.

She touched the phoenix mantle resting on her collar. "They gave me more."

Rycus shook his head. "The softness, the innocence—it's gone."

She let her wings envelop them both, so they were in a cocoon of warmth and light. "Do you know how they make glass?"

She didn't wait for him to answer. "With fire. I might be different, Rycus, but only because I have had the impurities burned out."

He stepped toward her and settled the necklace over her head. She let him, for she sensed he needed this bit of familiarity about her. When he was ready to handle another shock, she would tell him about his son. He reached out and carefully took her face in his hands. Tipping her head back, she tapped her lips.

A smile broke out across his face. "You're still you."

He kissed her, and her wings deepened to garnet.

EPILOGUE

Nelay was right. Her allegiance with the fairies cost Idara more than they were willing to lose. The fires burned for weeks, and when they finally died, little was left. Those who departed Thanjavar spread out, taking on the century-long task of rebuilding what once was into what would be.

Another temple was built around the charred stone road where Nelay's wings had left an outline. The melted courtyard where her wings had first appeared was made into a shrine where pilgrims came to see for themselves the palace where the Goddess of Fire was born.

In the clanlands, a few men returned, among them a man named Harrow. He told of a holy woman with fire wings, lightning in her palms. The Clansmen who hadn't seen the devastation might not have believed him, for his father was a known traitor and his mother a ruined woman. But there were more stories by others—stories of battles in the sky, battles of fire and ice. Of voices in the storms.

Stories of another face in the storm surfaced. Stories from twenty years ago. Of a girl wearing a frozen wedding dress, her wings the color of an aurora. Her name had once been Ilyenna.

The only thing both nations could agree on was that the war had just begun. And the price for winning would be too steep.

ACKNOWLEDGMENTS

I wrote this book during perhaps one of the hardest times of my life. My middle child was in and out of hospitals with a noncancerous bone tumor. He had three surgeries, broke his femur and tibia (at separate times), was in a wheelchair, and not allowed any type of physical activity for months. At one point we were told he might be in a wheelchair until he was sixteen.

He's doing much better now. He's able to do many of the things other kids can. Fingers and eyes and toes crossed that it continues to improve.

We also moved to another state, I broke my leg, had surgery, and played single mom while my husband was away for a couple months. Insurance was, and still is, a nightmare (I'm looking at you, Humana).

So I'd like to thank all those who helped my family through this hard time. Our family and neighbors who brought us meals and cared for our other children. Bloggers and booklovers who responded when I sent out a call for Christmas in the Mail (run by Children and the Earth and headed up by Jodi), a program where bedridden kids are sent books and cards to cheer them up.

I can't tell you how much your kindness lifted our hearts during those dark days.

As for *Summer Queen*, thanks go out to JoLynne Lyon— love that girl; Charity West, whose talents have taken my books to another level; Linda Prince for her amazing editing skillz (she would want me to let you know the "z" was a stylistic choice and

403

not a part of *The Chicago Manual of Style*); Lara Sava for her fabulous artwork; Devon Dorrity for his graphic design savvy; and Julie Titus for the smokin' interior formatting.

Thank you to my street team, the Argylers, especially Anna Weimer, Wendy Riggs Burr, Kayla Swilling, and Frida Petersson.

Thank you to my husband, Derek, for his love and support. Thank you to my children for driving me crazy (sane people are boring, don't you think?). Thank you, God, for sending me the people I need when I need them.

And thank you, all my lovely readers. For reading my books, for leaving reviews, and for your lovely letters and notes.

Mwah!
    Amber

Amber Argyle is the number-one bestselling author of the Witch Song Series and the Fairy Queen Series. Her books have been nominated for and won awards and have been translated into French and Indonesian.

Amber graduated cum laude from Utah State University with a degree in English and physical education, a husband, and a two-year-old. Since then, she and her husband have added two more children, which they are actively trying to transform from crazy small people into less crazy larger people.

Visit Amber Argyle's website to sign up for her free starter library or to learn more: amberargyle.com

OTHER TITLES BY AMBER ARGYLE

Witch Song Series

Witch Song
Witch Born
Witch Rising
Witch Fall

Fairy Queens Series

Of Ice and Snow
Winter Queen
Of Fire and Ash
Summer Queen
Of Sand and Storm
Daughter of Winter
Winter's Heir